Chester's Last Ride

by

Nathan Wright

Nathan Wright

This is a work of fiction. All of the characters, organizations, and events portrayed in this novel are either products of the author's imagination or are used fictitiously.

ISBN: 9781081363383

Chester's Last Ride

South Dakota is a cold lonely place to spend an entire winter. Hell, it's a pretty lonely place in the dead of summer too. I had wintered there through the coldest days of December 1891 and right on through January 1892. I was after brown bear. The pelt of a brown bear could bring upwards of a hundred and fifty dollars, not to mention the claws and head. Hunting was good and by the middle of that January I had bagged seven browns and one unfortunate grizzly that happened into camp late one night with the intention of killing one of my horses and also me if I interfered. I had seen upwards of twenty other bears during this time but let them pass. No need of killing an undersized bear unless it was absolutely necessary. Let em grow another year or two.

Everything about this trip had been pretty much a non-event. A non-event means I wasn't nearly killed either by accident or on purpose, that all changed about two one morning. On a rather warm night for this time of year; it must have been at least fifteen degrees, I was sleeping soundly all curled up in my blankets and topped off with a brown bear hide. The fire had ceased to matter and all that was left were hot embers, no flame.

Nathan Wright

Hazel stirred first; I heard the big horse snort and when I looked over at her she was standing at attention, head up high, ears perked and eyes big with fear. She and Rusty, my other horse, were tied about twenty feet away in a stand of dried sage grass that hadn't been flattened already by the snows.

I could tell that she had sensed something and it was probably something that meant trouble. Horses have a keen sense of what certain kinds of sounds mean. Everything that stirs in the night makes a sound that is particular to that animal and that animal alone. A horse, with its keen eyesight, hearing, and smell, can detect anything that gets within range before a man ever does. Just by the look I knew something was up.

Checking the loads in my .45-.75 Winchester I eased from my warm cocoon of blankets and scanned the surrounding area. Rusty was now keen on the scent of something along with Hazel. Both horses were starting to pull against their leads which held them in place. I made sure my Colt slid freely in and out of its holster. One of the first things I learned a few years back while wintering in the cold high country was that a gun stuck snuggly in a leather holster while a man slept in his blankets would accumulate a little moisture during the night. When you stepped out of the warm blankets on a really cold night the moisture would frost over almost instantly and if you weren't careful the gun would freeze solid to the leather.

On this night there was a heavy cold fog and I knew the moisture in the air was high. The gun would no doubt be holster froze within seconds of me stepping from the covers. I looked in the same direction the horses were staring and there it was coming straight for me, a big bull elk that must have decided to take a short cut straight over top of me on his way to see a lady friend no doubt.

Chester's Last Ride

The horses had awakened me in time to jump up right in front of the charging bastard. All I could think of was to fire a quick shot at his head but to my horror the holster wouldn't release my gun, it had frozen solid. I only managed to get clubbed by one of the big antlers as he charged by. I was knocked at least ten feet. I landed in a heap against a pile of brush.

The elk was turning to come back around and have some more fun with me. I tried again to pull the Colt but the holster wouldn't give it up, the gun and holster had become one. All I could do was put both arms over my face and head and wait to get crushed.

If it hadn't have been for the big dog that traveled with me and the two horses I'm sure I would have been killed. Right before the bull elk made it to my spot Ben sprang from the brush and caught him behind the antlers at the top of his neck. Now Ben is a big dog, on a slow day he will go at least a hundred and fifty pounds, but seeing him attached to the neck of a thousand pound elk made him look like a stuffed toy a child might play with.

The big elk stopped dead in his tracks and started slinging his head from left to right but Ben wouldn't let go. Ben was doing what I had seen him do before when he brought down game. He was twisting his head and trying to bite into the animal's neck to kill it. But this was an elk, what was the dog thinking? Ben was doing all he could but even David wasn't this out matched. I tried to stand but there was pain in my ribs, no more had I gotten to my knees than I collapsed back to the ground. I knew the elk would kill the big dog once it got him on the ground and then probably dish out some more to me of what I had already gotten earlier.

Nathan Wright

All I could think of was to get to the rifle which was still beside my bedroll. Crawling on my hands and knees with tremendous pain in my ribs I finally made it. The big Winchester was right where I had left it the night before. I pulled it to me and managed to roll over on my side just as Ben was thrown free by the elk. He landed on his feet and looked like he was mad as hell. He bared his teeth and pounced again at the snorting monster. This time the elk was ready for him and batted the big cur away as if he were nothing more than a buzzing mosquito. Ben landed this time not on his feet but on his back and just rolled a couple of times, he didn't move after that. I raised the gun and hoped it too hadn't been affected by the cold temperatures.

The shot rang out and the bullet travelled true. I had aimed for the back of the head right where it joined the massive neck, the same spot where Ben had tried to chew through. The noise of the gun and the smoke expelled by the big slug made everything seem to stop as if by magic, everything that is except the bull elk. It had been in full charge toward the spot where Ben had landed. The dog was either unconscious or dead and would have been shredded by the massive antlers the elk sported. As it was the elk dropped to the ground and slid a few feet further before it went quiet, the only movement now was a twitch from one of its back legs from time to time. Ben still didn't move. I feared the worst.

I looked at my two horses and they were safe although startled either by the elk or the Winchester, most likely both. When I was sure there were no other angry elk close by to avenge the death of a family member I put the rifle on the ground and tried to move onto my knees. After I successfully accomplished that I tried to stand but found the effort too painful at the moment. Instead I crawled over on hands and knees. Ben hadn't moved and didn't appear to be breathing. I fought through the pain and made it to the big dog. I gently laid my hand on his side and held very still hoping to feel the up and down movement of his breathing.

He was alive but just barely. He was taking rapid shallow breaths. I stroked his forehead and called his name. After a minute or two he slowly opened his eyes and looked at me. All he could do was wag his tail; I now suspected his back might be broken. We both just lay there and tried to catch our breath. I could tell as I tried to breathe that I must have more than one broken rib, the pain was tremendous. If anything else in there was damaged or broken then I would most likely die right here in this camp.

The thought of my horses tied to a tree and me passing away was more than I could bare. I slowly made my way to where they were picketed. Hazel and Rusty both watched as I half crawled and half drug myself toward them. Once there I pulled out my knife and cut both sets of reins. If the two horses took off then I would die for sure and if they stayed and I died then at least they were free to roam for food and water. I fell to my side and just lay there. Before long I passed out.

The sun rose bright in a cloudless sky. The warmth on my face felt good. I opened my eyes and surveyed my surroundings. Hazel and Rusty were standing nearby and chewing on some tall dry grass that stuck up through the snow. Ben wasn't where I had left him, he was gone. He must have drug himself off into the brush during the night to die. I managed to roll onto my hands and knees and began to crawl back to where the fire was. My chest hurt like hell but I was cold. If I could make it to the fire I could see if there was any way to warm myself by reviving the embers.

Nathan Wright

As I moaned and groaned my way forward I heard a weak bark, more like a yelp than anything. It came from the direction of the fallen elk. Once I made it to the fire pit I could see Ben. He had come to during the cold night and made his way to the warm carcass of the big elk and snuggled up just behind its front legs and against its warm belly, hell he was smarter than I was. He was wagging his tail to beat the band and was holding his head up as he looked at me with his big Ben grin. I was glad to see he had made it.

The fire had grown cold; I took a stick and stirred the ashes until I spotted some red embers. There was a small stack of wood nearby which I had gathered the previous evening so I reached as far as I could without actually moving my body. I grabbed a long limb that stuck out from near the bottom of the stack. Slowly I pulled that limb toward me and to my pleasant surprise several small pieces of wood were drug along with it. I took one of the driest and smallest branches I could find and broke it into even smaller pieces for tinder. I then gently pressed the pieces into the sparks I had found and waited.

First nothing, then a little smoke, then more smoke, finally there was a small flame and then more flame. I quickly added more small pieces of wood and then some of the larger ones. The fire caught. Within a few minutes I had a warm fire and in my entire life I can't remember one that felt better. Ben sat the entire time snuggled up to the dead elk and watched. When the fire caught he raised his head and looked like he might try to give up his spot by the elk and join me. I watched and wondered if he would try.

Slowly he rose up onto his front legs and sat there for a while. Then slowly again he managed to raise himself onto his back legs. He stood there on all fours and looked at me. After a few seconds he started taking small cautious steps, at least none of his four legs seemed to be broken. With a few wobbles and a stop or two he made it to where I lay and stood there beside me and the fire. I patted his head and rubbed his back. He collapsed beside me onto the ground, no doubt exhausted by his efforts.

I checked out the big dog as best as I could. There was no blood that I could tell. His four legs didn't cause him pain when I probed and that was very good. His right shoulder looked a bit larger than it had been the day before. I gently patted that area and he whimpered. I didn't think anything was broken or he wouldn't have been able to make his way over to the fire. My guess was that he was just bruised up pretty bad.

As for me I knew I had some broken ribs, hopefully that was it. Any other internal injuries would make themselves known in a day or two. The only problem was that both me and Ben were laid up pretty good and unable to travel, even if we could travel we were at least a week's ride from anywhere with a roof over it.

I had broken some ribs when I was younger at home on the farm. I remembered lying in bed for the better part of two weeks. That was bad news. Two weeks in this weather and me and Ben would surely starve to death. The horses would do fine. They were free to forage in the tall dry grass that was everywhere. There was a shallow stream nearby that was frozen hard on top but at one spot went through some rocks at a really steep grade and at that spot the water wasn't frozen, there was plenty of water for Hazel and Rusty and it wasn't in the form of ice.

Food was going to be the only problem. As I thought of the predicament me and Ben were in my eyes wandered to the carcass of the elk. Hell we weren't going to die, that collision I had the previous night with that four legged locomotive must have shook something loose up there. We had enough food right here in camp to last two months and at the temperatures we were experiencing it wouldn't spoil. The meat hadn't been gutted and drained of blood properly but I could deal with that.

Both Ben and myself rested for the better part of the day. Late in the evening I paid a visit to the elk. With my big skinning knife I carefully carved away at one of the flanks. The skillet from the previous night's supper was lying near the fire and was easy enough to get to. I put two big chunks of lean elk meat into the pan and slid it onto the fire. Ben watched and knew the drill, what I ate he also got a portion of. Within thirty minutes I had the meat nearly done, turning it occasionally with my fingers. As it sizzled in the iron skillet it reminded me of steaks I had eaten in some of the fancier establishments back east. I doubted if there would be any cloth napkins with this meal though.

When I thought the food had cooked long enough I took a piece of wood I had sharpened with the skinning knife and speared one of the two 'Steaks'. Not wanting to wait for it to cool on its own I rubbed it in the snow for a few seconds until it was still hot but not too hot. I tore off a few small pieces and tossed them to Ben who sniffed once before gobbling them down. I tried a small piece and let me tell you, no seasoning, no salt, no nothing, but it was still delicious. I had expected it to be a little tough but to my pleasant surprise it was mostly tender.

It didn't take long before the two of us finished what was in the skillet. It wasn't long before I was back at the elk carcass carving more supper from the same flank that I had gotten the first mess from. Ben waited patiently for his share. When we both had our fill I scrubbed the skillet with some snow and put it back beside the fire. I then carved for an hour on the big elk and when I was finished I spread the strips of meat in the snow to freeze. Having some food in me and Ben seemed to revive the both of us. I knew the big elk carcass would freeze solid in the next day or two so I was determined to carve as much meat as possible as soon as I rested a bit, easier to carve now than to wait for the meat to freeze hard as a rock.

My ribs hurt like hell and I had yet to stand up straight since my encounter the previous night with that big bastard. My main concerns now were for two things. One was the distinct possibility of a bear catching the scent of blood in the air from the freshly killed elk. Second was the lack of fire wood.

I replaced the big Winchester cartridge that I had used to bring down the elk and checked the Colt. Both guns were where I could get to them by only reaching, not walking. I left the Colt out of the holster for the time being, no more frozen firearms for me please. I had used the last of the wood preparing what Ben and I had just ate and that was another concern for the moment.

Scanning our campsite I noticed some low hanging limbs that were near enough for me to crawl to. Taking the Winchester along with me I headed for the nearest one. Most of the bottom branches were dead and easy to break off. The effort was painful but I knew without wood for the fire I would either freeze to death or get killed by a bear, the fire was the best defense against both. A roaring fire might just keep a bear out of camp and away from the elk.

I worked until dark pulling branches back to where I could safely keep the fire fed during the night. Ben had actually walked a little while I was doing this. He had gone to the nearby stream and drank the cold clear water. Once he drank his fill he returned to a spot near the edge of the fire and settled down. He was doing much better than me.

Nathan Wright

When I figured there was enough wood to do until morning I took my coffee pot and filled it with the cleanest looking snow I could find without moving off into the darkness. Once I had it filled I sat it in the fire and then managed to get to the coffee and before long I had steaming coffee and more elk meat. Ben appreciated his snack and then settled down for the night. I slowly chewed my dinner and drank coffee. I was not feeling too bad for a man who had been run over by a thousand pound flesh covered locomotive with four legs traveling at full speed.

Both Hazel and Rusty stayed close to camp all day foraging on the tall dry grasses that stood near the timber line and hadn't been broken down and covered by the snow. Those two knew there were bear about and didn't want to be wandering around in the darkness without me. I decided to stay awake the entire night and keep watch. Most bear are opportunistic hunters and would not hesitate to sneak into camp under cover of darkness and kill anything that stood in the way of it and the elk carcass. Ben could probably escape but I could not although I knew he wouldn't flee from a bear knowing I was unable to make my escape with him. He would stand and fight even in his current condition before he would abandon me.

The night was cold but thankfully uneventful. At around three in the morning I did hear the sound of something big near camp. It was probably another elk. If it had been a bear I'm sure it would have investigated the fresh kill. I managed to stay awake the entire night and was entertained by both Rusty and Hazel who stayed close to camp. Hazel even came over once and butted me with her head before going back to stand beside Rusty. Ben slept like a new born puppy and at first light he was up and moving around, he sure was one tough critter.

With the arrival of a new day I felt safe to try to grab a couple of hours sleep. Ben was moving about and if I didn't know he was hurt I really wouldn't have been able to tell by his actions. The two horses were again munching on whatever was available. I fell asleep hoping the three would warn me if danger was about. By around ten-o'clock that morning I awoke and was pleased to see my three traveling companions close by. I slowly got to my feet for the first time in a day and a half, the effort brought tears to my eyes and sweat to my brow. I stood there for the longest of time taking in what our surroundings looked like and what they had to offer.

The water was close and by the looks of the stream it wouldn't freeze solid unless it got a lot colder. A little farther off from camp, maybe a hundred feet was a fallen tree that looked like it had been down for a year or two. I would move camp nearer to that spot in order to access the dead branches for fuel. I would also need to make some sort of brush tent to provide shelter for both me and Ben. It was farther away from the water but that would only be a problem for me not the horses or Ben. Then I thought of the elk. If I moved camp a hundred feet then I wouldn't be able to guard our food, which for the next several days was the elk. I carefully considered the need for a better camp and the need for food, I decided camp would remain here for at least another week or until I felt I could ride.

I hobbled around camp for a few minutes before returning to the fire and the skillet. Before long I had elk steaks sizzling in the skillet again and coffee boiling in the pot. Again Ben got as much as me. When he finished his portion he went to the stream for another drink. The meat I had was good but I would need to get to my saddle bags soon to get that sack of corn meal. I liked meat as well as Ben but I also like a little skillet bread to go along with it, tonight at supper I would have bread to go with my steak. When I had stripped the gear off the horses the night before the elk had charged camp I had put everything against a big pine tree which was about fifty feet from the fire. I made up my mind to grab both saddle bags before nightfall.

About an hour before dark Hazel snorted and moved to the other side of camp. Rusty looked around and soon followed the younger horse to the other side of the camp as well. Both had their ears perked and were standing with heads held high. They had either caught the scent of something or heard something, probably both. I slowly stood with the big Winchester rifle in my hands. I had also put the Colt in my pants pocket not wanting to strap on the gun belt. I listened hard but heard nothing. Ben was still sleeping by the fire.

Both horses were starting to get edgy and were backing away from camp. I knew that something was out there and pretty well knew which direction it would be coming from, which would be opposite Hazel and Rusty. Suddenly Ben raised his head and let out a low growl. He stood with an agility that masked his injuries. He stepped around the fire and slowly and silently stepped toward the tree line. There was the snap of a tree branch and seconds later another. Ben continued to advance but with extreme caution.

I was slowly backing to the trunk of a big tree which stood no more than fifteen feet from the fire. I leaned against the tree for support and also to steady my aim. If I had to fire a shot I knew it was going to be painful. The .45-.75 Winchester had a severe kick and with busted ribs I doubted if I would be able to get a second shot. If it was a bear and if that bear was running into camp then it would be on me before I could get a second chance to fire.

I took a quick look around and saw that both Hazel and Rusty had abandoned camp and were running at a full gallop in the opposite direction of whatever it was making the noise in the timber. I returned my gaze toward the tree line and waited for whatever it was. There was more breaking of branches. Whatever was coming at me was either too big to fit between the trees or was breaking branches in anger or as a warning. I could see some of the smaller trees shake. Ben had stopped advancing and was standing in a low crouch ready to pounce. The hair on the back of his neck stood straight up and said he welcomed whatever it was.

Finally the brush parted and a large brown bear stepped into the small opening but stopped when he saw the dog. No more than fifteen feet separated the bear and Ben. Both stood and stared. Most people think a grizzly is the biggest meanest bear in the forest but in these parts a North American Brown Bear can go nearly twice the size of a grizzly and also match the ferocity.

I braced myself against the tree but held my shot waiting for the best opportunity. At this distance there would definitely be only one chance. The standoff between Ben and the bear was lasting longer than I would have guessed. I thought about taking the shot but Ben was actually in my way. If I tried to shoot over the dog he might at the last second jump up into the shot. No, I wouldn't take that chance.

The bear had his lower lip stuck out and began scratching the ground with his left front paw. I had seen this before when hunting grizzly but had never been this close to its larger cousin, which at the moment felt too close. The bear began to step to the side of the dog but Ben matched his every move. Suddenly the bear roared and advanced a few steps. Ben howled in anger himself but gave ground to match the advancing bear.

Nathan Wright

I steadied my aim and started to apply pressure to the trigger of the Winchester. Both Ben and the bear had stopped moving and again tried to stare each other into submission. I knew the monster had come after the elk but was probably finding it a little harder to acquire than it wanted with the big snarling dog in the way. The bear lowered its head and began to turn. It looked one last time at the elk carcass and then moved off into the brush and timber. I could hear it snorting and breaking limbs as it went. The sound grew faint and I knew the danger was over, at least for a while.

Ben still held his position. He sniffed the air and then went into the brush where the bear had gone. I relaxed my grip on the Winchester and it was only then that I noticed the sweat running down my face. It was no more than twenty five degrees and here I was sweating. I wanted to call Ben back but let him follow the bear a little while. The bear had a really good sense of smell and would know the dog was still about. Finally after a few minutes when I was pretty certain that it was alright I called Ben. He came bounding into camp and ran straight to where I stood by the tree. I reached down and patted the big dog on the head.

Now why would a bear that big turn away from a dog. I stoked the fire and made some more coffee. Ben walked over and lay close to the heat and soon was sound asleep again. I stood slowly and whistled for the two horses hoping that they hadn't gone too far. Within minutes Hazel came out of the tree line followed by Rusty. Both walked to camp and I patted their heads, glad to not be stranded this far away from civilization on foot. I wouldn't tie out either for another day or two. With me barely able to move and now with an oversized brown bear about I felt they needed to be able to run if danger overtook us. I was sure each would come back once the danger had passed.

Chester's Last Ride

As I sat by the fire I wondered why that big bear had given up so easily. He may have had a fresh kill in the last few days and just wasn't that hungry. He may have encountered a man before and even been shot at, bears are not just dumb animals. I had hunted them now for four or five years and knew they could think and reason for themselves. But if that bear had truly been hungry then the sight of Ben wouldn't have slowed him down for a minute, the sight of me either for that matter.

I wondered why he was out anyway. This should have been the time of winter when he was in hibernation. I had seen bear before at this time of year and wasn't that surprised to see this one. They just wake up and start looking around. Hopefully he was on his way back to his den and wouldn't give me any more trouble, but I doubted it. He might den up a day or two but he would dream about that big elk carcass and soon wake back up and give me another visit. The next time he would really be hungry and one of us would surely die.

Darkness came on tonight with a purpose. The sky had grown cloudy and by the looks of it a snow storm was beginning to brew. I was caught out in the open without the slightest bit of shelter. I had decided to stay awake again tonight for fear of the brown bear paying us another visit. While I sat there and looked around I decided that tomorrow I would try to make a lean-to for shelter.

The wind had picked up a little and was blowing down from the Northwest. I eyed the big tree that I had backed up to when that big brown bastard came growling into camp and done some thinking. There was another much smaller pine tree right next to that big fir. With a little work I could place a small pole through the lowest branches of both for support. The limbs that were in the way could be stripped away and used for the back of the shelter. Yep I had just figured out my shelter. Come first light I would begin construction, if that is what you could call it.

The night was cold and windy. I kept up the fire in hopes it would warn off another bear visit, it must have worked. The next morning dawned cold and cloudy with snow starting to fall light at first but as the day progressed it became heavier. By noon the elk carcass was frozen solid and covered in snow. Maybe that would help mask its scent. I worked steadily on my new shelter and before long it was finished. I eased back inside and tried it out. The wind was blocked pretty well and I could almost feel heat from my fire. I would need to move the fire just a little bit closer in order to benefit fully from its warmth.

Breakfast that morning had again consisted of elk steaks but they were accompanied this time with skillet bread. Ben was enjoying his elk so much that he had given up on hunting rabbits and just hung around camp waiting on his next meal. I didn't mind, there was way more elk than he and I could hope to eat in a month or more. I spent the rest of the day gathering all the loose wood I could find. A big fire at night was my best defense against bears.

I wasn't worried about trappers or Indians seeing the fire. My camp was well positioned in a gorge and had good timber around. If I did have visitors they would hopefully be friendly but if not I was well armed and besides that, there was Ben. He could smell trouble just as well as he could smell the jack rabbits he loved to chase.

My chest was feeling better than it had any right to be. The broken ribs that I thought I had were probably just bruised really badly. By the third day I was moving around much better, almost as good as if I had never been injured. Ben was also acting good as new. He snored by the fire and ate elk meat three times a day. Now how difficult is that?

Chester's Last Ride

I decided to give it one more night in the woods and then I would break camp and head for civilization. I was also afraid to stay to long because that big brown bastard would start to feel his stomach rumble and he would pay me another visit very soon. I had given that bear a lot of thought since he had left the previous day. As big as he was it would take a very lucky shot to drop him on the first try, and there would be no second. I might get two or even three shots away with the Colt but even if the bullets later caused the bear to die he would kill me out of sheer anger and rage. He would be on me before I had a chance to flee. Ben would be right in the mix and he too would die trying to save me. No sir, tomorrow we were leaving.

At first light the next morning I was exhausted. I had again spent the night on guard duty. I stoked the fire with most of the remaining wood and then me and Ben had breakfast. I called in Hazel and Rusty and both horses came right up to me. I saddled up Hazel and fixed the pack on Rusty. Both horses were tied close to the lean-to and Ben was up and about so I felt relatively safe. I decided to grab a few minutes rest before breaking camp. I put the remainder of my wood on the fire and soon had a good blaze going. As soon as I lay down in the lean-to my eyes clamped shut from exhaustion.

Within thirty minutes of going to sleep Ben woke me by licking my face. It was probably the breath that really woke me but who was I to complain? He only disturbed me while I was sleeping if he had a good reason. I immediately got to my feet with the Winchester in hand. Everything was quiet but I could tell that Ben and the two horses were a little uneasy. I quickly finished loading the two horses and prepared to leave.

A man on horseback in big timber was no match for a hungry brown bear, especially one as big as our friend from the other day. If he was out there, and I was almost certain he was, then I was in trouble. Thinking fast I grabbed the small axe from the pack that Rusty carried and went over to the elk. I quickly chopped off a complete hind quarter and drug it ten feet from the carcass. I then did the same to a front shoulder and drug it ten feet in the other direction. Once done I put the axe back in the pack with Rusty and climbed in the saddle. I had just put the scent of blood in the air and if our four legged friend was out there waiting on me then I would know real soon.

Ben was acting real fidgety and wanted to leave but that would not be a good idea until I knew where the bear was. No more than ten minutes had gone by when I heard the snort and knew he was close. He had caught the scent and was coming hard through the trees. Limbs could be heard snapping not far off in the distance. This was what I had been waiting for, I knew right where he was and I was now going to go in the opposite direction. I tapped Hazel and we moved off at a good pace. Ben followed and he and I both kept a good watch on our campsite until it could no longer be seen.

When the big bear found the freshly carved elk he must have stayed with it, as we moved the sounds he made grew less and less. I wasn't really sure if chopping up that elk would have any effect on a big brown bear but it was the only option I had and as of now I think it worked. The bear was happy to stay there and I sure as hell was glad to be gone. After a couple of miles the horses had grown complacent and Big Ben seemed to also be at ease. We had survived.

It must have been very late in January as best I could tell; I didn't think it was February yet. My best guess was January the twenty-seventh but I really wasn't sure, I could be off four or five days in either direction. Every year I made myself a promise to keep a record of the days spent out on the trail and every year I managed to misplace a few. When out in the nowhere I found it easy to get caught up in the beauty of the country I traveled in and lose track of my days. It just didn't seem as important when there were no people around. Hazel and Rusty didn't care what day it was and for that matter neither did Ben. The more time I spend with them in the wild the less the days on a calendar meant to me too.

We traveled the entire day at a slow pace. Rusty was loaded pretty heavy with the pelts I had accumulated over the winter and also with what meager supplies we had left. I had managed to carve out about twenty pounds of elk meat the night before we left and it was frozen solid inside a burlap horse blanket. I never like to leave anything out in the open while traveling that might put off a scent. Hopefully the horse blanket would mask things a bit. I had a few sheets of waxy parchment paper left and used it to wrap the twenty steaks; I don't like my dinner to have been touching a fuzzy horse blanket, although I'm sure Ben wouldn't care.

Camp that night was in a shallow draw that possessed only slight cover from the wind. There was snow about six to eight inches deep on the ground and a semi frozen stream running nearby. The ice was thin in the middle, no more than two inches deep, under that was clear ice cold water. I used my axe to scrape away the top and then filled my coffee pot before letting my four legged companions have a drink. I had drank after both horses before and even Ben at times but never if I could help it.

There was a small stand of fir trees nearby and I made my camp under the healthiest looking tree in the bunch. There wasn't much in the way of standing grass but after I scraped away some of the snow I found what I was looking for, grass and hay covered and protected by an early snow. I staked out the two horses and they each began to munch on the frozen treat. When each horse finished a spot then they would rake away the snow with their noses or even a front hoof to get to more, the two were content to do this for hours. I had learned years back that grass that had been covered by early snow would kind of ferment and the horses loved it.

After I was sure that Hazel and Rusty were in good shape I started a fire and sat the coffee pot right in the middle. Another gift from Mother Nature was the fact that a large old fir tree had fallen the previous year. The branches were easily lopped off with my axe and would make good fire wood to last the entire night. The big deadfall would also make a convenient wind break for my blankets. It wasn't long before I had the skillet in the fire and two big elk steaks sizzling, along with a big pone of skillet bread. I was hungry, especially since we hadn't stopped for lunch. In cold climates like we were traveling in I rarely stopped for lunch, it just took too much time and made it that much longer until we could make final camp for the night.

Ben stayed close waiting for his supper. He watched the pan and rarely took his eyes off it. He knew that anything in the pan was half his. As the meat cooked I took my big knife and cut little chunks off the one that would be his. I regularly tossed him a small piece so he could enjoy his meal a little at a time. If I just threw him the entire portion he would be finished in ten seconds and be looking to share what I had the whole time I tried to eat.

When it was nearly finished I took a little pinch of salt and rubbed it onto the top of both steaks although the one Ben would get was nearly half gone already. I wished I had something other than salt but I didn't, just be happy with the salt I told myself. Ben got the remainder of his steak which was cut into very small strips and also half the skillet bread. When finished he seemed happy but looked at me just the same as I ate my share.

"Alright Ben here you go." I tossed him the last bite of my meat and then showed him the empty skillet that I had used as my plate. He inspected it and was finally convinced that the meal was truly over. I used some of the hard packed snow to scrub out the skillet and laid it near the fire to use for breakfast the next morning.

As I lay on my blankets sipping coffee and looking at the fire I wondered if I would ever be able to settle down somewhere with a roof over my head. I had been doing this for the last few years and had grown quite used to sleeping under the stars. The only time I ever missed home was late November and late December. Thanksgiving and Christmas were always happy times with lots of food, family and fun back in Kentucky. That was really the only two times during the year that I ever felt lonely, Thanksgiving and Christmas. As I lay there thinking about home I decided it was time to head back to Sioux City, Iowa to pick up my mail.

Ever since I had gone west I had visited the Sioux City Post Office at least twice a year and if it was handy maybe even three times. My family had used that address for the last five years and knew I would write back each time I was there. As I thought about the trip ahead I tried to remember the last visit I had made there for mail. It was either June or July, most likely July that I had been in that sizable town. Sizeable considering that anything with more than five sheds and two houses was considered a town out this way. Yes the more I thought about it the more it made sense. Hole up in Sioux City for the remainder of the winter and then see which way the wind was blowing come spring. I was sure Hazel and Rusty could use a little grain and molasses instead of frozen fermented grass that they had to dig loose with a hoof.

Now Ben was a different story. He didn't like towns and more than that he didn't like town dogs. He always managed to have him at least one showdown per day and on a good day maybe two. He had yet to lose a fight but two years back he had come close. Seems a big bulldog looking monster had crossed him in the street and the fight was on. I heard it from the stable where I had gone to check on my horses and I knew by the sound of it this was not just your regular dog fight. I ran around from the stables onto the main street and saw where a crowd had gathered. When I investigated I found Ben, he had his hands full with a muscle bound brute that looked like it should be wearing a Derby hat and smoking a cigar.

The crowd had apparently gathered to watch the fight and some of the men were even taking side bets on which dog they thought would win. It looked like a fight to the death. Ben was taller and looked only slightly heavier. The shorter dog looked like he was at least a hundred plus pounds and Ben, having just come off the range, was lighter than his usual weight of around a hundred and forty pounds. But Ben was lean and strong having just traveled six hundred miles in the last twenty-five days. The bystanders were back from the melee by at least twenty feet in any direction and that was when I noticed the men placing wagers on the side.

I was at a loss of what to do. If I marched into the middle of this heavyweight event then I might lose a leg. If I did nothing then one of the two dogs was going to get hurt badly or even killed. Now the last thing I wanted to do was lose my old trail partner but I also knew if I broke it up too soon Ben might have his feelings hurt. Before I had a chance to make a decision Ben made it for me.

Chester's Last Ride

His opponent had gone in for Ben's throat but the big cur simply raised up on his hind legs just enough to allow the shorter bulldog to go under him. As his opponent's body went under Ben came down and grabbed the shorter dog by the back of the neck and clamped down hard. He then picked the front part of the bulldog's stubby body up by the nap of the neck and shook hard.

I knew that if I didn't step in now the bulldog was a goner. Just as I was shoving my way through the crowd that had gathered a man on the other side of the fight betting on the outcome stepped forward.

"That long haired bastard is cheating and about to kill Bruiser. I'm going to kill that ugly mutt," he said.

As he said this he was going for his gun. Now I wasn't in the notion of killing a man over a dog fight but this wasn't just any dog fight, it involved Ben.

I took one last long step and made it through the crowd. The man who said he was going to kill Ben was straight across from me and saw my entrance into the center of the ring of people. He also saw how fast my Colt was drawn and his was just clearing leather.

"Stop right there mister," I demanded.

He stopped dead in his tracks and looked at me. His gun was in his hand but it was still pointed in a downward position toward the ground, he hadn't finished his draw.

As I stared at the stranger who was holding the gun I couldn't see how the fight was going. Ben was, for the moment, on his own. What I couldn't see with my eyes I could hear with my ears though. There was a crunching sound and a raspy yelp as the big bulldog had his neck broken and was then dropped to the ground by Ben.

Nathan Wright

"Ben," I shouted in hopes that he would leave his fresh kill and come to where I was standing in case anyone else wanted to shoot him. Within seconds he was standing in front of me and he was looking at the man holding the gun. Ben was still operating on full go and wanted nothing more than to do to the man with the gun what he had just done to the big bulldog.

"Mister, if you don't holster that iron then one of two things is going to happen," I told him.

He looked mad as hell but finally managed to ask, "What two things you talking about boy?"

"Number one is if you move that gun an inch in any direction other than back toward your holster I will blow your shooting hand clean off. Number two, and this one is much worse, Ben here will consider that bulldog over there just a warm up for the main event, which is you."

The man's eyes dropped from me to Ben. "Alright you bastard you, we'll just let the sheriff handle this."

I didn't like being called a bastard and the man still hadn't put his gun back in his holster so I slowly pulled back the hammer of my Colt and let the metallic click do the talking for me. Everyone heard the sound it made and a few even saw me cock the Colt; the sound it made truly meant business.

The man just stood there and held his gun. I wasn't sure what was going to happen until I heard a voice say, "This is the sheriff, put down those guns, both of you."

I waited for my opponent to put his away. He started the whole thing by drawing his gun first. He didn't make a move; he just stood there like a statue.

"Sheriff, this man drew first and I want him to put his gun away before I do anything," I told him.

Chester's Last Ride

The sheriff walked over to the man and slowly reached over and took the gun from his hand. It wasn't until then that I holstered my weapon.

The sheriff looked at the dead dog in the middle of the street and then at Ben. "What happened here anyway?" he asked.

The man who had his gun taken now decided to talk. "It was that young feller's fault sheriff. He sent that big dog of his after Bruiser and before I could intervene they started fighting. When I pulled my gun to kill his dog well you saw what he did. He drew down on me. If I had been drawing on him instead of his dog then he would be dead now instead of standing there with that sick looking smile on his face."

I was amazed at how far from the truth the story was but waited to see what the sheriff's response would be. The crowd was quiet for the moment and I really needed to tend to Ben. I still didn't know what kind of injuries he might have sustained in his run-in with the bulldog.

The sheriff looked at me and asked, "Is that true mister?"

"No Sheriff, as a matter of fact it's the farthest thing from the truth. Anyone here in this crowd will tell you that he is lying."

The man started to step in my direction until the sheriff held up a hand and said, "Whitley, why don't you tend to your dead dog over there, if I need anything more from you then I'll send for you later."

The man named Whitley looked in my direction and said, "This ain't over by any means stranger. Before you leave this town I intend to even the score."

"If you fight as good as your dead dog over there then I look forward to it," I told him.

This was more than he could stand, he charged toward me and the sheriff only caught him at the last second or there would have been another fight right there in the street.

"Now Whitley, this is your last warning, get that dog of yours off the street and I don't want to hear another word out of you," the sheriff said.

This time Whitley did as he was told but still couldn't manage to keep his mouth shut, "You're up for election again this November Sheriff and I think it's about time someone other than you won that election. Starting right now I will make it my soul purpose in life to get you defeated in the fall. And as for that bastard and his dog over there I intend to settle the score real soon." With that said he went over to his dog and knelt down. I supposed it would take a wagon to remove the body from the street.

The whole time this had been going on Ben sat to my left and caught his breath. I still hadn't had a chance to check out his injuries if he had any. As ferocious as the fight was I felt certain he was hurt but at least he wasn't the one laying in the street dead.

"Alright Mister, you mind following me over to my office so I can get your side of what happened? Shouldn't take too long, oh, and by the way, you better bring that dog along with you. By the looks of things he might need some tending to," the sheriff said.

I looked down at Ben and noticed he had blood coming from one side of his mouth and there were a couple of big patches of fur yanked clean off of him. Where the fur was gone it looked like some skin was gone along with it. I motioned for Ben to follow as I started down the boardwalk with the sheriff.

The sheriff's office was a little run down building made of wood frame with some sort of clapboard siding attached. There was a front porch along with the usual assortment of ladder back chairs facing the street. There was even a spittoon between two of the chairs that looked like antique rockers.

Chester's Last Ride

This being the middle of summer found two ancient men wearing bib overalls and smoking pipes sitting in two of the chairs with a checker board between them supported by an old wooden crate of some sort. As we approached one of the two reached over and knocked the hat off the head of his opponent. In response that man took out his pipe and threw it cross the checker board and hit the other man in the chest. Sparks and tobacco went every which way.

"What do you mean knocking my hat off like that you old fart?"

"You were taking too long to move you old goat. At my age I only got so many games of checkers left, and by the way, your pipe landed out in the street in a fresh steaming pile of horse shit. I hope for the rest of your days your pipe tobacco reminds you of the sweet aroma of horse shit. Now move your next checker before I knock you out of that rocker."

The sheriff walked over and gently picked up the pipe, careful not to get anything on his fingers. "Here you go Sam, you might want to give that thing a good scrubbing before you load any more tobacco in it."

The sheriff walked in through the front door of his office and paid the two checker players no more mind.

"Grab yourself a chair over there while I grab us a couple of coffee tins. See if that dog of yours needs any medical attention while I start the pot."

I sat down and motioned for Ben. He walked over and stood in front of me, eyeball to eyeball you might say. I took both hands and opened his mouth as gently as I could. The teeth were all bloody and his tongue had a slight cut on the side. I patted him on his head and then eased a hand inside. A few of the teeth were a little loose. When he had picked up that big dog by the neck he must have nearly pried a few out. His teeth all seemed to be accounted for though. The loose ones would tighten back up in a few weeks but he would have a real hard time eating anything tough for a while because of the soreness. The bite marks were another story. That big bulldog had bit off big chunks of fur along with some skin.

While I was checking Ben out the sheriff came back in from a side room carrying two tin coffee cups with steam coming off the top. "How bad is it?" he asked.

"Well, I think he's going to be having a hard time eating for a few days and he has some pretty bad bites on his back and shoulder. Is there anyone in town that works on dogs and such Sheriff?" I asked.

"Sure is. We got us a man in town that used to be a real people doctor but gave it up a few years back. Said he enjoyed working on animals better. He said people will pay to have a horse or dog patched up but when it comes to their own medical bills they just don't seem to be in any hurry about settling up the bill.

"Don't worry about that situation out there in the street. Whitley has been a bully ever since he landed in town a couple of months ago. I asked you to come to my office to get you away from everyone. His damn dog, the one he called Bruiser, has either killed or run off every other dog in the county I think. Good riddance to that big bastard if you ask me."

"Thanks Sheriff. I believe I'll take Ben over to that doc's place and get him patched up if you can point me in the right direction."

"Just go to the street back of this one and you'll find his place, big barn looking building. He's got a sign over the door that reads, *'Four legged friends come on in, everybody else wipe your feet first.'*" The sheriff laughed as he said this.

"Oh, and another friendly piece of advice, everyone in town will be glad that your dog bested Bruiser, everybody that is except Whitley. While in town don't turn your back on him," the sheriff said.

"Sounds like a good thing to know Sheriff. By the way I didn't get your name."

The sheriff stuck out his hand and said, "Names John Allen Messer, everybody around calls me John Allen, they never call me sheriff."

"Well it was nice to meet you John Allen; I'm Zeke Conley from Kentucky. I won't be in town to vote but I hope you win your re-election."

With that I thanked him for the coffee and then headed for the back street.

The barn was easy enough to find and the sign was just the way the sheriff had said it was. The building had two big sliding doors in the front; one was standing about three feet open so me and Ben walked on in. I did brush my feet on the boardwalk first though like the sign said. Inside looked like some sort of a zoo or traveling carnival, besides horses and mules there were cats and dogs, all either in a stall or a cage. There were two small bear cubs in one cage and a big raccoon in another. There was even a horse there that had big black and white strips which made it a zebra. I had seen pictures of that funny looking African horse before but was surprised to see one in Sioux City. I found out later that the animal had been left behind the previous year by a traveling circus.

The zebra had nearly broken its right front leg when a ramp used to load and unload the animals from a train car gave way and dumped the startled beast to the ground. At first it looked as if the leg might have been broken which would have spelled death for the animal, but it only turned out to be a sprain of some sort. The man who owned the circus was forced to proceed on to the next town without one of his main attractions. The doc had sort of adopted the zebra and was caring for it until the circus returned. After this much time it appeared the animal would stay there forever. The zebra had a name and it was the name that surprised me the most, the name was Zeke, Zeke the Zebra. Now if that didn't just beat all.

There was a man in a side room working on another dog. When he saw me and Ben he told me to have a seat and he would be with me shortly. I took a chair and Ben sat down between my feet. He seemed to be as surprised as I was by some of the strange animals in the barn. Within minutes the man finished up with what he was doing and came over to where I sat with Ben."

"Oh my goodness, looks like your dog has been fighting with a bull moose or something. Bring him on in and let me have a look at him."

He pulled a short stool from under his work table and placed it on the floor. "Have him to use this as a step so he can get up on the table."

I motioned for Ben to climb up on the table and then knew why the stool was there. Ben had trouble getting up on the stool and then from the stool to the table.

"He looks like hell mister, what happened?"

"He got in a fight with some dog the sheriff called Bruiser."

The doc stopped and looked at me. "You telling me this dog of yours tangled with Bruiser? No wonder he's hurt. Good thing you broke up the fight, for your dog's sake anyway."

"I didn't break up the fight doc, too many people in the way. By the time I was able to do anything it was too late."

Chester's Last Ride

The doc looked at Ben and then at me. "You telling me that Bruiser let your dog go? I never knew of Bruiser ever letting a dog go before."

"Bruiser didn't let Ben go Doc. Ben killed him."

The doc smiled real big and then patted Ben on the head. Now Ben is big and mean but he never turns down a friendly pat on the head. The doctor looked at Ben's shoulders and then at his back. He picked up one of the front paws and placed it in the center of his hand. The paw completely covered the doc's palm. He then put the paw down and stepped back.

"I've been waiting for at least two months for either Whitley to leave town or some dog meaner than his to show up. I guess this is the dog. Bruiser has been bad for this town and bad for my business. Everybody likes a dog around but that big monster has either killed or run off every canine in town. I make most of my money off horses and dogs but lately the dog business has been bad because all the dogs are gone. Bruiser was one tough critter."

"Well Ben here needs some looking after Doc. I don't know what needs to be done but just check him out good if you don't mind. I will pay in cash if that helps any," I told him.

"I'll take good care of him and you won't be paying in cash because this one is on the house." The doc looked at Ben's mouth and then at the bite marks on his back and shoulder.

"You're going to have to leave him with me for a couple of days. He can't eat anything solid for at least that long. His teeth have been nearly yanked out. These bites are pretty bad too. I wouldn't want the wounds to get infected and if he's outside running around that is exactly what is going to happen. I can fix him up some real good meals that he can more or less drink and let me tell you that dog of yours is going to enjoy what I make. By the way, he won't turn on me when you leave will he?

Nathan Wright

I mean I've got to treat him and some of what I do might cause him some pain." The doctor had a bit of a worried look on his face when he asked me this.

"Tell you what doc, how about I stay here with you and Ben while you work on him. He knows you are trying to help him but he is part wolf and that is the part that is unpredictable."

The doctor smiled and said, "That sounds like the thing to do. He killed Bruiser and he might still be a little excited. It takes a dog a few hours to really get over a fight like that."

I stayed there while the doc done his magic. He clipped away the fur around the bite marks and then had me to hold Ben's head while he put some sort of burgundy colored liquid on the wounds. Ben squirmed and yammered but otherwise held still. He knew he was being fixed up. Within thirty minutes the big cur was all patched up and ready to go but there would be no going for Ben. He would stay with the doc to make sure he didn't get his wounds infected. I both hated to leave him there but was also glad he was going to be alright.

Within three days Ben was starting to heal pretty well and the doc said it would be alright for him to leave. As we walked toward the big door to leave Ben stopped and looked at the doc. He then walked back over and brushed his head and neck against the man's coveralls as if to say thanks. Doc patted him on the head and then we left. True to his word I didn't owe a penny for Ben's treatment. I offered but he said no.

I gathered Hazel and Rusty at the stables and settled my bill there. We headed out a few hours before dark and went back west. That was two years ago. I had been there maybe four or five times since to pick up my mail and always looked the old doc up. Each time Ben and the doctor were glad to see each other.

I found out the next spring that the sheriff had won his bid for re-election and was glad of it. He seemed like a respectable man and handled his job with fairness. The man named Whitley had left town the next day after Ben had killed his bulldog. The sheriff told me that he suspected Whitley fell in with a gang of outlaws that were suspected of robbing three different trains. One eyewitness had described him well enough for the sheriff to suspect who it was.

I finally dozed off to sleep with thoughts of Ben's big fight with that bulldog from two years prior. The way I had it figured, we would be roughly two weeks on the trail before making Sioux City. There were a few small settlements we would pass on that two week trip that would allow for the purchase of some much needed supplies. Once I traded for the bear skins I would replace some of the weight Rusty now carried with a fifty pound sack of horse feed. Rusty and Hazel would appreciate a little snack other than the frozen grass each were forced to rake and scrape for.

The next morning was clear and cold with a heavy frost. I was actually excited about going to Sioux City. Mail was always a treat. I fixed up another big breakfast of elk steaks and skillet bread. Ben had gotten so used to having breakfast with me that he had pretty much given up on hunting rabbits. I didn't mind. I would actually share my last bite with that critter.

I broke camp and left about thirty minutes after sunrise and headed along the trail that I had used the previous year, knowing it would be about a five day ride to the first of the small settlements we would pass through on the way to Sioux City.

The next five days passed uneventfully. There were no more bear encounters and for that matter no people encounters either. The land we traveled through was barren and cold. Whenever I came across anything the horses could eat I would stop and make a small fire for coffee. Hazel and Rusty needed the rest and the food. As they picked whatever they could find I would sit by the fire and enjoy the hot brew, knowing that another day or two would see the last of it.

As each day passed I found myself thinking more and more about my mail run and the hopes of letters from home. In the evenings as we rode I was always on the lookout for any stands of grass that hadn't been covered by snow. If it was late enough in the evening and a stand looked promising I would go ahead and make camp for the night. Horses in winter needed a little more feed and a little less travel than they got during the summer months.

We made it to the first of the little settlements about two days after my coffee ran out. It was a town called Shasta. There was a small store and two saloons. It was a stage stop on the trail west, no railroad and no telegraph, just a stage stop. I noticed a barn with an office in front which meant it was probably a stable that rented stalls by the day. I walked in the front door and was met with stove warmed air, the first I had experienced in at least four months. The room was empty. Toward the back was another door which must have went into the barn. I opened it and looked inside.

"Howdy partner, you lookin for me?" The question was asked by a middle aged man wearing coveralls and a big checkered coat.

"Yes sir I guess I am. I was wondering if you rented stalls."

Chester's Last Ride

"Well yes I surely do, but to horses and mules only, not people. If you're looking for a place to stay there is a couple that lives by the general store and they let out rooms for fifty cents a night. You got horses?"

"Yes sir I do. They been on the trail more than four months and are in need of a day or two of rest and some oats if you got any."

"I got just the thing if you can pay. The stage pays me extra anytime the temperature drops below zero for more than a day. And guess what, a twenty-four hour zero arrived here more than three months ago. What they pay me extra for is the molasses I mix in with the oats. They like me to add molasses to the oats and grains I usually feed the horses when the stage arrives. Seems the molasses helps keep the animals in good health during cold times like this. I charge seventy-five cents a day per animal. How many you got?"

Zeke knew about the molasses and felt a little guilty knowing his two horses needed it. "I think that is a fair price. I got two horses and a big dog, how much for the dog?" I asked.

The hostler laughed. "I ain't never been asked that question before, how big is the dog?"

"Well he is smaller than the two horses, but not by much."

Again the man laughed. "I can feed him some scraps from the store; it's the closest thing we got to a diner or restaurant. They got four tables in the back by a big potbellied stove. The store owner's wife fixes meals every day and they are different every day. I'll check with her and see if she might have something for your dog. I won't charge you anything for that. Go ahead and bring in your horses and dog so I can get them situated."

The barn looked bigger standing on the inside. There were six stalls on one side and four on the other. There might have been three other horses penned along with a bunch of chickens which were running loose. I noticed a coop where a stall would have been and figured the man raised chickens to eat and also for the eggs.

Ben had been around chickens before and never paid them no mind. But now you go and fry one up and that big dog was always first in line, I just hoped he didn't take to eating the ones in the barn that were walking around. I walked back through the office and out to where I had Hazel and Rusty tied to a hitching post. Ben was sitting on the boardwalk looking the small town over. I led both horses inside the big front door which had just been opened by the hostler. As soon as we were inside he closed the door to keep out the wind.

"Nice pair of horses you got there. Looks like that older one is loaded pretty heavy."

"Yea, he is but he ain't been carrying the load the entire trip. I switch horses each morning, let both take turns to help keep them fresh."

"That's the way I would handle it if I was out in this kind of weather. What kind of load is it anyway if asking ain't being rude?"

"Bear skins, got all bear skins and two wolverine pelts. This is all I got to show for over three months of winter work."

"Well you might have hit a little streak of luck. The man that owns the general store pays good money for bear skins. Anytime someone in town needs a little extra jangle in his pocket he just goes off for a few days and hunts bear. A good hide will get you a hundred and fifty dollars. A poorly one can bring maybe seventy-five. I don't know about the wolverine hides you got but you might ask."

I liked what I had just heard. A hundred and forty-five was the most I had ever gotten before but the usual price was about one thirty-five to one forty. "Why is he paying that much for a bear hide if I might ask?"

"He works them up real good. People say he is the best at curing out a hide and making it presentable for a front room rug, you know the kind they put in them fancy parlors. People from back east have standing orders for every bearskin rug he can make. When he gets a few hides he works them up and then freights them back east on the stage, makes a pretty good wage for the work he puts into it. If you go to the general store and ask around I think you might be able to strike a deal, that is unless you want to haul these hides all over creation trying to find a better price than the one you'll get here in town."

I thought about what the hostler had said. "Can you keep the hides here while I go to the general store?"

"Be glad to help out if you'll just lend me a hand unloading everything. We can stack it up in the corner over there till you figure out what you're going to do."

I helped unload the furs and then headed for the door. I stopped and reached the man two three dollar gold pieces and then called Ben. We headed down the snow covered street toward the store. As I approached the building I noticed it was actually bigger than it first looked. There was a front porch with a long wooden bench. I had Ben to stay outside and then opened the door. I was met with the feel of stove warmed air again and the aroma of fresh baked bread, the first I had encountered in over four months.

"Howdy stranger, come in and warm yourself by the fire." The voice came from the side of the store where a counter was. Behind the counter stood a tall man with a handlebar mustache who was wearing a leather apron.

"I saw you come across the street from the stable. If that big dog that was with you wants to come in I don't mind as long as he's friendly. I hate to see him standing out there all by himself," the man said.

In all my years I had never had anyone to invite Ben inside unless I asked first. I turned and opened the door and snapped my fingers. Ben came inside and began looking the place over. "Sit boy." Ben took a seat on the rug by the door and looked as happy as could be.

"That is some dog you got there mister, what do you call him?"

"Ben, his name is Ben," I told the man.

"Well if I give him a piece of chicken jerky he wouldn't take offence would he?"

"Mister, if you give him a taste of anything to do with a chicken then he will probably be your friend for life."

The man grinned and went toward the back. In less than a minute he came back with what looked like small pieces of white dried chicken meat. He approached Ben as most people did, with great caution. Ben was looking at what the man was carrying in his hand. As the man spoke some calming words to Ben he laid the pieces of meat on the floor by the big dog. Ben started to wag his tail and as soon as the man's hand was clear he scooped up the treats with his teeth and tongue. Now anyone who has ever been around dogs will tell you that a dog can smile as well as a man and the look on Ben's face was definitely a smile.

"Nice dog you got there, he looks part wolf."

"You might be right about that. Me and Big Ben covered some miles together in the last few years."

"What can I help you with today?" the store clerk asked.

"I just stabled my two horses across the street and the man over there said you might be interested in a few bear skins."

The man's eyes lit up. "You got bear skins young man?"

Chester's Last Ride

"I got a few along with two big wolverine pelts."

The man drew back and slapped me on the shoulder. "Well can you bring them in, I would be glad to make you an offer on all of it if that suits you."

Now this was looking better than I had hoped. I was nearly out of money and fully expected to not be able to sell the hides until I got into Sioux City which was at least ten more days. I would be willing to sell them a little cheaper here if I could. Funny how being broke and out of coffee makes a man lower his price.

"Might be easier if you walked over to the stables with me, I dropped them in a corner over there. There are enough that I would need to reload them on one of my horses to get them over here."

The man looked toward the back of the store and when he didn't see whatever it was he was looking for he headed that way. Once back there I heard him say, "June, could I get you to watch the front for me? I got a man up there that has some bear skins I need to have a look at."

"Can you give me a minute or two; I just put two pones of cornbread in the oven," she said.

"Sure can, you know I would never want you to burn the cornbread you are so famous for." He laughed after he said this.

Within three or four minutes the man came back up front and indicated he was ready to go. Once we made it over to the livery stable I pointed at the big stack of furs. I paid close attention to the man's expression as he opened and then unfolded each. I knew the bears I had killed were of good size and good quality. The South Dakota bears were always a little bigger than their more southern cousins. After he finished inspecting the brown bear furs he opened the two wolverine pelts and the grizzly. He felt the texture of the fur and then the quality of the hides.

"I've never had the opportunity to work up a wolverine before. I don't believe they are suitable for rugs, maybe a woman's shawl though. Looks like seven browns and a grizzly. What were you thinking as a fair price mister?" He asked me.

I could tell that he wanted the hides by the way he looked at each during his inspection. "I asked what you would pay when I came into your place over there. I just want a fair price, you make some money and I make some money."

"Tell you what, looks like you got four really good hides and three more that are not as good, but close. How about we call all seven the same and my best offer is one fifty-five each. How does that sound?"

I wasn't expecting more than one twenty-five each this far from Sioux City, all the time I had been in the wild must have seen the value of hides increase. "How about the grizzly and the two wolverine hides?" I asked.

The man looked again at the three hides which were sitting to the side of the seven browns. "I don't really want them. Grizzly is a hard bastard to work up and I have no idea about something like a wolverine. Let's just deal on the seven browns if that would be alright with you."

I really didn't want to pack just three hides all the way to Sioux City and try to make a sale. I had found it hard in the past to unload just a hide or two. I think the man from the store knew this and wanted me to just throw them in with the seven browns. "Tell you what, if you want the browns then I will agree to your price of one fifty-five each but you will have to make me an offer for the other three or no deal." I really didn't want to lose the deal on the browns and would back down fast if I was pushed.

Chester's Last Ride

The man went back over to the three hides and picked each up. He was thinking hard and I hoped he would see things my way.

"Tell you what, the seven browns comes to a little more than a thousand dollars. I will take the whole lot for eight hundred cash and four hundred dollars store credit. You can spend the four hundred on anything I got. If you find that fair then let's shake on it," the store clerk said.

I had done a quick count in my head and knew the price he offered me for the browns was a thousand and eighty-five dollars. That meant I was getting a hundred and fifteen dollars for the two wolverine and one grizzly pelt and four hundred of the money would need to be spent in his store. It was an excellent deal for him but at the same time it wasn't such a bad deal for me either. I had intended to spend a little money in town anyway but didn't know how I would spend four-hundred dollars in his general store. At any rate I knew he had a deal.

"You got yourself a deal as long as you carry over any of the four-hundred that I don't spend this trip. I travel through here two or three times a year and will spend it during future visits, if you think that is alright."

The man didn't have to think about that at all, he stuck out a hand and said. "Get these brought over and I'll have you the eight hundred waiting."

As we shook he added, "I got something over there that a man like you might be interested in. I noticed you got a Winchester .45-.75 and that's a good gun. But if I was making my living hunting browns and grizzlies then I might be tempted to carry something with a little more stopping power. When you get the hides carried over then I'll show you what I got."

Nathan Wright

As I carried the hides over to his store, one at a time of course, I thought about what he said about a bigger gun. Now a .45-.75 is a pretty big bore but more than once I had shot a brown only to see him continue to charge me. Two shots had always done the trick but if a brown ever got close enough before I shot him the first time then he would be on me before I had a chance at a second shot. A bigger gun might be nice but I wondered what he had. This far away from civilization made the chance for a really nice gun purchase a little unlikely.

I made eight trips for the bear hides and one for the two wolverines. By the time I was finished I had worked up a sweat even though the temperature outside wasn't even twenty degrees. After the last trip I went to the back of the store and found the tables and chairs I had been told of earlier. As I sat there catching my breath I suddenly found myself hungry. What had triggered this was the smell of something good and also the sight of men and women at two of the other tables eating out of big bowls. It looked like beef stew.

Not long after I sat down the man came back and sat down in the chair across from me. He slid over a white envelope and said to check inside but then he whispered to not be too obvious about it. I eased open the flap and without taking the money out counted eight one-hundred dollar bills. After reclosing the envelope I put it inside my coat pocket. Five minutes ago I had exactly eight dollars and twelve cents to my name, now that amount had grown by another eight-hundred dollars.

"Me and my wife run this store and live in the house out back. Next time you pass through town if you can't find me here then come around and knock on the front door. I am always either here or there," he said. "If you like I can bust up one of them hundreds into some smaller bills and three-dollar gold pieces. I always like to make my deals in big bills but after the deal is done most people like something smaller to carry around. Not everyone can bust a hundred."

He was right about that but I was lucky if I ever had a hundred to begin with. I noticed he hadn't mentioned the four-hundred dollar store credit and this had me a little suspicious. Maybe he hoped that I wouldn't need anything this trip and if I never made it back then he just made himself another four-hundred dollars. Maybe I should try to spend as much of the credit now as I could.

"You mentioned a gun earlier," I said.

I noticed the man's reaction and couldn't help but notice that he looked a little surprised. I didn't know this man and really hoped he wasn't going to try and beat me out of the other four-hundred dollars he owed me. I made up my mind right then to try and spend as much of the store credit I had coming as I could.

"Well I did, didn't I? Tell you what I got in the back if you're interested. I traded a man out of a Sharps Big 50 buffalo gun. I could let it go for two-hundred dollars plus a little extra for the ammunition, that is if you think you can handle a gun that big."

I knew of the Big 50 and to tell you the truth I had always wanted one but when I had the money one wasn't available and when one was available I didn't have the money. Now as luck would have it I had the money that I really needed to spend and this man had the gun.

"I just might be interested if it's in good shape and hasn't been fired too much. Let's have a look at it."

The man smiled and went in the back. Within a couple of minutes he was standing in front of me holding a really nice leather gun rug. When he unbuttoned the rug and spread it out in front of me on the table I was extremely impressed but tried not to show it. The Sharps looked brand new but in reality was at least fifteen years old. The stock was shiny and didn't show any sign of abuse. The barrel was etched with a buffalo design, four bison one behind the other. I picked up the gun and was impressed with the weight. All buffalo guns were heavy because the weight also helped with the recoil caused by the big ammunition.

"How much ammunition you got that matches this gun?" I asked.

"When I traded for this rig the man had eight boxes with twenty rounds to a box, all full, he had twelve more cartridges loose. If you like the gun I can make you a deal on the rug and the ammunition and also the cleaning rod I got for it. What do you think?"

I thought a minute. I knew the ammunition was going to be expensive and probably hard to find. If I was going to buy the gun then I would definitely need the rug and all the cartridges he had for it.

"Make me a price for the whole bundle and let's see what we come up with."

The man didn't move he just sat there and figured in his head.

"Them bullets cost fifty cents each for a gun like that. Let's see now a cleaning rod, a leather rug, a hundred and seventy-two rounds of ammunition and the gun. I figure I can let you have the entire rig for three hundred and twenty-five dollars mister."

I knew he had made me a fair price for the lot and I would take it if for nothing else than to use up the store credit he owed me but I also wanted to haggle a little.

"Make it three hundred even and you got a deal."

Chester's Last Ride

He didn't frown or smile at this offer. He just sat there and looked at the pot-bellied stove.

"Well how about me and you split the difference, three hundred and twelve-fifty?"

I knew I could save a little money if I tried, and I had just saved twelve dollars and fifty cents.

"You got a deal," I said as I stuck out my hand.

After we shook hands I said if my calculations were right then I still had a store credit of eighty-seven dollars and fifty cents. He agreed and said if I was interested that he had a brand new Smith & Wesson thirty eight caliber revolver he could let go for sixty five dollars. This sounded pretty good to me. I told him to make up the other twenty two dollars and fifty cents with ammunition for the Smith and also my Colt. That took care of my store credit and it also took care of any doubts I had about the man. We were even. I found I liked the store keep and I also liked his store. I usually passed Shasta up when traveling through. I had only been in this town on two other occasions but now made up my mind to visit any time I was near.

With my hides sold and the credit spent I was feeling pretty wealthy, if only for the moment. When the store keep returned from his stock room this time he was carrying a brand new Smith & Wesson revolver and a cloth sack full of cartridges that fit my Colt and also the Smith.

"My name is Clarence Lloyd; I don't believe I got yours," the store keep said.

"I'm Zeke Conley from Kentucky," I told him.

"Well Zeke, me and you done us some swapping this morning. If there is anything else I can do just give me a shout."

By now Ben had decided that he had sat on the rug by the front door long enough. He came back to where Clarence and me were and peeked around a shelf. I wondered if dogs were allowed this far back in the store especially where people were eating but Clarence answered that question when he looked at Ben and patted him on the head. Ben sat down and looked at me as if to say, 'I'm here, now find me something to eat.'

Just then the store keep's wife came out of the back room and said, "Oh my goodness, what a dog."

"This here is Ben and I think he wants to have some dinner. You got anything back there that might fit this critter's stomach?" Clarence asked.

She looked at the dog and said, "I think about everything I got back there would fit in that dog's stomach. Let me go and have a look, but in the meantime could he wait back up front?"

I smiled at the woman and said, "I'll take him back up front ma'am. And I think I want to have some food myself, but in a separate plate."

Everyone laughed as I led Ben back to the rug by the front door. When I returned to the back of the store I took better notice of my surroundings. The woman who I took was Clarence's wife was cooking on a big cast iron stove. There was a name plate on the top where the flue pipe was located which read *Chief National Excelsior Stove & Mfg. Co.*

It was a fine looking affair with several cooking surfaces and even what looked like a warming oven to the side. On the top was any number of pots and each was steaming. The woman quickly stirred some broth and flour together to make thick gravy and then put a big stew bone in. Clarence came in a side door and was carrying a small bucket that looked like it was used to carry off scraps. He held the bucket as the woman gently poured the thick contents into the bucket.

Chester's Last Ride

"Here you go young man. I think that big dog of yours will like what I fixed him. If you will take it to him then I will set your place on a table," she said.

I thanked her and headed for the front of the store. Ben was sitting where I had told him to and from the look on his face he knew I had his dinner in the bucket I was carrying. I sat it down in front of him and he immediately went to eating. Whatever it was he was sure enjoying it. I hurried back to the table where I had been and sat back down. The lady was busy waiting on the other two couples but I did notice a plate sitting on a counter beside the stove and hoped it was going to be for me.

In no time at all she had the plate filled and sat it down on the table in front of me. There was a big slice of buffalo meat surrounded by cooked potatoes and corn. There was a small side dish which contained some dried fruit and bread, not cornbread but actual wheat bread baked brown and still steaming. After looking over the food I looked up at the woman. "This is the most pleasant looking meal I have seen in many a month."

"Well you dig right in and I will get you some coffee. You want any cream in it?"

I hadn't had cream in at least four months and I hadn't seen any cattle around or in the stable where I left the horses so I asked her, "Where on earth do you get cream ma'am?"

"Oh, it's something new we get on the stage coach from time to time, they call it condensed milk and it comes in a can. You need to use it up in a few days after you open the can but around here it never lasts that long anyway. Wait till you try it in the coffee, you are in for a treat," she said.

She brought the coffee and it was as good as I hoped. The cream from the can was just like fresh, what would they think of next? When I was about finished she topped off my coffee and asked if I wanted dessert. I told her I would love some but I didn't ask what it was; I was looking forward to the surprise. Soon she brought over a big slice of baked squash that was lightly covered with a dark brown sugar, she called it brown sugar. It was delicious and I had no trouble finishing every bite, except for the rind. When I asked her how much I owed her she said seventy-five cents would do just fine. I gave her a dollar and thanked her for such good food. Ben heard me and came back; he stood looking at the woman and wagged his tail. It was his way of saying thanks.

I spent the rest of the day gathering up what supplies I would need for the rest of my journey into Sioux City. Besides the four-hundred dollars I had spent on the two guns I added another fifty-five for supplies, even managed to get a fifty pound sack of feed and a gallon of molasses for the two horses. Hazel and Rusty were going to be two happy critters for the remainder of our journey.

I pulled out of Shasta town two days after I had arrived there. Hazel and Rusty had spent two glorious nights in a barn stall eating oats and molasses along with lots of hay. Ben too looked better. He was more perky and rested after two days of sleeping in the same barn with the two horses. The hostler had taken a liking to Ben and I really think he hated to see the big dog go. The weather during the two days we had spent in town had been cold and snowy. The morning we left the skies had cleared up considerably, but it was still cold. I thanked Clarence and his wife for the great food and friendship. I never did know what her name was and neither she nor Clarence had bothered to say. It seemed he had called her June the first day I was there, but I couldn't be sure.

With the provisions we now had I could make it all the way to Sioux City without any problem at all. We could take our time and arrive there in about seven or eight days if we weren't presented with any difficulties along the way.

As the day progressed, the sky darkened and soon light snow began to fall. I decided to find suitable shelter for the night which out in the open meant a fallen tree for fire wood and a few fir trees to keep the snow off me and the horses. By five in the afternoon we still hadn't passed any spots along the trail that looked suitable. I pressed on deciding that if we hadn't found what we wanted thirty minutes before nightfall then I would make camp anyway.

As luck would have it thirty minutes before dark I could see in the distance a good stand of timber and what looked like a small stream that wasn't completely frozen. The problem was that by the time we got there it would be well past dark. I had made camp many a night after dark. It wasn't the best way but tonight with a storm brewing it was the only way.

As soon as we made it to the timber I unloaded the pack Rusty was carrying and then unsaddled Hazel. The time it took to do this allowed the two horses to cool down before I led them to the small stream for water. There was brush and timber on both sides of the stream so it wasn't too difficult to tie the two up where I could keep a close eye on things.

As the horses drank I quickly picked a spot for my fire and began to gather wood. In the distance I could hear a mountain lion and then I heard Ben barking. Surely he wasn't thinking about mountain lion for supper. I called the big dog and within minutes he came bounding into camp. After I got the fire going and filled my coffee pot with water, upstream from the horses of course, I led Hazel and Rusty back to the tree line. We were in a big stand of timber so it wasn't too difficult to find a spot close to camp that wasn't covered in snow. There was some standing dry grasses and weeds for the two horses to nibble on during the night but the main course for the two was going to be a portion of the horse feed from the fifty pound sack with some of the molasses poured on top for good measure.

Snow had started coming down much heavier now and I was certain that it wasn't going to stop soon. I started to think that maybe I should have stayed in Shasta another day or two. Too late to worry about that now, we were here.

Supper on the trail tonight would be buffalo steaks I had purchased from Clarence at his General Store. While the steaks sizzled in the skillet I made stick bread. In times when you have only one skillet it is possible to make bread dough up a little stiff and then wrap it around a sharpened stick. Put the stick in the ground near the fire and turn it every few minutes and soon you have a big biscuit you can eat right off the stick. Ben got his usual share of the steak and I even gave him some of my biscuit.

I noticed that during the night Ben stayed close to camp, no doubt wary of the big mountain lion that he had heard earlier. Ben was big and mean but let's face it he wasn't stupid.

I had an abundance of firewood thanks to a fallen tree that had been down long enough to get brittle but not so long as to turn spongey. I kept a good fire all night and slept little. I had noticed in years past that anytime I had spent more than a day in a town then my return to the trail was always accompanied with camp jitters. After a day or two out in the open I would settle back down, at least I always had before.

The next morning dawned cloudy and cold. The snow had slacked off to just light stuff but by the looks of things it could start back up at any time. After a quick breakfast for me and Ben I started putting away the camp. I had already given Rusty and Hazel their bait of corn and molasses about an hour before first light. During the night each horse had nibbled on the dry brush and tall sage that was within reach of their tethers. One thing I had noticed about the two was that during the night only one horse would sleep at a time while the other nibbled. It was actually very smart for the two to work together like that; one was always on guard for danger. It was also good for me knowing that at least one horse was awake, just in case.

We pulled out about an hour after first light with a strong wind blowing and more than a foot of new snow on the ground. The horses didn't have any trouble but I could tell that the day would prove hard on Ben. Each step for the big dog would require more effort and therefore more energy. I decided to take advantage of any standing grasses under the timber along the way to allow the horses to munch and rest; this would give Ben a chance to catch his breath too.

During the remainder of the trip into Sioux City we continued to hear a cougar at night. I doubted it was the same cat but you never know. This might have been one that didn't have a territory of its own and was tracking me and my horses. Stranger things have happened. I never did get to see the animal but it was there. One morning we even crossed fresh tracks in the snow. By the size of the footprints it was a really big cougar. Ben was smart to stay close during the night; he never really strayed far during the day either.

As it worked out the snow never let up the entire trip. By the time we made town we were traveling in eighteen inches of snow. Instead of eight days it took ten.

We got into Sioux City at three in the afternoon on February 21st, 1892. I was off by four days on my mental calendar, not bad. I headed straight for the livery stable hoping it wasn't full up. The man that ran the place was a friend of mine named Chet Brimley. He had been stabling Hazel and Rusty on and off now for the better part of five years. He also knew and liked

Nathan Wright

Ben and Ben liked him. Hell, Ben liked anybody that gave him food.

I walked into the front office of the livery stable and to my surprise there was a man sitting at Chet's desk that I didn't recognize. He was wearing a sharp looking set of duds and smoking a thick cigar. He looked up at me when I walked in and through a haze of cigar smoke he asked, "Can I help you?"

"I was looking for Chet, would you know if he is around or not?"

The man leaned back in his chair and that is when I noticed he was wearing a fancy holster and in it was an ivory handled Colt .45. He crossed his hands across his chest and asked, "What do you need him for?" As he said this he looked down at my Colt.

Now it's funny how a man can make up his mind about a complete stranger in no more than thirty-seconds and less than two sentences but let me tell you right now that is exactly what I had done. I could tell that I didn't like this man and by the way he was acting I doubted if he liked anybody.

"He stables my horses when I'm in town, can you tell me where I can find him?"

"Well he won't stable them this trip or any other for that matter," the man said.

I was really starting to get a bad filling about this stranger sitting in Chet's office.

"What happened to him, if I might ask?"

"He retired. I bought the livery stable off him a little more than a month ago. If you got horses that you don't want to stay out in this weather then you need to talk to me. I'm the new owner, now what will it be?"

Chester's Last Ride

In all my years and all my travels I had never been spoken to so bluntly by a man who was in the business of trying to rent me a stall. "Mister, can I ask you one more question?" I asked.

"Well, if you just ain't full of questions young feller. Tell you what, you go ahead and ask. I might answer and then again I might not. My time is too valuable to be wasted on tumbleweed like you anyway," he said.

Now I was getting steamed. This man was trouble and something told me he came about the livery by less than honorable means. Chet was not near old enough to retire and from what I could tell he loved his work.

"My question is this, why would Chet sell out to you when he ain't even forty years old and loved this place. Now before you answer let me add that you're right, I might be tumbleweed, but a man like you is not the one to be saying something like that to a man like me. Now I was going to leave my horses here for a few days but after speaking to you I would rather they stay someplace else."

The man pushed back from the desk and stood up. He was slightly taller than me and at least twenty pounds heavier. I didn't think he would try to draw on me but if he did then I was probably going to be slow. I had been ten days in below freezing weather and I could feel it all the way to my bones. My hands were also very cold. Not a good spot to be in right now.

"Now you listen to me tumbleweed. You ain't coming in here and talking to me like that. Now if you don't come up with an apology, and I mean real fast, then I'm going to give you a good thrashing right here and now," he said.

I expected this and wasn't going to take it. I straightened up a bit and faced the man just in case I had to draw. Before I had a chance to speak another man came through the door behind me and as he did Ben ran through and put his front feet up on the man's desk. The big dog had been looking through the front window and must have seen the man jump up from his chair. Ben had a nose for trouble and could tell if someone was being unfriendly. Ben looked at the stranger standing behind the desk and for the moment it was eyeball to eyeball.

"What the hell?" the man said as he went for his gun.

I had expected him to draw on Ben and as cold as my fingers were I knew I needed to draw first. I was right, the cold made my draw as slow as sap running in winter. I still managed to get my Colt out before he did.

"Now mister, if you think you're going to shoot a dog that only came in out of the cold to get a good look at a city slicker like you then you better think again."

The man eased his gun, which was only part of the way out of its holster, back down and then slowly put his hands up, palms out toward me.

"You will have some explaining to do to the sheriff mister. And if this dog of yours bites me then he will be taken out and shot by one of the deputies," the man said.

"Oh, you don't need to worry about Ben biting you mister, he don't like the taste of shit."

With that I eased back toward the door. When I had my hand on the handle I opened the door and called Ben. When we were both safely outside I headed in the direction of the sheriff's office. I had first met Sheriff Messer just after Ben had killed that big bulldog a couple of years back. Each time back to town I paid him a visit to see if there was anything I should know about, when a man is in the timber for months at a time it's good to keep up on events from time to time. The sheriff had always been knowledgeable and likable. Some sheriffs were ignorant and snotty, but not Messer.

Chester's Last Ride

I made it to the front porch of the sheriff's office and remembered back to the two old men playing checkers. I had asked about the two each time I was in town and it was last summer that I found out that both had died the previous winter, the flu had taken them. I would always remember the one saying to the other that he didn't have that many games of checkers left, I guess he was right.

Sheriff Messer was seated at his desk drinking coffee and looking through a bunch of paperwork. When Ben and me entered he looked up and said, "Howdy young Conley, how have you and that big dog of yours been getting along this winter?"

"Fine John Allen, never really had much trouble till we got into town and tried to stable the horses."

The sheriff pushed back in his chair and rubbed his chin. "Let me guess, you met the new owner of the livery and things didn't go so well."

"That's a pretty good guess. I went in expecting to find Chet but instead was met with some dressed up store bought cowboy. We damn near had us a fight right there in his office until Ben walked in."

The sheriff got up and grabbed another cup and filled it with coffee from the pot on the stove. "Here Conley, you look like a man who could use something hot to drink." He reached over and patted Ben on top of the head. Ben had always liked the sheriff.

"What happened to Chet Sheriff? I thought he was too young to just up and retire like that."

The sheriff sat back down at his desk and then propped his feet up. "He is too young at that Conley. I asked him when I heard the news and he seemed real nervous about answering me. I think the man you met in the livery somehow got the

57

edge on old Chet Brimley and used it to take away the stable. Not many people in town use the livery now just for the reason that they can't stand the new owner."

"If no one is using the livery Sheriff then how is the man staying in business? He made sure he pissed me off before I even got fully in the door."

"That is a good question and damn if I got an answer. He has a lot of traffic in and out but it's mostly people that I've never seen before. Damn if anyone in town uses that place now. What business he does get is from strangers and it ain't just your run of the mill strangers either. There are some mean looking men coming and going from there. That's what I was doing when you came in, checking my wanted posters. I do it every day and have yet to recognize anyone that is using the stables. You know Chet pretty good, maybe you can pry some information out of him. I really don't think he wanted to give up the livery and if someone used unlawful means to get it from him then I would really like to know."

I sipped my coffee and thought about what the sheriff just said. Before I got to speak Ben stood and let out a low growl. The sheriff looked over at the big dog and asked, "What do you think has Ben riled up Conley?"

Just then the door opened and the man from the livery stomped in ready to start shouting, that is until he saw Ben. "What in hell is that damn dog doing in here Sheriff? I want that ugly bastard out right now so I can file a complaint against that little bastard sitting there drinking up the taxpayer's coffee."

Ben was looking at me all the while so I gave him a wink; it was something the dog was waiting for. Before the man said another word Ben was on him. He didn't bite the man he just raised up and put both front paws on his shoulders and then let out a tremendous and vicious bark. The man was backing up and as he did Ben went back down on all fours and advanced on him with as vicious a racket as anyone could imagine. The man had made it back to the door but was stopped there and couldn't retreat any further. As this was going on the sheriff looked over at me and said, "Looks like it might snow some more tonight, what do you think Conley?" As he said this he had drawn his Colt and pointed it at the man Ben was barking at.

I snapped my fingers and Ben stopped barking and went over to lay beside the pot-bellied stove.

"You know Sheriff, I believe you're right. It has snowed on me and Ben for the better part of two weeks now and I doubt if it's ready to stop anytime soon." When I finished speaking I looked at the man standing by the door. He looked like he wanted to kill both of us right here and now, but the sheriff had him covered with his gun.

Sheriff Messer spoke next. "Wade, I think you were about to say something else before that big dog got in your face. As a word of advice I would like you to knock on the door next time and then if you hear someone on the other side say come on in then it is safe to proceed. And if you come in here cussing someone I'm talking to again then I can promise you that I will not be as polite as I'm being now. Do you understand everything I have just said Wade or has Ben got you a little hard of hearing right now?"

The man named Wade looked like he was going to blow up right where he stood. "Damn you Sheriff. I refuse to be talked to that way. I plan on running for mayor of this town come next election and when I am sworn in there is going to be a few changes made around here. Now I want that man arrested for being a vagrant and I want that dog of his shot. This is the second time he has attacked me in the last hour."

I decided that this man was trouble no matter where he was or who he was talking to. After what he said when he came through the door I felt like provoking him a little more. "If Ben had attacked you then you wouldn't be here talking to us now. He has killed men in the past a lot bigger and a lot meaner than you. For that matter he may not even consider you a man at all. He might think you would look better if you wore a shawl instead of a hat."

This was more than the man could stand. He walked over to the sheriff's desk and pounded his fist on the top. "Messer, quit pointing that gun at me and arrest that smart ass little tumbleweed right now."

"What should I charge him with Bowers, assaulting you with harsh language?" the sheriff asked.

"No dammit, he is a nuisance and a troublemaker. He had his dog attack me twice and I want something done about it right now."

"Tell you what Bowers. You go over to the livery and see if you can act a little more civilized when a man comes in there to rent a couple of stables for his horses. The weather is bad and you got the only place in town where animals can be sheltered," the sheriff said.

"You can't tell me how to run my business Sheriff. If you ain't going to earn your pay then I think it's time someone else wore that badge. I plan on calling a special meeting of the town council this very evening to have you removed from office. And as for that little bastard sitting over there I plan............"

Before he could finish I jumped from my chair and hit him square in the jaw with a strong right. He stumbled a bit but didn't go down. I grabbed him by the collar of his fancy jacket and slammed him against the door. "I don't like the names you been calling me ever since I met you not more than an hour ago. You are not a nice person and I think you could use a good ass-kicking every day for the rest of your life, it might help your disposition." I wasn't worried about the sheriff, he had nodded at me when the man was giving me the bad speech so I did as I was told and jumped up. I released the man's collar and returned to my chair. Ben hadn't moved from his spot by the warm stove but he was paying attention.

The man straightened his coat and rubbed his chin. He smiled at the sheriff and then at me. "You two just fell in a little further than you realized." With that he turned and went out the door.

Messer looked at me and asked what in the hell Bowers had meant by that.

"Sounds like he's going to get even Sheriff, what do you know about him other than what you have already told me?" I asked.

Messer took his cup and went to the stove. As he stood there pouring more coffee Ben reached over and grabbed the cuff of his pants with his teeth and pulled. From past visits the sheriff had learned that this was Ben's way of asking for a snack. "When is the last time this dog has been fed Conley? Reason I asked is I don't want him to start chewing on my leg." The sheriff reached down and patted Ben on the head.

"This morning, we were going to go to one of the diners in town after I stabled Hazel and Rusty but that little plan got scrambled up by the man that just got his jaw busted."

"Well don't worry about that too much. There is a man not far from here that has a big barn and for the last month he has taken all the business that Bowers has turned away with his sorry-ass attitude. Leave Ben here with me while you get your horses squared away. His is the barn directly back of the one where the animal doctor works. Tell him I sent you and he will see that them horses are put inside and taken care of real quick. I brought some soup beans and cornbread from home for my supper this evening but I think I'm going to give it to Ben. Will he eat it?"

"Ben loves soup beans Sheriff. He likes his cornbread crumbled up in with the beans if you don't mind though. Since you're going to give Ben your supper then how about I buy supper for the both of us at the café after I get my horses situated? That is if you don't mind being seen around town with a tumbleweed like me?"

The sheriff laughed and said I had a deal. I headed out the door as Messer went to get Ben his supper. I knew where the town vet had his practice. It was in a big barn at the edge of town near the sheriff's office. I had been there numerous times but never paid much attention to what was behind it a street or two back.

Once I made it to the vet's office I walked around and down a side street and there it was, a building that had about the same footprint as a large barn but instead of a big loft where you would normally store hay it had a slant roof not much taller than a normal house. Behind it was another smaller building with the two front doors open and inside those doors I could see the hay. There were two large corrals and a farm house which sat to the side directly behind the barn. It was a neat and pleasant looking place; it reminded me of a place a man would want to retire to after he had done all the traveling his body would allow.

I approached the front door of the big slant roof barn and slide it open. Inside was nearly as bright as the outside thanks to a large window to the left where a man sat near a squatty stove warming his hands. I had never seen a neater barn in my life. There were even curtains hanging beside the big glass window. The part of the barn where the man sat must have been some sort of office, although it wasn't partitioned off in any way from the long center hall and the stalls on either side.

"Howdy stranger, come on over and warm yourself by the fire," the man said.

"Thanks, that wind outside will cut right through a man if you stand out there and let it," I said.

"I reckon so. You look like a feller that might need a place to keep a horse out of the weather. Would I be far from the truth in that statement?"

"No sir, you hit the truth pretty much dead center. I got to town an hour or two ago and have two horses to shed if you got the room?"

The man pointed to a coffee pot sitting on top of his funny looking stove and asked if I would like a cup. I had just finished my coffee over at the sheriff's office but when it was free and already hot I found I couldn't resist.

"Thank you kindly." I picked up an empty cup from the stack and filled it. "Arbuckle, this is my favorite brand. It's hard to find though out in some of the smaller towns where I've been." I pointed my thumb in a westward direction.

"You know, I used to travel the wilds out west a ways. That was quite a few years ago. It was a life I truly loved. After two much snow and too many droughts I finally settled here and found me a good woman. This kind of weather is hard on an old man. Anyway, up until a few weeks ago all I kept in this big old barn was mostly chickens. I love raising chickens and the folks here abouts like the fact that I do. I make me a pretty good living just selling eggs, and that don't even count all the birds I sell for people to fry up on Sunday."

Nathan Wright

The man must have been in his sixties and maybe even rubbing seventy but still looked like he could put in a good days work. "I got two horses and one big dog that need a place to stay for a few days. The sheriff sent me this way, said you might have space."

"I do. This is a big barn and I mostly got rid of my stock a few years back, that is except for the chickens, lately though I have been taking in business that used to go over to Chet Brimley's place. Somehow old Chet lost his livery to some out of town man that don't have much in the way of friendliness. In the last month, which is about how long that new feller has been in business, I have been busy as can be. I first started taking in horses for free just to help folks out but I soon figured that I had to charge or go broke. Now I charge the same as old Chet used to get and from what I hear it is still less than half what that city boy who took the place over gets. It's fifty cents a day and that is for hay. If you want oats for your horse it is twenty-five cents extra. How does that sound?"

"That sounds pretty good to me. How about my dog, he usually stays close to the horses when I stable them."

"Is he friendly? The reason I ask is a few years back we had a feller land here from somewhere and he had a big bulldog that traveled with him. That damn bulldog either killed or ran off every other dog in town, that is until some young man came to town with a monster of a brute that he claimed was a dog. I never seen him but from the stories around town he was more of a wolf, although twice as big. Anyway, that big bulldog picked a fight with that wolf and that was the end of the bulldog, and as far as I am concerned good riddance."

I sat listening to the man and realized that Ben was a little bit famous. "Well I heard about that fight, as a matter of fact I seen the whole thing. The dog you are talking about is named

Ben and he is over at the sheriff's office right now eating the sheriff's soup beans and cornbread."

The man took his foot and kicked me in the shin in a friendly way. "You don't say, well I sure would like to see that animal, and if he is friendly then he is more than welcome to stay with your horses, and the dog stays for free."

So far in the last few years Ben had gotten his vet bill for free, he was eating the sheriff's supper for free, and now was going to be put up in one of the nicest barns I had ever seen for free. If that dog was a man then I'm sure he would manage to get elected president of these here United States. Leave it to Ben.

"You got yourself a deal. I'll get my two horses and bring them on over. Ben will eat about anything you feed him except hay. He even tried that once but I don't think the taste took." I reached the man two three dollar gold pieces and thanked him for the coffee. I slid open the door and just before I went out I noticed a few men had gathered on the side street about fifty feet from the stable. I paused just long enough to see one of the men point at the barn where I stood. I was in a hurry to get my two horses and really didn't give the group of men much thought, they were in the opposite direction that I was going.

After making it back to the sheriff's office I quickly made my way to the stove, the wind had picked up and snow was falling at a really good pace. It almost felt like sleet. I knew the horses would be alright for a while but I was still anxious to get them both inside the barn. Ben was asleep beside the big desk and the sheriff was back at his task of looking over wanted posters.

"Howdy Zeke, you find that barn I told you about?"

"Sure did. That is the nicest barn I reckon I was ever in. Why do you think he has a wood burning stove in there other than to keep warm? It seems like he lives close enough that he could just go home from time to time."

"You probably didn't notice but at the back and to the left of that barn is a long hall that is attached to his house. He can come and go without ever going out in the weather. He told me he built that little addition just so as he got older he could check on his livestock and do it in his house slippers if he wanted to. I think that was a pretty smart thing for him to do, especially with the kind of winters we get around here. Anyway, his wife told him that if the barn was attached to the house then he better keep it as neat as he could. She is the one that insisted he put that wood burning stove in there a few years back. She knew how much he liked to tinker in his barn and she didn't want him getting too cold while he was out there. No matter how cold it gets outside it is always above freezing in there, maybe even closer to forty degrees. I think it's good for the horses too."

The sheriff thought a minute as if his mind was in a faraway place and then he said in a low almost solemn voice, "In all my years I don't ever remember a woman that cared that much for me. The one I married sure don't give a damn whether I come home or not and she don't care if I'm cold either."

I could tell the sheriff had momentarily drifted away and wasn't coming back until he got through cussing his wife in his thoughts. "Well Sheriff, I got to get my horses into that barn and I need to do it pretty quick, it's starting to look like a blizzard out there."

The sheriff snapped out of his trance and walked over to the window. Snow had begun to blow along the street and was piling up at the corners of buildings. "It does at that Zeke. You need help, I don't mind, in weather like this the sherriffing business is usually pretty slow. Funny how people just like breaking the law in good weather."

"Thanks Sheriff but me and old Ben here can make it just fine. Rusty and Hazel will gladly come along to get out of this storm. Say, I never thought to get the name of the man who has that new stable."

"His name is Thurman Bishop. His wife's name is Rhoda. They will take real good care of the horses and if they don't want Ben in there then you just bring him back here. I would be more than glad to have his company while you're in town. Me and that dog will break bread three times a day."

Again I thought of all the people that would do about anything for Ben. He was getting to be a hell of a lot more popular than anybody I had ever known.

"Thanks Sheriff but Mr. Bishop said he already knew about Ben from that big fight a couple of years back and he wants him to stay there with the horses. You know Sheriff; I reckon Ben has become pretty famous because of that fight. I don't think I'll ever hear anyone talk that nice about me."

The sheriff turned back from the window and looked down at Ben. "Lot of people in town know about that fight and them same people think Ben here done the town a good deed. Hell if Ben ran for sheriff I think the people of Sioux City would vote me out and vote him in." Both me and the sheriff had a good laugh about that.

I hurried to where Hazel and Rusty had been tied up down from the sheriff's office. Both horses looked glad to see Ben and me. They each had a good coating of snow on their backs but not on their heads or necks. They had both managed to keep that slung off pretty good. I unhitched both and walked them around to Bishop's barn. By the time we got there the storm had turned into a full-fledged blizzard.

Nathan Wright

As I approached the barn for the second time today I noticed the same group of men I had seen earlier. They were now standing at the front sliding door and they were talking to Mr. Bishop, actually it sounded more like they were shouting at Mr. Bishop. Before I had made it half way there one of the men grabbed Bishop and shoved him to the ground. Another of the group then began kicking him.

Ben had noticed the commotion and was starting to growl. I knew I wouldn't be able to do much while leading the two horses and I was still at least a hundred feet away. I slapped my hands together and shouted 'Ben.' He knew the drill. The big dog took off and within a couple of seconds he was in the mix. He grabbed the man doing the kicking by the seat of his pants and gave a vicious yank. As far away as I was I could still hear the fabric of the man's trousers ripping. Ben pulled so hard that the man fell backwards screaming. By the sounds of the screams I think Ben must have latched on to more than just trousers.

When that man hit the ground Ben went after the next closest one and grabbed him by the arm that he was using to go for his gun. I counted five men and Ben had already done away with two of them. By now I was at a full run, having released the reins of Hazel and Rusty. I made it to the fight just as Ben was going after a third man who was trying to kick him off his friend. I knew Ben could handle that man just the same as he had handled the first two so I devoted my attention to the last two. Both had drawn their guns but hadn't seen me coming up from behind. I didn't think either would fire on Ben because he had pulled the third man down and was going after his throat. If either fired at Ben then they would kill the man on the ground for sure.

Chester's Last Ride

I grabbed the one that was closest and spun him around, hitting him in the face with a wild right. It was the best I could do in all the excitement. The punch landed where I intended, on the end of the man's nose. Blood immediately gushed. The last of the five was startled by all the damage being done to his friends by the big dog and now by me. Before he could respond I hit him with a solid left to the face and he fell straight back into a fresh pile of horse shit that had started to freeze but was still producing a little bit of steam. He would surely need a bath after this little fight was over. Ben had just finished up with the third man. He could have killed him by ripping out his throat but once he saw that me and him had everything under control he let up. The first man that he had attacked was now going for his gun but he was too late, I already had my Colt out and pointed at his face. He dropped his to the ground and started trying to pull the tattered remains of his pants back up to his waist.

Now seeing that the five no longer posed a threat I went around and gathered their guns. Unless one of the five had a hideaway gun, or a knife, then I pretty much figured they were as harmless as babies. Mr. Bishop had made it to his feet and was dusting the snow and ice off his cloths. I asked if he was alright and he looked at me and nodded.

"Good thing you got here when you did mister. I think them five were going to take turns beating the shit out of me," Mr. Bishop said.

I looked at the five and then back at Bishop and said I believed they would. Just then a woman came through the barn and out the open door. I assumed this to be Rhoda Bishop. She ran up to Mr. Bishop and helped dust him off.

"What on earth is going on out here Thurman? I could hear hollering all the way to the house. Are you alright?" she asked.

He stood a little straighter and stiffened his shoulders. He was a proud man who must have been in a fight or two in his time and didn't want his wife to think he couldn't take care of himself.

"I think so. If it hadn't been for this young feller and Ben then I doubt if these sorry bastards were going to stop anytime soon," he told his wife.

I hadn't told the man my dog's name but he must have heard it from the stories about that fight with the big bulldog from a couple of years back. The woman looked at Ben who was standing and looking at the five men as if he wanted to have another go at them.

"That is Ben; you mean to tell me that Ben saved you from these men?" she asked.

"That's right Rhoda, this dog just saved me from a beating and by the way he's looking at them five he might not be done yet."

The five men heard this and were now looking at Ben. As the man and woman were talking Ben had been slowly advancing on the five, small steps and a killer stare that meant he wanted to finish what he had started. The five men were slowly stepping back as Ben approached.

"Stay Ben," I said.

Ben stopped but didn't take his eyes off the five.

"Look at that Thurman. Ben was protecting you. That big dog is a hero," Mrs. Bishop said.

She had yet to notice that I had taken part in the fight and was now holding a gun on the five men. As usual Ben was getting all the credit and something told me his legend had just grown by a sizable amount. I didn't mind, Ben had surely saved my ass a time or two in years past.

Chester's Last Ride

As I held my gun on the five men and Thurman's wife fussed over him I noticed a young man slipping and sliding down the frozen street. He looked to be about thirteen or fourteen years old and was having fun in the new snow.

"Here comes Thomas. Why don't you let him tend to the chores while you go home and get yourself sorted out Thurman? It looks like you got a knot starting to rise up on your forehead," Mrs. Bishop told her husband.

"Can't go just yet Rhoda, I got to see what the sheriff thinks about what these men tried to do to me."

Just then the boy named Thomas made it to where we were standing. He was looking at Ben and wasn't paying much attention to anything else.

"Oh my goodness Mr. Bishop, that wouldn't be the dog everybody talks about would it? Is it Ben, tell me it is. I done heard how he tore up that big old bulldog a few years back and rescued those people that were stranded in the big blizzard of ninety-one."

"Yes Thomas that's Ben and he just saved me from them five no-goods standing over there. How about you run and fetch the sheriff and tell him he might want to bring along a deputy. Get them back here as fast as you can," Thurman said.

As Thomas turned and sprinted his way toward the sheriff's office I asked Mr. Bishop, "Did I hear him say something about Ben saving some people in a blizzard?"

Bishop looked at me and said, "Seems some of the parents around these parts might have exaggerated a bit about all the things that dog of yours has accomplished in his lifetime. Moms love to tell the stories and children love to hear em. The lady who runs the library in town has even written a children's book that tells all about the heroics that Ben has done. The stories get a little taller each time I hear them."

Nathan Wright

I looked at Ben, he was still standing guard on the five men and they weren't taking their eyes off him either.

One of the five finally got the wind to speak. "Did I hear you right Bishop? Is that the dog that saved them people from the blizzard?"

Another one of the five added, "I heard he killed a man that was beating up his wife, he had damn near killed her before that dog killed him, is that the same dog Mister?"

Bishop looked at me and smiled. "You damn right it's the same dog. If this man hadn't made him stop then I figure he would have took turns chewing the five of you to bits, now how about the five of you shutting the hell up until Sheriff Messer gets here."

The man that Ben had first attacked and had his pants nearly ripped off was starting to look a little pale. I noticed there was red snow where he stood and I could see blood dripping from his pants cuff.

"Is there a doctor in this town? I think that dog damn near tore my ass off," the man said just before his eyes rolled back in his head and he passed out. He went straight down and didn't move another muscle.

One of the five started to check on him but I motioned for him to step away. I knew the man needed attention but I was afraid there might have been a hidden gun on the man that was passed out and this feller trying to help might have known about it.

"Let me check on him mister before he dies," the man said.

"Just leave him be until the sheriff gets here. He probably just fainted from the sight of his own blood." I didn't know much about medicine and hoped Ben hadn't torn off more of the man's back side that he could afford to lose.

Chester's Last Ride

Just then the sheriff and two other men wearing badges rounded the end of the street and were running in our direction but also trying to not slip and fall. When he got there he saw the four men standing and the one lying unconscious on the ground. He also noticed Bishop being tended to by his wife.

"What happened here Mr. Bishop? You look like you've been in a fight."

"Sheriff, these men came to my place a little while ago and threatened to burn me out unless I stopped taking in horses. Said there was already a livery in town and there wasn't room for two. Before I got a chance to say anything they shoved me down and started kicking me. If it hadn't been for that young feller and his dog then I figure they were going to give me a pretty good whipping." He looked at his wife and then added. "You know I can't fight five men all by myself Sheriff." He looked back at his wife who was now patting him on the arm.

The sheriff looked at the five men and then at me. "What happened to that man on the ground? Is he dead?"

"I don't think so Sheriff. He's the one that was doing most of the kicking so he's the one that Ben took on first. I think if you check you will find bite marks on his ass. Couple more of these men were also bitten. You got anybody in town that knows anything about rabies sheriff?" I winked as I said this.

The sheriff knew I was only funning but decided to play along. "No Zeke we surely don't. I don't think there is a cure anyway. If these three start showing signs then I will have no choice but to put them all in the same cell. If they start howling and foaming at the mouth it's better that they kill each other than to infect anyone else."

The four men that were still standing started looking real nervous. "If that dog has the rabies then shoot him right now Sheriff before he attacks us again," one of the four said.

Nathan Wright

The sheriff looked at one of his deputies and told him to take two of the men to jail. The other two he ordered to pick up the unconscious man before he got frost bite on his ass.

"Zeke, you get your horses and Ben settled in with Mr. Bishop and then come over to my office so I can get some information and try to figure out what these men were trying to do here. I'll leave this injured one with the doctor along with a deputy to make sure he doesn't cause any more trouble when he comes to. I'll be over at the jail after I leave the doctor's office," Messer said.

I told the sheriff I would be on over in a half hour or so. Mr. Bishop was looking a lot better now that the danger was gone. He had a goose egg knot on his forehead but other than that he looked fine. During all the commotion Hazel and Rusty stood pretty much where I had left them. I always wondered what they were thinking when they saw old Ben and me tangling it up with some no goods. It had happened more than a few times over the years and I guess they had pretty much gotten used to it.

The storm hadn't let up a bit and the two horses were again covered with snow and even had some ice pellets frozen to their manes. I grabbed the reins and led both through the open door of the barn. I turned to get Ben but noticed he was going along with the sheriff. I didn't mind, Sheriff Messer and Ben were now fast friends who had just shared supper together.

Once inside I slid the big door shut and then wiped the snow off the horses. There was a saddle blanket hanging over a rail to a stall and I took it to wipe down Rusty. He was older than Hazel by about five years so I always tended to him first. Hazel never seemed to mind, she was smart enough to know that whatever Rusty got then within a few minutes she would get the same.

Chester's Last Ride

Mr. Bishop seemed to be alright, he had even sent his wife home. After I was sure he was fit to take care of my two horses I headed out the door on my way to the sheriff's office.

The snow was deep and getting deeper. I wanted to make my way to the post office before it closed to collect my mail, it was the main reason I was in town to begin with. Now thanks to some no good sorry sons-o-bitches I was plodding through a damn blizzard back to the sheriff's office. When I entered I saw that the deputy that had brought the first two back was in the front office sitting at the big desk. He was cleaning a couple of Colts and drinking some strong looking coffee.

"The sheriff made it back yet?" I asked.

"Not yet, shouldn't be long now though. Say, did you know them fellers you had the tangle with?" the deputy asked.

"Never saw any of them in my life, first I ever laid eyes on em was when they started beating up Mr. Bishop. They been around town long?" I asked.

"I questioned them two I brought over and locked up, said they got off the train yesterday. Said this was the first time any of them have ever been in Sioux City."

"Well it didn't take them long to create some trouble. I just find it hard to believe that they would just get off the train and the very next day start beating on a man that has been here for years," I said.

"It seems to me they came here to do some work for that new feller that took over the old livery. Something tells me they came here to work for Wade Bowers. My guess is that Wade got these fellers in here to scare old man Bishop bad enough that he would stop taking in horses. I been around a lot of bad men in my day and let me tell you I can pick one a mile away. I don't need any spy glass to figure out that Bowers is as mean as they come. The sheriff keeps looking through old dodgers trying to find one on Bowers, so far though he ain't had any luck."

Just then the big door opened and a strong gust of icy wind blew in. Sheriff Messer, along with the other two men that had carried the man with the bite marks on his ass to the doctor, came in and pushed the door shut behind them.

"Lucky, how bout you showing these two to a cell, I can't stand to be around either of them another second," the sheriff said.

The man called Lucky jumped up from the sheriff's desk and ushered the two men toward the cells in the back. Both went along complaining and cussing. After Lucky got them locked up he came back out and slammed the big cell room door shut.

"What in the hell is wrong with them two Sheriff. I never heard such swearing, why don't you let me go back in there and shoot a couple of em, might do the other two some good," Lucky said.

"Now you know how I feel. Just walking over here from the doctor's office was about more than I could stand," the sheriff said.

"How is the one doing that Ben grabbed by the ass Sheriff?" Lucky asked.

"Not too good. Doc said he will survive but doubted if he will be sitting down normal anytime soon. Said Ben tore him a new one." With that the sheriff started laughing. "Tore him a new one, get it?" The sheriff said between laughs.

It was then that I realized Ben hadn't come back with the sheriff.

"Where's Ben? He went along with you when you were taking that man to the doc's," I asked.

The sheriff was trying to warm his hands by the fire which looked like it was growing cold. "When I left the doc's to bring them nice talking bastards to jail he headed toward Bishop's place. I figured he was looking for you since that's the last place he saw you."

I didn't want Ben out in the middle of a blizzard in a town that he wasn't familiar with. I stood and headed for the door. "Tell you what Sheriff, I think I'll head back over to Bishop's place and make sure Ben is alright. I won't be gone long." Before anyone could answer I went out the door and headed back down the street. Within minutes I was at Bishop's and there was no sign of Ben as I approached. I was a little worried to say the least. The weather was getting worse and I surely didn't want Ben to spend the night out of doors, or even worse, lost in the storm.

I walked over and slid one of the big doors back and hurried in. There by the fire was Mr. and Mrs. Bishop and standing by the stove was Ben chewing on a big ham bone. He looked up and seemed glad to see me but not glad enough to walk over to where I was, he just went back to chewing on that big old bone. Mrs. Bishop was patting him on the head. This was Ben's second meal in as many hours and I hadn't had a scrap of anything since we hit town this morning. I looked at the big bone and wondered how he would feel about sharing.

"Howdy there young feller, bring yourself over and warm by the fire. How would you like a big cup of hot coffee with a taste of fresh cream and a spoon full of sugar throwed in for good measure?" Mr. Bishop asked.

"That sounds real good to me. I just came back to make sure Ben had found your place alright after he left the doctor's office."

"He sure did, about ten minutes ago I heard his scratch on the door and I let him in. He came straight back to the stalls and looked in on them two horses of yours. Once he seen they were alright he came back up here too warm by the fire. The wife went into the house and brought him out that big ham bone and he's been happy as a cat trapped in a cream factory ever since."

As he was saying this Mrs. Bishop was making the coffee. When she had it the way her husband had described she reached it to me. I took a slow sip because of how hot it was and let me tell you it was good, real good.

"I don't reckon I got your name cause of all the commotion going on earlier," Bishop said.

"It has been some kind of day I reckon with the blizzard and all, not to mention them five no-goods earlier. Names Conley, Zeke Conley from out Kentucky way." I stuck out a hand and we both shook.

"Well it's a pleasure to meet you young Conley and it is also a pleasure to meet your famous dog. He sure saved me earlier, and you helped a little too." He looked at me and grinned as he said this.

"Wish it could have been under better circumstances but at least we were here when you needed us," I told him. "How are the two horses doing?"

"Oh just fine, I put both in their stalls and gave them a fresh bucket of oats and a little hay. I think they have been on the trail for quite a while. Both looks to be in great shape but I was amazed at how they each went after the oats. I decided to give them a little corn later and in the morning they get molasses with their oats. Now what do you think of that?"

"I think that all sounds good. There is part of a sack of corn over there in the pack Rusty was carrying. Use it up if you like; I plan on buying a brand new sack before we pull out," I told him.

Chester's Last Ride

"Pull out, you just got here. How long do you figure on staying?"

"Just long enough to pick up my mail and some supplies, might be a couple of days, maybe three."

"Well you at least need to let this blizzard blow over, that might take a few days. And anyway, the mail didn't come in yesterday. Might be all the bad weather we been having lately," Bishop told me.

"I thought the mail came in on the train. Unless the snow is really deep the trains still run don't they?"

"The train did run yesterday and the day before too. The mail doesn't all come in on the train though. All the southern mail comes by train only so far and then they put it on a stage and run it on up to us. If your mail is coming from Chicago, or say New York, then it came in on the train. I believe you said you're from Kentucky and all the Kentucky mail comes in on the stage. Stage didn't come in yesterday and I doubt the way the weather is turning if it will come in anytime soon. As long as you been out west though you probably got some mail. If you want the latest then you might want to stay in town a few days, wait on the next stage."

I thought about this and also about the weather. It would be a shame to leave town with only the mail that came in on the earlier stages and not get the latest. If something had happened at home and I missed the letter then it would be at least four months before I got back here to get it.

"You make a good point Mr. Bishop. I would surely like to get the latest mail while I'm in town. How many stages does the town get a week anyway?" I asked him.

"It varies, sometimes when the weather is good we get a stage every day. In times like this though, with all the snow and the cold temperatures, that can drop to only once a week. Add in the trouble we been having with outlaws on the trail and you could be waiting for a long time on the next mail wagon."

"Outlaws on the trail, how long has that been going on?"

"Started about two years ago, you know right after you and Ben came to town and your dog killed that big bulldog bastard. It seems that the man that owned that bulldog left town right after his dog got killed. Sheriff Messer seems to think that man, I believe his name was Whitley; well it seems the sheriff has some evidence that links Whitley to a gang that is holed up outside of town. Whitley might even be the leader of the gang."

I thought about what Bishop had just said as I finished my coffee. I reached the empty cup to Mrs. Bishop and thanked her. "You think you'll be alright here, after what went on outside earlier Mr. Bishop?"

Bishop reached under a horse blanket that was lying on his work table and pulled out a brand new Colt revolver. "I went to the house and got this little baby while you were gone. Next time anyone comes in here that I don't know then I plan to have this in my pocket. Plus if you ain't forgot, I got Ben staying here. I feel better just knowing that big dog is a friend of mine. Only problem is the wife is planning on keeping him fed a lot better than she feeds me. In a couple of days he might be so fat he can't get up." Bishop must have thought this was funny by the way he started laughing.

"I think Ben could use some good food and a little rest Mr. Bishop. Well, I need to be getting back to the sheriff's office. I just came over to check on everything. I'll be back early in the morning."

I left the Bishops and my three trail partners and headed back through the snowy streets. Ben stopped chewing on his bone just long enough to come to the door before I left and bit my hand. He just about brought blood but I knew it was just his way of saying so long. He immediately went back to his bone as I rubbed my hand. Hope I don't get rabies.

The sheriff didn't want to talk about the five men, he wanted to go and get the supper I had promised to pay for earlier. We ended up in a saloon that served food and not a minute too soon. It seemed that ever since we had gotten into town everybody we met wanted to fight me and feed Ben. I was starved. The sheriff picked a table toward the back and we both took a chair.

"What's good Messer? Course as long as it's been since I have eaten anything it probably doesn't really matter."

"They actually serve a steak here that I hear is great but I've never been able to afford it. As a matter of fact this is only the second time I've ever eaten here. Tonight I plan on having the steak, that is if you can afford it?"

I looked at the sheriff. In all my days I had never met an honest sheriff that had anything. The crooked ones though had money to burn. You can always tell an honest lawman, he is the one that's poor.

"Sheriff, you gave your dinner to Ben and I promised you I would buy supper for the both of us. I can afford it."

The sheriff gave me a funny look.

"Don't worry Messer; I came about the money honest. I sold a bunch of hides back in Shasta nearly two weeks ago. I got money."

The sheriff started laughing. "You sure did spill that story fast. Don't worry Conley; I didn't suspect anything unlawful on how you got the money. I reckon I've known you and Ben for a little over two years now and you are one of the few people I trust. Plus I sent a letter off to your paw a while back. He vouched for everything you said about yourself."

Nathan Wright

"Well if that don't beat all Messer. You trust me so much you wrote to my paw to see if the story I told was true or not." I just looked at him and then started laughing. "That was probably the smart thing to do. I would probably have done the same thing myself."

"In my line of work it doesn't pay to take many chances Conley. Here comes the waitress. Try to not let your jaw hit the floor when you see her."

I turned just as she came around the bar. She was tall and shapely, that was obvious even with her wearing an apron. Here hair was long and the color of honey. Her face and arms were dark like she might have been part Mexican. I had never seen such light colored hair on such a dark skinned woman before. When she got closer I noticed her eyes, they were a brilliant shade of blue. They were bright, even to the point that I thought they glowed. When she made it to the table she smiled. Her teeth were white as the snow outside and perfectly straight. Her smile seemed to brighten the room.

"Hello Sheriff Messer. Never see you in here much."

"No Suzie, I tend to eat at my desk over at the office most of the time. I brought a friend with me, his name is Zeke Conley."

"Well nice to meet you Zeke Conley, you must be new in town."

"I am, I come through couple of times a year."

The sheriff said, "Suzie, you may not know Zeke here but I would bet anything that you've heard about his dog."

She looked at me and then back at the sheriff.

"His dog, what do I know about a dog Sheriff Messer?"

"The name of his dog is Ben," the sheriff told her.

I looked at her face and the change was immediate. She smiled and said, "Ben, you mean the stories about that dog are true. I can't believe it. I always thought those stories were just for children to hear."

"Naw they are true, well at least most of them are anyway. And Ben is here or at least over at Thurman Bishops place. Ben done whipped five men that were giving Bishop some trouble today. I got four of them arrested and in the jail and the other one is over at the doctor's office recovering from what Ben done to him," the sheriff said.

I noticed Messer didn't mention me in all the heroics, not that I cared.

"I would surely like to see that dog; he is the closest thing to a celebrity that has ever been in Sioux City," Suzie said.

"Well maybe tomorrow you can go over to Mr. Bishop's place and meet him. He probably wouldn't mind getting patted on the head by a pretty girl, I know I wouldn't," Sheriff Messer said.

Suzie reached over and patted Messer right on top of the head and then started laughing. "How was that sheriff?"

"Makes me want to lick your hand."

"Down boy," she told him.

With that I started laughing. We ordered the steaks and all the fixings and sweet tea for the drinks. I hadn't had tea in almost a year and really didn't want it now but Suzie said I should try it, said it would probably go better with the meal than coffee.

It didn't take long for the food to arrive and we both dived right in. I counted up and realized that it had been almost twelve hours since I had eaten breakfast and it was starting to show.

The food was good and Suzie was right, tea went better with the beef than coffee, or at least it seemed that way to me. I decided right then and there to buy me a small sack of the stuff and some extra sugar to have on the trail. Maybe tea for supper and coffee for breakfast. Just because I was on the trail didn't mean I had to have only coffee. As we ate and talked I asked the sheriff about the stage robberies that had been going on.

"Now how did you hear about that Conley? You only got into town this morning."

"Mr. Bishop over at the barn was telling me that I might need to wait here in town a day or two if I wanted to receive the latest mail. He said someone has been giving the stage a bit of trouble lately."

As the sheriff chewed his food he thought of my answer. "Well Mr. Bishop is exactly right except it ain't just a bit of trouble it's a lot of trouble. In the last two years there have been five murders on the trail the stage uses. They started putting an extra man up top with a shotgun but that didn't work. Whoever was running that gang put a man on a cliff with a Winchester 73 and all they had to do was shoot the man holding the shotgun.

"The stage company figured on trying something different after that. They tried to speed up the stage by using a six horse team instead of four. That helped a little but the problem now is that there ain't many men that can handle a stage and six."

"Why did they only use a shotgun Sheriff? Seems to me it would have been better to use a rifle so the guard could return fire from a distance. Shotgun is only good for close work," I said.

"I told them the same thing. The solution they came up with was that since it was the mail for Sioux City that was being robbed it was a matter for the sheriff's department of Sioux City to fix. So now I furnish a deputy to ride on that stage. It cost the town some extra wages but the people got to have their mail. Instead of a shotgun I sent a 73 with the deputy. So far they have exchanged a few rounds but it still didn't solve the problem. Two passengers have been hit and one even died."

I thought about this for a minute and then came up with an idea. "You know Messer, I think what you need is a bigger gun on that stage. Something that will allow your deputy to hit somebody before the stage comes into range of a 73."

"That sounds like it might work Conley but a gun like that is hard to come by. Winchester makes a .45-.75 but those guns are rare and the ammunition is even harder to find than the gun is," the sheriff said.

"I got a .45-.75 over at the barn with my stuff but that ain't the gun I think you need. What I think you need is something even bigger than the seventy-five. You need a Sharps Big 50."

I could tell I had gotten the sheriff's attention. He was thinking over what I had said and chewing away on his steak. Finally he looked over at me and said.

"A Sharps Big 50 is a hell of a gun. It will bring down a buffalo at a half a mile and I heard that feller Dixon hit an Indian at over a mile away with a Big 50. They still call it the shot of the century. I don't reckon I ever seen a Big 50 though, only heard stories about it."

"If you want to see a Big 50 then after we finish supper I can show you one. I traded for it when I was up in Shasta town and I got it right over there in my kit at Bishop's place. I got a bunch of ammunition to go along with it too, that is if you're interested?"

Again I could tell that I had the sheriff's attention. He didn't speak for the longest time until finally he said, "If you got a Sharps Big 50, what would you be asking for it? The sheriff's department is on a pretty limited budget but I might be able to convince the mayor to make a special purchase. How much does a gun like that go for anyway?"

I really liked the deal I had gotten on the Sharps and wasn't looking to unload it this quick. But the town needed it and the fact that it just might save a man's life was an incentive to get rid of it.

"Tell you what Sheriff; I got about a hundred and seventy rounds of ammunition and the cleaning kit for the gun. It comes with a leather rug to carry it in. The gun itself is about fifteen years old but is in pristine condition. You need it and I got it and don't need it. You can have the entire kit for four-hundred dollars."

I knew I was bumping the price up a hundred more than I had paid but the extra hundred would go a long way for a man who made very little during an entire year.

"That was quite a sales pitch Conley. If you ever get too old to chase bears through the woods then I think you got a great future selling used horses." We both laughed.

When the meal was finished Suzie asked if either of us wanted a big slice of homemade pumpkin pie. She said it would be the last pumpkin pie until the next fall, they had just field dressed their last pumpkin of the season. Both the sheriff and myself ordered a slice and this time we both wanted coffee. I hadn't eaten a dessert in so long that I forgot how much I liked it. When the pie came it was covered in whipped cream and the whole thing was warm like it just came out of the oven. Neither me or the sheriff said a word during the dessert and for good reason, it was delicious.

Once finished Suzie said the bill was three dollars and fifty cents so I gave a three-dollar gold piece and another dollar bill. I was glad I had traded in one of my hundred dollar bills back at the General Store in Shasta for the gold pieces. It seemed that a three-dollar gold piece could come in real handy for just about everything a man needed. We both thanked Suzie and then headed for Mr. Bishop's place. The sheriff wanted to fetch the Sharps Big 50 so he could make his case to the mayor. I could tell he really wanted the gun.

Outside the saloon the storm had seemed to pick up strength. Snow was still coming down hard and the wind seemed more ferocious. It was then that I realized I didn't have a place to stay for the night.

"Sheriff, where would I find a room this late in the day?"

"You didn't book yourself a room when you got to town earlier Conley? With the blizzard and all I would say you are out of luck, everything in town is rented out by now. Tell you what though, you can stay at the jail until you can make other arrangement's tomorrow, how does that sound?" the sheriff asked.

"Well Sheriff, I doubt I would like sleeping in a jail cell, especially since the five prisoners you got back there might still be a little mad just by the fact that me and Ben helped to put them there in the first place."

"Conley, you won't be sleeping in a jail cell, we got a bunk room where the night deputy sleeps. There are four bunks in there and it's real nice. We make sure the room is kept clean and it doesn't get all that cold in there either. One of the night deputy's duties is to keep the fire going and the coffee fresh and hot. The bunk room is mainly for when some of the men are putting in too many hours. You'd be surprised how a twenty minute nap and a strong cup of coffee can perk a man up," the sheriff said.

"Well you got yourself a deal Sheriff. It sure sounds better that building me a camp outside of town in weather like this, although I have done it a time or two in my life."

"Alright then, as soon as we look at that gun of yours then you can bring your kit back to the jail and get settled in for the night," the sheriff told me.

I was actually glad for the offer. The thoughts of being in a town of this size and still having to make camp outside was not appealing at all. I had slept in barns before with Hazel and Rusty but I knew Mr. Bishop only rented space for animals, not people.

Once we made it to the barn we had to knock real loud on the door and when it slid open we were met by the business end of a Colt revolver and Mr. Bishop was holding it. Behind him stood Ben and he looked like he was ready to rumble again until he saw who it was that was making all the racket.

Ben was glad to see me, I could always tell this when he put both of his front paws on my shoulders and tried to lick me in the face. I knew what to expect and managed to turn my head just in time. His breath smelled of ham. Ben was eating as good as, if not better than, me.

"What in hell are you two doing out on a night like this?" Bishop asked. "Even old Ben here knows better than to be outside during a blizzard." As if to prove Bishop's point Ben walked over and sat down by the wood burning stove.

Once we made it inside and closed the door I noticed how warm the barn felt. I wondered if the old man had designed his barn with the low slant roof in order to keep the heat down in the stalls. Whatever it was it worked, this place was nice and cozy, not too warm by any means but at least a little above freezing. As the sheriff warmed his hands by the stove I went to my pile of stuff and retrieved the Sharps and all the ammunition that went with it. When I reached the gun to Messer I could see by the look on his face that the town of Sioux City had just purchased a Sharps Big 50.

Chester's Last Ride

The sheriff looked over the stock and the etching on the barrel. He balanced the heavy gun in both hands and even sighted down the barrel. I sat the cloth sack that contained the ammunition on Mr. Bishop's table, along with the cleaning rod. "What do you think Sheriff?"

"Not bad Conley. In all my days this is the first time I ever got up close and personal with a Sharps Big 50. I believe a man with good eyesight and steady aim could pick off just about anybody before the gun they used could return fire." Sheriff Messer reached into his coat pocket and pulled out a pocket watch.

"Looks like it ain't even seven o'clock yet. How about you and me head over to the mayor's house and see what he thinks of the plan?"

I was getting pretty tired and was starting to think about that bunk that had been promised to me at the jail.

"Alright sheriff, let me dig out my kit and bedroll first. If the trip to the mayor's house takes us by the jail maybe I can leave my stuff there."

"That's a good idea. I need to check on the prisoners and the night shift deputy anyway. Grab your stuff and let's get going."

I made a quick check of Hazel and Rusty. Both looked content as sheep in their nice cozy stalls. On the way out I scratched under Ben's neck and then patted him on top of the head. Me and the sheriff hurried out the door and back to the jail. On the way back to the jail we never met anyone else out of doors, hopefully no one in his right mind would have any business outside on a night like this.

The deputy who worked nights was standing by the stove and I noticed a Greener shotgun lying on top of the big desk. "You expect trouble on a night when a full blown blizzard is blowing Sheriff?" I asked.

"Standard policy Conley when we got more than two prisoners, the night deputy has got to have a Greener within reach at all times," Messer said.

I stashed my stuff in the room I was pointed toward. It was sort of small but neat and clean, two bunks on each wall and one table in the middle with a kerosene lantern sitting on top. There were two ladder back chairs against the same wall as the door. "Looks better than a campsite out in the timber Sheriff by at least two to one and on a night like this I would say it's more like ten to one."

"It ain't bad is it? The city likes to keep its deputies well rested, well fed, well-armed, and underpaid." He busted out laughing when he said this; the night deputy began to laugh too.

When he finally caught his breath he looked at me and said, "Well, let's get over to the mayors house before the snow gets any deeper."

Within ten minutes we were on the porch of one of the nicest looking houses I had seen in years. Sheriff Messer knocked on the front door and within seconds the door opened.

"My goodness Messer, what are you doing out on a night like this?" A short round man wearing a house coat asked.

"Needed to ask your opinion about a little matter mayor," the sheriff said.

"Well come on in before you freeze to death right here on my front porch."

We both entered and were met with the view of a well-lit parlor with a grand piano sitting in one corner. It was a large room with fancy furniture and several pictures hanging on the walls.

Chester's Last Ride

"Sheriff, you have been here before do you remember where my study is? If so why don't you and this gentleman head on in and I will have my wife fix us some hot eggnog to drink. I assume both of you like eggnog?"

The sheriff looked at me and then said, "I'm sure both of us would love some mayor." With that the mayor disappeared into another room.

"Come this way Conley. If you ain't never tried eggnog before then you are in for a treat. I don't know the recipe the mayor uses but I think it contains a little bourbon. Anyway it will warm you right up," the sheriff said.

We entered another fancy room but this one had much more of a man's touch than the parlor by the front door. The room was big enough for a large desk and several chairs. The most dramatic thing about the mayor's study was the sight of a billiards table. On the wall was a rack that contained a number of pool cues. It was the first billiards table I had ever seen west of the Mississippi River, but then I was never one to visit mayor's studies.

"Gentlemen have a seat; my wife will be in shortly with the eggnog. Now Sheriff, what is it you wanted to talk to me about?"

"Well Mayor, it concerns the robberies of the stage from down south that brings the mail. This man here is Zeke Conley and he is from Kentucky. He came up with the idea of arming the guard on the stage with a weapon that might just give us the advantage."

I stood and shook the mayor's hand.

"What kind of a weapon is it Messer?" the mayor asked.

"Well, have you ever heard of a Sharps rifle Mayor?"

"I have. Matter of fact when I first came out west I owned one. It was called a Sharps Big 50. I sold it to a feller though about ten years ago. It kicked too hard for me. Damn thing hurt my shoulder it kicked so hard. It was a fine looking gun though. I had it engraved with four buffalo, one behind the other; it made the four look like they were running in a stampede. It was one beautiful gun I will have to admit. I always wondered what ever happened to that gun and the man I sold it to, funny how a man's mind likes to look back on things that are long gone."

I was startled by what the mayor just said. He had just described the gun I had traded for in Shasta. The sheriff looked at me and said, "Why don't we show him the gun Conley and see if he still remembers what a Sharps Big 50 looks like?"

I took the gun out of its leather rug and reached it to the wide eyed mayor. "Mayor, I don't believe I got your name when we shook hands," I said. If his name had been mentioned then either I hadn't heard or had just plain forgot.

"It's Evan Carter," the mayor said as he looked at the gun he now held in his hands. Both the sheriff and myself paid close attention as he turned the gun in every direction. When he looked at the side where the four buffalo were engraved he stopped and stared for the longest time before looking back at us to speak.

"I don't believe it. This is the gun I sold ten years back. It looks the same now as it did all those years ago. Whoever had it has taken very good care of it, how did you come about it Sheriff?"

"It belongs to young Conley here Mayor. He bought it over in Shasta a couple of weeks ago."

The mayor looked up from the gun and his gaze fell on Conley. "Are you looking to sell it, is that why you have come to see me?"

Chester's Last Ride

I looked at the mayor and said. "Mayor, I heard about all the trouble the stage has been having due to the bandits on the road. The sheriff and myself thought a bigger gun might give the man riding shotgun a better chance to defend himself if he could throw a little lead at the robbers before they could return fire. That gun would be about the best hope of accomplishing that."

"Oh no, this gun can't be used out in the open, especially in this kind of weather. This gun needs to be put away as a keepsake. How much are you asking for it?" the mayor said.

The sheriff spoke next. "He said he will take four-hundred dollars for it and all the ammunition he has."

"Sold Sheriff, I will get you the money now." The mayor rose from his chair and started to go to his desk.

I wanted to sell the gun but only to serve the purpose of protecting the men and women that rode the stage. "Mayor, I intended on selling the gun to the sheriff here so his deputy that rides the stage as a guard might have a better chance of stopping the robberies. I really don't want to sell it if it ain't going to the deputy."

The mayor returned to his chair and sat down. Surely he was a reasonable man and could see the need I was referring to.

"Yes Mr. Conley I see your point. In my excitement I guess I failed to appreciate what you and the sheriff were saying. How about the three of us work out a little compromise?"

Now this was getting interesting. I had come here intent on selling my gun and now it appeared that sentimentality had intervened. It was anybody's guess as to what the mayor had in mind.

The sheriff must have known the mayor pretty well. He sat back in his chair and crossed his right boot over his left knee.

Nathan Wright

He looked at me and then at the mayor. "Alright Evan, let's hear it."

The mayor stood and said, "Not before we have our eggnog." He exited the room but before he was out of sight he was met by his wife. She was carrying a tray with three cups along with a teapot of some sort. He thanked his wife and sent her away but not before giving her a kiss on the cheek. When he returned to the room he sat the tray down on his writing table and then closed the door to his study.

"I like to sweeten up my wife's eggnog. She doesn't know I add a little libation, it helps to ward off blizzards." He chuckled as he said this. The mayor took a key from his pocket and used it to open a wall cabinet. Inside was any number of bottles. He picked one out and came back to the tray. He poured a liberal shot into each glass and then filled the remainder with the hot eggnog from the china pot. I was starting to wonder if I would like the funny looking drink. He reached a glass to each of us and then said cheers. We each took a sip and I was surprised at how good it was. The texture was thick and creamy. The taste was a little sweet with the strong presence of bourbon, or maybe even Tennessee whiskey. As it went down I could feel it warming me up from my throat to my stomach.

The mayor, to my surprise, emptied his glass in one long gulp and then went back for another. Before doing so he went and rechecked the door to make sure it was locked. "You know one time I thought I had locked the door to my study but found out I hadn't when my wife came in and found me doctoring up her eggnog. Let me tell you something about that couch in the front parlor, it doesn't sleep near as good as you would think. I also got burnt eggs and raw bacon for the better part of a week. I might be the mayor of Sioux City but my wife is the dictator of this house, I try not to cross her."

Chester's Last Ride

He refilled his glass and then sat back down. "Here is the compromise I want to offer. I will have the sheriff to order a brand new gun from the manufacturer and have it delivered at all possible speed. In the meantime he can use this gun to protect the stage, but only under one condition."

The mayor didn't finish he just leaned back in his chair and sipped his eggnog. "How do you two like my wife's drink, kind of hits the spot on a cold night like this don't you think."

I had to shake my head in the affirmative, I could feel my face starting to heat up and my throat was on fire.

Sheriff Messer took another sip of his drink and then said, "Yes mayor it is delicious, what is the rest of your little compromise?"

"Oh yes, the one condition I have is for you to deputize young Conley here and have him ride with the stage, carrying his Sharps cannon of course, until the new gun arrives. Then I will purchase the gun from him and your deputy that normally rides with the stage can have the new gun. How does that sound?" the mayor asked.

Sheriff Messer looked at me. I could tell he really didn't care; I was the one that would be riding on a cold stage with the strong possibility of getting shot. "I guess that is up to Conley here."

Now I had a decision to make. Ride shotgun for a stage which is something I had never done before, in terrain I had never traveled before, in weather that could kill a man if he wasn't both careful and lucky.

"I'll do it." What the hell did I just say? It must be the eggnog talking.

There was a big look of surprise on the sheriff's face. There was nothing but a smile on the mayor's face. I'm sure if there was a mirror around I would see the look of a dumbass on my face.

"All right then Sheriff. You get this boy signed up on your payroll and I'll approve it. How long before the new gun shows up do you think?" The mayor asked. He looked like a kid who had just been promised his first gun.

"Last time we ordered anything in the way of a gun was them two new Colts. Best I can remember it took three weeks for them to arrive but it was summertime then. Now in this kind of weather I just don't know. Throw in the fact that the stage is two days late as of today and I would doubt it showing up for another day or two because of the blizzard."

"Well I guess it don't matter. Send the telegram first thing in the morning. And Sheriff, the train will deliver the new gun because that comes from St. Louis. Only the southern mail gets delivered on the stage."

"Oh yeah, I guess that is right. Should be three weeks or less then, you alright with that Conley?"

"I guess so. I don't intend on heading back west for a few weeks anyway. I wanted to get my mail and then write a few letters to send back home, plus my horses could really use the rest."

"You know, I was thinking about that. Wouldn't it be better if you took one of your horses and went along with the stage on horseback? You could scout around if need be and if a gun battle took place you would have the benefit of being able to run off the bandits," the sheriff added.

Did he really just say I could run off the bandits? One man on one horse with one gun could run off the bandits. "Sounds good to me sheriff." Now why the hell had I just said that? No more eggnog for me tonight.

Chester's Last Ride

"Then it is all agreed. Sheriff, where is this man staying while he's in town?" the mayor asked.

"Well for tonight mayor he is put up over at the bunk room at the jail. The way the weather is outside everything is sold out. Both hotels and even the boarding house is full. I checked with Miss Burke earlier today."

As the sheriff was talking there could be footsteps heard coming up the front steps of the big house. A moment later and there was a vicious knock at the door.

"What in hell is going on out there?" the mayor said as he got out of his chair and headed for the front door.

Before Mayor Carter could even make it out of his study there was another harsh knock at the door. Sheriff Messer jumped from his chair and headed to the front room right behind Carter.

"Better let me open that door mayor. You don't know who's on the other side and by the way they're knocking it can't be anything other than trouble."

Carter stopped and allowed Sheriff Messer to open the door. It was the deputy named Lucky and he was completely out of breath. He came in as the sheriff shut the door.

"Sheriff, you had better get to the jail quick. The four men we locked up earlier today have managed to escape. They shot Felix," Lucky said.

"Shot Felix, is he dead?" the sheriff asked.

"Naw sheriff, he got hit in the shoulder and looks like another bullet might have grazed his thigh. I got Sammy over there looking after him now. He's the one that told me where you were. I stopped by and told the doc to get over there as fast as he could and then I came here." Lucky's face was red from the biting wind and cold and he was completely out of breath, probably his run here was also not helping things.

Mayor, I better get back to the jail. How early can you stop by in the morning?" Messer asked.

"I'll be there first thing, how does daylight sound?"

"That will work. I don't intend on following them bastards until it gets daylight anyway. In this kind of weather we would most likely just be riding into an ambush. Conley you are now a full time deputy for Sioux City. Bring that Sharps and let's get back to the jail. Lucky how about you stay here and catch your breath for a few minutes. Have the mayor serve you some of that eggnog, make sure it's the same recipe he served us."

The mayor took Lucky toward the study as the sheriff headed out the front door and toward the jail, I was right behind him. We were there in less than ten minutes and the doctor must have beaten us by at least five.

"How is Felix Doc?" the sheriff asked.

"He's going to be just fine. The bullet that hit his shoulder didn't hit any bone. I got the bleeding stopped and plan on stitching it up in a minute. The wound to the leg is only a scratch. Man's been shot twice and he could still put in a full day's work tomorrow in my opinion," the doctor said.

I could tell the sheriff was relieved. It would be a hard thing on a man to have one of his deputies killed by some no-goods, especially when he thought they were locked up safe and sound.

"Sammy, what happened here anyway?" Messer asked.

"Well sheriff, I was on my way back to the jail after I walked the town and checked everything out. I heard the two shots and came running. I saw five men heading out of the jail at a full run when I got close enough but I was still too far away to fire a shot. I shouted but they just kept going. When I got in here I found Felix over there on the floor. I thought he was dead at first but then I saw him breathing. I locked the door just in case them fellers tried to come back and then went to him. I think the shot to the shoulder must have spun him around and his face connected with the wall. It must have just knocked him out."

"Were the cells empty when you got here?" Messer asked.

"Empty as my pockets Sheriff, Lucky got here within a minute or two so I sent him to get you and the doctor."

"How did they get Felix though? Did he say anything when he was coming to?"

"He said he didn't hear anything until the door swung open and a gun fired. He said the first shot hit him in the shoulder and that is all he remembers. Don't know how he got grazed in the leg unless it was a ricochet. Second shot must have bounced off the wall and that is what got the leg. Anyway, he was out cold and they must have taken him for dead. They yanked the keys off the wall by the door and unlocked the two cells. I would say Felix is one lucky bastard to have been shot twice and live to tell about it."

"Sounds about right Sam, Lucky will be here in a minute or two. I want you two to take a couple of Greeners and head out to see if you can track the bastards. Don't go farther than the edge of town though, don't need anybody else shot tonight. If you find where they might have gone in town then come back and get me and Conley here. If the tracks lead out of town then don't follow them just come on back. I plan on hunting them down at first light."

When the deputy named Lucky came in the door he looked much calmer than he had been when he barged into the mayor's house. I think he must have had two glasses of eggnog. The sheriff sent the two men back out into the cold to hunt for tracks. I was pretty sure the prisoners and whoever it was that helped them escape were not stopping anywhere in town for the night. I wondered if they had anything to do with the stage robberies that had been going on. There seemed to be a lot of mischief going on for it not all to be associated in some way.

The doctor finished up with Felix and headed for the coffee pot. He looked like a man that knew what he was doing. He was never nervous as he worked on his patient. His voice never rose or was even shaky. His hands were as steady as could be as he poured his coffee. Funny how a little gray hair can make a man sure of himself.

"Your deputy will be alright Sheriff. Might be a little sore in the morning but I want you to keep him here and keep him busy anyway," the doc said.

"Why should he stay here doc? If he is alright why not let him go home where he can rest," the sheriff asked.

The doctor was busy pouring his cup half full of sugar and then started to stir it in with a spoon that had been left beside the bowl of sugar for just such occasions. He took a sip and then sat the cup back down and started adding more sugar.

"Well Sheriff, the reason I want him here is because I don't want him anywhere near his place or that woman of his."

The sheriff looked at me and was as puzzled as I was.

"I don't follow you Doc. Again why don't you want him to go home?" the sheriff asked.

The doctor continued to fuss over his coffee which was probably more like a cup of sugar by now. Finally he got it sweet enough. "You ever been over to his house Sheriff, for that matter have you ever met his wife? Well I just bet you haven't because if you had then you would know why I don't want him there until his wounds heal. That is the nastiest place I have ever seen. That woman of his is no housekeeper. And I'll tell you something else you probably don't know, she's mean. He made me promise not to tell anyone but twice I've had to stitch him up where she went after him with a butcher knife. I guess I just broke my promise to him but that was a promise I should have never made in the first place."

Messer went to the coffee pot himself, it was empty and so was the sugar bowl. "Tell you what Doc; I'll keep him here for a few days till his shoulder heals a bit. You're right, I didn't know about the situation at his house and I never met his wife and from the description you just gave I don't think I ever want to. You think he can do some stuff around the office here while he is on the mend?"

"Oh yes, he can do anything he wants as long as he don't strain that shoulder of his too much, might be good to keep him busy anyway. After a man has been shot he tends to dwell on it for a spell. He tries to figure out how it happened and maybe starts to figure he brought it on himself for not being more alert or not being fast enough. It's just human nature to sit and stew over something that happened, especially if that something was bad. Now I ain't no scientist of the human brain mind you but I do read a lot and I read that somewhere once. It sounded right and I am sharing it with you now. So pay attention to me, I'm a doctor." The doc chuckled at that last remark.

I grabbed the coffee pot and went for the water which was kept in a big covered bucket sitting on a table where a half empty sack of sugar sat along with two small pouches of Arbuckle coffee. I filled the pot and put it on the stove and waited. It seemed anytime I saw the name Arbuckle it made me want coffee.

"Sheriff, what do you want me to do now that I'm on the payroll as a stagecoach guard; as far as I can tell there ain't a stagecoach in sight?" I asked.

Nathan Wright

The sheriff was deep in thought and seemed not to hear my question. I waited for the water to heat up and for the sheriff to speak. In my mind I bet the water would win, I was wrong.

"Tell you what Conley, you seem to have a pretty good head on your shoulders, how about you look around the jail here and see what you can learn about what happened. Any clues you find put them down on paper. If we ever catch them five then the case will be brought before Judge Runyon. Runyon is a man who likes all the facts straight."

I checked the coffee water one last time before it dawned on me that we still had one of the five men from the trouble earlier; he was over at the doctor's office. "Sheriff, what about the fifth man you arrested today. You know the one that Ben bit on the ass."

The sheriff looked up from his thoughts and then said, "That's right Conley. In all the excitement I plum forgot about him. Doc what kind of shape was he in when you came over here?"

The doctor was still playing with his coffee and it really looked like he was going to add some more sugar the way he was looking at the sack. "He was out cold Sheriff. I had to give him a strong dose of laudanum to keep him still while I sewed up his asshole. That big dog of Conley's tried to either tear that one clean off or make him an extra one." Again the doc chuckled.

The sheriff picked up the lid to the coffee pot and looked inside. "Slowest damn pot I ever seen, how bout we go over there and check on him in a minute Conley? I'll lock the door behind us and let Felix rest a bit. Surely with only one wounded deputy here nothing else can go wrong."

The sheriff kept looking in the coffee pot as if he could make the water boil just by shear willpower. Finally he filled his cup and added some sugar. This town used more sugar in its coffee than I had ever seen before. I went in and checked on Felix. He was sitting on the edge of one of the bunks and if it weren't for the bandage on the shoulder he wouldn't have looked hurt at all.

"Howdy Felix, I don't know if you heard us talking out there but the sheriff wants to go over and get the man that is laid up at the doctor's office and bring him back here for safe keeping. He is one of the gang that just escaped," I said.

"Yeah I heard. Before you go I would like someone to bring me my gun. I don't want to be here all alone after what just happened without something to shoot back with." He tried to laugh when he said this but by the look on his face it brought on some pain.

"I'll get it for you; by the way my name is Zeke Conley. The sheriff and the mayor have done made me a temporary deputy for the next three or four weeks."

"Welcome aboard Zeke Conley. We always schedule for at least one deputy to get shot around here each week and I was the last one for this month. That puts you at the front of the list for next month." This time he did laugh even although he paid a price for it.

"I'll try to keep that in mind Felix. Are there any rules against ducking when someone points a gun at you? I noticed that you didn't," this time I laughed.

I grabbed the gun and holster and took both to the wounded deputy. He was still trying to laugh. "I'll just put it on the edge of your bunk here. The sheriff is going to lock the door when we leave. Please don't shoot when we come back in, the new month don't start for another day or two." If laughing is good for healing then Felix would be good as new in minutes.

Nathan Wright

The sheriff, myself and the doc headed out into the blizzard and up the street toward the building that was used as the town's hospital. When we got there we were greeted with a wide open front door. I pulled my gun and the sheriff did the same. We entered the building with the doc close behind. After we determined the place was empty I struck a match and lit a lantern.

"Doc, it looks like your patient has gotten up and walked out on you," Messer said.

The doc lit his kerosene lamps and soon the place was lit up like Christmas. The three of us continued to look around for clues as to what happened to the patient. I noticed the rooms were all extremely cold and there was a serious draft.

"Doc is there a back door to this place?" I asked.

"There is Conley; if you're thinking what I'm thinking then maybe we should have a look."

The three of us headed toward the back with the doc in the lead. Once there we found the back door wide open, which explained the draft. I noticed some blood on the floor and once I stepped outside there was blood on the snow. It looked like a man had been dragged through the snow; there was even a place where it looked like they had dropped him.

The sheriff stepped forward and asked if either of us had just heard anything. We all got real quiet. All I could hear was the blowing of the wind.

"Doc, do you hear anything, maybe like a man's voice," the sheriff asked.

"I do, sounds like two men talking and it also sounds like they might be heading this way."

I had finally heard what the other two had heard; it really was two men talking. "You recognize who that might be Sheriff?"

Chester's Last Ride

"I think so Conley, it sounds like Lucky and Sammy. Let's just put out these lanterns and see what happens."

We did as Sheriff Messer asked and stepped back inside the building but left the door open so we could hear. Within minutes two men came around the corner of the next building up and they were not trying to be quiet in the least. It was evident they were tracking whoever had been drug through the snow. When they got to within twenty feet of the backdoor of the building the sheriff shouted out, "You two, stop where you are and be recognized."

"Is that you Sheriff? One of the two men asked.

"It is, is that you Lucky?" As the sheriff asked this he stepped outside but he still had his gun drawn.

"It's us Sheriff. We were following a trail that leads right to where you are standing. How come you two are here and not at the jail with Felix?" Lucky asked

"We came here to get the man the doc worked on earlier today. Did you two find anything while you were scouting the town?"

"We did Sheriff. We found that man you came here to get." Lucky said.

"Well where is he?"

"We left him a few doors back. We found him lying face down in the snow. Looks like somebody stuck a knife in his back, he's dead."

The sheriff looked at me. "They came here to rescue him. I guess when they found out what kind of shape he was in they decided to kill him instead. Didn't want him talking and revealing who they are," the sheriff said.

"Sounds about right Sheriff, let's go and have a look at the body," I said.

Nathan Wright

"Lucky, why don't you and Sammy show us where you found that body, we need to get it moved off the street before coyotes get the scent of fresh blood," the sheriff said as he and the two deputies started down the street.

Before I followed the three men I turned back to the doctor. "Say Doc, you wouldn't have a stretcher around would you? I really don't want to be trying to move a man without one, especially one that has just been stabbed to death."

"I got one in the side room, might be a good idea at that young Conley. You go on in while I get this place all shut up for the night. Both the fires have even gone out. I keep a little heat going all the time in the clinic, can't have all my stuff freezing solid you know." The doctor pointed toward the side room and I hurried after the stretcher. As I was leaving he was shutting the front door. I went out the back door and hurried after the sheriff.

We hadn't gone more than a hundred feet when we came upon the body. It was lying just as Lucky had described, face down with a neat hole in the back of the coat where the knife had gone in. When they rolled him over we stood there looking at him for a second. When he opened his eyes the three of us nearly had matching heart attacks.

"What the hell, he's still alive," Lucky said.

"Hurry up boys and let's get him back to the doctor before he freezes to death," Messer said.

I quickly put the stretcher beside the man and we eased him over as gently as we could. I took off my coat and covered the man as best as I could. Sammy and Lucky had already grabbed the ends of the stretcher and were lifting while I got him covered.

Chester's Last Ride

"Sheriff, I think I'll run back and help light the two fireplaces at doc's place." I didn't wait for a response, I was already moving.

When I got to the clinic the back door was still open and I hurried in. The doctor was putting some wood in the fireplace in the front room and heard me come in. He pulled a two shot Derringer from his vest pocket and met me in the long hallway ready to fire.

"Hold on there a minute Doc, it's me Conley," I shouted.

He quickly put the Derringer back in his pocket and said, "I just about shot you Conley. Then I guess I would have had to sew you back up. What the hell are you doing running back in here like that anyway?"

"Thanks for not shooting me Doc. That man that got drug out of here a little while ago and was stabbed is still alive. The sheriff is on his way back here with him now. Lucky and Sammy are carrying him on your stretcher."

"My God, how on earth could he have survived, you start the two fireplaces and then the cook stove in the kitchen. I'll finish lighting the kerosene lamps in my operating room. When they get here send them on back. Fix a big pot of coffee and also heat some water, real hot because I'm going to need plenty," the doc said as he turned and headed for a room that I hadn't been in yet.

Just as I was getting the fireplace lit I heard the sheriff coming through the back door. "Conley, where are you?" he shouted.

I stepped from the front room to the kitchen. When he saw me he asked where the doctor wanted the man on the stretcher. "He went into that room off the right of the hallway. He said it was his operating room."

Nathan Wright

As Lucky and Sammy carried the stretcher by the wounded man on it looked me square in the eye. He didn't speak but you could tell he wanted to say something. Once they got him situated on the big table the doctor used for his work they came back with the stretcher.

"You two take that thing outside and rub the blood off with some snow. I hope it isn't needed anymore but at least it'll be ready if it is," the sheriff said.

I began fueling the cook stove in the kitchen and before long I had it nice and hot. I put on a big pot for coffee and then a couple of buckets about half full of water for the doctor to use. I really didn't know what hot water had to do with operating on a man and I wasn't going to ask. Before long the room smelled of fresh brewed coffee.

The sheriff sent his two deputies back to the jail to check on Felix and told them to stay there; it was just too cold to search anymore tonight. I just sat at the kitchen table and drank coffee; with a little help from the sheriff we finished the entire pot in only an hour. As I was finishing up a brand new batch the doc came out of the operating room.

"How's he doing doc?" the sheriff asked.

After filling himself a cup of coffee the doctor looked at the both of us and said, "You two wouldn't believe how easy it was to patch that bastard back up. He was wearing his undershirt and shirt and a vest when they brought him in this afternoon. I never took any of that off him because that big dog of yours never bit him up there, only his ass. Well, when those fellers broke him out of here they put a big coat around him so he wouldn't freeze to death. When they figured he was going to slow them down too much they dropped him in the snow and then stuck that knife in his back. Anyway, it must have been a short bladed knife and with all the clothes he had on it never went more than an inch under his skin. And the best part is it was over to the side and never hit anything that would have been fatal. They were in such a hurry to get out of town they never checked to see if he was dead or not. That's the short of it.

"Sheriff, I would appreciate it if you could leave a deputy here until that man is well enough to take to jail." The doctor took a big drink of his coffee after he finished talking. He smacked his lips and then made a sour face, "Damn if I didn't forget the sugar."

"After all that has happened today I believe that might be a good idea, Conley do you mind staying here until I can get either Sammy or Lucky to come back over?" the sheriff asked.

"Sounds like a plan Sheriff. Once them outlaws find out that man is still alive I would bet they'll make another attempt on his life. You might want to have whoever you send over for the night to bring a Greener. I don't think a Colt can hit much after dark and especially in the middle of a blizzard."

"Good idea Conley. Doc when do you think I can get to talk to that man back there? I would like to as soon as possible. I really don't know how long he has to live with that bunch after him."

"Right now I got him all drugged up with Laudanum, hell he was still pretty drugged up from the Laudanum I had given him earlier. He doesn't know whose little boy he is right now. Check first thing in the morning. I'll have him sobered up by then. He might be in some pain but hell he's an outlaw, who cares."

"I reckon that'll be just fine Doc. I'll stop by a little after daylight. You think he will be able to talk by then?"

"I can almost guarantee it. I might even give him a little strong coffee to help wake him up. He'll probably want something to eat too but you had better speak to him first.

Food might make him sick and if that happens then you don't want to be in the same room with him, hell you won't want to be in the same building when he starts throwing up."

The sheriff left and headed back toward the jail. The doc asked if I knew how to play chess and I indicated I did though it had been five or six years. He dug around in a side room and brought out a chess board and a cloth sack which contained the pieces. As he sat the game up on the table I fixed myself some more coffee although I didn't dare use any sugar, the doc might take offence.

"Alright Conley, let's get started cause I know neither one of the deputies that get sent over here know how to play."

I did manage to stir in a little cream before I was ordered to sit down and play. The doc was starting to remind me of the two old men who were playing checkers on the front porch of the jail a few years back. I just hoped he wasn't as mean as those two. We played for nearly thirty minutes and I could tell I was about to get my ass handed to me, the doc was a good chess player. Just about the time I was going to make one of my last moves before check mate the door opened and in walked Lucky. He went straight for the stove and began to warm his hands.

"Looks like you two are playing them fancy checkers. I never did learn that game," Lucky said.

"Well you're going to learn tonight Lucky. After Conley here gets his ass beat then it's your turn," the doc said.

"You got yourself a game Doc, but let me warn you right now, I'm a fast learner. You just show me which piece jumps the other pieces and how you get a king and I bet I can win," Lucky said.

The doc looked up and frowned at Lucky. "Well if that ain't about the dumbest thing you ever said Lucky. This is chess not checkers. Do you really think it's just a fancy game of checkers or are you just that stupid?"

I could tell by the way the two were going at each other that this must be some sort of ongoing feud.

"You better just watch it doc. When them outlaw fellers come back here to finish up on that patient of yours back there then I'll bet you are a little nicer with that smart tongue of yours," Lucky said.

"Yeah, when them outlaw fellers, as you call them, shoot you then maybe I'll just remove the bullet without giving you anything for the pain. Move Conley so I can beat your ass. I got me a game waiting with that babbling idiot standing over there by the stove," the doc said.

Lucky filled himself a cup and then walked over to the table. "Did you just call me a babbling idiot Doc?"

"You damn right I did and when I fillet you out over a game of chess then you will probably agree with me."

Lucky looked at me and winked, "Conley, now might be a good time to upset the board there. If all the pieces land in the floor then I would say it's a draw."

The doc reached over and moved a piece and then slapped his knee, "Checkmate Conley. Now get out of that chair so I can cut this idiot down a notch or two."

I practically jumped out of the chair and Lucky immediately sat down, rubbing both his hands together like he couldn't wait to play.

"Doc, if you think you and Lucky here won't kill each other then I believe I'll head back over to the jail. I can hear my bunk over there hollering my name." Neither man looked up or for that matter even acknowledged that I had spoken. I grabbed my hat and pulled on my coat. When I went out the back door the two were arguing about where the chess pieces went.

Lucky might have never played before but it was apparent that he still had an opinion.

The weather hadn't improved much, if anything it had even gotten worse if that could be possible. The temperature had to be near or below zero and the wind was ferocious. I hurried along and made it to the jail right before I thought I would freeze to death. I slammed the big door shut and headed straight for the stove. Sammy was sitting at the sheriff's desk.

"Where are the sheriff and Felix?" I asked.

"The sheriff is in the bunk room sleeping. Felix was too but the snoring got too bad so he went into one of the cells to sleep."

I could hear heavy snoring coming from the bunk room and understood why Felix moved. The room we were in wasn't that warm and there was a steady draft. I checked the fire and seen that it was about to go out.

"Is there a reason why the fire is so low Sammy?" I asked.

"Not really Conley. I was going to stoke it up a little while ago but I sat here and fell asleep, when you opened the door I woke up. It is a little cold in here."

It wasn't just a little cold it was damn near freezing. I put in a couple of average size logs and before long the place started to heat back up. I checked the coffee pot and found it empty. What kind of a jail was Sheriff Messer running here anyway? After getting the coffee going I looked around what would be my new home for the next month, it wasn't much. I could tell that the mayor never wasted any of the taxpayer's money on extravagances.

As I snooped around the place I noticed that Sammy had fallen back asleep at the big desk. I dug out my pocket watch and saw that it was a little past midnight. As I fixed my coffee I wondered how the chess game was going back at the clinic. I hadn't heard any gunfire so I suspected it was still civil, at least for the moment.

As I sat in one of the ladder backed chairs and sipped my coffee I wondered what the policy was on locking the door. I really didn't want to fall asleep and get surprised by someone who wanted to cause some more mischief like the kind that had presented itself to Felix earlier. I decided to go over and lock the door anyway, if someone needed in then they could just knock. The night was uneventful. I had dozed off leaning back in my chair and finally after I couldn't stand the snoring coming from the bunkroom anymore I picked out one of the cells in the back that looked the cleanest and fell asleep.

Just before daylight I was awakened by the sound of someone stocking up the stove. When I entered the front room I found Sammy by the fire and the sheriff standing in front of a mirror shaving with a straight razor. I don't know how I slept in the cell area; it had to be at least twenty degrees colder than the big front room.

"Morning Conley, I trust you found some sleep during the night," Sammy said.

"I did. This place is about as cold as sleeping outside though. At least outside I can warm my hands by an open flame. That cell block back there is like an icebox."

Sammy laughed. "Well the smart deputies always try to sleep in here like civilized folk. It would take a bear in hibernation to want to sleep in one of them cold jail cells." He must have thought he said something funny by the way he started laughing.

Sheriff Messer finished up at the mirror and put on his vest and hat.

"I'm heading over to the doc's place to see if our prisoner feels like talking. Conley, why don't you head over to the telegraph office and see if they have any news about the stage. I'll meet you back here and we can figure out what to do about the jail break." With that the sheriff turned and headed out the door carrying his coat in his hand.

By the way the snow had piled up in front of the building I figured it must have snowed at least a foot during the night. Before the sheriff got the door closed a blast of cold air blew in along with a little snow. I decided to use the wash basin to shave before I headed out myself. I changed the water and took out my soap and razor from my kit. Within a few minutes I felt, and looked, like a new man. I yanked on my coat and headed out to find the telegraph office.

From my previous visits I knew it was near the railroad tracks. I knew they had moved it from where it used to be in years past but didn't know if they had moved it from the depot or to the depot. I decided to head there first and then to the post office. The trip there was bitter and my hands were starting to get cold even through my gloves. When I found the depot I saw the wires attached and that indicated that the telegraph had been moved there. I made my way up the steps and hurried inside. The depot was much warmer than the sheriff's office and I was glad of that. There was a window where a ticket man worked but I didn't see any telegraph or for that matter, an operator.

"Excuse me but could you tell me where the telegraph is located," I asked.

The man on the other side of the window was reading a newspaper and when he heard my question he looked up. "My goodness you scared me mister. I never heard you come in. Can I help you?"

He must have been reading something really interesting because he never heard my question, only the sound of me talking. "Yes, can you tell me where the telegraph for the town is located?" I asked again.

"As a matter of fact I can. It used to be located here but somebody thought it would be handier if it was in the post office. Easier for the people that work in the courthouse to send and receive messages than walking all the way over here," he said and then went back to reading his paper.

"Well, can you tell me where it is, the sheriff wants me to check on some messages." I wondered why I would now be asking for the third time.

Again he looked up from his paper and after a moment said, "You looking for the telegraph office?"

I could communicate with Ben and my two horses better than I could with this man. "Yes I am and before you look at that paper again please tell me."

The man didn't act any different this time than he had before. He looked back at his paper and read for a few seconds before he finally stood up and walked over to the window. He stuck his arm through and pointed at the back wall of the depot. "You'll find it that way about a thousand feet from the end of my finger." He then went back to his seat and continued reading his paper.

I decided to leave that thick headed bastard, and his paper, and go in search of the telegraph office without his help. As much as I hated it I ventured back into the freezing cold and headed toward the center of town. There was a speck of sunshine here and there and the light of it on the new fallen snow was truly blinding. I pulled my hat down low and proceeded to any building that looked like it might have people moving around in it.

I saw through the window of a barber shop that the proprietor was inside and already had a customer. I walked in and went straight to the stove that sat near a side wall. The room smelled of talcum powder and lilac water.

"Morning there young feller, you be interested in a haircut on this fine February morning?" he asked in a jovial voice. In all my travels I had found that barbers were most always in a good mood and they also seemed to increase the mood of anyone they talked to.

"Maybe later, right now I need to find the telegraph office. The man over at the train depot could only read his paper and point," I said.

The barber laughed. "That would be old Ted. Did you ask him two or three times what it was you wanted?"

"I did as a matter of fact. I asked him three times and never did get a straight answer."

Again the barber laughed. "Old Ted is deaf. He ain't heard anything anybody has said in years. He lost his hearing back in the war, he was an artillery man. Almost all artillery men from the war are now deaf."

Well that certainly helped to explain the man at the depot but this barber still hadn't answered the question either. "Thanks, now do you know where the telegraph office is?"

I could tell by the look on the barber's face that he was a prankster. He looked out the window and only pointed. Both the barber and his customer busted out laughing. I was a stranger in town and didn't expect much help from anyone but this was starting to rub me the wrong way.

"That is real funny. Sheriff Messer hired me as his new deputy last night and now he wants me to go to the telegraph office to check on some messages. I wouldn't want to get back to the jail and tell him that I couldn't fine the telegraph, so please, if it ain't asking too much, can you tell me."

Chester's Last Ride

The barber straightened right up when I told him I was a deputy. "Well, I was just having a little fun. Tell you what; you see them wires hanging on that pole over there?"

I looked out the front window and saw the wires he was pointing at and then nodded.

"Well, if you go over to that side of the street and then follow them wires they will lead you right to the telegraph office." With that both men busted out laughing again. Seemed that I got a lot more respect when Ben was around, him being famous and all. I thanked the two men and left, glad to leave the two silly bastards behind.

I followed the wires and sure enough they led me straight to the place I was looking for. I guess the smartass barber was right after all. The telegraph office was inside a spacious new post office building. There were double front doors which were each half glass. Etched on one door was the word *Post*, and on the other *Office*. I turned the knob fully expecting the door to be locked but to my pleasant surprise the knob turned and the door opened. I stepped inside to find a large front room, so large that it had two wood burning stoves instead of one. There were three men inside each wearing the standard headband with a bill or visor in the front. I had seen them before but usually on tellers or bankers. Two of the men were tending the fires in the stoves and the third was placing letters in slots in a wall that must have had hundreds of openings. The room was very cold which indicated that they had just opened up and were only now tending the fires.

I walked over to the nearest man and presented myself as a new deputy. I explained that the sheriff had sent me over to see if there was any news about the stage.

"Well mister, if you are a deputy then where is your badge?" he asked me.

Nathan Wright

This was a truly great question and I was sure my answer would do nothing to ease his suspicions that I was just a common criminal trying to obtain information that I wasn't entitled to.

"I was appointed last night by the sheriff and the mayor. We had a deputy wounded last night and the sheriff hired me for a month until his deputy is back to full duty." This was partially true in that a deputy was wounded and I was hired for only one month. I knew I would never be able to explain the story of the Sharps Big 50 and me riding shotgun for the stage.

"Well how do we know you are really a deputy without a badge? I ain't never seen no lawman without a badge before," the man said.

I knew I was licked. Seems I had spent the last hour talking to idiots and smartasses. "I tell you what, since it doesn't look like you are going to believe I am a deputy then I would at least like to check my mail."

The man straightened up from his fire and pointed to the third man, the one that was shoving envelopes into slots and said, "Then you need to talk to Frank over there. He's the postmaster for Sioux City." With that said the man went back to stoking his fire.

I walked over and introduced myself. I did remember this man and he had given me my mail before but I wondered if he remembered me.

"You say you're Zeke Conley? If that's so then where is your dog Ben? I remember that the real Zeke Conley don't go anywhere without that monster of a dog by his side. He travels with two fine looking horses too. One by the name of Hazel and the other is Rusty. I look at you and don't see any of them. You give me a good reason why I should believe what you just told me," the postmaster said.

"I hung my head, truly defeated. I had been a lot of places in my time but couldn't remember ever having this much trouble trying to talk to people. I decided to head back to the jail and see if I could scare up a deputy's badge of some sort. If I couldn't then I intended to bring back either Sammy or Lucky to let people in this town know that I was legit.

"Well thank you kindly mister. If I was to bring back one of the other deputies, or even the sheriff, then would you believe that I am Zeke Conley and let me have my mail."

The man rubbed his chin and then said, "You bring back anybody wearing a badge and I recognize them then you can have the mail. How does that sound?" the man asked.

I tipped my hat and headed for the door. I remembered this to be a friendlier town in my previous visits but I also remembered having Ben with me everywhere I went. I headed out the door and back to the jail. As I walked by the barber shop the barber was looking out the window. He waved and I swear it looked like he was laughing. I guess when it's zero outside with a foot and a half of snow on the ground then a man will laugh at about anything.

I made it back to the jail and went immediately to the stove. My toes were starting to get cold. I stomped my feet and clapped my gloves together trying to get some blood circulating. Just then the sheriff walked in.

"Damn nation if it ain't cold this morning. Conley, what did you find out over at the telegraph office?"

"Nothing Sheriff, seems nobody wants to talk to me. I can't really blame them though, me being a stranger and all. One thing that might help is if I had a badge to wear."

The sheriff was holding his cold hands so close to the stove it looked like steam was coming off them. He turned and backed his ass up to the stove and damn near caught his pants on fire. After he felt he was sufficiently cooked he walked over to his desk and pulled out a side drawer. He pulled out a deputy's badge and tossed it to me.

"There you go Conley, now as soon as you get yourself warmed up head back over there and find us out some news."

This time when I went into the Post Office I was met with about the same reception as before.

"Did the sheriff really give you that badge or did you buy it at the general store," the head postmaster asked.

I decided that I had just about had enough this morning, "Tell you what, how about I arrest you and when we get to the jail then the sheriff can fill you in?"

The man smiled and held out both hands, palms forward. "I only been funning you Conley. I remember you from your previous visits. How come you ain't traveling with that big dog of yours? If anything has happened to him then it would surely ruin my day, I like that big wolf."

"Ben's alright. As a matter of fact he's doing a sight better than me. Everybody in town treats him with respect while I get run up and down the street in zero weather trying to find someone that believes who I am."

The postmaster slapped me on the shoulder and said, "You come on back where we sort the mail. I got a big pot of coffee and an entire squash pie back there."

"Squash pie, what on earth is that?" I asked the man. I hadn't had anything since dinner the night before and the mention of food made me realize just how hungry I was getting.

"Well, I'm sure you know what pumpkin pie is. Squash pie is kind of like pumpkin but not as sweet. It makes for the best breakfast you ever had. Come on back and warm yourself up while I field dress that pie."

Chester's Last Ride

We walked through a door that was to the right of all the mail slots he had been filling earlier. It was warm back there too thanks to another wood burning stove. This was one of them big cooking stoves with an oven underneath to one side and a big flat cooking surface on top where a huge coffee pot sat. I could tell that I had missed my calling. Working for the United States Post Office was the way to go. There was even a big icebox that almost looked brand new although I was sure it wasn't used much during this kind of weather.

I asked the postmaster his name and he said it was Ancil Hughes.

"Well Ancil, you know by now that my name is Zeke Conley," I told him.

He looked up from the stove and asked, "Wouldn't that be Deputy Zeke Conley?"

The other two men who worked there started laughing. I could tell that these three men must enjoy their jobs; they seemed to always be happy.

"I stand corrected Ancil. Since you offered I think I will accept a slice of that squash pie." I could see it sitting on the side of the stove, which would mean it would be at least warm, and right now, after my trips back and forth outside, I could really use it.

The other two men came over and each poured coffee. There was a rectangular table with four chairs they used for their meals where the two men sat down with their cups. Ancil must have been the one who brought the pie from home because he was the one who sliced it and put it on parchment paper. He carefully cut the pie into four equal parts and took a big flat spoon to lift each piece onto the paper. He left the last slice in the pan. He sat a piece in front of each of us and then the pan, which contained the last piece, he sat down where he would sit. Inside the ice box was a pitcher of either milk or cream which he also sat on the table. I stand corrected, ice boxes can be used even in zero weather.

After he was satisfied that each of us had our coffee and an equal portion of pie he sat down and then asked for a prayer. He thanked the Lord for the Squash Pie and the coffee. When each of us had said Amen, we picked up our forks.

The crust was thick and flakey. It had a top crust and a bottom crust. The filling looked a light brown color instead of the orange you would see in a pumpkin pie. I tried a bite and noticed a hint of brown sugar. He was right, it wasn't too sweet but it was still sweet just the same. The other three men ate like hogs and I noticed that I was falling behind. I quickly caught up though. When finished Ancil looked at us and asked what we thought of his wife's creation. All agreed it was good, really good.

"Has there been any word about the stage Ancil?" I asked.

He was rolling a cigarette and as he struck a match he said, "Got word this morning, they are heading out this morning. With no trouble they will be here by four this evening."

"You got to be joking. It's damn near zero outside and there is over a foot of snow on the ground."

"Weather is warming. By noon it should make it up to the freezing mark. The ground is frozen so the stage pulls easy and that snow is light stuff. Not thick and mushy like it will be in a day or two. Nantz is pulling with a six horse team. They won't have any trouble."

"How do you know the snow won't keep coming down, and how do you know it will warm up by noon?" I asked.

"The railroad gets telegrams about the weather every day from all over and they got a man that takes the information he gets and puts it all together, that man can tell you when it's going to rain and when it's going to snow. He can even predict how warm or how cold it's going to get," Ancil said.

Sounded like something that might work; what would people think of next? A man that could predict the weather might as well call himself a weatherman. After thinking about it I decided it was the craziest thing I had ever heard of, a weatherman.

"Thanks for the pie Ancil. If I can pick up my mail then I better get back to the sheriff's office."

The three men stood and put the parchment paper we had used for plates in a big barrel that they used for trash. "Come on around to the boxes Zeke and I'll fetch your mail. You got a few letters but we ain't got a stage in over a week so there might be something else in the mailbag when it gets here," Ancil said.

He went straight to a box and pulled out four letters and a bunch of flyers. When he reached them to me I asked what was with all the flyers.

"That is something new. If someone is running for political office then they pay a small fee to put one of these flyers in each mailbox. If a store is wanting to move a particular kind of merchandise that they might have too much of then they pay to have more papers stuffed in each box that tells what they got and how much they want for it. It's called advertising," he said.

"Now that is about as crazy as that weather stuff you mentioned. Why do people want to go messing with stuff when it's working fine the way it is?" I asked.

"Conley, it sounds like you been in the wilderness too long. These things I'm telling you about are the future and you just as well get used to it. It's coming whether you like it or not. Maybe you need to spend a little more time in town and less out there chasing grizzly bears."

Nathan Wright

I was looking at my letters while Ancil was lecturing me about the future. There were three letters from my paw back in Kentucky and one from the sheriff of Floyd County, the county where my paw lived. As bad as I wanted to open all four letters I had a job to do first. I again thanked Ancil for his hospitality and then headed back toward the jail. Once outside I could see the sky had cleared and the sun had some power to it. It felt good on my face. The wind had completely died down. Maybe the man who predicted the weather for the railroad knew what he was doing after all. I would still need more convincing though.

Back at the sheriff's office I found Lucky and Messer. Felix was still asleep in one of the jail cells.

"What did you do with Sammy Sheriff?" I asked.

"I sent him over to the doc's place to guard our prisoner. Doc says if everything goes well today then we can bring him over here and put him in a cell and I agreed. He would be a lot safer here locked up than over there. Doc said for us to clean up one of the cells real good, clean sheets and pillow, sweep the floors and get down all the cobwebs. Doc said he will spend the first night here to see how his patient does. What did you find out about the stage?"

"Stage is on the way Sheriff. Ancil over at the post office said they sent a telegram early this morning and said to expect it about four this evening. By the way, is Ancil the postmaster and also the telegraph operator?"

"No, Ancil is just the postmaster. The man that operates the telegraph is Lester, Lester Burrows. He helps with the mail from time to time. There ain't been a stage here in over a week so I guess life at the post office has been pretty boring lately."

"Well Ancil was putting up mail this morning. I guess people still bring their letters to the post office everyday whether the stage runs or not," I said as I took a seat and pulled the mail from my pocket.

I separated the leaflets from my letters and then shoved the sheets into the stove. For some reason I felt the need to open the one from Sheriff Barnes first, the letter contained a single sheet of paper and on it was written a single paragraph. It read,

Zeke Conley,

I write to inform you that there is trouble brewing in your home county. Some strangers from up north are in the process of acquiring every scrap of land that can be had by either hook or crook. Your father has been approached by these men and from what I gather they have threatened him. Haskell is a proud man and doesn't need to sell. Rumor has it that he will be forced off his land if he refuses to come to terms. I think that at times like these it would be wise for you to be here to assist your father.

Sincerely, Sheriff Barnes

I read the letter from the sheriff twice before I folded it back up. Trouble at home? If Sheriff Barnes wrote to me then I was sure there was something to it.

I looked at the other three letters and opened the oldest one first. It was just the usual stuff about how the family was doing and hoping I was well and that they wanted me to come home.

The second letter was pretty much the same. The third letter, which was also the most recent, was more in line with what the sheriff had said in his letter. The only difference was this letter didn't ask for me to head home but more or less insisted I return to Kentucky. It told me to use caution and not let anyone know who I was or where I was going. I folded each letter and returned it to the envelope it had come out of. I put all four into an inside coat pocket and then leaned back in my chair.

"Everything alright Conley?" the sheriff asked.

"Not really Sheriff. I got some trouble back home that I need to attend to. I don't know if I'm going to be able to ride guard with the stage now after all," I said.

"Well if you got to go then I'm sure the mayor will understand. One way or another I still think he will buy that Sharps off you though. The way his eyes lit up when he held that gun, it was like he was being carried back in time," Messer said.

"You know Sheriff, what's the chance that he would ever have seen that gun again anyway, pretty slim if you ask me. If it kicked too hard back then it will kick too hard now. That doesn't change over time."

"I really don't think he wants to shoot that gun at all Zeke, he just wants to put it up on his wall over the fireplace so he can look at it from time to time. As a man starts to look toward the last years of his life he wonders how much time he's really got left. In the mayor's case, he probably figures he has ten years left at the most and he probably won't like the last five of em. I was talking to him a few days back and he was telling me this. Then you came along with that Sharps rifle that he used to own."

"Well I believe the mayor deserves to get his gun back even if I have to give it to him Sheriff. The reason I say that is by the looks of these letters I got to get back to Kentucky and I really can't wait a month to start the journey."

The sheriff thought about what I had found out in my letters and had just shared with him. "Conley, why don't you put off leaving for at least a day or two, make sure the weather doesn't get worse. Out here it can throw you a blizzard without more than a few hours warning."

"Who will you send to guard the stage now Sheriff if I can't go?"

"Lucky used to carry a Sharps a few years back when he was a little farther West hunting buffalo. He mentioned that he would like to go with the stage and carry that Sharps if at any way possible, said he was ready for a little excitement. I reckon if you head on out then I'll give Lucky the job. He's a good deputy and if the rumors I hear carry any weight then he truly is a dead shot. You go ahead and plan on heading back to Kentucky in a couple of days and I'll let Lucky tag along with the stage," the sheriff said.

So it was settled, I was released from the bargain the mayor had hung over me. Lucky when told of his new assignment was elated.

When the mayor came in about half past eight in the morning he was brought up to date on all the happenings of the previous evening. When told of my need to head east he agreed. Apparently he thought well of a man who came running when his family needed him. Before noon the mayor had gone home and retrieved the four-hundred dollars for the Sharps Big 50. I reached in my pocket and returned the deputies badge to the sheriff.

"My career as a lawman lasted a total of eighteen hours Sheriff, which has got to be some sort of record," I told him.

"Oh I think your career as a lawman is going to last just a little longer Conley. The mayor wants you to go along with the stage on its way back out of town. Once you are out of town your deputies badge wouldn't have been any good anyway, you would have been out of the town's jurisdiction. Anyway, Mayor Carter was so glad to get his Sharps back that he talked to the judge and had him to appoint you as a Deputy US Marshal. He thought you could ride with the stage on its way back out of town. He knew you were heading back to Kentucky and he thought that maybe when your business was done there you could come back here and help put a little law and order back in this area. How does that all sound to you?"

I had been a Deputy US Marshal a few years back but when I decided to hunt bear hides I resigned my badge and headed for bear country. I had been in a few scrapes while I wore that badge but managed to stay alive anyway. I wondered if they knew about this, it would be odd for a judge to swear me in otherwise. They just don't pin those badges on strangers.

"Sheriff, how is it they would make me a Deputy Marshal, I just blew into town yesterday?" I said.

"We know who you are Conley. You hunted down and arrested the Hembree brothers. Those two had already killed two other lawmen that tried to bring them in but you managed to do it all by yourself. And you brought them in alive, not an easy task if you ask me," the sheriff said.

I was surprised that the sheriff knew so much about that little incident. Bringing in those two outlaws was one of the reasons I resigned my badge. One of the two brothers, I never did figure out which, had managed to shoot me before I managed to arrest and bring them both in. That was the closest I ever came to losing my life, that is if you don't count bear and moose encounters.

"When did you find out about all this Sheriff?"

"Oh, I had my suspicions when I first saw you. You don't remember me but I was one of the deputies that relieved you of the two Hembree brothers when you brought them in. You had been shot and were just barely hanging in the saddle when you made it to town with those two. It's been a few years. You were in one sorry shape when you finally did make it to town, damn near dead. It took me a while but I figured it out."

I thought back to when the sheriff had mentioned. I really didn't remember much about bringing them two in. I had lost a lot of blood and was ready to kill both of them before I would allow them to get away. I had made up my mind the morning before that if I didn't make it to town by nightfall then I would shoot both of the Hembrees and then allow myself to pass out. I found out later that I had made it to town about an hour before dark. It was real lucky for the two Hembrees; they got to live two more days before they were both hung.

"I don't remember much about that Sheriff."

"I reckon you don't. When they pried you out of the saddle and took you to the doc's you were damn near dead. I heard later that you never came to for three days after the doctor removed that bullet from you. Later I heard you turned in your badge and headed west after bear hides. That's been nearly five years ago. You never even waited for your last month's pay. It's been sitting in a bank all this time earning interest. The mayor had me send off a telegram a little while ago, didn't take long to get a reply. Anyway when my suspicions were confirmed I told the mayor and he talked to the judge. The marshal's badge is yours, all you got to do is accept," the sheriff said.

I was deep in thought. If I was heading back to Kentucky then a badge might help me get there. And the good thing about being a deputy marshal was that I would have a little authority when I got there.

"Thanks Sheriff, I'll accept. It's been a long time since all that happened. I really tried to forget about it, but I guess a man can never outrun who he is can he?"

"No Conley, I reckon he can't."

Nathan Wright

After being sworn in by the judge I headed over to Thurman Bishops to check on Ben and the horses. The weather had warmed up substantially; it must have been nearly twenty-five degrees. The sun even had a little power. When I entered the barn there sat Mr. Bishop by the stove. Ben was working on another big hambone but this time he came running over to greet me.

"Morning Mr. Bishop, how did everything go last night?" I asked. He looked to be in pretty good shape after his run in with the five men the previous evening. All I could see was a slight knot on the side of his forehead which had turned a little blue.

"Went fine young Conley, I doubted if anyone would want to come in here knowing Ben was inside. The wife fixed scrambled eggs and biscuits for breakfast and then fed it to Ben. I got a glass of milk," he laughed as he said this. He had said the night before that Ben would eat better than he would and I guess he was right.

"Old Ben does have a way with the ladies don't he?" I said.

"He does at that Conley. My wife fed him and then patted his forehead; she ain't laid a hand on me in years." Again Bishop laughed so hard that tears came to his eyes.

"The stage is going to make it to town this afternoon. I reckon when it leaves I'll be going with it. I never did get a schedule, does it leave back out the same day or will it be in the morning?"

"In the morning, they've been running them animals pretty hard trying to dodge them outlaws that have been causing the trouble lately. I feed and water the team and then they leave about an hour after first light the next day. You say you're planning on heading out with them?"

Chester's Last Ride

"Yeah I reckon so Mr. Bishop. After I make the run with the stage I plan on heading back to Kentucky, got some family matters there to tend to."

"That is a good thing to do Conley. A man has got to see to his family. Lots of men I've known in my life just left home at the first chance and never looked back, hard thing to do to a father and mother though. You see to your family and if you're ever back this way then you make sure you stop by here."

"I'll be back, it might be a year or two but you can count on it." I walked over and checked on Hazel and Rusty. Both were as content as sheep in their stalls. Again I left Ben with Mr. Bishop and headed back to the sheriff's office. I was a bit curious about what he was going to do about the jail break from the night before.

Before I made it back to the jail I had decided that since I was now a Deputy U.S. Marshal again I might as well look the part. I took the badge from the pocket in my coat where I had placed it when the judge swore me in earlier. I pinned it to the left front of my coat. The sight of the familiar badge on my chest brought back memories, a lot of good ones and even a few bad. As it worked out having that badge out where people could see it was about to save me a lot of trouble. As I walked toward the jail I saw Wade Bowers coming out of the saloon where I had eaten the night before. He was accompanied by two other men that I hadn't seen before. He looked across the street and noticed me, the way I was heading he couldn't see the badge on my coat.

"Conley you son of a bitch wait up a minute," Bowers shouted.

I done as I was told and stopped, I was actually looking forward to continuing the conversation from the night before.

He came bounding across the street with the two strangers in tow.

"Fellers, this is the bastard that sucker-punched me last night at the sheriff's office. That no good Messer didn't even arrest him, now I think it's time to settle the score," he said.

I really didn't like the names he had just called me and intended to settle a score myself. As they got closer I timed my reaction just right and wheeled around and hit Bowers square in the same place I had hit him the night before. The other men with him came at me but stopped mid-step, they had seen the badge.

"What are you waiting for, you saw him attack me again," Bowers said through busted lips.

I turned on around so he could see why they had stopped; it was now my turn to talk. Both of Bower's friends were wearing guns so I eased the front of my coat to the side so as to show my Colt. It also would allow me to draw in case any of these men didn't like what I was about to say.

"Bowers, or whatever your name is, I don't like the way you talk. I don't like the way you act and I don't like the company you keep," I said this as I looked at the two men still standing.

"Now you shut the hell up and listen real good, it just might save your life." I was silent for a second to allow this to sink in.

"I came to town to stable my horses and get some rest. The first person I met when I got to town was a big mouth lying cheating bastard and just in case any of you don't know who I'm talking about it's that snake sitting on his ass in the street rubbing his chin." I turned now so Bowers could actually see that what I wore was a marshal's badge, not just a city deputy's badge. He looked at it and stopped rubbing his chin.

"Bowers, you been running your mouth about me and the sheriff. Now you tie a knot in your tongue and listen for a change. This badge I'm wearing states that I am a Deputy U.S. Marshal. I don't know how you swindled Chet Brimley out of his livery stable but you can damn well bet that I'm going to make it my life's work to find out. Something else that I strongly suspect is that the robbery of the stage coach has something to do with you." I only said this to give him something to think about, the look on Bowers face was one of pure guilt. The two men with him also looked like the gig was up. I continued.

"I'll be riding out first thing in the morning with the stage. I plan on either arresting or killing every man that looks the wrong way at that stage, you hear me Bowers?" He shook his head violently.

"Now as far as your two daughters here, I'm going to give them until sundown to get the hell out of Sioux City."

Bowers was slowly getting to his feet and started to get a little backbone.

"You can't run these men out of town Conley, they haven't broken any laws," he said.

"Actually they have Bowers, they were getting ready to attack a U.S. Marshal and it was on your directions. Now that is a Federal Offense but I'm going to do the gentlemanly thing and let them ride out of town. The next time I see either one of them though I won't be nearly so gracious. In addition there was a jail break last night and one of the town's deputies was wounded as he valiantly defended himself and the jail. That would be considered attempted murder of a lawman. It carries the penalty of hanging. I intend to hunt down the four escaped prisoners and the man who assisted them."

The two men and Bowers didn't speak, they just stood there with their mouths open. I thought I would put a little emphasis to what I had just said.

"Come with me Bowers, you're under arrest."

"Under arrest, what's the charge?" he asked.

"Being an asshole mainly, the rest is for inciting violence against a peace officer, now come along before I knock your silly ass unconscious and drag you over to the jail."

Suddenly the wind had gone out of Bowers' sails. He came along peacefully without all the lip I had become so accustomed to. The other two men made a hasty retreat toward Bower's stables, no doubt to gather their horses and head out of town.

We entered the jail and I grabbed the key from the peg where it hung. I led Bowers back and put him in the dirtiest cell I could find. Once inside I slammed the door shut.

"How many horses you got over at Chet's Livery?" I asked.

"Just three Marshal. Mine and the two that belong to the two men you just ran out of town," Bowers said in a tone that said he was a defeated man.

"You want out of here anytime soon then you better figure on a way to give the livery back to Brimley," I told him as I started back toward the front office.

"You say that I can go if I leave the livery?" he asked.

I knew Bowers had most likely stolen the livery from Chet Brimley and wondered how on earth that little problem could ever be made right. Surely it wouldn't be this easy.

"That's right Bowers. I don't know how you ever got control of the livery in the first place, but right now all I care about is for it to be given back to its rightful owner and that is Chet Brimley."

"Alright Marshal, you let me out and I'll get gone in less than an hour," he said.

Now this was way too easy. Why would Bowers fold his hand and leave town in such a hurry? I had a suspicion and there might be a way to find out. I turned and left the cell area and headed out to find Sheriff Messer. I didn't have to look far; the sheriff was standing in the big front office.

"I saw you bringing Bowers up the street, what did he do?" the sheriff asked.

"Not much Sheriff, but enough to get him arrested. While you were looking through your wanted posters did you ever find anything with Bowers' name on it?"

The sheriff looked at me and said, "Not with his name on it Conley, it just dawned on me, his name really isn't Bowers is it?"

"I don't think so. When I arrested him he was pretty surprised. He even offered to leave town and give the livery back to Brimley if I would let him go. Now why would a man be so anxious to leave town that he would abandon an investment as valuable as the livery?" I asked.

The sheriff thought a minute and then smiled. He had just figured it out. "Something tells me that Bowers is a wanted man hiding behind an alias and didn't want to be identified by being arrested. How about we take another look at those posters I got in my desk."

Sheriff Messer pulled out the drawer and got out a handful of wanted dodgers and reached them to me. I started thumbing through them as he headed for the coffee pot. It didn't take long before one caught my eye. It was of a man wearing a business suit of some sort and he had a neatly cropped beard. I sat the others down and reached it to Messer. He sat the coffee pot back on the stove and glanced at the poster.

"Harpo Hamilton," the sheriff said. He continued to look at the face on the dodger.

"I believe this is the man. I never noticed before due to the full beard and name. Let's go and have a little talk with our man." The sheriff stopped and thought a second.

"Conley, bring him out under the notion that you are letting him go and then I will spring this dodger on him. If we catch him off guard then he might give up the scheme," Sheriff Messer said.

"Sounds good to me Sheriff." I opened the door to the cell area and took the keys back off the peg.

"Come on Bowers, the sheriff said for me to let you go."

Bowers didn't speak but he did smile. I opened the door to the cell he occupied and pointed toward the front of the building. As he walked into the front office the sheriff motioned for him to come over to his desk.

"Have a seat Hamilton so I can sign you out of jail," the sheriff said.

To my surprise, and I think the sheriff's too, Bowers sat down without contesting the name used. Messer picked up the wanted dodger and slid it toward Bowers. When Bowers looked at the dodger in front of him his head just dropped and his shoulders sagged.

"Your name is Hamilton isn't it?" the sheriff asked.

Bowers didn't answer he just looked at the paper. Finally after a few minutes he looked at Messer. "What happens now Sheriff?"

"I'll hold you here until the weather is good enough to have you sent back to St. Louis where you can stand trial for bank fraud. Embezzlement should keep you in jail for at least ten years. By the way, how did you come about the livery stable in town anyway?" the sheriff asked.

Bowers, or Hamilton, who he had just admitted he was said, "I just told him that I was with the war crimes department from Washington and had evidence that he had profiteered during the war. I didn't tell him what kind of profiteering it was. He folded like a cheap suit and told me if I would look the other way then he would give me his livery stable. I accepted. In this matter I am only guilty of telling a lie but the way he caved I would say he is guilty of something. And by the way, I am also innocent of the crime described in that wanted poster you possess. I'm actually glad that now I can go back and prove my innocence."

"Well Hamilton, if you can prove your innocence then I am glad for you. As for ever returning to Sioux City in the future, I doubt that would be a wise move on your part. Now if you would kindly march back to your cell I will have a telegram sent to St. Louis and see what they want me to do with you," Sheriff Messer said.

The man we knew as Bowers turned and went back to the cell he had just left. After locking the door I asked what we should do about the livery.

"Tell you what Conley, I better send Sammy over there pretty quick to let Chet know he's got his livery back and he has a horse or two over there that need to be looked after."

After Sammy left I asked the sheriff about Chet giving away his livery so easily in the first place.

"You know Conley, if Chet is guilty of a crime in his past and that is why he gave Bowers the livery, then I say we forget about it. In my opinion, I think Chet Brimley is so gullible that he probably believed Bowers had something on him even if he didn't. Anyway, Brimley has been an outstanding member of the community for a lot of years. If he did do something way back when then I don't care," the sheriff said.

Later that day the rumor of a stage showing up had a lot of the town in a buzz. It had been at least a week and people wanted their mail. They also wanted to see if the stage had made the trip without any trouble. I was waiting in the sheriff's office when Lucky came running in.

"The stage is coming up main street Sheriff. You told me to let you know as soon as I saw it."

The sheriff rose from his desk and grabbed his hat. We all stepped out onto the covered porch of the jail. The sun had managed to get the temperature up above freezing and water was beginning to drip from the front edge of the porch roof. As the stage approached I could tell it was being pulled by a team of six stout looking horses. The driver was a man with solid white hair and a bushy white mustache. It gave him the look of one of the cowboys you read about in the dime novels.

The stage stopped in front of the sheriff's office and the driver set the brake. The horses were not breathing hard at all. You could tell that they hadn't been run hard on this trip.

"Howdy Sheriff," the driver said as he jumped down from his seat. He wore a leather gun belt and had an ivory handled Colt stuck in the holster.

"Howdy William, you have any trouble on the way up today?" the sheriff asked.

The man named William pulled a big red handkerchief from his coat pocket and rubbed his forehead. When he took off his hat the sun sparkled off his solid white hair. He couldn't have been more than fifty years old but the white hair and mustache made him look a lot older.

"No trouble Sheriff. I did run into a couple of fellers riding well rested mounts though. I had the Greener shotgun ready as they got close. The team pulled hard as the two riders approached. I had some speed as we met just in case they decided to turn and give chase but they never gave me a second glance after they saw that Greener," Nantz said.

Chester's Last Ride

"How do you know they were riding rested mounts?" I asked.

The man looked at me with cold gray eyes and said, "They were riding their horses too hard. Where we passed was in a draw and the snow had piled up to more than a foot. Those two horses were running like they enjoyed it. I better get on over to the post office, I got a wagon load of mail." Nantz climbed back up on the stage and released the brake. The six horses pulled away as if they were pulling nothing at all.

"Well that's good news Conley. I'll bet the two riders he met are the two you run out of town earlier," the sheriff said.

"That would be my guess Sheriff. Reckon why the stage got through without any trouble this time?"

"Might be that they didn't want to mess with Nantz. You saw those new handles on that old Colt of his. Well let me tell you why he had to replace those handles. The other pair had thirteen notches, one notch for each man he had ever shot."

I looked at the stage as it rounded the corner and headed toward the post office. "You telling me that white headed feller has shot thirteen men Sheriff?" I asked.

"He did at that Conley. He used to be the sheriff in a little town about a hundred miles south of here. Seems there was a range war going on and somehow he managed to arrest the man that had started the whole thing. Well, the man he arrested worked a big crew and the crew he worked was some of the meanest bastards that ever put on a cowboy hat. Anyway, they decided to break their boss out of jail and then hang the sheriff, namely one William Nantz. You know old Nantz managed to hold that bunch off until some Deputy Marshals made it to town and broke the whole thing up."

"You telling me that man killed thirteen men while holed up in his jail guarding the man they wanted to bust out?"

The sheriff laughed. "I didn't say he killed thirteen men Conley, but he did shoot thirteen though."

"Well Sheriff, how many did he kill if you don't mind saying."

"None, and that is the damdest thing, he actually wounded thirteen and not a single one died. The marshals arrested all thirteen of the men he shot and two more that didn't have a scratch. I asked Nantz once why he tried to wound all them men without trying to kill any of them. He said he was shooting to kill but just couldn't manage it. Just between me and you I think the man needs glasses. I'll bet the outlaws said to each other not to mess with William Nantz unless you want to get wounded." The sheriff started laughing at what he said.

"I don't know Sheriff, thirteen men in one gun battle is quite a feat," I said.

"You know Conley it truly is. Odds like that usually get a man a visit from the undertaker, but he survived. He gave up being sheriff, said he wanted to do something a little more tame like driving stage coaches, and now he's getting shot at all the same. A man just can't pick and choose how he's going to die can he Conley?"

"I reckon he can't Sheriff. Between me and you I hope my death just sneaks up on me while I'm sleeping. If I see it coming I would probably put up a fight."

"Me too, I do love being alive." Again the sheriff started laughing.

The sheriff went back inside the jail and I walked over to the post office. I was really anxious to see if there were any more letters from Kentucky. The driver and the three men from inside were carrying in big canvas sacks which I assumed were filled with mail and parcels. I grabbed one of the sacks and carried it inside. There were twelve sacks in all and two crates. Once the mail was safely inside the driver said he was heading over to Bishop's place to stable the six horses until the run out of town the next morning. I wondered how Bishop would feel when he heard that Chet Brimley had gotten his livery stable back from the thief Bowers. I doubted if he would care much, I think he enjoyed raising chickens and selling eggs about as well as he liked stabling horses.

I was told to come back in two hours and the three men that worked the post office should have all the mail sorted. I used this time to replenish the items I would need for my journey to St. Louis, the first stop on my journey back to Kentucky. I carried everything I had purchased at the general store over to Bishop's and packed it away. It took two trips for my supplies and another for a fifty pound sack of grain and a jar of molasses for the horses. I had a feeling that Hazel and Rusty had taken a liking to this little treat. It would be several more weeks before they could find better grazing along the trails we would be following.

Having this little job complete I headed back to the post office. Once there I was handed a single letter. It was from my paw and as usual it was written using his homemade ink recipe. I quickly opened the envelop and read the contents. It was the same as the other letters but I could tell the tone was more urgent. The warnings about secrecy were there except this time it was more of a demand than a request. I was warned to watch my back and tell no one who I was or where I was headed. I refolded the letter and put it in my coat pocket along with the others. I thanked the three men at the post office as I headed back to the sheriff's office.

The street had become busy as people tended to business that had been neglected due to the weather. The man who sold firewood from the back of a wagon pulled by two stout looking mules was doing a booming business as was the man in charge of refilling the oil lamps along main street. It looked as if everyone was preparing for another bad storm. At this time of year blizzards could be lined up for weeks, as soon as one blew out of town another could take its place within days.

When I went in the front door of the jail I could hear men talking and laughing. The sheriff was there along with both Sammy and Lucky. Felix was sitting by the fire drinking a cup of coffee. The doc was there tending to the injured prisoner who had been carried over sometime earlier. The only other person there was the stage driver, William Nantz. He was playing a game of checkers with the sheriff, and by the sound of things it looked like a fist fight might break out at any minute.

"Lucky, what on earth is all the hollering about?" I asked.

"Nantz don't like to lose and usually he doesn't. Somehow the sheriff has him backed into a corner and things are starting to get loud."

"Does this always happen when he is losing?" I asked.

"Don't know, I never seen him lose before," Lucky said.

Just then Nantz got up and went to the stove.

"Your move William," the sheriff said.

"I quit Messer. I don't like the way you play," Nantz said.

"Alright then, you lose."

"Ain't no way Sheriff, I said I quit."

"Okay then you quit and you lose," the sheriff said.

"Don't matter none to me Sheriff, I figure you won this one and I won the other hundred we played."

Sheriff Messer smiled, "I never did keep count but you might be right Nantz. I don't ever remember winning before but I sure will remember this time."

Nantz just poured himself a cup of coffee and went over to a chair and sat down. Lucky whispered that he would cool off before long, said Nantz and the sheriff was brother in laws and neither would stay mad for long count of the wives. That was good to hear because I would hate to see two grown men in a fist fight over a simple game of checkers. Again I thought of the two old men playing on the front porch from years past.

Lucky looked at me and asked, "You want to play?"

I declined, this was high stakes checkers and I was just a poor Kentucky boy.

I checked the pot and found probably one more cup of coffee in it, so I grabbed a cup and filled it. When Lucky came over with his empty cup he frowned and went for more water.

"What time are you pulling out in the morning Nantz?" I asked.

"Exactly one hour after sunup. I never like to head out of town with the sun in my eyes. Sheriff says you are riding in with the stage and Lucky is riding shotgun, is that true?"

"It is, I want to check the trail along the way to see what I can find. I got a pack horse that is getting on in years and was wondering if I could tie him a lead to the back of the stage?"

"Fine by me, I don't run the team hard. I like to save the power in case there's trouble. You would be surprised how fast a team of six can go if they're fresh. I figure we will go at a fast trot. You reckon that will suit your pack horse?" Nantz asked.

That will suit old Rusty just fine. He can still raise some dust but I like to take it easy on him if I can. If my pack horse is following the stage I can do more scouting around," I told the silver haired stage driver.

After me and the horses left the stage coach without running into any problems the next day I settled into the trip ahead. Rusty was loaded pretty heavy with the supplies I had bought in Sioux City. It would lighten down pretty fast as we traveled, especially the grain and molasses I had purchased for the horses.

It took nearly two weeks to get to St. Louis. I was satisfied with the progress we had made but was still anxious to get back home. The weather was less than pleasant and the miles seemed to go by a little slower than I would have liked. Ben had done well for himself during the journey; he had fresh rabbit almost every night. I sometimes thought it was his purpose in life to reduce the rabbit population, he was trying his best.

We stayed in St. Louis for the better part of three days with two full nights thrown in for good measure. The horses needed resting and I needed a bath and a haircut. I turned down the barber shave though preferring to put the razor to my own throat instead of letting a stranger do it.

The letters I carried had me a little spooked and I was starting to imagine all sorts of mischief. The craziest thing I done while in town was to allow myself to get a little drunk while playing five card poker. The bunch at the table seemed harmless enough, before I knew it though I had drunk a couple of beers more than I should have. I was lucky that night and no trouble decided to show up although I did manage to lose a couple of hundred dollars. What a dumbass.

As the days went by the weather slowly began to improve. I was heading a little south and it was getting on toward spring. At times I could see a few hints of color in the foliage in the distance. I noticed the horses were also starting to investigate some of the greenery that was trying to sprout up.

As we traveled I started to take more notice behind us. For some reason I felt I was being watched but from extreme distance. A couple of times I thought I had seen movement but decided it was probably a deer, or maybe an elk.

Chester's Last Ride

The farther we traveled the more the landscape started to take on the beginnings of spring. The trees had started to bud and leaves were beginning to decorate the ends of the branches. I was as content as a sheep traveling with only my two horses and Ben. The four of us were actually starting to enjoy the trip. Ben had managed to shake off the winter blues and was actually starting to romp in the new grass each time we stopped for camp.

We were making good time and I was hoping the trouble back home had somehow managed to fix itself. I knew I was not being realistic. Trouble just didn't go away because a man hoped it would. As I thought of these things the landscape we traveled through drifted by at the pace of a walking horse. It was getting on in the day and I was starting to feel the miles pile up on me. I started looking for a good place to camp for the night. It didn't take long before I found what I was looking for. We were in hilly country and there were small streams in the low valleys. I found a good spot where the horses had good water and the grass had started to reach for the sky. There was a light breeze and as it rocked the grasses it reminded me of waves on water.

I rubbed down the horses and then gathered wood for a fire. By the time it started to grow dark there was a big fire going and hot coffee in my cup. Ben was out and before long he ran through camp with a big jack rabbit in his mouth. I was really glad he decided to eat it outside of camp and away from me. I had never been able to really enjoy my supper if he was nearby crunching on a rabbit carcass. As the sky continued to darken, and just before the moon came up, I drifted off to sleep. What in the world could be better?"

Late in the night I found myself awake and looking up through the trees. The fire popped and cracked as the dim light danced on the overhanging branches. Leaves gently rocked on the limbs as a cool night breeze moved through the trees. By the position of the stars it must have been two, maybe even three o'clock in the morning. I could hear the horses cropping grass several yards away and by the sound they made and the peacefulness of the night there was no reason for me to be startled, or even awake at such an early hour. Instinctively I had drawn the Colt revolver I always carried, even while I slept.

As I lay there, I kept looking to my left in the direction from which I had heard the noise that had shaken me from my sleep. Nothing moved, not a sound could be heard now that seemed out of place. After several tense moments I realized that it was probably nothing, just an over-worked imagination.

After a few minutes I put my head back down on my saddle, the same saddle I had been using as a pillow for more years than I cared to remember. I placed my gun back in its holster and tried to relax. If someone or something was out there, my horses would warn me in plenty of time. I smiled at the thought of me being out here alone and far away from anyone. Peace and solitude was what I enjoyed most about being on the open range with only my horses and gun to see me through. The gentle breeze lulled me back into the half-sleep I was accustomed to. The horses would stir and wake me if a danger did exist; a comforting thought indeed.

Suddenly a terrifying awareness jerked me back to my senses; the horses hadn't awakened me this time, so what on earth had? I was up and moving toward the nearest tree with the big Colt revolver back in my hand. As I moved into the darkness away from the firelight I noticed that the horses were still cropping grass and showed no sign of danger. They didn't even seem concerned by my own dash for cover. Something just didn't feel right and darkness was the safest place to be until I could calm down and figure out what it was that had me so spooked.

I reached the nearest tree and went to a crouching position with the Colt in my right hand. I became very quiet. Not even the sound of my breathing could be heard. As I scanned the surrounding area the Colt moved with my line of sight as if both were one and the same. Years of close calls had made my hand and eye move as one. I realized that my Winchester was still near the spot where I had bedded down for the night, and now I wished I had brought it with me.

The horses had finally taken notice and stopped eating after I made my mad dash to the trees. After only a moment or two they both resumed cropping grass. They still seemed to be unconcerned about any possible danger. My senses told me that something was wrong, but I just couldn't figure out what it was.

Suddenly, something touched my gun elbow which sent a cold tingle of fear running up my spine. I spun around, gun in hand, ready to fire at whoever, or whatever, had brushed up against me. Just as I made my turn a huge mouth, full of shining teeth stained bright red and dripping with the blood from its last victim, gaped wide and grabbed my gun arm just above the wrist. Hot breath almost toasted my skin as my wrist was gripped in the creature's mouth.

"Ben, you scared the hell out of me boy, where you been anyway?"

Ben just wagged his tail and slobbered all over my shirt sleeve. "Turn loose dog." Ben released my arm and took a couple of steps back and sat down. I thought a second and then said to Ben, "Scout boy." With that the big hound moved off into the darkness to make a sweep of the area. If nothing was found he would be back by my side and expecting a piece of jerky for his trouble. With my arm back in one piece I tried as best as I could to wipe the dog drool off my shirt sleeve, damn dog.

I felt a little better knowing Ben was on the prowl. The big cur could be quiet and extremely deadly. After only a couple of minutes he was back which meant that everything was alright. I reached into my pocket and grabbed a small piece of jerky and tossed it into the open area of our camp near the fire. Ben knew the drill; he had earned many a treat in this way during our adventures together. The big hound bounded across the opening toward his well-earned treat. Before he made it even half way to the piece of jerky that lay on the ground I was startled to the bone, my breath caught in my throat.

On the other side of the fire there stood a big black horse without a rider. In less than a heartbeat my gun was up and I was back behind the protection of the tree. The hair on the back of my neck tingled with fear. I watched Ben run up to the jerky I had thrown and pay no attention what-so-ever to this saddled horse without a rider. I glanced at the other two horses and was amazed to find that they were also paying no mind to this new horse that seemed to appear from nowhere in the early morning gloom. Something was terribly wrong and I could feel the sweat running down my neck. I was overwhelmed with fear and it was a feeling I was unaccustomed to. In my entire life I could never remember such fear.

The black horse stood motionless as if it were a statue. As I watched the horse I noticed the right ear flutter. The motion then moved down the mane as if a man's hand had just stroked the stallion's neck. The right stirrup moved down and out slightly as if it had just taken weight. The saddle pulled slightly to the side and then compressed down on the horse's back. A rider had just mounted but all I could see was the black horse and on its back, an empty saddle.

Then, to add to my terror, the stirrups that hung below the saddle moved back and touched the horse. The reins, held up by invisible fingers, pulled the horse around to face me. With a steady gaze the head continued to move until it was looking straight at me. In its coal-black eyes was the red glow of fire. I realized that the glow in its eyes was the reflection of my own campfire.

This had to be the end of the road for me. The Black Prince had come to collect his due.

And then I woke up. I jumped to my feet and done a complete turn as I quickly scanned my campsite. My heart was pounding as if it were going to jump from my chest and do a dance all on its own. I looked at Ben, he was sound asleep a couple of yards from the fire. The horses were standing off about ten yards all three legged and content as sheep. It had all been a dream, just a dream.

I took a few deep breaths and tried to calm myself. After several long minutes my breathing was starting to return to normal, although my chest was still trying to hold on to my wildly beating heart. I moved closer to the fire and added some dry branches for fuel. My mouth was dry and my hands were cold and clammy. I rubbed both palms together as I held them closer to the fire. For the longest time I simply stayed by the fire and replayed the dream I had just had. I used the time to calm my nerves and gather my thoughts.

This wasn't the first time I had had that particular dream. The big black stallion, missing a rider, had visited me once before late in the night. A few years back, while on a job up in Utah, I had experienced that same dream, the dream of a black

Nathan Wright

rider-less horse, and paid it no mind.

Suddenly it dawned on me that the night I had experienced that same dream up in Utah I was almost shot in my sleep by a pair of hard luck gunmen who wanted my horses and saddle, along with everything else I was carrying. All that saved me that night was when, by the grace of God, one of the bandits own guns misfired. That was all it took for me to grab my own gun and shoot him in the chest while Ben tore the throat out of the other hapless bandit. I did do the Christian thing the next morning and bury them both in a common grave with no marker, didn't want to make it too obvious for the Indians, who would just as soon take a scalp from a dead man as a live one.

Now I had a decision to make. Move camp because of a dream or forget about this whole silly thing and go back to sleep? I sat there and told myself that under no circumstances would I ever be frightened so much by a dream that it would make me want to move my camp in the middle of the night. I continued to tell myself this while I moved everything about a thousand feet away. This time my camp would be on a ridge where I could keep an eye on the original campsite. It wouldn't hurt to use a little extra caution this time around.

I guess you could say I was a mite curious as to whether this dream had been some kind of warning, as it had been before, or just my imagination run wild. Before moving to the new location I added some more wood to the fire and threw my spare blanket over some brush to make it look as if I were still there, and still sound asleep.

It only took about thirty minutes to move to the new site and ground hitch my two horses. Both horses immediately started cropping grass knowing that daylight was only about a hour off and we would be back on the trail soon after. I leaned up against a deadfall to keep an eye on the fire at my previous camp site while Ben went off on the trail of some unlucky rabbit. No more than ten minutes went by before Ben was back carrying the limp body of a large rabbit in his mouth. One thing about old Ben; while on the trail he always ate good and what he loved to eat most was rabbit.

As I sat at my cold camp and looked over at the warm fire, still burning at the old campsite, I began to feel a little foolish. Why all the concern? Nothing could be seen moving but the flames flickering from the fire on the opposite side of the hill. All that could be heard was Ben, crunching noisily on his breakfast. Now why would a grown man who had seen his fair share of trouble in real life suddenly start to also expect trouble from his dreams? After all, wasn't that what it was, just a dream.

Sitting there with such thoughts I started to chuckle at myself over my newfound foolishness when, over at the foot of the hill just below the fire of the old campsite, I saw movement. I scanned hard all along the hills and the ridgeline, trying to see the movement again or anything else out of the ordinary. Sure enough, I soon saw it again on the back trail that had led me to the first campsite the previous evening.

I sprang to my feet and grabbed my spyglass from the saddlebags. It was an old glass my father had given me from his days as a Colonel in the War Between the States. Perched against the deadfall, with the glass resting steadily on a limb, I began to peer at the adjacent hill for the movement I had seen only a few seconds before. The full moon was high in the nearly cloudless sky and I could see almost as well as if it were only a cloudy day.

It didn't take long before I spotted three horses and riders, each with a Winchester slung across his saddle. They were moving slowly, using more caution than should be expected from men just traveling from town to town. The three riders stopped about a quarter mile from my old camp site under cover of some pine trees and tied their horses to a few low hanging branches.

Neither the men, nor their horses, were in view of the fire. They could probably still see the glow of it from where they were. This trio must have felt safe in the assumption that they were out of sight from anyone in the camp. They were unaware that I had taken up a new position not more than an hour earlier. And from this new position, I had both a spyglass and a Winchester, pointed in their direction.

The three stood there for a few minutes and it looked like they were talking to each other, probably working out a plan. The horses the men rode in on were well positioned out of sight and ready for a fast get away if need be. It was apparent that these three were up to some sort of mischief by the amount of stealth they were using and also by the fact that each carried his Winchester ready for action. The three spread out about five yards apart and headed up the hill toward the fire light. They moved with the utmost of caution, using pine trees and deadfalls for cover. I had used this time to saddle my horse and tighten the cinch on the saddle just in case there was any need for a fast getaway on my part. The two horses I had knew something was about to happen. We had been on the trail together for too many years.

Upon completing this, and making sure both horses were ready for a run, I renewed my observations with the spyglass. I was very careful not to position it where any moonlight might reflect from its lens and give away my position. A sparkle of moonlight on glass was not what I needed at the moment. I also unclipped my badge and slid it into my shirt pocket. What a target I would make with a shiny marshal's badge pinned over my heart. I was two states out of my original jurisdiction but with a marshal's badge if you were on United States soil then you had jurisdiction. Out this far though, and all alone, a badge wouldn't improve my chances in the least.

The sun would be up soon and even now the blackness of night was giving way to the light gray of morning. I looked around and took stock of my situation. My own position wasn't bad. There was good cover if any bullets came this way, and I was on the higher ground with an excellent field of view in case a firefight developed. One man against three from high ground with good cover evened things out quite a bit. I would still be badly outnumbered if shooting started but my position helped my confidence. But the biggest advantage was that these three bushwhackers had no idea where I was and I knew exactly where they were.

What happened next completely took me by surprise, as any cold blooded murder would. The three came within sight of the fire and the bedroll that covered the brush instead of a sleeping man. They each took positions behind cover. Two of the men looked at the third who I figured must have been the leader or boss of the outfit. This third man gave an up and down nod of the head and with that all three leveled their rifles and fired what I figured was two shots apiece at the empty bedroll.

Ben let out a low growl beside me, he had been watching the whole thing and with his good eyes he could probably see it better than I could with the spyglass. "Quiet Ben," I said as I tightened the grip on my Winchester and took a bead on the one who I figured must be the man in charge. They were a mite over three hundred yards away and even if I didn't hit one it would at least give them something to think about. I held my fire, not wanting to give away my position, at least not yet.

The three cautiously walked over to the bedroll, the man

who I assumed was leader of the outfit, kicked it over. They must have surely expected to see a badly shot up body, but instead all they found was some brush and short tree limbs. Each then jerked back and scanned the area around, waiting for a shot from the darkness. They started stepping back and continued to retreat toward the spot where their horses had been picketed, all the while scanning around to see if they were being watched. Each now knew that they were probably in a bad predicament with what was most likely a Winchester aimed their way.

They moved quickly now back to their horses and climbed into the saddle. They didn't try to track me to find out which way I had gone. They knew that I had set them up and the safest place for them right now was back the way they came, putting a few miles between themselves and this situation that had, for the moment, gotten so badly out of hand.

When the three were out of sight I climbed up in the saddle of Hazel, having put the pack on Rusty. I grabbed the reins of his bridle and led him up the hill, all the while keeping Hazel well below the top of the ridge. Me and the two big horses would be easily outlined against the morning sky if we ventured to close to the top.

Cover was good among the late winter, early spring foliage of oak, pine, and poplar trees. There was the occasional bloom of a redbud or a dogwood tree that helped to break up our outline from the view of anyone else who might be close. The trail I chose kept us in the shadows of the forest and away from the ridges. The going was pretty good as there wasn't much brush, just trees and a lot of freshly sprouted Kentucky bluegrass.

Chester's Last Ride

My trip back East, up until the previous morning, had been pretty much uneventful, nothing other than the firelight shooting had happened to speak of in the past two weeks. There was that stop in St. Louis to pick up supplies along with a couple of boxes of extra cartridges for my Colt. In trying to find shells for my .45-75 Winchester though I was out of luck. I only had fourteen rounds left, and these I would use sparingly. I was starting to wish I hadn't sold my Sharps Big 50 back in Sioux City along with all eight boxes of ammunition I had for it. The Winchester would have to do.

As I rode I tried to think of a reason for what had happened at the campsite. Why would three men who I didn't know try to kill me? Could it have been just a random robbery with a killing thrown in for good measure? Not likely, these three knew who they were hunting and had undoubtedly been tracking me for some time. But how did they know who I was and which way I was heading? It must have been that stop in St. Louis. They saw me there and followed me.

Now who did I talk to and where all had I been while in that cow town, the saloon that Friday night, the hotel, the general store? I had had a bath and a hot meal at the hotel and then a card game at the saloon...that was it. I knew there was more to those two cow-punchers than just chit-chat. And I wondered how two gents just off the trail could afford such as they were wearing. Too clean, too neat, and too well dressed for a couple of trail hands. All the while they must have let me win and kept buying the drinks just to loosen up my tongue and get a little information out of me. And I was winning but when I woke up the next morning I was missing two-hundred dollars. Whiskey, beer, and cards, don't make for a good outcome.

That last letter from my paw had warned me not to talk to anyone about my business or where I was headed. Paw had mentioned a detective outfit by the name of Baldwin-Felts. He said that Baldwin-Felts was a big company and that they had detectives out over the entire country looking for information that would help them with some of the dirty deeds of which he would tell me more when I got home. These men worked for big coal and where big coal money went so did Baldwin-Felts, the largest detective agency in the country.

Rumor had it that more than once a man had been gunned down, shot in the back, or just woke up with his throat cut at the hands of some Baldwin-Felts men...but never any proof, just a body of someone who for any number of reasons had something to do with coal or oil. And now was it possible that they were after me? I was on my way back to Floyd County in Southeastern Kentucky which was down deep in the heart of Appalachian Coal Country. And this area was rich in coal.

Paw never mentioned many details about the trouble back home, he just said to stay quiet and get there as fast as I could. That must be it, in one of the letters he had mentioned some big interests had approached him a few months earlier with an offer on his farm but he told them he wasn't interested. Later on when they returned with some tough looking guys and started pushing Paw around, one of my younger brothers, along with the big bunkhouse cook, fired off a Greener twelve-gauge shotgun at their feet. A prior letter from Paw told all about it and how they had lit a shuck for Prestonsburg, the county seat, but before they left they said this wasn't over by a long shot. The letter from Sheriff Barnes had also talked of trouble.

In St. Louis I had signed the hotel register with my full name, Zeke Conley. When I checked in those two, who I thought were gamblers, must have been keeping an eye on that register which told them exactly who I was and where I was heading. I sure didn't know Paw raised a boy who could be so foolish as to sign his full name and where he was from on a hotel register, knowing that he was heading back home on account of trouble. But then he also never told me how much trouble was brewing, that would have helped a mite. Maybe he was afraid that all of his mail was being opened and read and that might be why he never gave any mention of serious trouble.

I fished into my saddlebag and retrieved one of the letters from back home. Looking it over closely as Ben led the way and my two horses trotted along after him, I read the entire thing again. It was sure enough my sisters writing. Paw could write, and he could write well. When it came to the children though, Paw always had my sister write the letters. He always said her hand was a mite easier to read than his. My sister helped keep the books on the farm. He would just tell her what he wanted written and then after she was finished he would read over it himself just to make sure she had it all down just the way he wanted. The last letter even mentioned that he was sending her up north to spend some time with relatives. Now I realized he was sending her away to protect her.

After I had read the whole thing through again and noticed nothing new I folded it up and it was then, when I was putting it back in the envelope, that I noticed the writing on the envelope was different. Someone had tried to write like it was sis's hand, but it was different somehow. Oh whoever it was had done a pretty good job of it but there was some slight differences. But the biggest difference of all was the ink. Back home Paw made his ink from mulberries and coal oil in the wood-working shop, but what was on this envelope was not that at all. Probably store bought ink that they thought some poor dumb hick from the hills of Kentucky wouldn't notice. Paw could afford anything he or the farm needed but he took pride in his ink recipe and said any number of years wouldn't cause it to fade.

Now I began to worry, this Baldwin-Felts outfit knew who I was, and where I was going. Not only that, from what had happened so far I was pretty sure they would stop at nothing, including murder, to keep me from getting there. From this moment forward I would have to stay on my toes, trust no one, and use only back country trails if I expected to have half a chance to make it back home alive.

I was in Kentucky now and knew the lay of the land as well as anyone. Plus, I noticed that Ben had become more alert after seeing what had happened that morning at the campsite. He was on his toes and very quiet about it. He loved to bark as much as the next dog, but he was also smarter than the next dog and knew that any noise now might draw attention to us, and that had become a bad thing.

That night we made a cold camp in a small holler that was covered by low hanging tree limbs. I picketed the horses close by in some freshly sprouted Kentucky bluegrass, short but thick and dark green, in no time at all Hazel and Rusty were cropping grass and slapping flies with their tails. Ben was off hunting his supper and I built the smallest of fires under the trees for some hot coffee and bacon. I used the driest fuel I could find and let what little smoke it produced wander up through the tree limbs to help hide any sign. As soon as the coffee and bacon was finished I put out the fire and ate. I hadn't realized how hungry I had become, before I knew it the bacon was gone and I was digging around in the saddlebags for some hardtack. Now anyone who has tasted hardtack will tell you that it is about as lacking in taste as tree bark, but I was hungry and the tack was all I could have without making another fire.

As I struggled with the tack Ben came back with the biggest rabbit I'd seen him with in quite a while. Now when me and Ben are on the trail I always try to have my meal finished before he starts on his. The noises that hound can make with his fresh kill, crunching and slobbering on whatever it may be, can surely take a man's appetite away in a hurry. This evening was no different; Ben made more noise crunching that rabbit's bones than a lumberjack chopping down a tree.

After I finished the last of the coffee I built a smoke so as to have it lit and finished before dark. I leaned back against the saddle and thought about the day. I also thought about the black rider-less horse which had saved my life. Funny how a man's mind works, all the while I had all this information from back home and the danger that was building there. It was all in the back of my mind not doing anybody any good. Somehow it all got put together in my sleep and my mind conjured up that rider-less horse in a dream…and it saved my life.

Sleep was difficult that night. It seemed every noise was amplified in my mind a hundred times. Finally about four in the morning, or there bouts by the look of the sky, I just gave up on sleep and sat back on my bedroll and looked up at the stars. Ben was sound asleep and the horses were quiet, any movement and at least one of the three would alert me.

I was up early and saddled Rusty for the days ride, putting the pack on Hazel. I liked to alternate pack and saddle on each horse for each day. It gave the pack carrying horse a lighter load and seemed to keep both horses a bit fresher in case of trouble. Again I built the smallest of fires to heat coffee. For breakfast I had heated beans and fried bacon, and let me tell you it was quite a treat. Within an hour of daylight we were on the trail all the while keeping a wary eye both in front of me and on my back trail. I traveled now with the Winchester across the saddle, not quite over the scare of the previous day.

We were about a day's ride from E-town when it dawned on me that the three men had probably went back to the nearest town in order to telegraph ahead to a few towns to let anyone there know that I was on the way and probably how long it would take me to get there. This thought became a little unsettling, but knowing that I was going to stay off any main roads should keep me safe and out of sight from any more Baldwin-Felts people. The only problem was going to be food. I had loaded up pretty good in St. Louis but what you can carry on one horse won't get you very far. There was enough for one more day and that was it. With that thought always in mind I decided to swing near E-town and stop in the first general store I came to and load up on enough for a seven day ride, which, with any luck, would put me in Floyd County.

Later on that day, near dusk I came to a small town with a couple of stores and three or four saloons. There was also a railroad depot, a hotel, and two churches. This meant that there was probably a telegraph office. As much as I hated to, I had to chance it. Coming in on a side street I found a livery and paid the hostler to keep Hazel, Rusty, and Ben, for the night. It was too late to get supplies and head out of town to find a campsite, especially with men who might stop at nothing to keep me from where I was going. With that thought in mind I decided to get the supplies tonight and leave an hour before sunrise. I went into the general store, which seemed to be a well-stocked affair, and approached the storekeeper. As he and I gathered the few things that would be needed for the next few days I thought also to add a couple more boxes of cartridges for my Winchester, a .45-.75, not knowing how easily these could be acquired in a coal town like Prestonsburg.

Chester's Last Ride

"Sorry sonny, quit stocking forty-five seventy-five rounds last year. Damn things are too expensive and don't sell that fast. You're the first person to ask for that big ammunition in at least a year."

I thought about this for a minute and decided pistol cartridges would have to do. "I guess I will just take an extra box of Colt forty-fives then. I'll just make due with a few extra pistol cartridges and hope the few forty-five seventy-fives I got will do." There were usually twenty five rounds in a box of Colt ammunition and that would make me about a hundred. Paw always said that if you're in a spot that needs more than ten rounds then you're probably dead anyway, you just haven't started bleeding yet.

As the store keep was weighing out a pound of Arbuckle Coffee, which I had requested, two men walked in, each wearing tied down guns. One of the two approached and noticed my supplies. Now what the hell had I gotten myself into?

"Looks like you been on the trail a few days son, mind if I ask where your heading?" He was a big man with the look of someone who could handle himself in a tough situation. The look on his face was one of suspicion. I finished up with the storekeeper and as he was putting my belongings into a cloth sack I turned to the man and said

"Who's asking?"

With that the other man came over and with a smirk said, "You just answer the question sonny!"

I looked back at the store keep "How much I owe you mister?"

"Bout ten dollars and fifty cents ought to do it," he said.

After I paid the man I quickly turned without any advance notice of what I was about to do and hit the second man who had spoken right on the end of his nose. He went down with blood flying everywhere, seems when a nose bleeds it bleeds a lot. The other came in with a wild right that I just ducked under and then rose up right in this man's face. This was my kind of fight; these two had the advantage of two on one, which tends to build just a bit too much optimism in the two, and a lot more desperation in the one, the one being me.

At such close quarters all I had to do was chop down the man still standing with a flurry of lefts and rights. It didn't take long before he joined his partner with the bloody nose on the floor. As soon as he hit he went for his gun and fired a shot that just nicked my shoulder. Before he had time to fire again my Colt was in my hand and a bullet had torn out his throat. Bad thing though, that .45 slug just kept on going and didn't stop until it had hit the other man in the right forearm. This turned out to be a mighty good piece of luck for me because that busted nose son-of-a-bitch had his gun out and it was leveled at my head. When the bullet hit his arm he dropped the gun, and just yelled out "Don't shoot mister, I'm done."

I went over and picked up the two guns and handed them to the store keep.

"Can you keep these until the law shows up?"

"Sure thing, but what are you going to do?"

"I'm leaving; you saw the whole thing, that dead feller there drew down on me and put this crease in my shoulder."

"Yea, I reckon it was self-defense all right, but if I was you, I'd be gittin some miles between me and this town, do you know who those two work for?"

"No, I reckon not."

"They're Baldwin-Felts detectives and by tomorrow morning this place will be swarming with more of them fellers than you'd care to throw a cat at. I'll let the sheriff know what happened here, don't you worry any about that," the store clerk said.

With that I picked up my supplies and headed for the livery. The hostler was there and he helped me saddle and outfit the two horses. Leading Hazel and holding Rusty's reins I threw the hostler a couple of dollars and then headed out of town letting the horses have their run with Big Ben hot on our heels. We went all out for about ten minutes or so and then I had to rein in on Hazel. Being the younger of the two she liked to show Rusty what she was made of and Rusty, though he was getting up in years, still could give as good as he was getting. I think those two would have run each other to death if I weren't around to put the brakes on every now and then.

We trotted hard for another two hours and then I slowed them down to a slow walk to let'em cool a mite. Ben was starting to tire and it was beginning to show on the big cur. His walk was slow and he was slobbering something awful. It was time to start looking for a place to rest for a few hours. Another fifteen minutes and I found what we were looking for. A thicket of bushy evergreens with a few oak here and there would do the job just fine. Near this was a small stream and good grass. I jumped down and tied out the two horses. Using some of the dryer bluegrass I rubbed down both horses and after they had cooled down sufficiently I led them to water and they both drank their fill.

Soon I had my bedroll down and collapsed on top of it. Big Ben was so tired he didn't even chase down a rabbit. As tired as I was I hoped it would be safe to sleep. Ben and the horses would alert me of any trouble. And then there was always that black rider-less horse.

Next morning we were on the trail before first light. Two reasons to hurry; stay ahead of any more Baldwin-Felts men and also to get back to Paw's farm as fast as possible in case trouble had erupted since that last letter had been sent.

The sun came up bright and hot. The sky was a brilliant blue with only the occasional white puffy cloud throwing patchy shadows across the ground. A slight breeze blew from the west which helped quite a bit as far as the heat was concerned.

Big Ben was up ahead, no-doubt looking for his next meal. Leaving before breakfast I had tossed him a bite or two of jerky. Ben liked his jerky but what he really loved was his fresh rabbit. It wasn't long before he showed up with a limp rabbit in his mouth. He dropped it at the foot of Rusty and looked up at me. I always thought he was offering it to me first when he did that. I said, "Good hunting Ben, good boy." He just gave me that big Ben grin of his and wagged his tail. Me and the two horses rode on by to leave Ben to his breakfast. He polished it off in only a few minutes and then took up his position again at lead.

We were making good time without the use of any roads. The path we took was not the most direct route but one that led through thick stands of oak, pine and small spruce. We forded quite a few streams and creeks with hardly any difficulty at all. Hazel and Rusty were both unafraid of the water and Ben liked nothing more than a cool dip on a warm day.

I headed a bit south toward Leslie and Harlan counties as to throw anyone off our trail. Most would think that we would go down through the Red River Gorge to throw off any pursuit but I didn't want to do the obvious. Plus, to be cornered in there might not be a good situation. Any trail through the Gorge ran through the valley itself giving a man with a rifle a good field of view. I just didn't want to give that view if at all possible. At least in the low hills of the Boone horses were better suited and it gave me more options.

Chester's Last Ride

From E-town we headed south toward a small town called London, in Laurel County. I knew the sheriff there from a few years back. Paw and I sold him ten horses to use for himself and some of his deputies. That was one thing Paw was known for around all of eastern Kentucky; his horses. He had for years raised some of the finest riding and draft stock in the state. Men would come from as far away as Cincinnati, Ohio and Huntington, West Virginia to purchase Paw's stock. In all those years of raising horses and mules Paw had become one of the wealthiest men in the state. He had done well selling horses to the North during the war and in the process made another small fortune.

He also acquired large land holdings in several Eastern Kentucky Counties amounting to almost thirty-five hundred additional acres besides what the farm sat on in Floyd County. Most of that acreage was used for horses and hay. The family farm now consisted of a large and substantial home adjacent to a good size vegetable garden. There were two large barns that could stable fifty horses each and in nearby pastures several hundred head of cattle roamed alongside the fenced in acres of corn.

Usually there were twelve to fifteen hands working the farm. There was a good size bunkhouse with a fully stocked kitchen and full time cook, a man that my paw had known from back in the war. The mountains were pastured to the top with the crops in the bottom land. Everything was separated by stands of timber.

Just thinkin about it made me want to hurry all the more, that and the fact that I hadn't been home in over eight years. I left at the age of sixteen to try my hand at the world. You name it; I had done it, anything from working on a riverboat out of New Orleans to panning for gold in California. The most fun though, not to mention the hardest work was a cattle drive out of Texas. Now I was headed home to help Paw and settle down a while to raise horses and rest a bit.

I reached Laurel County about three in the afternoon on my third day out of E-town. The thought of a cold beer had been on my mind for days. With any luck I might be able to ease into a saloon without drawing too much attention.

Approaching the town I noticed my trail crossed the railroad, which was now a double set of tracks that lead to a large depot for both freight and passengers. There was a freight train pulling cars out of the depot as we approached. I had to sit my horse and watch as the big Baldwin 2-8-4 engine labored with its load out onto the main line. There were several cars of freight but in the lead, just behind the tender, were four big Pullmans. As they went by I noticed two new Pullmans painted in identical colors. A bright red and yellow paint scheme almost seemed to glow in the afternoon sun. As they went by I couldn't miss in large black letters, 'BFDA' which as it turned out was an acronym for the next line written under it, 'Baldwin-Felts Detective Agency.' Acronym was one of those fifty-cent words that Paw made us kids learn during our home schooling classes, he even hired a tutor every winter when there was less work to do around the farm, to make sure us kids got an education.

No one in the cars appeared to pay me any notice. After the train passed I crossed the tracks and just rode right on through town and into the Daniel Boone forest. For all I knew that detective bunch might have a murder warrant out on me after what had happened back in E-town. If big coal and big money were involved then I'm sure the story that storekeeper told about the shooting wouldn't keep me out of trouble. Money had bought the law many times before and would many times after.

As me and the horses rode away from town I noticed a sign that read *Whistle Stop Saloon*. The sight of the saloon sign and knowing that there were probably at least ten more in town made me all the more thirsty. I took my eyes off that sign and rode on with thoughts of a cold beer bouncing around inside my skull.

We traveled well into the night and made another cold camp deep in the protection of the Boone. The Daniel Boone Forest, not an official name but what local people called it just the same, had some mighty scary stories and rumors floating about and most people didn't travel this part of it, especially at night. Quite a few strange and unexplained things had been told about the Boone over the years and as each year went by some of the stories just grew bigger and bigger. Paw attributed most of it to the moonshiners who operated there and wanted to keep their stills hidden and out of reach of competing men with stills of their own. Tonight it was the perfect place to hide out and catch a few winks just in case anybody in those two BFDA cars might have seen a lone rider with two horses and a big wolf-like dog cross the tracks back in London.

The night was clear and cool with just a hint of a breeze out of the west. After giving the horses their rubdown and picketing them for the night I sat down to cold beans and hardtack. By the time I started to eat Ben came out of the trees with a good size raccoon and by the look of things it must have been some kind of fight. Big Ben had blood coming from his nose and two or three big scratches on his face. There was a cut on his shoulder and by the look of it a pretty bad bite mark on his right front leg. He seemed to pay it no mind. Before I could finish my cold supper he was crunching and pull-in and tearing at that thing like it was an Angus Steak. It was quite the most grisly sound you ever heard for a while and I could feel my supper starting to back up. I took a short walk so he could finish his meal in peace.

The night was restful knowing that the rumors of the Boone were watching over me. I rose early and saddled up Rusty, then threw the pack on Hazel. We had been on the move for more than an hour before the sun came up. Moving along at a good pace I noticed the wind had picked up and the clouds back to the west were growing quite a bit darker. This was good because a thunderstorm would wash out my trail making it almost impossible for anyone to track me. The closer to Floyd County I got, chances were, the more people there would be searching for me.

Riding along with my slicker on waiting for the rain I began to think of how to get through that last hundred miles without being spotted. This problem had been on my mind for the last couple of days and no easy solution as yet had presented itself. A lone man, two horses and a big wolf dog were about as easy to spot as the morning sun. In this country I figured I was covering about thirty miles a day. If I traveled as far as Harlan County I could hole up during the day and travel by night.

About twenty miles from home at a place called Rowdy I had a friend who raised a little tobacco and made a little whiskey. If I could get him to keep Rusty and my pack, then Hazel, Ben, and me, could make that last eighteen or twenty miles at a good pace and a dead run at times if the situation called for it. Before anyone was the wiser we would be at the family farm. I could send one of my brothers back to bring in Rusty a few days after the dust settled.

Old man Haywood Jones had been making whiskey for more

than forty years. Some said that men would travel as far to buy Haywood's whiskey as they would to purchase Paw's horses.

Haywood had fought for the South during the Civil War and made the rank of Colonel in a Cavalry regiment. He'd lost a foot in the Second Battle of Manassas when his sword glanced off a Yankee's rifle, nearly severing his own leg just above the ankle, during a Cavalry charge. The regimental surgeon finished the job and then commented on what a fine surgeon old Haywood would make.

Old man Haywood was rather proud of that story and never missed a chance to tell it to whoever was within earshot. He said he had a whole tater box full of new boots to fit a right foot, seems that since the war he only had need for the left ones.

When I was about a day's ride from Rowdy I came across two men heading west in a hurry. They came up over a ridge and were heading toward me at a full run. As they came within earshot I ordered them to stop and they both were more than glad to obey as I had them covered with that big Winchester .45-.75. When we had gotten to within about fifty yards Big Ben decided he would close up and get a better look. Now that big cur went up with teeth bared and fur standing in a rather menacing how-do-ya-do. I let him get to within about twenty feet of their horses and then ordered him to stay. He stopped dead in his tracks and those two strangers were mighty glad he did. Ben looked back at me and let out a low growl. It was just his way of letting me know he was none too happy about being stopped before he could have his fun.

"Mister, why are you aiming that gun at us, we don't even know you," one of the two men said.

"Let's just say I don't feel comfortable being approached at a full gallop."

"Step aside and let us pass."

"Can't do it, don't believe I want to turn my back on those guns of yours. Now you two fellers just un-strap those hog legs with your left hands and let-em fall to the ground real easy like.

"Now you wait just a minute mister, we ain't going…"

I pulled back the hammer of the Winchester, and the noise was just enough to stop the words in his throat.

"Okay mister, we're doing it, just take it easy with that rifle."

Slowly, and with the utmost of care, the two strangers loosened their gun belts and dropped them to the ground. As soon as the guns hit I hollered, "Fetch Ben." Now you could imagine the surprise on the faces of those two strangers when Ben walked over and picked up a gun belt in his mouth and brought it over to where I could reach over and take it out of his mouth. Then without any pause he walked back and picked up the other belt and did the same. With Ben's work done I tossed him a piece of jerky. He picked it up and walked back to his previous position in front of the two strangers.

"Now you two mind telling me where you're going in such a hurry?"

"Mister, we don't have to tell you nothing, cause we work for the biggest detective agency east of the Mississippi and as soon as some of the other boys find out what you done here today then they'll be on your tail same as that Conley feller we were sent to catch. That is until you stopped us."

With that the other stranger drew back and knocked his partner clean out of the saddle.

"For somebody who doesn't have to tell him nothing Powder you done told it all, and who knows he might even be Conley for all you know."

Chester's Last Ride

At that both men looked at me and then one of them said, "One man with two horses and a big mean dog. Mister, please tell me your last name ain't Conley," the man called Powder asked.

"Might be at that, now tell me why you two were sent after this Conley feller?"

"Cause they said he killed one of our agents and wounded another up near E-town." This time it was the man still on his horse that spoke.

The other man, the one knocked to the ground spoke up and said, "Then he killed the storekeeper, the only other witness. The wounded detective was still putting up such a good fight that Conley just high-tailed it out of town before he got himself arrested."

The man still in the saddle spoke again, "You are that Conley feller aren't you? And now you're going to kill us in cold blood, just like you did those two up in E-town?"

"It was a fair fight and your man drew on me first. The storekeeper wasn't shot, Hell, he was holding their guns until I left."

The man on the ground looked from his partner to me and said, "You did shoot him right between the eyes and then lit a shuck for the nowhere in-betweens."

I knew I was in a pretty bad fix. Undoubtedly when those other Baldwin-Felts men showed up they killed the storekeeper and when the authorities showed up they said I did it. I was now wanted for murder in Kentucky.

First thing to do now was put these two afoot and try to make my way to Floyd County. The sheriff there owed my paw a few favors. Not only that, he rode a Conley horse.

"Alright boys, tell you what I'm going to do, first take off your boots," I said.

"No way mister, I ain't going to die here without my boots," Powder said.

"Now you make a real good point there friend, I wouldn't want to die in my stocking feet either. But if you don't take your boots off, and I mean right now, you are going to die right here with your boots on."

Both men looked at each other and then took off their boots. Each man threw them down halfway between where they stood and where Ben stood.

"Fetch Ben!" With that Ben brought the boots over to me and I tied each pair to my saddle horn.

"Now step off that horse and slap both of them on the rump as hard as you can," I told the two.

"Mister, you ain't going to kill us are you?" Powder asked.

"Not at all, but I am going to set you afoot. By the time you two get to anywhere in particular I'll be long gone and you can tell how the both of you had me beat but I managed to escape. I figure this detective agency you work for only hires liars and killers anyway. By the sound of that story you just told about the storekeeper up in E-town one more lie won't make any difference. And anyway, I would never want it to be told that I ever shot a man with a name like Powder."

The two strangers slapped their horses and watched both run into the woods. They then looked at me as meek as mice hoping I wasn't the killer they thought I was.

"You two can buy some new boots when you reach the next town, which ought to be about day after tomorrow. And don't get any ideas about hollering your fool heads off hoping someone will hear you and come to help. I hear any noise and I'll ride back just to watch Big Ben tear your throats out." Both shook their heads in the affirmative and then I added.

"You boys ever up around Lexington way you can call on

your guns and belts at the sheriff's office." Course I wasn't going to Lexington, but those two could think I was.

Before I left the two I just had to ask, "What kind of a name is Powder anyway?"

The men were acting a little relieved now no doubt knowing I wasn't going to kill them.

"Once when I got drunk in a saloon some of the boys put powder and lipstick on me while I was passed out. I walked around town for an hour or two before I realized I was wearing the stuff, so the name Powder just stuck," The man said sheepishly.

With that I tapped the hocks of my horse with my spurs and moved on, leaving Ben to watch over those two for a little while. After I had gone about a mile I let out a loud whistle and before long Big Ben showed up. We traveled about an hour past dark and found a nice little dry gully to hole up in until daylight.

During the night I took all the cartridges from one of the gun belts that me and Ben had taken off those two Baldwin-Felts hard cases. I put this extra ammo into one of my saddlebags along with the Colt, which was brand new. I looked at the gun in the other holster, it was a Whitney .36 caliber, also new. Apparently this Baldwin-Felts outfit bought every man a new gun when he hired on, but only an idiot, with his choice of any gun made, would choose a Whitney .36 caliber. I would toss it, along with the two holsters, to the bottom of the very first creek we crossed the next day.

Again we enjoyed all the comforts of a cold camp, cold beans and cold coffee, which are about as far from the comforts of home as a man can get. All the while I kept thinking about that poor storekeeper back in E-town. They must have listened to his story about the fair fight and thought that wouldn't help their case at all. Also by killing him I would go from a man who had only defended himself in a fair fight, to a man who had committed a double murder.

Those Baldwin-Felts boys were now going to have help from every lawman east of the Mississippi River. Hunting me down now would be so much easier. A man with a murder warrant on his head wouldn't have many places to hide. I liked it a lot better when I was just a loner drifting from town to town or up in the high country hunting bear. Also, my credibility would be shattered whenever they did catch up with me. Who would listen to anything from a man with a double murder warrant on his head? I would have a tough time helping Paw now with all this to answer for. It seemed things were pretty well stacked in the coal operator's favor.

The next morning I found some dry oak branches and started the smallest of fires, letting the smoke get lost in the early morning fog. I fried half of what was left of my bacon and had three cups of coffee, not intending to stop for any lunch. With any luck I would be at old man Jones's place just after dark and could make arrangements for my twenty mile run to Floyd County the next day. Only problem with that was going to be old man Jones himself. Moonshiners tend to shoot first and ask questions later when they hear any noise after dark. It was a chance I would just have to take. With all that had happened so far on this trip I was going to need to be extra careful.

I saddled up Rusty and put the ever-lighter pack on Hazel again, hoping a two day rest without a saddle on her back would give her the energy she needed for our twenty-mile run tomorrow. As we moved along through thick undergrowth and burned-out deadfalls I kept a close eye on my back-trail. Big Ben led the way and would alert me of anyone heading in our

Chester's Last Ride

direction. As we moved out of the flatlands of Central Kentucky and got more into the foothills of the Appalachian Mountain Range, our progress started to slow substantially. The Gorge area of the Kentucky River, in places, was as rugged as the Breaks, which bordered Kentucky at the Virginia State line.

Not being able to use any of the main trails which crossed the river at the most desirable spots was a substantial inconvenience. Rusty and Hazel, being sure footed as mountain goats, still had very little trouble. Our river crossing shouldn't be any problem this time of year.

We soon found a deer or elk trail which took us down to the water. I allowed both horses to drink their fill at the water's edge and cool down a bit before we went across. I didn't want either horse in the water before a cool down. Big Ben used the time to swim to the opposite shore and scout around. He exited on the opposite bank and shook himself off. He disappeared into the thick undergrowth, but soon reappeared full of energy and ready for his return swim.

As Ben started to swim back there was the sudden crack of a Winchester. A water spout shot up not five feet from the big cur. I couldn't see the shooter, but from the sound of the shot it was up river and on top of the Gorge.

"Swim Ben, Swim," I called to the big dog. Ben was swimming hard and seemed to realize that he had been shot at. The big cur was in serious trouble. Each second meant he was that much closer to our position and safety. Being the strong swimmer he was I knew now that he would make it.

And then there was another shot. This time the shooter had Ben dead in his sights. There was a yelp from Ben and then he slowly sank from sight. Within seconds I could see a spot of crimson where the big dog had, just seconds before, been swimming for his life. He was gone.

175

Nathan Wright

My concern for Ben was now replaced with an uncontrollable fury. I raced to Rusty and pulled my .45-.75 Winchester out of its leather rug. Some son-of-a-buck had shot Big Ben and he was going to pay. With all that had been happening in the last few days and knowing that I was accused of a murder I decided to make it a reality instead of only an accusation. I was going to kill the man who had killed Ben.

The .45-.75 is a big game gun used to bring down critters as large as elk or buffalo at long range. My only problem was to find the shooter. I began to ease up the bank toward the sound of the last shot when both horses let out a little snort. I turned to spot Ben coming out of the water about fifty feet downstream from where he had gone under. The current had undoubtedly carried him down that far before he managed to claw his way out.

I ran over and grabbed the big hound, and pulled him to better cover near the horses. After I turned him loose he stood and shook. Both water and blood covered me and the horses. He was so glad to see me that he reared up and put both paws on my shoulders and licked me square in the mouth. Any other time and I would have gagged but I was so glad to see him I just let it pass.

Upon inspection I found a graze along his right hip. Just a fraction more and his hip would have been shattered. He would have undoubtedly drowned.

As it was the impact of the shot just took him under and he swam the last several yards under water. That may have saved his life because whoever was doing the shooting had him zeroed in and the next shot would have had him.

Blood still oozed from the wound but it was very slow. I knew he would be alright.

With Ben safe now I could take my time and work on the

shooter. I ordered Ben to stay with the horses and then moved off in the direction of that, dog-shooting son-of a-bitch. The cover was good with tall oak and poplar trees, and the occasional pine and sycamore at the edge of the river bank.

It didn't take long before I came to a spot where a big deadfall lay partially in the water and the large trunk would offer some protection. I eased up through the pines and took a position to observe the cliffs. The sun wasn't on this section of creek bank so there was no worry of a glint off my rifle that might give my position away.

I scanned the creek and the cliffs looking for any sign of movement. I tried to work out in my mind where the shot had originated from. It had to be high up or the bullet would have just pan-caked off the surface of the water. Both bullets hit the water at such an angle as to go in and not bounce off the surface.

I began to scan the top of the ridge and within seconds I found what I was looking for. Three men were at the skyline of the ridge not taking much effort in concealing themselves. One man, the one in the middle, had a rifle with one of those rare scopes attached to the top. These three must have been new to the dog shooting business and just weren't expecting any trouble to be heading back in their direction.

The shot was about two-hundred and fifty yards and uphill at that, a tough order for any man. Shooting uphill at that range was a gamble at best but I wasn't going to let these three off with attempted murder, even if it was just a dog. A dog that I held in higher regards than a lot of men I had known.

I lined up the shot with the big .45-.75 resting on the deadfall. I suspected the man in the middle with the fancy rifle as the one who had shot Ben. The range was nothing for a 210 grain bullet with a tapered case. I started to apply pressure to the trigger and then something made me stop. I couldn't do it; I just couldn't kill a man, even if he had almost taken the life of Ben. I thought about it for a second and then lined up my shot on a scraggly pine tree that was behind the men. With slow steady pressure I eased in on the trigger. That big cartridge escaped the end of the Winchester with the sound of an artillery piece.

Now the sound of a .45-.75 alone is enough to take a man's breath away, but when that big bullet hit the tree you could see large chunks of bark explode in every direction. Now I don't know if a man can jump and duck at the same time but I swear that's what it looked like. Not knowing where the shot came from, all that those three doggie bush-whackers could do was just run for cover. Instinct from years of trouble had taught me to move as soon as I had fired in case anyone saw my muzzle flash. I moved about ten yards to my right and waited for a while to see if there was any more movement from the ridgetop.

With nothing else to shoot at, or scare off, I hurried back to tend to Ben. The big cur was right where I left him, standing there with Rusty and Hazel. I took some flour out of my saddle bag and put it on his wound to stop the bleeding. He was in pretty good shape for a dog that had just been shot. The score between me and Ben was now even at two and two, with both of us now being shot twice over the years and both still none the worse for wear. I counted Ben's graze as a gunshot but for myself I never counted grazes. It kind of gave Ben an edge as far as the count went.

I saddled up and moved off down river away from those bush-whackers. We moved downstream about a half a mile until I found a good place to cross and climb the other side of the gorge. When we hit the top I was careful to stay in the trees, not wanting to get sky-lined. Men were hunting me and now it looked like they were hunting Ben too.

The traveling was rough with low limbs and undergrowth. The delay at the river had cost us more than an hour, not counting the detour downstream to avoid any more trouble. It would be nearly midnight before we reached Haywood Jones' place now. I for one didn't like the thought of that old man shooting me with that twelve-gauge Greener shotgun of his in the middle of the night. We would hole up a few miles from Haywood's place and go in at first light.

After rubbing down the horses and settling into the third cold camp in a row I thought about the events of the day. I for the life of me had never heard of anyone shooting a dog unless it needed it. Paw had shot one or two over the years, but these were dogs that we knew, and he always had a good reason. Once he shot an old hound that had been in a fight with a big coon. After a few days that dog began to act real strange. Paw, being afraid of rabies, took his twenty two and put it out of its misery.

Then another thought came to mind and it made a cold chill run down my back. What if them three were Baldwin-Felts men and they were trying to draw me out. The more I thought about it the more it made sense. That big fancy scoped rifle looked like something a Baldwin man would be carrying, and anyway, that fancy target rifle wasn't something any old farm boy could afford. The three weren't dressed like Kentucky farm boys either. One even looked like he was wearing a Bowler hat.

That evening I searched out a good campsite that would offer both seclusion and several different ways out in case the need arose for a quick get-away. I was being particularly cautious now with all that had happened. There would be no hot coffee tonight and no fried bacon. I had a piece or two of hard tack and one piece of biscuit bread in my saddle bag, along with several pieces of beef jerky. I gave Ben the biscuit bread which he loved due to the fact that it was fried in bacon grease. He polished it off as soon as I reached it to him. I had a pretty good stash of bacon left and knowing that I couldn't fry it without giving away my position I dug it out and fed it to him one piece at a time. He was one happy puppy after that.

After the horses and Ben were set for the night I spread out my blankets next to a big pine tree. I always love the smell of pine needles and they make for a soft bed. As I lay there thinking about the events that had led me to where I was I wondered about Paw. It had been a long time and I was really starting to miss home. After being gone all these years I wondered if he had changed much. I wondered how much the farm had changed over the years; going by what I had read in the letters it was probably a lot. I drifted off to sleep that night with thoughts of my paw and my family on my mind.

William Haskell Conley, the father of Zeke Conley, was still a powerfully built man despite the toll that fifty plus years had taken on him. In all those fifty-eight years he had been shot, stabbed, kicked by a horse, and had broken more bones than he cared to remember. He always claimed that the local doctor made more off him than all the other patients in the area combined. Still though, even with the years and the injuries, he felt as strong as ever and had an optimistic outlook on life that only comes after years tempered by hardship and struggle.

He was a self-educated man who enjoyed the classics. Each evening after dinner he would retire to his study with a glass of Kentucky Bourbon, a cigar produced with some of the area's finest leaf, which happened to be raised on one of his own tobacco farms, and read for an hour or two. He was up to date on current affairs thanks to a steady stream of mail along with several newspapers that were delivered by rail to the depot in the town of Drift, and then delivered on horseback each day to his farm office twenty miles away on Beaver Creek.

In one corner of his office there stood a small gaming table made of Wormy Chestnut. The wood for the table had been milled from a tree that once stood twenty paces from Conley's front door. During one particularly pleasant sunny spring day a bolt of lightning from a nearly cloudless sky had struck the tree, splitting it in half and killing one of Conley's prize horses, which had been ground hitched nearby. Within minutes the sky filled with black clouds and soon a springtime deluge erupted. Conley mourned not only the death of such a fine horse but also the loss of his shady Chestnut tree.

Conley loved the game of chess. He had taken up the habit while still a young man and found himself quite good. After nearly thirty years of practice he discovered that his style of play could hardly be beaten. His most worthy opponent at the present was a graying lawyer from West Virginia by the name of Stanley Rooms.

In the eight or so years that Conley and Rooms had been playing Conley had only lost to Rooms four times and been played to a draw twice. Now this wasn't to say that Rooms was a poor chess player, far from it. Stanley Rooms was the only man to beat William Conley in over six years. As it was Rooms was a very worthy opponent indeed. His game, which wasn't bad to begin with, had improved immensely due to his highly competitive nature and a bit of guidance from the old Sage of Floyd County, William Haskell Conley. Conley and Rooms played a slow game which was built around the strategy of strong defense and the slow attrition of the other player's pieces. Each man enjoyed sipping bourbon and enjoying one of several types of cigars that Conley kept stocked in his handmade humidor.

Most evenings in his study now Conley found himself looking back to ponder the past. With age it seemed came more and more reflection on a life filled with both happiness and hardship. The way he felt now he figured he had twenty more years left, although he probably wouldn't like the last five, after that whatever was left of him could sit on his big front porch, whittling on a piece of dried Kentucky cedar, and looking out over his massive farm and fences full of cattle and horses. These were not just any cattle and horses he would be spending his last years looking at, they happened to be some of the finest stock in the country.

Now if there was one thing Haskell Conley knew how to do, and do well, it was raising horses. Some of the best thoroughbreds east of the Mississippi river resided on his farms. His horses had won many a race during peacetime and carried many a Union Officer during war time. Why it was even said that any picture taken of General Ulysses S. Grant or General William Tecumseh Sherman sitting a horse was probably a William Haskell Conley horse.

Conley had become quite a wealthy man during the war supplying horses to the north. He was a strong Union man and would never have considered selling anything, especially his prize horses, to the South. Oh, he had offers as high as six hundred dollars a head to ship horses down to Dixie, but he continued to supply officer grade stock to the North for two-hundred and fifty dollars a head when he could have more than doubled his money by shipping that same stock southward. Conley thought his horses favored the Union is what he jokingly told friends and relatives.

Chester's Last Ride

The stallions that Grant and Sherman rode were said to have cost as much as a thousand dollars apiece, but price was no object when it came to President Lincoln's generals. He was even once quoted as saying that even if, heaven forbid, the North lost the war, it wouldn't be because of a lack of quality horses. Horses couldn't lose a battle but they could damn sure help win it, especially if the stock was of a higher quality than anything the opposition could put on the field.

Yep, old man Conley knew his horses, but there was something else he knew too, trouble, and it was beginning to brew in Floyd County. As far back as the previous year there had been rumors of big interests up North wanting to tie up all the land, timber, and coal rights, in the area. Anything that could be bought, bribed, or stolen, was up for grabs. Strangers had been flooding in now for several months.

Crime was up considerably, especially murder. The local county Sheriff, along with his five deputies, seemed helpless to do anything about it. The sheriff once told Conley that he and his deputies would do their best to prevent crime, but as far as solving a serious crime or murder his small force were not detectives. He went on to say that his five deputies couldn't solve a murder even if the man or women who had committed it wore a sign around their neck. Sheriff Ezra Barnes had finally convinced the county government to fund the hiring of a detective who brought his force up to five deputies, one detective, and the Sheriff.

It wasn't even April and Floyd County alone had experienced twelve murders. Five were the usual stuff, drunken fights, cheating wives, or husbands and the such, which was about normal for three months into any given year, but seven of the murders were unexplained and no one had been arrested as of yet. More than anything else the unsolved murders were what had the people who lived in Floyd County most scared.

Men had been back-shot or found with a knife wound that had proven fatal, and in one case, a hanging. And these weren't just any men who were being found bushwhacked; they were well respected, law-abiding citizens in their communities and neighborhoods. One was even a preacher who had made the mistake of standing up to some Baldwin-Felts men. The Baldwin-Felts Detective Agency had been sent into the area to help find out who was behind these killings that the local law 'couldn't solve'. The Agency, as they became known in the area, also worked to settle any deed disputes that might arise between local land owners and any out of state buyers, almost always in favor of the out of state buyers.

The preacher that had been killed was a tough old sky-pilot who knew how to handle himself. He had known some rough and rowdy days before finding the Lord. Story had it that he had whipped two detectives who had been trying to evict a member of his congregation from his home. Seems a long lost deed had mysteriously shown up that gave full ownership of the property to the County Attorney in the town of Prestonsburg, the county seat. That County Attorney, Preston Blair had gone before a judge and had the deed declared valid, although the judge involved, one Isaiah Helton said he was puzzled as to how Blair, who had only been in Floyd County for little over a year had come to possess this new deed in the first place.

When Blair tried to have the judge's order enforced, the sheriff said he was too busy to be evicting people so the County Attorney had two of the Baldwin-Felts boys deputized against the sheriff's wishes. When those two started throwing that man's belongings off the front porch it was more than the good preacher could stand. The preacher, who had once been a prize fighter in his younger days, gave those two rented deputies the thrashing of their lives.

Next morning he was found hanging from his own front porch with his Bible under his toes. Seems that whoever had done it had stretched him up just high enough so that he could hold himself up by his tippy-toes only. After so long though, when he couldn't hold himself up like that any longer, he slowly strangled to death under his own weight. He was found like that the next morning, just after the fight with the Baldwin boys, hands tied behind his back, hanging over his Bible. His Bible was still there, lying on the porch under his feet.

The story was told that when a deputy picked that Bible up it was as cold as ice. Crying out in pain the deputy threw the good book back down faster than he had picked it up. When the others came over to the deputy he was just standing there holding his left hand in a handkerchief with a frightened, puzzled look on his face. When the handkerchief was pulled away why that hand was blistered from his palm all the way down to his fingertips. No one else would touch the Bible until a preacher from the next town over was sent for. When that other preacher got there he asked for a moment of silence and then said a small prayer. He then picked up the Bible and examined it. It had the imprint of a hand branded right into its leather cover. That Bible is still in the church for anyone to look at who doesn't believe, and brother when you see it, you'll believe.

Things in Floyd County just weren't the way they used to be, and that was for sure. Most people wouldn't talk to strangers. People had started to lock their doors at night, something that was unheard of only a year before.

Nathan Wright

The county courthouse was being overrun almost every day by people checking on their deeds to see if a problem existed that they hadn't know about. The deeds office, which usually had only one employee, now employed three, and business was booming. The deed room alone was as busy as ever, and getting more busy each day. During any given day it was elbow to elbow, with a line waiting from the door, clean out the front of the court house onto the front steps and down onto the lawn. Business was so good for the local attorneys that they were competing and discounting their fees in order to get the most business. A few of the town lawyers were said to be working twelve to fourteen hours a day to keep pace.

Old man Conley pondered all these happenings each night as he sat in his study with his books, his bourbon, and his hand rolled Kentucky cigars. It seemed that the quiet of his study was the best place to think things over, and in doing so he had started to formulate what all this meant, and a plan was beginning to take shape.

He had lived here all his life, having inherited his home and adjoining acreage from his father. The elder William Conley, or Big Bill as he was known for years, had been a part time farmer and rancher, while also being a full time coal miner. Conley's dad had gone into the mines at the age of eleven and by the age of twenty it was told that he was the biggest, strongest man in the entire county. But by the time he was forty he was dying of a disease known locally as Dust-Lung. His robustness of youth was now gone, only a thin shell of a man remained to replace what had once been. The family's mother had died when Sara, the youngest of the children, was born.

When a man works underground for that many years and breathes in all that coal dust it eventually lines the inside of his lungs and cuts off his breathing. Conley had seen his dad cough for hours at a time all the while trying to catch his breath. The elder Conley had died at the age of forty-three when Haskell was twenty-two. One thing Haskell's father told his son, shortly before he died, was to never, never, let another Conley go underground and die the death that he himself was dying of.

Those words had changed Haskell's life, and probably saved it as well. Haskell had been working in the mines for more than five years alongside his father and after his father died he kept the promise he had made to him by quitting the mines and never setting foot back under the mountain again. He also made sure that his three younger brothers were taken care of, all the while cautioning them of the dangers a man faced if he chose to work underground. As time went by Haskell managed to keep that promise he made to his dying father, not a single one of his brothers had gone inside the mines to earn a living. Farm life proved rough at first, but all four boys and an only sister had managed to make a go of it.

From the beginning things didn't look good for the family. The meager income that mining had given to the Conley's through the labors of Haskell and Big Bill was sorely missed. They made due as best they could with the farming and the livestock. Their younger sister Sara, by the time she was ten years old, even took in washing and sewing to try and help out. Each year crops, horses, and cattle, were tended to with all the tender attentions the young farmers could provide, and in not so many years their efforts were beginning to pay off.

It seems that young Haskell had a knack for raising cattle and horses. As time went by his reputation grew, along with that of the family's, because of the fine stock which was produced each year on the farm. Haskell bought only the best horses he could locate, and in doing so, raised some of the finest stock which could be had in the entire state.

Nathan Wright

But the real financial gains came from selling trips he made to adjoining states. Haskell would leave each spring and travel far and wide advertising the quality of the Conley horses. He sold horses in Tennessee, Virginia, (West Virginia was still part of Virginia at this time and didn't become a state until the beginning of the Civil War when it broke away from the confederate state of Virginia in order to stay with the Union), and Ohio. It didn't take long before people came from all around to Eastern Kentucky to look over the Conley stock and make their purchases. As his reputation grew for being one of the finest breeders in the business, so did his clientele. He was getting a hundred and fifty dollars on average per horse, when most were selling for half that much.

These trips took anywhere from eight to twelve weeks and covered as much as fifteen-hundred miles. While on these trips the farm and stables were looked after by Haskell's younger brothers and their sister. This turned out to be very good training for the youths, and as time would tell, each would eventually run an individual aspect of the Conley Farm's businesses.

It wasn't many years until the family had acquired several large tracks of land along with timber and mineral rights in Eastern and South Central Kentucky. The farm had grown with the addition of a substantial house and gardens, along with two large barns, which were used for both horses and cattle.

Haskell's abilities weren't limited to horses though. He had experimented with different cattle breeds to see which could produce the best quality beef. His farm was home to two herds of about five hundred head each of Herford, and Black Angus stock. The Herford, or White Face as the locals liked to call them, thrived in the Appalachian climate. His Black Angus stock took a bit more effort though, but the payoff was in some of the best beef east of the Mississippi River. He had buyers from as far away as Boston ordering a hundred Black Angus at a time and then shipped them by rail to the East Coast.

With the coming of the War Between the States Haskell had fallen strongly behind the Union cause. Some of his neighbors though were strong Southern supporters, and needless to say, tensions ran high in all of Kentucky, especially in the more southern counties.

When confederate soldiers would sortie into Floyd County, a local militia, which was headed by Colonel Haskell Conley himself, helped to protect the county from confederate scavengers as he called them, who were sent in to pilfer anything of value in the area.

The horses and cattle on the Conley farm would have been a prize that no confederate officer could resist, but Colonel Conley and his militiamen fought like demons to protect the homes and property they were entrusted with. A man will always fight harder to protect what's his and in this case it was no different.

Conley had paid out of his own pocket for some of the best rifles and pistols produced by northern factories. His militia was well trained and better equipped than most and could, on average, outshoot and outfight anything that came across the Kentucky-Tennessee border. In the entire war he estimated he never lost more than ten percent of his stock due to southern scavenging.

His three younger brothers stayed with the farm during the war, along with the twenty or so hired hands. Each day all the farm hands got twenty rounds of ammunition and a shooting contest was held. The winner always received four hours off each day without any cut in wages. This was a great incentive to excel and also helped to keep the crew a little more rested.

Nathan Wright

With an incentive like that it didn't take long before each man had attained a very high level of proficiency with firearms. Whenever ten or twelve confederates made a raid on the Conley farm and stables, they were met with a very hot and accurate hail of lead. It didn't take long for word to get around, steer a wide path around southern Floyd County, and the Conley farm in particular.

When a congressman from Kentucky met with President Lincoln early in the war, it was mentioned that the area around Floyd County, which had supplied a substantial number of fine horses to union officers, was under steady attack from southern raiding parties. This news alarmed the President. At this time in the war the President was still trying to keep Kentucky in the Union. In order to prevent another state from possibly sliding to the side of the south he ordered a small Union garrison to be posted in the area around Eastern and Southeastern Kentucky. This garrison moved from town to town to show its presence. Once near the county seat of Prestonsburg it was discovered that a Confederate sortie into the area was going to happen soon.

That posting of the Union garrison led a short time later to the Battle of Middle Creek which was billed as a Union victory. Whether argued as a victory or a defeat, the North used it as another example of the righteousness of its cause. Shortly after the battle there was a substantial reduction in the number of southern incursions into the area.

The Conley farm now was free to move as many horses and cattle as it could produce to the north to help in the Union cause. The quantity, and quality, of the stock being shipped from Conley's farms by rail through Ashland, Kentucky terminals, and then on to the north, was unmatched by any other Kentucky farmer, and his efforts were richly rewarded.

Chester's Last Ride

Conley managed to ship over five-thousand head of cattle out of Kentucky to the North during each year of the war.

But the real benefit of the Conley farm was the officer grade horses it shipped. His Eastern and Central Kentucky farms produced, on average, over a thousand horses a year, with almost four-hundred of those horses being of the quality required for the Cavalry and Officer Corps.

Through his shrewd acquisition of land and breeding stock, and then marketing that stock all over the east, Conley was set to supply the war effort with a portion of its needs at a time when a man could name his own price. The war had made Conley rich beyond his or any of his family's wildest dreams.

Now it seemed that all of this was in jeopardy. No one could figure out who or what was behind all the trouble of the last year. It was a given that coal had something to do with it. But would men fight and die over something as troublesome to get out of the ground as coal? Would these newcomers to the area who had been buying every scrap of land that they could get their hands on resort to murder to obtain the deeds that they wanted? And who was backing them? Big money was changing hands every day, and someone had to be fronting all that money. Rumors were rife about a group of men from the northeast who had their sights set on the region.

Conley was also made aware of interests out of Chicago that had bought up a surprising amount of property in Eastern Kentucky as well. At times it seemed as if these two groups were at odds with each other. Even some of the Baldwin-Felts men were using caution around anyone they thought had Chicago ties.

And it seemed that if the land either of these two groups of Northerners wanted wasn't for sale, then a strange new deed would appear and the local owners would almost always lose in court, giving up not only their homes, but their livelihood as well. William Haskell Conley knew that it was only a matter of time before men in city suits came knocking on his door. He had received correspondence in the mail wanting him to put a price on his holdings. The only way to respond to these letters was through a return address only, no name. Conley had simply thrown the letters in the fireplace in his spacious study. As he watched each one of the letters being consumed by the flames he told himself that his land wasn't for sell at any price.

He had already done what any good businessman would do in a situation like this; he had contacted his attorneys in Beckley, West Virginia, and notified them of the trouble in and around Floyd County. These were men he trusted from back in the war days, and they were some of the best lawyers that money could hire. They had sent a man to each of the counties that Haskell owned property in and solidified the existing deeds. Nine out of ten of his deeds were solid and most of the others were touched up with any necessary legal jargon that might be required. More than one family had lost the land they lived on because of a hastily or poorly prepared deed.

The law firm of Parsons, Wiggle, and Rooms, or Wiggle-Room as Conley liked to refer to them when none of the attorneys were around, had been on retainer with the Conley Farms for over ten years. In that time they had handled anything and everything that came up concerning Conley's vast holdings, and had been very successful in the process. The firm was considered one of the top law firms in the nation and old man Conley was one of their best clients. Anything Conley-Farms needed was handled at once and almost always with very favorable results.

Joshua Parsons, Herbert Wiggle and Stanley Theodore Rooms, had each spent time at the Conley farm enjoying deer, elk, and grouse hunting. Once they had managed to track a large bear for two days but were finally forced to give up the chase when they found out the bear had cubs and Conley wouldn't allow the momma bear to be killed.

Over the years Conley and Rooms had enjoyed a number of chess matches with Conley usually being the winner. Each considered Conley not only a business client but also a personal friend. This trio of Harvard trained lawyers enjoyed nothing more than a good challenge, especially one that came with a good fee.

The Triplets, a more pleasant name Conley used from time to time, that handled his legal matters, had eight other lawyers and a staff of assistants that numbered more than thirty. They were well acquainted with the Conley holdings along with the timber, cattle, horses, and anything else to do with farming or ranching in Kentucky. The law firm also dealt with heavy industry such as steel, rail, and coal operations. They were perfectly suited to deal with the trouble that had begun to brew in Southeastern Kentucky.

The telegraph lines between Beckley and Drift, which was the closest telegraph office to the Conley farms, had been humming as of late keeping the Triplets and the farm updated with any and all news that seemed important. The firm also subscribed to all local newspapers in the counties around the Conley Farms and had a man assigned with the task of scanning them and keeping updated files on all the latest happenings. If there was one thing the Triplets believed in, it was well organized files on anything that affected their clients.

All the local elections for as far back as the year eighteen-twenty four were on file at the home offices of the Triplets. Any race of significance was cataloged, with a heavy weighting toward the judiciary. Files were also kept on the losers. Any reason that might shed light on why they lost was duly logged in the files for each county where Conley had holdings.

Court cases that had anything to do with coal or transportation by rail were being heavily researched. The Triplets had a vested interest in Eastern Kentucky, primarily because of William Haskell Conley. If it was a matter that affected the Conley Farms then the Triplets wanted to know about it and already have an open file with all the necessary information at hand.

They knew about the run on the county offices and the shakeup of deeds in the area. For the better part of the year a local attorney had been hired by the Triplets to dig into the courthouse activities and determine who might be behind the growing trouble in the area. So far all indications led to big money from the northeast and northern mid-west. The Triplets had been pooling money and resources in the hopes of averting a takeover of the politicians in the area. It was widely known that politicians were bought and sold by the wagon load for those who could afford the price.

The biggest fear for the Triplets, and Conley, was if a crooked politician teamed up with local law enforcement. Throw in a judge or two and the situation would spiral out of hand in a hurry. The Floyd County Sheriff and the county judge were already suspected of coercion, although Conley liked Judge Helton and Sheriff Barnes and still wasn't convinced the two had any involvement other than what the law called for. The Triplets had tracked some of the money from the northeast into the largest bank in Prestonsburg. The battle lines were being drawn with much at stake for not only the winners but also the losers.

The man in the county seat who was president of the bank just mentioned was one Samuel J. Reed. He was not a tall man by any means and his girth had managed to grow by four or five pounds each year until he was considered both short and fat. He considered himself to be an honest man and by most standards he was. The only problem with bankers is that what they see as perfectly honest might seem to others as dishonest. In a time before strong banking legislation and government oversite these local banks were notorious for playing by their own rules.

Reed had tried to take a middle road in the affairs of the local people of Floyd County and the men from the northern regions that were interested in coal. If a sweet profit was to be made then it was more likely that the bank president would side with the northerners over his own neighbors. Reed was a wealthy man who had made the bulk of his money fair and square. But these profits that were starting to materialize at the expense of the local residents were beginning to bother him. He laughed at himself when he thought of a banker that would question where his money might have come from.

The problem was that there were other men who held a portion of the bank and they together held more of the bank's stock than he did. He was certainly the largest single shareholder but if the others banded together then he could be forced out and that was something he could never let happen. He tried to reign in his partners whenever he felt they had overstepped their boundaries but the profits involved from the northeastern investors had him at a disadvantage. Sure he was set to profit more than any of the other owners of the bank but this did little to soothe his conscious.

Mr. Reed's wife had died a few years earlier and this event had shattered him. He tried to busy himself with work but soon found that piling riches on top of riches would actually do him no good and certainly brought no additional pleasure. He just couldn't justify the money grab his partners always demanded over the well-being of the local residents.

The last straw for Samuel J. Reed was when he was forced to evict a man by the name of Stanton Hatfield from his fine old home. Mr. Hatfield had made a fortune selling land to the railroad in the mid-eighteen hundreds. When the Civil War erupted Mr. Hatfield fell squarely behind the South and in doing so converted his sizable fortune into Confederate dollars. When the South lost the war Hatfield lost everything but his house and his pride. Now twenty-seven years later he was about to lose the house and what was left of his pride too.

Word was sent down from New York to have the old man's property taxes raised to the point that he would lose the house. It seemed that an operative would be arriving in the near future who wanted the house for his own personal use and the only thing preventing this was Stanton Hatfield. Reed had known Mr. Hatfield his entire life and was reluctant to have the old man evicted. The bank's board overruled Reed and made the arrangements required to have the house vacated.

Reed felt bad at first but eventually managed to accept what had happened when told that once the man from New York finished with the business at hand then he could acquire the house if he wanted it. This idea had at first soothed Reed's conscious but soon the feelings of guilt returned.

About an hour before first light I saddled up Hazel and put the pack back on Rusty. Ben was somewhere off in the brush scouting around for what must have been his breakfast because before long he appeared out of the forest with a very skinny little rabbit. In all my years I had never seen him settle for such a meager meal. "Ben, are you getting old, or just losing your touch?" I asked the big cur. He just looked at me with a sad face and then began to tear into his meal, fur, hide and all.

Then it dawned on me that he was probably pretty sore from his gunshot wound the previous day. It must have been all he could do to chase down that sickly little rabbit in the shape he was in. Now I started to feel pretty bad for my old trail partner, him being wounded and all. I searched in my saddlebag and got out the rest of the beef jerky and the last piece of skillet bread and went over and sat it down beside what was left of his rabbit. I reached over and patted him on the head. Ben looked up with what had to be a big doggie grin and began to lick my hand. I gave him another pat on the head and went back to tending the horses. I took a little extra time this morning, giving Ben a chance to finish that rabbit along with his jerky and biscuit. If he had a good meal in him maybe he could make better time on the trail.

Once the horses were ready I checked on Ben's wound. It didn't look near as bad as the day before. Once he had finished eating his rabbit I climbed in the saddle and we moved off into the darkness. It was almost daylight and we were only about five miles from Haywood's place. Old man Jones would already have been up more than an hour or so by the time we made it to his cabin. I hoped he had a little extra breakfast ready since I had given all I had left to Ben.

I approached the cabin with caution and at about twenty yards away I shouted, "Hello the cabin." No more had the words left my mouth than I heard the double hammer of a Greener being cocked back. Old man Haywood must have heard Hazel's hoof beats as we were making our way to the cabin. A low voice from the trees to my left said "Who in the Sam-Hill are you boy and what are you doing out so early?"

Nathan Wright

Now I hadn't seen old Haywood in many a year and hoped the voice coming from behind the shotgun was his. "I'm Zeke Conley looking for a man by the name of Haywood Jones. He used to trade horses and such with my paw."

Not a sound could be heard for the longest while. I began to wonder if maybe old Haywood had cashed in his chips and this was someone else living on his farm. Finally the voice holding the shotgun asked, "You talking about old man Haskell Conley from over Floyd County way?"

"Yes sir, that's the one, and I would feel a good deal better if that shotgun you're holding was pointed in another direction."

Next thing I heard was laughing and then the voice walked out of the brush. Sure enough it was a man who was missing a leg. He walked with the help of a cane and was wearing some sort of homemade wooden leg or peg like a pirate would wear.

"Calm down boy, I was mostly just a funning ye. I been expecting you for the last three days, what took you so long anyway."

"Some trouble along the way has got me going real slow and cautious. I had to travel every back woods trail between here and St. Louis. What do you mean you been expecting me anyway, nobody knows where I'm going or where I'm coming from."

"Oh now you might be a bit more popular than you think there young feller. Been some of them Baldwin-Felts boys here a couple of times in the last few days asking about a man traveling with two horses and one frightful big dog. I reckon you would fit that description real good, and so would that dog." Haywood eased down the barrel of the Greener. "Not only that, one of your brothers came by day fore yesterday and filled me in on what's been happening over in Floyd County, and I reckon it ain't very good, no sir, ain't good at all."

Chester's Last Ride

I got down from Hazel and tied her and Rusty to an old hitch post beside of a split rail corral. Beside the corral and attached by a gate was a substantial barn with a dormer window on the second floor. Ben walked over and stretched out on some loose hay beside the corral. I could tell that the five mile walk this morning had done him in.

"What's wrong with your dog there Zeke?" Haywood asked.

"He got shot by three no goods up in the gorge yesterday. I thought they had killed him but it was only a graze. It's affecting his ability to keep up and there is no way in hell I will ever run off and leave him."

"Shot you say, by three men." Haywood rubbed his stubbly chin and then asked, "What did these three fellers look like anyway?"

"Wore city clothes, one was carrying a rifle with one of them new type scopes, you know the type that helps you shoot straighter at a long distance."

"Zeke, maybe we should put those two horses of yours in the barn, rub them down good and give them a little grain, looks like they been living off too much Kentucky Bluegrass and not enough oats. I got a big ham bone in the house for that animal you call a dog, I think he would appreciate a little pork instead of what he's been getting off the trail you two been on these last few weeks."

"Be much obliged Haywood, we been moving pretty hard for longer than I care to talk about. The last few weeks I think have mostly worn out the four of us."

"Yeah, I heard about your troubles from those Baldwin-Felts men, cept I heard it the way they wanted me to hear it. Your brother asked me to give you any help I could and your paw would square things up once he got back from Cincinnati. I told him there wouldn't be any squaring up. I reckon me and your dad go back a long way and plus I don't take kindly to them city-slicker detectives pushing folk around. Come on in the house, I reckon you look like you could use some home cooked grub for a change yourself."

"I sure could Haywood, been a few days since I've seen anything that came out of a skillet. Why is my paw in Cincinnati?" The old man moved about his stove with the skill of an old chuck wagon cook. He was fixing skillet bread and bacon. He got out four big hen eggs and with the skill of his years showing, he broke each on the edge of the skillet and dropped them in the pan with one hand and tossed the empty shells into a bucket beside the stove. Wasn't long until the smell filled the cabin and with each minute that passed I could almost taste what was being cooked. Just before it was finished he grabbed a big hambone that still had a goodly amount of meat on it and walked to the door.

"You say your dog's name is Ben?"

"Yep, Ben it is, sometimes I call him Big Ben," I told Haywood.

He eased the door open and whistled. Ben looked up from what must have been a nap and looked at Haywood. He either smelled the ham or saw it but you can bet it didn't take him long to limp over and take it from Haywood's hand. "That's a good boy," Haywood said as he rubbed Ben's head. Ben headed back to the spot where he had been laying and started working on his meal.

Haywood came back and washed his hands in a bucket of water that was sitting on a side table. He then finished cooking what he had on the stove. The old man scooped up the food and put it in a big tin plate. He sat the meal on the table in front of me and then poured a cup of some of the best coffee I had ever tasted; it was so strong it probably didn't even need the cup.

Haywood then decided to answer why my paw was in Cincinnati. "Don't know, your brother didn't say except that Haskell had an old friend from the War who was now a federal judge up in Cincinnati. It seems your paw was going to call in a few favors."

The food was good and I ate my fill and then some. While I was working on my feast, old man Jones went out and got my saddle bags. As I ate he busied himself filling them with grub, some home grown Kentucky Leaf and coffee.

"I see you got you one of them Winchester .45-.75 big game guns, how you fixed for cartridges?" Now I had loaded up with an extra box of Colt .45 shells back in E-town and also took some off of those two fellers I set afoot, but the store keep didn't stock any .45-.75. That thought reminded me of the unfortunate storekeeper who had been killed at the hands of those no-good Baldwin-Felts boys.

"I'm good on the six shooter side but I only got about a dozen .45-.75 rounds, hard to come by that caliber when you're traveling in the boonies. How is it that you know about the .45-.75 anyway Haywood?"

"Well, when that new caliber Winchester came out a few years ago I just couldn't help myself but to ride into Lexington and pick me one up. I got that buffalo gun and ten boxes of cartridges with twenty rounds to a box. Reckon in all these past three years I ain't shot it more than a dozen times, kicks too hard for my old shoulder. You take half what cartridges I got, ought to set you up pretty good," Haywood said.

"Mind if I ask why you carry a cannon like that, instead of a .45-60? Shoots better with a lot less kick than the .45-.75, and is accurate up to three-hundred yards," Haywood asked.

"I got good eyes Haywood, and with that .45-.75 I can hit what I shoot at, at a range of up to and including five-hundred yards."

"But with the smoke that thing puts off anyone you're shooting at will know where you are. You ever think about that?" Haywood asked.

"Won't matter, it's hard for a dead man to shoot back," I told him.

"Yea, I reckon that's so, young feller, I reckon that's so. You hurry up and eat now; I got you all loaded up for a long ride," Haywood said.

"A long ride, I ain't going for a long ride, I'm going to Paw's over in Floyd County. That little trip is no more than twenty miles at the most."

The old man continued to busy himself around his house and didn't respond at first. Then Haywood stopped what he was doing and said, "It's too dangerous for you to go to Floyd County riding in from the west. Baldwin-Felts wants you dead and your brother said from here to there they got at least twenty men waiting for you to show up. From what he said I doubt it will be a standup fight, more like an ambush."

"I reckon I can handle myself around them store-bought lawmen."

"Naw Zeke, I reckon you ain't got the whole story. I'll fill you in later today after we put a few miles between us and this place," Haywood said.

I looked at old man Haywood and for the first time on this trip I realized that a lot more was going on than I had expected.

"Haywood, do you mind telling me what in blazes is going on and just what do you mean by us, are you expecting to come along with me?"

Chester's Last Ride

"You got it little feller, now finish your breakfast and let's get those horses ready for the trail." The words 'little feller' suddenly brought back memories. Haywood had called me that many years ago when I was just a pup and hadn't got my full growth yet.

Next thing I knew a horse came into the yard and Haywood said "You finish up while I go talk to Frank."

Still not sure what all this was about, I hurried up with my food and gulped down the last of the coffee. Haywood had made his way outside and I could hear him telling someone to help him with his horse and gear. I hurried outside and came face to face with a man who could pass for one of my brothers standing there listening to the old man.

As I came closer my astonishment was complete. This young man was almost the spitting image of me. The young fellow looked at me and said, "You must be Zeke!"

"Yeah, I reckon I am, and you would be?"

"Name's Frank, I'll be looking after the place while you and my old daddy here are off taking care of some business he mentioned to me yesterday. And by the looks of things down by the river you two had best be hurrying."

I looked at the young man and said, "What's going on down at the river?"

"Three Baldwin-Felts men are trying to track you and that big dog of yours, said you shot at them as they were camping out by the gorge yesterday."

"Well I reckon that's partly true, they shot at my dog Ben and then I just about killed the man I suspected that done it. I couldn't let something like that pass so I took a shot back and made it high and wide. Didn't even come close to them three, but they did take notice," I said.

"Yeah I figured something like that, them Baldwin boys ain't noted for telling the truth. Matter of fact I think they only hire outlaws and bushwhackers," Frank said.

The whole time we were talking Frank had been saddling up one of the finest looking horses I had ever seen.

"Nice horse you're working on there Frank, wouldn't be some Floyd County stock would it?"

"As a matter of fact it is. My dad and your paw do a little trading now and again. It took dad about a year to swing the deal on this critter. Seems your paw wouldn't let this animal go for neither love nor money, so they finally worked out an arrangement, they flipped a hundred dollar gold eagle, winner got the horse, and the loser got the gold eagle."

"You know that sounds like Paw, he would bet on just about anything, said it was his one and only vice. And he always told me that if a man ain't got at least one vice then he ain't much of a man," I told Frank.

As Frank finished up with Haywood's horse I saddled up Hazel and loaded up Rusty. Wasn't long before we were ready for the trail, and Ben seemed to be ready too after his little rest. That big hound was all smiles after finishing off that big ham bone that Haywood had tossed him. I checked his wound and noticed it had turned a little red. As I was poking and prodding he reached around and grabbed my arm with his mouth. He just stood there and looked at me. I knew that checking that gunshot wound had caused him some pain and he was just letting me know that he wanted me to stop. I took my other hand, the one that wasn't surrounded by big sharp teeth and patted his head. He released my arm and started shaking his tail. I guess it was his way of saying, 'No hard feelings'.

I still wasn't sure what was going on or where we were headed but old man Jones had a plan and that was way better than anything I had had for these last few weeks. I saddled up and watched with amazement at how Haywood pegged it over to his big horse and hoisted himself into the saddle. It seemed as if that old man had been pretty powerful in his prime and apparently had lost very little as age came after him. He was wearing an old army Colt single action revolver in a leather belt and holster and had that Greener in his saddle scabbard.

"Haywood, why are you taking that doubled-barreled shotgun instead of your Winchester?"

"Reckon my eyes ain't what they used to be Zeke, Greener makes up the difference for what my aim has lost. We had better be moving out before them Baldwin boys show up. It's been quite a spell since I pulled the trigger on anybody, guess you could say I'm putting it off as long as I can."

We moved out with Ben up in front scouting around and Haywood bringing up the rear. I was leading Rusty with a lead tied to my saddle horn. We headed away from the gorge where Frank said the Baldwin-Felts men had been scouting around for my trail. They must have been pretty poor scouts because I hadn't tried very hard to hide my trail, not knowing that those three from yesterday might have had any interest in me. I had hoped that .45-.75 cartridge would have scared them into another county, if not another state, by now.

We moved at a pretty good pace until about noon. The sun was riding high when we came upon a little holler with good cover and a small clear running stream between two low hills. Haywood said, "Zeke, what do you say to a little coffee and jerky while I fill you in on the plan."

I ground hitched the horses in some good grass and found some dry oak branches to build a fire that would put off as little smoke as possible. Haywood sat on an old deadfall that made about as good a seat as anybody would want. He pulled a piece of cedar from his old leather saddle bag and a two-blade Barlow knife from his pocket and after he got settled on that deadfall he began to whittle slivers as small as crow's hair from the cedar.

"Whittling calms my temper a might, maybe you ought to take it up yourself sometime young Conley."

I looked at the old man and just shot him a grin. When the coffee was ready I poured two cups and reached one to Haywood. He tossed me a piece of jerky as he took a sip of the coffee. I sampled the jerky, it tasted like deer meat.

"Haywood, you mind if I ask you a question?"

"Naw, I reckon I don't mind at all."

"How come your boy looks so much like a Conley?"

The old man thought about my question for quite some time before he finally looked at me with a big grin.

"You know Zeke, that ain't the first time I been asked that question and it probably won't be the last. I have been meaning to ask your old man the same thing. Just ain't got around to it yet. If you don't mind, let's change the subject."

I would find out later that Haywood had married one of my paw's first cousins and that was the reason me and Frank were so similar. Haywood liked nothing more than a practical joke and he just let me wonder for myself what the reason was.

"Sure thing Haywood, what do you want to talk about?"

"Oh I don't know, you make pretty good coffee, for a youngster. Most boys your age try to make the coffee way too strong, they think it makes them look tough or something I guess."

That got my attention pretty good. Not that old man Jones had liked my coffee, but what he had called me, youngster. It had been many a year since my paw had affectionately called me youngster. In a way, now that I noticed it, there were more than a few similarities to old man Jones and my paw.

I looked at him and said, "Yeah, I never was much of a whiskey or beer drinker, just coffee when it's handy. Now how about filling me in on where we're going and what happens when we get there."

The old man chewed his jerky and sipped the coffee for some time before he finally decided to speak.

"We're heading southeast into Tennessee, and then on over to Virginia. And starting right now we leave no sign. Whoever is tracking us probably ain't much of a tracker so let's not help them out."

"What's in Virginia?" I asked.

"It's not what's in Virginia boy, but what's not in Virginia, that being mainly no Baldwin-Felts men. Also you got a murder warrant on your head in Kentucky. Virginia and Tennessee ain't never honored a Kentucky warrant as far as I know, so you ought not to have any trouble out of the law when we get there. Seems there might still be some hard feelings between them two states and Kentucky you know. Mad cause Kentucky didn't bolt and run with the rest of the south."

"I reckon I been in trouble before Haywood, so this don't worry me much. How am I going to help Paw if I'm in Virginia?"

"I didn't say we were staying in Virginia Conley, we're just passin through, after we travel a few miles we'll double back into Kentucky. Those Baldwin-Felts boys won't be looking for two men and three horses coming out of the east from Virginia.

"Your paw went through Virginia and then turned north through West Virginia on his way up to Cincinnati to see that federal judge he knows. He was forced to take a very roundabout way to Ohio so he wouldn't be followed. Seems when your brother came by a few days back he said your father never made it to Ohio. Funny thing is that no one has heard from him since he left, no letter, no telegram, no nothing."

Ben used his time to sleep, seems his wound had taken something out of the big cur. Hazel and Rusty were trying to figure out this new horse and rider that was traveling with us. Hazel even reached over and nipped the big stallion a time or two on his back flank. The big chestnut never paid her any mind; I think that just made Hazel a little more mad. Hazel always liked to be in control, Rusty couldn't care less.

The horse that Haywood rode was a very fine animal indeed, such a big chestnut stallion. I looked at Haywood and asked, "What do you call that big chestnut of yours Haywood?"

"Chester, what else?"

I should have known; these old timers had a funny way of naming their mounts, and Chester just took the cake. "Good choice Haywood, I wouldn't have thought of that, but it does seem appropriate."

"Had an old dog once named Chester, best old hound a man could ask for, lived to be eighteen years old. One morning I went out and he was all curled up on the porch on an old rug that he liked to sleep on. I said Chester, ain't you up yet, but he didn't move, it seems he had passed on during the night in his sleep real peaceful like. I sat there with him for more than an hour, remembering all of those eighteen years he and I had spent together. Later that day I buried my best friend under the apple tree right there in the front of the cabin. Laid him to rest with his rug and an old leather rawhide he'd been chewing on for about a month. He'd lost most of his teeth over the years, but he still loved to work on an old rawhide. You know, after I buried him I brought out my old ladder back chair and just sat there with him under that old apple tree for the better part of the day. Even now it brings a tear to my eye. Won't be long though until me and my old friend will be hunting together again."

Haywood rubbed his eyes and then went back to whittling on his cedar. Neither of us spoke for the longest time. Finally Haywood got to his feet, or should I say foot, and said, "We'd best be on our way, with any luck we can be in Tennessee by midnight. The sooner we make it out of Kentucky the sooner them Baldwin-Felts boys lose their warrant power."

We loaded up and moved out with neither of us saying much. I believe Haywood was still thinking about his old dog Chester. We moved along in silence all the time keeping a close watch on our back trail. Ben moved with a slight limp and acted a bit stiff after his encounter with the bullet from the previous day. Still though, I had a great appreciation for the big cur and realized that most men had a dog in their life, just like Haywood had Chester.

We traveled the whole day and didn't encounter another rider on the trail. About two hours past dark I asked Haywood how much farther it was to the state line. Old man Haywood said, "Oh, it's about thirty minutes I reckon...behind us." It seemed we were already in Tennessee and Haywood was just looking for a good place to bed down for the night. It had been a very long day and I don't think Haywood had done this much riding in quite a spell. Big Ben was showing the strain too and was ready to stop right there on the trail if he could.

Haywood said he knew a good spot where we could picket the horses and build a good fire without any undue attention. Wasn't long before we turned off the trail and moved about a mile off into the woods to a spot with tall trees good water and grass in a slight depression where our camp and fire wouldn't be seen. Soon we had a fire going. As tired as we were we were even more hungry. Within a half hour we had coffee, bacon and beans and believe me rough grub never tasted so good.

The horses had already been rubbed down and watered. They were now happily cropping grass. Haywood had packed another ham bone for Ben and you never heard such a racket as that big cur made as he attacked his meal. It did sound a lot better than him chewing on a rabbit carcass though. It wasn't long before we were all finished and settled in for the night.

Our plan was to be on the trail before daylight but as tired as we were, and as late as we had traveled the day before, it was a good thirty minutes past first light before old man Haywood threw a stick at me to wake me up. "Just like young folk these days to go sleeping all the daylight hours away." I rose up and saw that Haywood had already made coffee and skillet bread.

"Well Haywood, it seems you might make someone a good wife someday," I told the old man.

"Very funny you young whipper-snapper, maybe I won't share this feast with you after all."

"Sorry Haywood, I ain't used to breakfast being ready before I even get up."

"Well the way you were sleeping, I thought you were waiting for breakfast in bed."

All I could do was laugh and dig into the biscuit bread and coffee and let me tell you that old man knew how to cook.

Haywood began to saddle up his big chestnut. As he did he began to whistle Dixie. All of the sudden he stopped and looked at me.

"Hey young Zeke, did you ever wonder what in blazes the War Between the States was all about?"

I looked at the old man and wondered where this was heading.

"Naw Haywood, I never gave it much thought."

"Never gave it much thought, damn-it Zeke, what kind of an answer is that?"

"I don't know Haywood; I just never did think about it much, that's all."

"Well if that don't just beat all Zeke. I gave three years of my life and my left leg to the Confederate cause. If you didn't think about it very much then you must have thought about it at least a little. So tell me about the little."

I could see that Haywood wasn't going to let this pass so I filled him in on what little I did know.

"Haywood, all I know is what I've heard."

"Well then Zeke, just what did you hear?"

"Paw told me that the War was all about freeing the slaves."

With that old man Jones began to laugh as loud as a man could. I began for a second to think that his years might have left him a bit touched.

"Zeke, you and Haskell got it all wrong. The War Between the States was about the South's right to govern itself and not be interfered with by them Yankees up North. We just wanted to be left alone and run each state as we saw fit. That slavery thing was just something that the North brought up to make their cause seem right. Hell it wasn't that many years before the War that those high and mighty office holders up in Washington D.C. had slaves of their own. Ain't about slavery at all, never was. Anyone who thinks otherwise needs to take a history class."

"Well Haywood, I am sure glad you straightened me out on that. Like I said, never gave it much thought before and I doubt I'm going to give it much thought now."

"Well at least now you know," he said.

"Now I know."

Nathan Wright

We traveled for a couple of hours and at each junction in the trail Haywood already knew which way to go, as if he were the one who had blazed these trails to begin with. There was something uncanny about his sense of direction.

"Haywood, how is it that you know these trails so good this far from your place?"

The old man just kept riding and didn't seem to pay me no mind. After about ten minutes I asked again.

"Haywood how is it that you know these trails so good?"

"I heard ye the first time boy, why is it you young folk like to talk so much, you mind telling me that?"

"Sorry Haywood, just trying to make the time pass."

"Boy, when you get my age the last thing you want to do is make the time pass. You want to make it slow down to almost a stop. Then again, I guess I would be putting off spending time with old Chester, wouldn't I?"

"Your horse?"

"No, my old hunting dog I was telling you about yesterday."

"You mean you ain't got any friendship built up with your horse Haywood?"

"Not much, horses ain't got the same kind of loyalty as a dog. Dog is truly man's best friend. A horse ain't much better than a house cat when it comes to loyalty. Horses just as soon kick your head off if you let em. Cats are the same way; claw your eyes out if you don't scratch their ears the right way. As a matter of fact if house cats weighed forty pounds apiece, instead of ten, I think the human race would become extinct, killed off by house cats."

Well let me tell you, I almost fell off my horse laughing. In all my days there had never been a story such as this one told to me, not even in my childhood when Maw and Paw would tell us kid's nursery rhymes before bedtime.

Chester's Last Ride

"Go ahead, laugh your silly ass off Zeke, but you think about what I just said. It's true, every damn word of it. House cat look at you all cute and such leading you into dropping your guard. They're just biding their time thinking about how nice it would be to fillet you out. Next time one looks at you and starts a purring you just remember, he's wondering how you'd taste."

"Oh I don't doubt you in the least Haywood. I just never had so much philosophy throwed at me in so short a time." With that both me and Haywood had a good laugh.

"Alright Haywood, tell me the plan."

We rode another mile before Haywood said another word.

"We just crossed into Virginia about a half mile back. There's a spot where Kentucky, Virginia and Tennessee all three touch near a town called Middlesboro. We're about thirty miles northeast of that, getting near a place called Appalachia. We travel this trail another fifteen or twenty miles and then we head back north into Kentucky. We'll spend one more night in Virginia and then go back north. Take two days through Southeast Kentucky and we should be at the Conley Ranch two days after tomorrow. It should be perfect timing to make a run for Haskell's place. The last ten miles will be fast paced. Think that wounded dog of yours can keep up?"

I turned and looked at Ben. He walked with a limp and instead of leading he followed, not able to set the pace.

"I don't know Haywood. If we outrun him he may never find Paw's farm. He's never been in this country before."

"Well then you got a decision to make young Conley. We don't haul ass that last ten miles then we might be in a gun battle with those Baldwin-Felts boys."

"Haywood, if the tables were turned and it was Chester, your old hunting dog you were telling me about, what would you do?"

Haywood looked at me and grinned. "No way in hell would I ever leave Chester on the trail, trouble or not. Never split up a man from his dog. I reckon I would go down with guns a blazing before I would have ever left Chester behind."

"You just answered my question. You make the run in with your horse and Rusty. They won't be any trouble for you. Me, Hazel and Ben will make the best time we can. Maybe they won't take much notice if I have only one horse. They're expecting a man and two horses."

Haywood thought about this for a while and finally looked at me and said, "Might just work Conley, might just work. Only problem is that big dog of yours."

"What do you mean Haywood? Ben is just a dog, nobody will pay him no never mind."

"Boy, when is the last time you had a good look at that dog of yours, are you blind or just plain foolish? That is one monster that I don't think anyone could mistake. You might be just another drifter looking feller but that dog of yours is about as unique as a catfish with legs. Any of them Baldwin-Felts bastards sees you and that critter they will know all at once who you are and where you're going."

I just sat my saddle and tried to absorb what old man Haywood had just said. "Yeah I reckon you're right Haywood, Ben is one of the biggest dogs I've ever seen. I'm sure they got his description out on the telegraph wires same as mine." He reached over and patted his old trail hand on the head. Ben just looked up and gave Zeke that big Ben grin of his. "Hear that Ben, you're the most famous dog in this whole country. What do you think about that boy?"

Ben sat down and started scratching behind his ear with his back leg. Both Haywood and me started laughing as we watched.

Chester's Last Ride

"Looks like your dog has picked himself up a flea there Zeke, now what do you think about that, fleas before fame I reckon if you're a dog."

We rode on for another hour before either of us said another word.

At about three o'clock in the afternoon we came across a group of riders headed in our direction. Before they made it to our position Haywood told me to let him do the talking. Told me to just keep quiet and let him pry some information out of these men. When they got within twenty paces of us they pulled up and stopped. Seven men on seven mounts, no pack horses. These men weren't traveling far.

"Howdy old timer. Where you headed this evening?" A tall thin rider asked.

Haywood looked the bunch over and finally answered, "That way, the way you just came from."

The rider who had asked the question eased his horse toward us but the other six stayed where they were.

"That ain't really an answer now is it? I think I'll ask again and this time try to be more specific. Where are you two headed?"

With one smooth fluid motion Haywood pulled the Greener from its scabbard and twirled it toward the man's face. "This specific enough for ya?"

The man's horse was startled by the flurry created by Haywood's movement and bucked a little before backing up. None of the seven men tried to draw; they all sat their mounts and looked at the Greener. Haywood tapped Chester and the big horse began to step backward. I had drawn my Colt when Haywood had pulled the Greener. Rusty knew the move and began to back up too. When we were a good hundred feet from the seven riders Haywood headed Chester off the trail and up on higher ground. We passed the seven riders and came out a few hundred feet behind the spot where they still sat.

The seven riders had just sat their spot and waited for us to re-enter the trail. As we moved on up the trail Haywood shouted, "You boys have yourselves a good day."

"What was that all about Haywood?"

"I recognized two of the older men in that group, bounty hunters from down south around Georgia. My guess is they are headed for Kentucky to pick up a little work."

"You think they're going to be working for Baldwin-Felts?"

Haywood looked at me and then just rode on. After a couple of miles we started to relax a little, it didn't look like they were going to follow us. "My guess is that they heard about you. By now I suspect there's a good sized bounty on your head and they heard about it."

"Well if there is a bounty out on me then why didn't they try to take me in, they just let us go?" Zeke asked.

"If they have heard about a bounty they probably don't know what you look like yet. They're probably going into Kentucky to one of the Baldwin-Felts offices, probably London to pick up any dodgers that might be out. Right now they don't know any of the details about you and us being in Virginia helped some too I suspect. They wouldn't think it was us, not yet anyway."

"Haywood, I think we need to head into a town that has a telegraph and send out for some information. How close are we to a town of any size would you guess?"

"Well let me think a minute, probably Big Stone Gap, naw wait a minute, Norton is closer, Norton, Virginia. They got a set of train tracks pretty close and I would guess there is a telegraph office too. Me and you will start heading that way.

Probably is a dry goods store there too. We probably should provision a little heavier."

Zeke looked at his new trail partner and asked, "Why should we provision heavier Haywood. We got enough for probably three more days if we skimp."

"Ever since we ran upon them seven riders back a ways I been thinking. If we try to head back in from the east toward your paw's farm then we will probably meet up with the same reception we would get if we were traveling in from the west. Something tells me this Baldwin-Felts outfit is playing for keeps. My guess is they'll have the entire area covered with detectives and bounty hunters who would shoot you first and then not bother with any questions later."

Zeke thought this over for the longest time before adding, "We have a little problem then Haywood. I don't have any money. I spent the last I had in E-Town. Before that I seemed to have lost a bundle in St Louis. Used what money I had left to buy the few provisions that got me to your place, you got any money Haywood?"

Haywood laughed and slapped his thigh. "Yes I do. I got all kinds of money."

"Well then we're set. First town we get to with a telegraph and a general store we'll be in business," Zeke said.

"That's right Zeke, just find me a store that takes confederate money and I can buy everything we need."

Zeke looked at Haywood and realized they were in a fix. "Are you serious, confederate money? That's only good for starting campfires Haywood."

"All I got. I've been carrying it for more than twenty-five years, never had the heart to throw it away."

Nathan Wright

"Well what are we going to do now? In a few short days we are going to be getting a bit hungry. And don't forget, to send a telegraph costs money. They don't do it for free you know."

The two men rode on for several miles without a word being spoken. The mountains were getting bigger and steeper. Luckily the trails they were on had been used for years and either went around the mountains or just followed the valleys. About an hour before dark Haywood said they would stop.

"Stop here, we still got daylight left Haywood." Zeke said.

"That's right, we are going to stop here but we ain't staying. We build a camp fire and have our supper and coffee. As soon as it gets good and dark we leave the fire and move on for a few miles. We let anyone who might be looking for us think we are still here. We camp later, miles from this place and no fire. We'll be up and gone before anyone knows where we are."

"Where did you ever learn a trick like that Haywood?"

"In the army, we did it all the time. Yankee scouts kept a close eye on our movements and usually had an attack or ambush planned for us in the morning. Always had a good laugh thinking about them dumb Yank's sitting off a mile or two watching our campfires while we were moving away."

Supper that night was meager. We had provisions for at least two more days but Haywood said it would be best if we cut them in half. "Rather be a little hungry for four days than starving after two," he said.

It made good sense. The old man had been through a lot in his life and I was starting to think I could learn something from him if I paid close attention. After we finished I loaded up the fire with some big wood and then we moved out. Within less than an hour we were at our new campsite. It had good cover and water for the horses. Ben went off in search of a rabbit as me and Haywood took care of the horses.

Chester's Last Ride

Next morning we were up well before sunup and started taking care of the horses when Haywood said, "Well, I'll be dammed. Zeke come on over here and take a look at this."

I walked over to where Haywood was gathering up our stuff. The canvas sack that contained our food was gone. "What do you think happened to it, you think a critter came into camp and stole our food?"

"That would be my guess Zeke. Why didn't that wolf dog of yours do something about it?"

Zeke thought long and hard of how any varmint could sneak into camp with Ben there, and then he remembered."

"Just figured it out Haywood, bout three in the morning Ben heard something and took off out of camp. I knew it was a varmint because I had waked up and heard something off in the brush myself. Must have been two raccoons and while Ben was chasing one the other came into camp and took that canvas bag with our food inside. Only way it could have happened."

"I would say that sounds about right. Me and old Chester was hunting once and a raccoon came into camp and cleaned us out good. I could tell because of all the tracks. Those little bastards are sneaky, maybe that's why they all got them bandit eyes."

"Well I guess our four days of half rations just got dropped down to zero, now what are we going to do Haywood?"

"I'll tell you exactly what we're gonna do, we're gonna get hungry and tomorrow we are going to get even hungrier and so on. You can bet on it. But I wouldn't let it worry me much, the Lord will provide," Haywood said.

We saddled up and headed out of camp. As we rode I wondered how I had gotten into such a mess. A month and a half earlier I was chasing big brown bears on the other side of the Mississippi River and now I was in Virginia with bounty hunters after me and raccoons stealing the last of my food. I think the raccoons might be forgiven because stealing food is just what they do, but the bounty hunters were another story.

As we traveled Ben began to fall back a bit. I tried to slow the pace and Haywood understood. It might be another full week before that big cur was completely healed. It wasn't helping things that he had to do so much traveling. Any other time and I would have let him rest up but now that was out of the question. I think Ben even understood that there were men out here who were intent on doing us harm, after all he had already been shot once. All we could do was move along at the best pace we could. Ben tried to keep up but was always back a ways.

"You boys stop right there and don't try anything foolish," came a harsh voice from the tree line.

Both me and Haywood stopped and looked in the direction the voice had come from. Out of the trees came three men, each holding a handgun. Haywood looked at me and I knew he had something in mind. "What can we do for you fellers?" he asked.

"You can shut the hell up old man," one of the three said.

The three looked like trouble warmed over. Each was filthy and had at least a week's worth of beard.

"Step down off them horses and stand where we can see ya."

We did as we were told. They hadn't asked for our guns yet but we knew it was coming.

"That is some fine lookin horse flesh you two are riding. I would say by the looks of things the two of you stole those horses. Me and my friends here are constables and have the authority to shoot either, or both of you, over them horses. The state of Virginia has appointed the three of us as horse thief investigators."

Chester's Last Ride

The three had spread a few paces apart and it looked like they were nothing but outlaws looking to take what we had.

"Tell you what, me and my friends here are in need of some good horses and I think them three you got will do the job just fine."

One of the other two spoke next. "We can't just set them afoot. They will tell the first law they come to."

The three still hadn't asked Haywood or Zeke to throw down their weapons. It was possible that they hadn't seen the old revolver of Haywood's yet because it was partially covered by his loose hanging shirt. Zeke was wearing a tattered vest that came down well past his gun belt. Both did have long guns stuck down by their saddles and it was possible that the three thought these were the only weapons they had.

"We ain't gonna set them afoot, where these two are going they won't be needing any shoes. Willard how bout you take those three horses while I march these two horse thieves into them trees over there. Pete you come with me. Alright you two, march your asses into that stand of timber. If you're wondering whether we're gonna hang you or not don't worry. We ain't got time to hang no horse thieves; a knife works just as good and is a whole lot quieter."

Zeke and Haywood started toward the trees desperate for some kind of a plan. Just as they made it out of sight of the man who was holding the three horses they were told to stop. The man that had been doing all the talking pulled a long shiny knife from his boot and then with his left hand felt the edge as he grinned at Haywood and Zeke.

"Now you two turn around and let's get this over with, Pete you keep that gun ready in case either one struggles."

Ben had finally caught up with the horses and saw the three newcomers. He was traveling slow due to the injury to his hip from the gunshot. Being the curious type he didn't come running up to Zeke but stayed in the brush. Ben could see the guns and knew that it was up to him now to rescue the two. The dog was smart enough to wait for an opportunity. As Zeke and Haywood were marched into the woods the big dog stalked the two men holding the guns, when the knife came out of the boot Ben made his move. Ben went low and fast, moving toward the man holding the knife with all the speed his injured hip would allow.

About ten feet away from the outlaw he launched himself into the air and with teeth bared he caught the man holding the knife by the throat. He clamped down hard and his momentum knocked the man to the ground. The jaws of a dog have incredible bite pressure and on top of that Ben was a big dog. When both dog and man went down Ben landed on top and crushed the man's throat. Zeke had seen Ben come from the brush and knew it was now or never. He wheeled around and drew his Colt. He could see the man with the knife going down with Ben latched around his neck. The other man was about to shoot Ben but wasn't fast enough. Zeke fired off a quick shot which hit him in the shoulder. The heavy slug spun him around and he fell, releasing his gun.

Haywood ran back through the trees toward the horses. He had his old revolver at the ready when he came face to face with the third man. He had apparently heard the shot and came running. Just before he pulled the trigger Haywood leveled his gun and shot the man. He fell to the ground holding his stomach.

Zeke saw Haywood take away the third man's gun. He wasn't hit as bad as it first appeared. The bullet must have passed through his side and hadn't hit anything vital. "See what I told you Zeke, my eyesight ain't as good as it once was."

Chester's Last Ride

The man that was shot in the shoulder wasn't hit that bad either. He was sitting up and holding a dirty bandanna over the wound. Ben was sitting beside his victim making sure he couldn't cause any more trouble. Zeke went over and kicked away the knife. He rolled the man onto his back and almost threw up. Ben had done more that crush the man's throat, he had ripped a large chunk away and the sight was truly gruesome.

Haywood and Zeke marched the two men back onto the trail and checked on the three horses, they were fine but nervous. "Now Haywood, what do you think about that? Hell these trails in Virginia are as dangerous as anything in Kentucky. We done met two unfriendly groups of men this morning. And this bunch was intent on killing the both of us and then taking our horses."

"If it hadn't been for that monster of a dog we would both be dead right now. Makes me wish I had another hambone to give him," Haywood said. I truly believed Ben knew the word hambone because when Haywood said it he walked over to where we stood.

Zeke looked the two wounded outlaws over. Both had rope burns around their wrists. He checked the third man and found the same injuries to both his wrists as well. He looked at the man with the shoulder wound and asked, "What is your name mister?"

The man looked at Zeke and through gritted teeth he said, "Pete Monroe. What do you plan to do with us mister?"

Zeke looked at Haywood, "I don't know, Haywood what do you think we ought to do?"

"Well it would be my guess that these three are criminals. Them injuries to their wrists were probably caused by handcuffs. My best guess is that they escaped and that would explain why they ain't got any horses." As Haywood said this he was keeping a careful watch on the two. He assumed by the expression of both men that he was pretty close with his assumption.

Zeke looked at Pete and asked, "Is that right mister, are you two escaped criminals from the law?"

"We are. The three of us were framed with a robbery and killing that neither of us had anything to do with. That's why we escaped. They were going to hang the three of us and we're innocent. You can't hang an innocent man, just ain't right, ain't that so Buster?"

The man with the gunshot wound to his side was shaking his head in agreement.

"If the three of you are innocent then why were you going to kill me and my friend here and then take our horses?" Zeke asked.

Neither man responded.

"Well Haywood, what do you think we should do?"

"We can't leave them here and we can't take them with us, especially that dead one over there. I ain't too keen on draping him over one of these horses; I wouldn't do a horse that way. I say we march these two over there off the trail and use that big knife on each of em." Haywood winked at me as he said this, I knew the old man would never do something like that; he was probably just giving them something to worry about.

Just then we could hear horses coming hard. Within minutes five riders came around the trail and pulled up about ten yards back. Zeke and Haywood were standing beside the two wounded men. Haywood had retrieved his Greener from Chester and was standing ready to blow hell off its hinges if this bunch was as unfriendly as everyone else he had met so far this morning. All five were wearing badges.

"Easy boys with them guns. I'm Sheriff Roy Gannon and these are my deputies. Looks like you took care of what we been chasing for the last two days."

Zeke lowered his Colt and put it back in his holster. "Sorry Sheriff, this just hasn't been our day and five men on horses riding hard just looked like more trouble."

"Well, my guess is that it has been your day. Them two you got there are as bloodthirsty a pair as I have ever run up against. Everyone else they been around is mostly dead. There was another man traveling with them two, you didn't happen to see him around did you?" Gannon asked.

"He's lying on the other side of those trees with his throat torn out. If it hadn't been for that dog standing with the three horses over there we would be dead too," Haywood said.

"Bill, how about you and Kermit go over and take a look. Make damn sure he is dead, I've had about enough surprises from this bunch," Gannon said.

"Sheriff, we ran into a group of riders a few hours ago, a real unfriendly acting bunch. You know anything about them?" Zeke asked.

"Bounty hunters would be my guess. Seven men left out of town yesterday morning looking for this bunch, but mainly trying to get into Kentucky. I hear they got a bounty out on a feller over there that amounts to five thousand dollars," Gannon said.

"Did you say this bunch got a bounty reward Sheriff?" Haywood asked.

The sheriff smiled and said, "You heard me right. These two are a hundred apiece and if that is the other one over there you say that has got his throat tore out then that would be another hundred. You two wouldn't be interested would you?"

Haywood laughed and said, "We shore would, we had all our provisions stole in the middle of the night by some thieving raccoons and we were a mite worried about where our next meal was coming from."

Just then Bill and Kermit came back to the trail and said, "Looks like that big dog took care of the other one Sheriff. He's laying over there with his head bout bit off." Everyone looked at Ben; the big cur couldn't care less.

Sheriff Gannon wondered how the judge in town would feel about paying a bounty to a dog. "Well Kermit, these two ain't in much shape for riding. How about you and Bill head into town and bring back a buckboard, we'll need it anyway for the body. Burnis, you and Luther stay here until they get back with the wagon, and don't take any chances with these two. If either one of them gives you any trouble at all then shoot em, and after you shoot em both then shoot em again."

The two deputies galloped away toward town. Sheriff Gannon looked at Haywood and Zeke and asked if they would want to go into town to collect the bounty they had earned. Zeke was a little leery about going along after hearing earlier about the five thousand dollar bounty on a man in Kentucky; he suspected it was for him.

"Sheriff that hundred dollar bounty sounds pretty good to me, you reckon anybody in Kentucky has a bounty on them too?" Zeke asked hoping to see if what Haywood said was true.

"Don't matter what them hillbillies got over there. We don't honor any warrants from Kentucky, they stopped sending them over here years ago anyway. We don't send them from here to there either. Never met many people from Kentucky that knew how to read so why send em?"

Chester's Last Ride

Haywood grinned at Zeke. He was right about the warrant situation and he would rub it in later. "How far is it into town Sheriff?" Haywood asked.

After Gannon made sure his two deputies were situated and the two wounded outlaws tied up under a shade tree he answered. "No more than two hours at a reasonable trot. We done spent two days rattling every bush between here and there and this is as far as we got, town is close. Luther, you and Burnis try not to kill them two before the wagon gets back. Give them a little water after a while; I would shore hate it if they died before the judge gets to hang them tomorrow." With that Gannon turned his horse toward town and Zeke and Haywood followed.

"What did them three do that got them the death sentence Sheriff?" Haywood asked.

"They killed one of my deputies about a week ago. Judge Stratton held a quick trial and sentenced all three to hang. Day before yesterday another deputy of mine named Estill Hayes was bringing the three from the jail to the courthouse yard where we were planning to do the hanging. All three were wearing cuffs but somehow managed to overpower Estill and killed him with his own knife. Before we suspected anything was wrong they had a good twenty minute head start. They managed to slip out of town on foot unnoticed and we been looking for them ever since."

"How do you figure they got out of them cuffs Sheriff?" Haywood asked.

"Estill didn't have a key that's for sure. We never allow a key on the man who is bringing the prisoners over from the jail. My guess is that someone helped them. As a matter of fact I am sure someone helped them. We had some other prisoners locked up at the jail and it's my guess that one of them must have had a key hidden. Those keys are getting pretty common," the sheriff said.

"Any idea why them riders we met this morning was so damn hateful Sheriff?" Zeke asked.

"They might have thought you were some of these men you caught. Really though, neither of you got the look of them three. They were probably treating everyone they met the same way. Those seven riders knew about the three hundred dollars offered but my guess is they wanted to get to Kentucky as fast as they could. Couple of Baldwin-Felt detectives was at the saloon last night spouting off about some bloodthirsty killer from out west that is wanted over there. Said he was wanted for a bunch of murders and robberies and such. Just between the three of us I wouldn't put much weight into what a Baldwin-Felts man says. They're worse than anybody they're after."

Neither Zeke nor Haywood commented; glad to ride on in silence. A little over two hours later they rode into a town that for the most part was squeezed between some pretty large mountains. The lower part contained what looked to be a thriving business section. The lower slopes of the hills contained quite a few houses. The town square was bustling with people out and about. "We get a bunch of people from out in the surrounding areas on Saturday. The courthouse is where we're heading; maybe we can catch Judge Stratton there. You boys probably will want your reward money for food since that raccoon stole all you had last night." The Sheriff knew the coon had taken their food but couldn't resist a little humor, "Some of them raccoons are pretty smart, never had one outsmart me yet though."

Haywood wasn't going to let this pass unchallenged, "I wouldn't worry about it much Sheriff, you're still young."

Chester's Last Ride

All three men tied their mounts to a hitching post and headed inside. Before leaving Zeke told Ben to stay with Rusty and Hazel. The big cur pouted a bit but obeyed and sat down on the boardwalk where a big Pin Oak tree provided some shade. Haywood made sure to tie Chester another hitch post down to keep him away from the bossy Hazel.

The courthouse was a one story wooden structure with a stone faced exterior on the front only. There was a bell tower at the center and the big double doors were right underneath. There was a foyer and two more doors facing the front. "In through those two doors is the courtroom. The judge's office is down that hallway to the right, last door on the left."

The three men walked down by several offices where people were conducting business. Sheriff Gannon knocked on the judge's door and was soon met by a bailiff. Once inside we could see that the judge had several people in the side office he must have used as his conference room. There was some shouting and cursing going on but the judge had three bailiffs inside and it was apparent the shouting was being carried on between two attorneys; the judge was just sitting there listening. At times when the cursing got a little too loud, and a little too out of hand, the judge would speak and then the shouting was lowered a notch, but only slightly. Soon though the sounds grew loud again and the judge would have to speak once more. Finally after the better part of thirty minutes the two lawyers shook hands and went out the door laughing and backslapping. Lawyers were sure a strange bunch.

When Sheriff Gannon felt the time was right he knocked on the door jamb and asked if the judge had a few minutes.

"Sure thing Sheriff Gannon, how about we head over to my office though. I need a taste of something to settle my nerves after that little battle that just took place. You know being a judge would be a lot more fun if it weren't for all the lawyers I have to put up with." Both he and the sheriff laughed at this.

"Who you got with you there Sheriff, they look like strangers to me?" the judge asked.

"These two men captured the three no-goods that killed my deputies' judge. They are traveling with one hell of a dog and from what they told me it was the dog that saved them from getting killed themselves," the sheriff said.

"A big dog, well where is this dog? I want to meet him," the judge said.

The sheriff looked at both Zeke and Haywood. "Are you sure Judge, I mean this is one big dog."

"Well yes I'm sure, I like dogs and if this one helped capture them three murdering bastards then I want to see him; that is unless he doesn't like judges." Again the judge laughed.

"Oh he likes judges, he likes them with a side of taters and some sweet tea," Haywood said. After everyone stopped laughing Haywood assured the judge that Ben was a good judge of character.

"Well now in that case I definitely want to see him. I want to see if I pass his character test," the judge said.

As soon as Zeke went outside to get Ben the judge sent one of his bailiffs to get what was left of his lunch, which consisted of mash potatoes and roast beef.

Haywood thought about this and asked, "Judge, if I didn't know better I would say you're trying to buy Ben's vote. I believe he would lick the devil's hand for a bite of roast beef."

The judge grinned at Haywood. "Well how do you think I got elected to my job four times in a row, I know how to please the voters."

The bailiff came in with what was left of the judge's lunch and sat it on the table. Within a couple of minutes Zeke walked in with Ben right on his heels. Both the judge and his bailiff were shocked at the size of the dog.

"Kind of makes me wish I hadn't eaten so much of my lunch. Mr. Conley, do you think it would be alright if I gave your dog a bite of roast beef and some mashed potatoes?" The judge asked.

"That would be just fine judge. We've all been on short rations for the last couple of days," Zeke said.

The judge stood and walked around the table. When he picked up the tray that contained the food Ben's ears perked up. The closer the judge got to Ben the slower he went. He gingerly sat the tray down on the floor and backed up a couple of steps. Ben looked at the food and then at the judge. The next thing Ben did even surprised Zeke; he walked around the tray and went over to the judge. I could see fear in the judge's eyes as Ben walked right up to him and then licked his hand. With that accomplished Ben went back to the tray and started eating.

The judge took a white handkerchief from his pocket and started mopping his forehead. He then went over and sat down exhausted. I could tell that he had been very frightened when Ben came over to him and no doubt the extreme level of fear he experienced had tired him out. No one had said a word as they watched Ben finish what was on the tray. When finished he walked over to the judges chair and sat down beside him.

Judge Stratton was overjoyed and reached down and patted Ben on top of the head. He had just made friends with the largest animal, other than a horse, that he ever had the experience of associating with. I knew that Ben had just helped out both Haywood and myself. It never hurts to have a judge on your side.

Stratton looked up from Ben and asked, "Where are you two staying while you're in Norton?"

The sheriff took the liberty to put in a word for us. "Judge, they just got into town. With your approval we need to talk to you about a matter or two without anyone else around if that would be alright?"

"That would be perfectly alright Sheriff." The judge sent the three bailiffs away and then he got up and closed the door to his office. Zeke and Haywood took the time to explain everything that had happened in the last few weeks. Zeke felt it might be a mistake but he knew he had to tell his side of the story to someone just in case anything happened to him before he made it back to Floyd County. The sheriff then told the judge his take on what Zeke and Haywood had been through that morning and when he was finished the judge just sat behind his big desk and thought about what he had just heard.

After a minute or two both Zeke and Haywood thought they had made a mistake by telling the story.

Judge Stratton had a disturbed look on his face and everyone in the room thought he didn't believe the story he had just heard. The judge reached into his desk and pulled out four thick cigars and passed them out, keeping one for himself.

"Gentlemen, please light up and let's figure out what our next move is," Judge Stratton said.

The tension had decreased by at least half but no one still knew what the judge was going to do.

"First of all, let me say that I know William Haskell Conley and as a matter of fact he was sitting in the very same chair you occupy now Haywood a little over a week ago. I know about the happenings in Floyd County. I advised Haskell to head on back home and allow me to contact the Federal Judge in Cincinnati. I doubted if he could make it without being overtaken by these Baldwin-Felts people he spoke of. As a matter of fact, I helped spread the rumor that he was still heading north and had somehow disappeared." The judge stopped talking and lit his cigar.

"So my paw isn't missing?" Zeke said.

Haywood thought this was a little more than he would allow himself to believe so he asked, "If he ain't missing then where is he? I talked to one of his sons just three days ago and he told me that Haskell had gone to Cincinnati a few weeks ago and hadn't been heard from since."

The judge smiled and continued. "Then our little ruse has worked. When he left here I told him to make it home and allow me to spin a rumor that he had gone missing. The only people that know the real story are the sheriff here and myself, along with his attorneys in Beckley, West Virginia. I felt he would be safer if no one knew where he was."

Zeke now spoke up, "Then how did he make it back home without being apprehended by the detective agency. They would like nothing more than to capture my father and make him sign over his property."

"That is where Sheriff Gannon here comes into the story. Sheriff I will allow you to finish."

The sheriff was wearing the face of a very good poker player. "I deputized him. He rode with me and two more of my deputies all the way to Wheelwright, Kentucky. We had to travel south through Tennessee due to all the flooding in Kentucky but we made it and no one was the wiser."

"They thought Paw was a deputy from Virginia? That doesn't make any sense. What would four deputies from Virginia be doing in Kentucky?" Haywood asked.

"Well, the way I see it one badge looks pretty much like all the others, that is unless it's a marshal's badge. No one asked us any questions and we didn't volunteer any information. You would be surprised at how far out of the way people will ride to avoid four heavily armed men wearing badges," the sheriff said.

Haywood started laughing and was barely able to stop. "You hear that Zeke, these two men have done your father a great service, I would even venture as far as to say they probably saved his life."

The judge was sitting in his chair laughing and rubbing Ben's head. Ben had fallen asleep shortly after his meal and during his head rub. He was one happy dog.

Zeke looked at Sheriff Gannon. "Sheriff, as we rode into town and told you our story you never mentioned anything about the trouble in Floyd County or the fact that you had helped my father."

"That's right Conley. This whole plan was arranged by the judge here and also by Mr. Conley, your father. I let you and Haywood talk for two reasons. Number one is that I wanted to hear your side of the story to see if I really trusted you. Number two is that I take orders from Judge Stratton and wasn't at liberty to give out any information, or for that matter to even let you know that I had helped get your paw home safely. For all I knew the two of you might have been operatives for the Baldwin-Felts Detective Agency. I believed the both of you but it was the judge's plan and I do take my orders from him," the sheriff said.

Zeke looked at Judge Stratton. "Thanks Judge for all you've done for my father."

"It was my pleasure. I have known your father for many a year and I feel like I know your friend Haywood there too, although I have never met him in person until now. As a matter of fact I have sampled some of that whiskey you make

Haywood and I have to say, for something that burns like hell going down, it is still about as smooth as anything I have ever drank, I am sad to say that in my time I have drank a lot. You wouldn't have a bottle out there on one of your horses would you?"

Haywood smiled and told the judge, "We don't but I promise to send you a couple of jars as soon as I make it back home, you can count on it."

"Well what's the plan now Judge? We've told you about the murder charge against me. I can't actually take the train back to Floyd County with that much bounty on my head, and we'll be caught for sure if we go by horse," Zeke said.

Haywood and Zeke both knew the judge was a smart man and probably had some sort of plan in mind.

"Well it's for certain that you need to make it back to your father's place, he can use the help right now. If they catch up with you beforehand then you can figure on getting arrested and then tried, that is assuming you don't get lynched by that outlaw detective agency first. I might be able to help with a few of the details though," the judge said.

Both Zeke and Haywood noticed the way the judge described the Baldwin-Felts Detective Agency and felt he probably disliked it as much as they did.

The judge spoke next, "I think the best thing to do is for me to contact the lawyers your father uses and see if they have any suggestions. They are already aware of the situation, at least up until yesterday. I have been sending them at least one telegram a day and on some days two. Why don't you boys go and get you something to eat and let me put together a message. I'll meet the three of you at the telegraph office in about an hour. How does that sound?"

Both Zeke and Haywood shook the judge's hand. As they left Ben got up and rubbed his head on the judge's pants leg. It was his way of showing he liked the judge.

"See there sheriff, this dog is a good judge of character. He done voted me into my next term." The judge was still laughing as Ben and the three men left the office.

"Come on over to the jail and I'll get you the money you earned for them three hard-cases you nabbed this morning," the sheriff said. "It will actually be a voucher but you can take it to the bank and they will draw the cash from the account."

The jail was just around the corner from the big courthouse. It was made of stone and had a front porch. Zeke thought of the two old checker players from a couple of years back and the argument they were having, both dead now.

Inside was the usual arrangement, big front room with a heavy wooden door that led to the cells in the back. The sheriff went to his desk and pulled out some papers. He filled out three, one for each man that had been apprehended.

"This is the bounty receipts for the three men. We can take them back to the courthouse and the clerk there will sign all three. After that it's just a short trip to the bank. They will make the payment to you out of the county's general account. Within thirty minutes your raccoon problem will be over," the sheriff said with a chuckle.

"Yeah, I reckon that raccoon did put us on starvation rations didn't he?" Haywood told the sheriff.

With the paperwork complete and some jingle in our pockets we waited for the judge at the telegraph office. When he came in the door he asked how we had enjoyed our meals. The sheriff informed him that we had been too busy so far to get anything to eat.

Chester's Last Ride

"Well, that just won't do now will it? Here Zeke, look over this telegram I wrote out for your father's lawyers and if it suits you then we can send it right away. After that how about I buy supper for all of us, that includes you too Sheriff. It will give me time to explain what I got in mind," the judge said.

"Well Judge, I don't know about these other two fellers but I like your plan. Don't ever remember having my supper bought by a judge before," Haywood said.

"Then it's settled," The judge said, and then he looked down at Ben. "And for Ben here I think I'll see if the cook can fix him up another tray with all the fixings, and it won't be any leftover tray like he got in my office earlier either. I figure whatever we get to eat is the same thing he'll get." The judge thought a second and then added, "Does Ben like beer?" They all had a laugh at that last remark although in the back of his mind Haywood figured Ben could hold his beer as well as the next man.

Zeke read the note the judge had prepared and said it looked fine. The judge gave it to the man that worked the keys and said to put the charges on the county's tab.

"The five of us will be over at the Steak and Syrup, when you get a reply please hand deliver it to me. As of now this message, and anything pertaining to it, are to be considered sealed by the court. No one sees or hears about what you send or receive concerning this matter except me. Is that understood?" the judge asked the man working the telegraph.

The man said he understood as he counted the men in front of him. "Judge, you said that five of you were going to eat but there are only four that I count."

Judge Stratton reached down and patted Ben on top of the head. "This is the fifth." With that said we all headed out the door.

Nathan Wright

"Judge, did you say steak and syrup in there? Now I don't want to sound ungrateful but that don't seem to be a pleasant supper. Don't get me wrong, I like steak and I love syrup, but I ain't ever tried the two together," Haywood said.

"Not together Haywood. That's just the name of the restaurant we're going to. They serve a great breakfast and they also serve a great supper, hence the name Steak and Syrup," the judge said.

"Well back in Kentucky we always have our breakfast first so why ain't the name Syrup and Steak?" Haywood asked.

"Oh, I really don't know Haywood, guess I never gave it much thought other than the fact that Steak and Syrup seems to roll off the tongue a little better," Judge Stratton said.

Again Haywood misunderstood. "Well judge, I guess I will just take your word on it, but if it makes the steak too sweet then I'm scraping the syrup off."

Zeke truly thought Ben understood what the judge was talking about better than Haywood.

"Judge, if Haywood and me could have a few minutes to take our horses to a livery then we will join you for supper. Which stable would you recommend?" Zeke asked.

"Just take them over to Ezra's place, it's close and he is very good with horses. Sheriff, how about you showing them where it is and I'll meet you in a little while," the judge said.

We left the judge and went to where we had tied Hazel, Rusty, and Chester. Ben ran up to the three horses and sat between Hazel and Rusty. I sometimes wondered if Ben actually thought he was a horse instead of a dog. With thoughts of food on our minds we hustled on over to the stable and paid the hostler. He had a nice looking operation and I was confident the horses would be well taken care of.

238

Chester's Last Ride

Haywood was hobbling along on his peg leg and I could tell he had picked up the pace a bit. We hadn't eaten anything since the night before and that was when we both had decided to go on half rations, not knowing that a raccoon would steal every last bite of food we had during the night.

"You two walk like you got all the time in the world, as for me my days are numbered and I don't intend on spending them following behind to young fellers that act like they're going to live forever. And more than that I'm hungry and the judge done promised to pay. Now move your asses, the both of you," Haywood said to Zeke and the sheriff as he hobbled past both at a trot.

"My goodness, what a bunch of mean talk that is there Haywood, you get a couple of dollars in your pocket and all of a sudden you're better than the rest of us?" the sheriff said.

"Not better sheriff, just faster, now put some quick in your step if you intend on eating at the same table as me and the judge."

The sheriff looked at Zeke and whispered. "How long has it been since you two last ate, he said yesterday but Haywood there is moving along like it's been a week?"

"I think he really just wants to show us youngsters that he is still fast on his foot, get it, foot." Both Zeke and the sheriff had a good laugh as Haywood made his way to the front door of the Steak and Syrup and went on in.

Once inside they found Haywood and the judge seated at the far back wall pretty much away from everybody else. The judge was holding a sheet of paper and looked pleased as we sat down. I was surprised when they let Ben follow us back to the table. Most eatin places wouldn't allow a dog anywhere near the front door.

"Howdy boys, what took you two so long? Me and Haywood here have already finished and were just about to leave," the judge said.

Sheriff Gannon looked at the table and said, "Looks like you two must have been eating finger food cause I don't see any plates. Me and Conley here are gonna need something a little more substantial for our supper; after all we work for a living." The judge started laughing so hard that two or three of the other patrons were starting to look our way.

It didn't take long before a lady came by and spoke to the judge and the sheriff. The judge said not to ask the three newcomers what they wanted to eat because he doubted if any of the knuckle-draggers knew how to talk. "Just bring five specials out here and make it snappy I got judge stuff to be doing."

The lady winked at the judge and said; "Now Judge Stratton, you really do know how to talk to a lady."

"That's right Sara, and there's more where that came from." When Stratton said this he winked back at her.

As the lady named Sara started for the kitchen she stopped and turned back toward the table. "Did I hear you correctly, you said bring five specials. Are you expecting somebody else to join you?"

The judge reached over and patted Ben on top of the head. He had walked over and sat down beside the judge's chair, Sara hadn't seen him. When Ben stood up Sara screamed.

"My goodness judge how did that bear get in here?"

"Oh Sara, this is my new dog Ben. He will be eating here from now on with me. If by some chance he ever shows up and I ain't with him just take his order and put it on my tab." Again Judge Stratton laughed until I thought he was going to pass out. I even thought it was a little funny myself.

Chester's Last Ride

"Judge, would it be okay if your new dog ate out on the back porch, might be a little more pleasant for the other guests, and a lot less scary?" Sara said.

The judge looked at me and said, "Conley, I have seen some people in here eating that look a lot less presentable than Ben but she does have a point. You mind if I take him out the side door over there and let him eat on the porch. He might like it better out there anyway."

"He's your dog judge," I said.

The judge got up and Ben followed him outside. Within seconds he was back. "That is not only the biggest dog I have ever seen but he is also the most intelligent. I pointed to a spot on the porch and said sit. He walked over there and sat down. If more people had Ben's manners then I would be out of a job."

Wasn't long before Sara brought out four big plates and sat one in front of each of us. She soon came back with another plate loaded with biscuits and cornbread, along with glasses of sweet tea. Haywood looked at me and then dug right in. I could tell the old man was getting pretty hungry because I was getting hungry myself. The four of us ate like freshly released prisoners.

I went out a time or two to check on Ben. He was working on a plate full of spare ribs; by the looks of it they must have given him a portion large enough to feed a crowd of miners.

"Judge, I noticed you reading a message when we came in. That wouldn't have been a response from the telegram you sent earlier would it?" Zeke asked.

"It is, and it contains what I believe is good news." The judge was speaking in a tone just low enough for us to hear but not anyone else in the room.

"The attorneys up in Beckley have a runner at the telegraph office that takes the messages to them and then immediately brings back a reply. They sent this to me not more than fifteen minutes after I telegraphed them."

The judge took a long drink of tea and then continued. "Let's finish our meals here and then go back to my office in the courthouse, and sheriff, you need to come along with us because the message pertains to you as well."

The sheriff indicated that he would, but then what other response could he give. We finished and the judge, good to his word, had the bill put on his tab. I pulled out a one dollar bill and laid it on the table for Sara. She had taken real good care of us, but then again there was a judge sitting there.

After we left the restaurant I whistled and Ben came running around the corner. It looked like he had barbecue sauce all over his face. When the judge seen him he again laughed, I noticed the judge liked to have a little fun from time to time. He would probably even laugh when he hung the two low-life outlaws tomorrow.

It was getting late in the evening and he had to use a key to get inside the courthouse. It was a much different place from when we were there earlier. The building was almost spooky without the hustle and bustle of day; very little light from the oil lamps on the street outside could penetrate the darkness. We followed the judge as he made his way to his back office. Once there he went about lighting his lamps and soon the room was lit up nicely.

"Gentlemen, please have a seat at the table over there while I get something from my cabinet," the judge said.

As we found a seat the judge opened a glass faced book cabinet that sat against one wall. From a bottom shelf that wasn't visible through the glass he grabbed a bottle of whiskey and four glasses. As he carried these to the table he looked at me and asked if Ben drank?

Chester's Last Ride

"Never while he's on duty," I told the judge. Ben had come in with us and was already snoozing on the judge's big rug that sat in front of his desk. I think that big plate of ribs he ate over behind the restaurant had pretty much done the big dog in.

Judge Stratton sat four glasses on the table and a bottle of Old Shawhan Bourbon. After he poured a generous portion into the four glasses Zeke picked up the bottle to read the label. He spoke out loud as he read.

Old Shawhan
Kentucky Straight Bourbon
Whiskey

86 Proof
4 Years Old

"This stuff any good Judge?" Zeke asked.

"Well, I don't think it compares to the shine that Haywood makes but it will do. Go ahead and have a taste and tell me what you think."

The three men took a taste from their glasses as the judge watched. Haywood was holding up pretty good but it looked like Sheriff Gannon and Zeke grimaced as they shut their eyes and tried to live through the pain. The sheriff must have prided himself on his toughness. He squinted and said through gritted teeth, "Not bad Judge." He let out a small cough and then said again, "Not bad at all."

Haywood tipped up his glass and finished it. "Thanks Judge, I believe I could use another little taste if you don't mind."

The judge poured more of the reddish brown liquid into Haywood's glass. Zeke was yet to speak, or open his eyes for that matter.

"Maybe one of you needs to check on that youngster over there," Stratton said.

Zeke finally opened his eyes and looked at the judge. With a hoarse low voice he managed to say, "No more for me Judge."

Haywood started laughing, "These children don't know what's good. You think this is strong stuff Zeke? In my professional opinion I would consider this 'woman's whiskey'. The stuff I brew back in Kentucky is so strong it don't even need a glass."

The sheriff had gotten back sufficient breath to ask the judge what the plan was. After Haywood finished his second glass he reached over and took the one from Zeke.

"Give me that before you hurt yourself."

The judge felt he had let the three have enough of his expensive whiskey so he recapped it and slid the bottle to the side of the table. "The message I got from the attorneys up in Beckley said that I should handle the situation here as I saw fit. They are working with the Federal Judge over in Cincinnati and said things were hopefully going to work out. The only trouble was time. It is a long way from here to there and the trouble is already there. The attorneys, and the Federal Judge, are working as fast as they can." The judge stopped to take a sip of his bourbon.

The sheriff finally managed to finish his drink and slid the glass to the side, glad that the ordeal was over. "Well, it sounds like the matters in Kentucky are starting to head in the right direction Judge, or is there more?"

"There is. As far as the federal authorities are concerned it looks like the lawyers have gotten their attention. The problem now is whether they can intervene in time to prevent bloodshed. It still won't settle the legal issues that seem to be at the bottom of everything, that will be a job for a bunch of lawyers and then for a jury to decide. I have no doubt that William Conley has valid deeds to all the property he possesses."

Again the judge stopped to taste his drink.

Zeke finally caught sufficient wind to put out the fire that the strong bourbon had started in his throat. "Judge, I need to get back to Floyd County. If there is going to be trouble at home then I need to be there to lend a hand."

"I agree Zeke. The only problem is that the trouble is already there and as we speak bad things are happening," the judge said.

"Do you have any idea how these two can get that far inside Kentucky without getting killed Judge?" the sheriff asked, but he already knew the answer.

"Well I am glad you asked Sheriff. The way we got Mr. Conley back to Floyd County worked pretty well. How would you feel about running that little diversion again?"

"I will do exactly as you tell me Judge, but do you really think that will work twice?" Gannon asked.

Judge Stratton thought about the question for a minute before he answered. "This time will be more difficult. I think they finally figured out how Mr. Conley got home last week. I have heard that they knew some Virginia lawmen assisted him and from what I gather the Baldwin-Felts agency has had some of the local sheriffs over there on the payroll for some time. I don't believe the sheriff in Floyd County is under their spell but you can never tell. All this information comes from the lawyers up in Beckley. They have had a few men there for some time for the sole purpose of checking out Mr. Conley's land deeds to make sure there isn't any loopholes. These same men are also keeping tabs on the elected officials and all this information goes directly to Beckley."

"If this detective agency is so big and powerful in Kentucky then how is the information getting to Beckley in the first place? They can't be using the telegraph in Floyd County." Haywood said.

"The county seat is a little town called Prestonsburg and you are correct in your assumption Haywood that the telegraph office there might be compromised. The information is sent by horse and rider to Williamson, West Virginia, and then telegraphed on to Beckley. The attorneys there know a thing or two about the value of up to date information and how to convey it without their opponents finding out," Judge Stratton said.

Zeke was glad to be getting all this help from the judge and the sheriff but something had really started to nag at him, what was a Virginia judge and a Virginia sheriff doing helping people from Kentucky?

"Judge, I need to ask something and I will try to word the question as not to offend anyone. Let me first say that I appreciate what you have done for my paw and also for me and Haywood. What I can't figure out is why you are doing all this; after all, we are from Kentucky."

The judge looked at Sheriff Gannon and said, "You told me they would figure out sooner or later that we are not in Kentucky." The sheriff laughed.

"I will tell you the reason and let me say up front that the question you just asked is exactly what you should have asked. First of all both me and the sheriff here believe in law and order. We are from Virginia but let me ask you a question, should I sit on my hands while a wrong is being committed even if it is in another state and I can do something about it?" the judge asked.

"No sir, I reckon not," Zeke said.

Chester's Last Ride

"Secondly, your father is a friend of mine. He may have never mentioned me but just the same we respect each other for what we have both accomplished and for our values. And lastly I would like to add that I am in the running for a federal judgeship myself and in doing so I must prove that I can provide justice not only in Virginia but in other states as well. The sheriff also has his resume out and about. He is pursuing a post as U.S. Marshal. I recommended him last year and I believe there is not another man more qualified. So you might say there are personal, and professional, reasons for the sheriff and myself to get involved."

Zeke was extremely pleased with what he had just heard. He had started to worry why these two strangers had wanted to help but now it all made sense. "Judge, I understand things more clearly now and let me just say thanks."

"You're entirely welcome. I hope I have convinced you that the sheriff and myself are both here to help."

"So what do you recommend we do Judge?" Zeke asked.

"With Sheriff Gannon's approval I would like to send you and Haywood back to Floyd County first thing tomorrow morning, along with the sheriff and one of his deputies. And I would like to add that the deputy will be appointed as sheriff as soon as the sheriff here is named the new U.S. Marshal. You see, everyone involved has a vested interest in doing what is right," the judge said.

It didn't take Zeke and Haywood long to figure out that their trip into Floyd County had been secured by two complete strangers.

The judge went on to ask, "Sheriff, can you and Deputy Fitch be ready to leave at first light?"

"It won't be a problem Judge. We will need to provision for four days though," Sheriff Gannon said.

"Go to Hoss's house and tell him you need to provision for a little trip. Don't let him know where you are going or who will be going with you. Try to get out of town tomorrow before first light so as not to let anyone see you if you can," the judge said.

Zeke asked, "What about us Judge? We don't even have a place to stay tonight and I really don't think it would be wise to check into a hotel this late, they would want me to sign the register."

The judge thought about this for a moment and then he smiled. "You, Haywood, and Ben, can stay right here in the courthouse. We got a couple of bunks in the basement where the bailiffs stay sometimes when we have a vicious trial. No one will be here in the morning so no one will know. How does that sound?"

Haywood spoke up now, "Sounds good to me Judge, and anyway, Ben has already staked out his claim to your big rug over there."

"Zeke, you go with the sheriff and secure the supplies you and Haywood will need for two days ride, use a little of that bounty money you earned this morning. The sheriff can get what he and Burnis needs and put it on the county's tab. Alright boys let's get to moving, it's late and we got stuff that needs to be gittin done."

Sheriff Gannon started for the door and then turned back to the judge. "Do the attorneys know about this plan Judge? If things go bad then we might need their help?"

"They don't know all of it but I am going over to the telegraph office now to send a wire. I like sending telegrams at night anyway, less people up and about," the judge said.

As the three men headed for the front door to the courthouse Haywood uncorked the lid to the bottle of bourbon and poured himself a little taste. "All this conspiring has made me a little thirsty," he said to himself.

Zeke and the sheriff headed down a couple of back streets toward the store owner's house. As they walked Zeke asked, "Sheriff did you see the two men standing across from the courthouse?"

"I did, I never thought much about it until I noticed they were trying way too hard to act like they didn't notice us. Hell, the best way to go unseen is to be right out in the street, looks a lot less suspicious that way."

"Are they from around here Sheriff?"

"Never seen either of them before in my life, you think they were keeping an eye on the courthouse Zeke, I mean they were standing close enough to a street lamp that I could make out their faces."

"I don't know why but for some reason I think they might have been right at the courthouse trying to listen through the walls, when we came out it was all they could do to get back cross the street," Zeke said.

"The judge has a bad habit of talking loud when he believes in what he is saying, which is all the time."

"Well Sheriff, I say we keep an eye out for them two between now and the time we leave in the morning," Zeke said as quietly as possible.

The two men made it to the store owner's house and the sheriff knocked on the front door. Within a minute a big man wearing bright red suspenders over his shirt answered the door.

"Well howdy Sheriff, what brings you out so late tonight?"

"Hoss, I hate to bother you at such an hour but we need some supplies from your store. Judge Stratton sent me over."

Nathan Wright

"Sheriff, you know it ain't no bother, and if Judge Stratton has something to do with it then that makes it all the less bother. Let me get my coat and hat and we'll head on over," Hoss said.

As he came out onto the porch the sheriff told him that they needed to be quiet about it. There might be some people about that are watching and listening. He also told him not to mention in the morning about what he and Zeke had gotten. That seemed to excite the store owner a little. Funny how something as simple as not spreading the word could get some people worked up.

"You got it Sheriff, we off on some sort of top secret trip again?" Hoss asked.

"Maybe Hoss, but it is real important that we keep everything quiet," Sheriff Gannon told him.

Somehow I wondered if telling Hoss to keep quiet was the best way to go about it. I was sure everyone in town would know what we got, when we got it, and what time we left town before the sun came up.

On the way to the general store Zeke and Sheriff Gannon kept a close eye on the side streets and alleys looking for the two men they had spotted when they left the courthouse earlier. Just as they were in sight of the store Gannon said.

"Zeke, take a look over there by the blacksmith shop."

Zeke looked right handed at a squatty looking building that had two sheds with open fronts where the blacksmith had his big fire pit and chimney. In the shadows he could see a couple of shadowy outlines, but no movement.

"You see anything that looks like it might be looking back Zeke?" the sheriff asked.

Zeke squinted harder and finally made out what it was the sheriff was talking about.

"Yeah Sheriff, I see what looks like two men. You think we should investigate?"

They walked on a few more steps.

"Let's just get the supplies we need and see if they are still there when we come out. Just watching us ain't against the law but if they follow us back to the livery then I might want to have a little talk with em," the sheriff said.

Zeke and Gannon quickly picked out what they would need. Zeke paid for enough to last him and Haywood two days and the sheriff got enough for four days, he put his on the county's tab. When the three men came out of the store there wasn't a soul to be seen on the street or even hiding in the blacksmith's shop.

Once the supplies had been taken to the livery Zeke went back to the courthouse and collapsed in one of the bunks that had been promised by the judge. Haywood had already given up for the night and Ben was still asleep on the big rug in the judge's office. The next morning everyone was up early and at the livery an hour before sunrise. By the time the horses were ready and the supplies loaded the four men, and also Ben, were able to make it out of town before first light.

The four kept a close eye on the trail behind them that led back to the town of Norton, Virginia. Sheriff Gannon had filled Haywood and Fitch in on the sighting of the two strangers from the previous night. Hopefully the four men had slipped off unnoticed this morning, but it wasn't meant to be. Ben stayed within earshot of the group of riders and could always tell which way they were heading. Even if he couldn't hear them he could always track the horses with his strong sense of smell.

It was nearly noon when the riders passed a run-down little store in a more run-down little town. The four men tied up the five horses and went inside. In the back they found a big flat top stove with any number of cookers on top, each with a different vegetable inside. It smelled good so the four men sat down at a table that seemed to have one leg shorter than the others, it rocked back and forth. As hungry as they were it really didn't matter.

"What'll it be?" A thin man wearing a cooking apron asked.

The four ordered a plate of vegetables along with boiled chicken, which the cook said was the meat of the day. Once the food was put on the table the four ate in a hurry in order to get back on the trail and make it to where Sheriff Gannon wanted to set up camp for the night. At different times one of the four riders would go back up to the front of the store to check on the horses. Each time they could see Ben sitting contently between Rusty and Hazel. Zeke had ordered a big chicken breast extra and had taken it outside so the dog would be finished when they were ready to leave. It had become his habit to share what he ate with Ben.

After the men paid and were just about to exit the building they saw a group of riders just outside on horseback. None of the four had worn their badges in order to try and not draw attention to themselves. Sheriff Gannon looked the situation over and turned to the other three.

"I think this would be a good time to put on our badges boys. It looks like that bunch outside might have business with us and I want to let them know up front that we represent the law," the sheriff said as he pinned on his badge.

Zeke pinned on his marshal's badge which neither of the other three knew anything about. The sheriff had deputized Zeke and Haywood just for the purpose of getting them out of Virginia and into Kentucky and in doing so had given them both deputy badges. Everyone knew that a man who possessed a Deputy U.S. Marshal badge had jurisdiction anywhere in the United States.

Gannon looked at the star on Zeke's chest and said, "Maybe if we get out of this little situation waiting on us outside you could tell me about you being a Deputy Marshal."

Zeke looked at the three and said, "It would truly be my pleasure, I just hope I get the chance."

Sheriff Gannon went out first followed by Deputy Fitch and Haywood who was also wearing the badge that Gannon had given him that morning. Zeke went out last and the four spread out in front of the store.

When Ben saw the group of riders come up to where the horses were tied he stood up, not knowing if this new group was going to behave themselves or not. When he saw the way Zeke and the others had faced up to the group he stepped forward and let out a low growl making sure everyone knew he was there. All it would take to start a stampede among the riders was for Ben to attack the horses they sat on. Ben knew how to handle men on horses.

The newcomers in front of the four were also wearing badges, but these were Baldwin-Felts badges which carried no authority and were only used to intimidate people. The man who now spoke was wearing a black suit of clothes not that much different from what a lawyer, or a judge, might wear. Again Zeke thought this was meant to intimidate anyone they ran up against.

"Well, it looks like the four of you got yourselves some badges in that store there. I can tell you right now that we don't put much weight in anyone who either bought a badge or for that matter stole one. The four of you throw your hands in the air and prepare to be arrested," the man in black said.

Nathan Wright

Before the words had finished ringing in everyone's ears Gannon and his three traveling companions drew down on the riders. There were nine in all and each was wearing the detective badges that were starting to be so hated in Kentucky. Gannon spoke next to the startled riders.

"Mister, I don't know your name and don't really care but unless you and your girlfriends there don't raise your hands then I might just shoot your ass right off that horse you're sitting on."

The man dressed in black slowly raised his hands. It was apparent that he had bullied his way before and this might have been the first time he had run into anyone that didn't respect his detective badge. Once all the men had their hands high over their heads Gannon spoke again.

"There you go, that wasn't too difficult was it? Now I'll tell you what we are going to do, I am going to point at one of you at a time and when I do I want that man, and that man only, to slowly use his left hand and unbuckle his gun belt and then drop it on the ground."

Gannon started pointing and guns started dropping. Once all nine had been disarmed of their pistols and belts Gannon stepped among the group and pulled the rifles from the gun rugs that hung by each saddle. Only five of the men had Winchesters which wasn't really unusual. Some men just never carried rifles.

The man in black decided to speak again. "You are in some serious trouble now mister. This group of men you're holding guns on has been appointed by the governor himself to hunt down and arrest anyone we think is associated with that bastard in Kentucky who goes by the name of Haskell Conley. It is our..."

Chester's Last Ride

Before the man could finish what he was saying Zeke rushed over and drug him off his horse. When he had him eye to eye he said, "I like to be face to face when a man is cussing my paw. Now I invite you to continue."

The man looked at Zeke and said, "Are you telling me that you are Zeke Conley, the man who murders innocent store clerks?"

Zeke was smaller than the man in front of him but that made no difference. The fight was on and it would be a short one. Zeke hit him with a flurry that startled everyone, even himself. When he actually heard the Baldwin-Felts man accuse him of killing that store clerk something must have snapped. Zeke hit the man with his bare fists until his opponent just collapsed onto the street. He then headed for another, fully intending on whipping all nine. Gannon grabbed Zeke by the shoulder and stopped him.

One of the other men in the group spoke, "The four of you are in for it now. You have just assaulted a Virginia Deputy, appointed by the governor himself. We will hunt down the four of you and if we can't arrest you then we are authorized to kill you."

Zeke had stepped back to where Haywood stood holding his hat. Haywood asked Gannon what they were going to do.

Gannon knew exactly what to do. "Well we're going to set every damn one of this bunch afoot. And after that we are going to take every gun they have." He pointed his Colt at the men still on horseback and ordered them to dismount.

All eight men climbed out of the saddle and then Gannon ordered them to start walking toward the other end of the street and not to look back. By this time the man Zeke had beaten was back on his feet, now though, he was unwilling to talk. The nine men started walking and not a one looked back.

Nathan Wright

William Haskell Conley had been spending more time than usual in his study each night. It wasn't unusual for a coal oil, or kerosene lamp, to burn into the small hours of the morning on the large walnut desk that sat facing the three large windows in his office. The map files in his office, which were some of the most up to date and best versions money could buy, were in constant use. He had four tripods of oak built with a movable top arm and side bar. On these arms was any number of clamps that could be used to suspend his maps for better inspection. The tripods could be configured into several different shapes by way of bolts and thumbscrews attached at the joints. The height could be elevated or lowered by using a center telescoping rod attached to the base. The entire design had been thought up by Conley himself and built by his own craftsmen in his woodworking and metal shops.

As an afterthought Conley had each unit sanded and then stained dark walnut to match his large desk. When the stain was sufficiently dry each tripod was then hand rubbed with three coats of gloss lacquer. The finish product matched the furnishings of his elaborate study nicely. *Take pride in your work, build what you are building well, and see if life doesn't become more enjoyable.* It was a directive Conley had used his entire life with amazing results thus far.

The project that had been consuming so much of Conley's time and thoughts these days were his tunnels through the head of Wheelwright Mountain. When complete it would allow rail service to continue from Bevinsville, on through to Knott and Letcher Counties. These two counties were only beginning to mine coal and rail service would allow the prosperity that had already begun in Floyd County to flourish in these adjoining counties as well.

Although Haskell Conley wasn't a fan of coal mining, he was a firm believer in the power of transportation, in particular rail transportation. It was a strong belief he had carried with him since the days of the Civil War. Transport by rail had been the determining factor in winning the war. Rail service during the war had made wealthy men of both Andrew Carnegie and John D. Rockefeller, two men who were destined to become titans in steel and oil respectively.

The Conley Farms had extensive experience with rail service. Most, if not all, of the livestock, produce, and tobacco, shipped by the Conley Farms went by rail.

Rail service was being extended now from the small mining community of Drift all the way through Bevinsville and on to the headwaters of Beaver Creek at Weeksbury. When the Conley tunnels, there would be three, were finished and twenty two miles of track laid, he would control transportation into the richest coal producing area south of Pennsylvania.

All the land required for the project had been acquired some years back. Conley knew land and he knew transportation. He had devised the tunnel project in his mind at least ten years earlier. He knew that as the country grew and it's appetite for things produced from factories grew, there would be a continued and ever growing need for coal.

Conley would own the entire line from Bevinsville into both adjoining counties. Although not actually owning any moving stock or locomotives he would receive a fee for each ton of freight or coal that travelled over his tracks. This would, over the course of several years, amount to tens of thousands if not hundreds of thousands of dollars in fees.

Conley would maintain his own track and tunnel crews to service his rail head. He was constructing his own double-track siding for his rail crew to work out of. Bunkhouses were under construction, along with cookhouses and a state of the art medical facility to deal not only with accidents that would go hand in hand with heavy construction, but also to deal with the overall health and well-being of the track crews and their families.

He also had a coaling station and a water tower under construction to service the engines that would be working the two counties. The fees from this enterprise alone would be enough to make a humble man proud or a proud man humble.

Conley's track and tunnel crews were overseen by a college trained engineer by the name of Winston Roy Martin. Martin was originally from New York but had moved fresh out of college to the Atlanta, Georgia, area.

He had gotten into a bit of trouble when he killed two men who, as it was later learned, had stalked and killed Martin's wife. Originally though, Martin had a bounty on his head for the murders of all three. If caught before the truth had been revealed it was believed he would have been hung on the spot due to the brutality of the killings. He was only proven innocent after a witness finally came forward and told of how the two killers had threatened to kill him if he talked. After Martin shot both men one night in a street fight, the witness, a few days later, mustered the backbone to go to the sheriff and clear Martin.

Martin, having escaped the hangman's noose, didn't fancy going back to Atlanta. His wife was dead and there were still people in Atlanta who would probably hold a grudge over the two men he had killed. He became a hobo, riding the rails from town to town for a while without a job or a destination.

Chester's Last Ride

One day he landed in the city of Beckley, West Virginia. Fully looking the part of a hobo he went to the town square and began inquiring about the prospects of finding employment as a railway engineer. Everyone he talked to only laughed, or worse, they threatened to find the sheriff.

At the offices of Parsons, Wiggle, and Rooms, a mail delivery man by the name of Simpson happened to mention the joke of a hobo on the street who was looking for employment as an engineer, of all things. Rooms, who overheard this, asked if the man wanted to be hired as a railroad engineer or a civil engineer. It seems Rooms actually knew of a railroad in Eastern Kentucky that was in need of a civil engineer for a tunnel project that was in the planning stage. The postal employee only laughed and said the man was neither; he was just a simple hobo.

Rooms never saw the humor in this. Feeling a bit intrigued with the story though, he asked the postal employee Simpson, if he could direct him to where he had last saw the hobo.

"I sure can Mr. Rooms," answered Simpson, "But why would you want to waste your time? This hobo guy is obviously a crackpot."

Rooms stood up and put on his coat. He looked at Simpson and said, "Because it is my time to waste and what if the man truly is an engineer and only down on his luck?"

The postal clerk thought this over for a second and said, "I suppose you're right, let's go have a look."

With that both the postal employee and Rooms went down the stairs, through the law firms lobby and onto the main street. After walking only a few steps they spotted the man sitting on a bench in front of the courthouse. As they approached, the man looked up and said hello. Rooms spoke first and said, "It is my understanding that you are looking for employment as an engineer, is this true sir?"

The hobo stood up. He was tall and lanky, the lanky part probably due to his hobo diet. His clothes were very loose, ill-fitting, and dirty. His hair had no trace of gray but was long and un-kept. The beard was at least a week old.

The hobo spoke with a voice that was clear and had the underlying tone of an education. "Yes sir, you are correct. My name is Winston Roy Martin, and I am originally from New York City. Both Rooms and the postal clerk were a bit shocked and surprised to hear not only the voice but also the words that had been spoken. The accent was northern but had a hint of the southeast, if that could be possible.

Rooms asked the next question. It was a question that would, depending on the answer, determine if the hobo was truly an engineer or just a smooth talking hobo.

"Where did you learn to be an engineer Mr. Martin?"

Martin smiled and looked past both men at nothing in particular. "I was enrolled at City College, New York, for three years before being accepted into Harvard for my final year. I didn't have the funds to pursue an education without also working full time in the process. My grades were sufficient to propel me to the top of my class. Some of the good professors at City College and my employer felt my talents were being wasted so a letter was sent to some men in Cambridge and I was put on a train the very next week."

Rooms absorbed what was said and then asked, "How were you able to study at Harvard for an entire year without any means?"

"My employer in New York was a Roosevelt, you see I worked for him in his plate glass business and he paid for my final education in full. Having such a generous benefactor I felt that the only way to repay him was to finish at the top of my class."

"Are you telling me that you finished the engineering program at Harvard, number one in your class?" Rooms asked in astonishment.

"That is correct. I am in need of employment, do you know of any jobs about, engineering or not would be acceptable to me in my present state."

Rooms looked at the postal clerk and said, "This may be the most amazing story I've ever heard."

The postal clerk looked back at Rooms and with a bewildered look asked, "You don't actually believe this man do you Mr. Rooms?"

"Well, there's only one way to find out. Mr. Martin, would you mind accompanying me to the telegraph office so a wire can be sent off to verify what you have just told me?"

"I think that is the same thing I would do if I were in your shoes Mr. Rooms." With that the three men headed over to the telegraph office and within thirty minutes Rooms had the proof right there in his hands. Winston Roy Martin, age thirty-two, had graduated from Harvard in 1879 at the top of his class with an engineering degree. Simpson looked at Rooms and said, "Who would have thought; this hobo looking feller is a Harvard trained engineer? I never would have dreamed it in a hundred years."

"This telegram has verified what you have told us Mr. Martin," Rooms told the lanky Harvard grad. "If I may suggest, there is a man in Southeastern Kentucky who is in need of a railroad engineer. Would you be willing to travel there with the promise of a job?"

It only took Martin a second to answer, "I would be more than willing to work anywhere except Atlanta, Georgia, Mr.

Rooms. There is a small problem though; I have no money or means. In the time it would take me to walk there I would most certainly starve to death."

Stanley Rooms felt a bit sorry for this skeleton of a man. "You let me worry about that Mr. Martin." With that the two men left the telegraph office. Rooms took the man to a clothier on Main Street where he had in the past purchased some of his own clothes. Here he purchased two complete changes of clothes and a pair of shoes. Martin got everything from his hat to his shoelaces. After Rooms signed the receipt he and Martin went to the Beckley Inn and Martin was checked into a room. He was instructed to bath, shave, and dress in his new clothes. Rooms would return in an hour and take the boney engineer to dinner.

Back at the law offices Rooms shared the story of Winston Roy Martin with the attorneys and some of the other employees. Another telegraph received and delivered to the law offices described the trouble that had been thrust upon an innocent man named Winston Roy Martin. The three attorneys knew a thing or two about the shortcomings of the local law in some areas. It was a wonder that Martin had survived long enough for the truth to be revealed. He was truly a lucky man indeed.

Rooms and the other two attorneys left and went to collect the hobo. When Martin met the three attorneys he was a changed man. Clean shaven and dressed in new clothes he truly looked the part of a well-educated man. Although rail thin he still carried himself like a man who at one time in his life had had it all.

The four men went to the Beckley Steak and Seafood Restaurant. After being seated and menus received the three attorneys ordered first, Martin ordered less than the other three. Rooms listened as the order was placed and watched as the waiter headed toward the kitchen.

"Mr. Martin, it seems that you ordered only very little, is there a reason for this. You do understand that you are a guest of me and my friends here and all your needs will be seen to until you are gainfully employed with your new employer in Eastern Kentucky."

"Please excuse me Mister Rooms. I haven't had a full meal in several weeks. I thought I should be a little careful with my feeble stomach. It might take a few days to build up my strength. Until then I plan to take it slow and easy."

It was doubtful that any of the three lawyers had experienced a day without food in their entire lives. Each man felt as if they had just experienced an example of how the less fortunate survived from day to day.

During dinner the four talked of life on the rails. After dinner and during dessert they brought Martin up to speed on the ambitious plans of his future employer, William Haskell Conley. Martin ate only two bites of his dessert and declared himself sufficiently stuffed.

With dinner finished Martin was asked to tell the story of how he had drawn the attentions of Mr. Roosevelt at the Glass Plant.

Winston started the story with the happenings in Atlanta first and then led them back to his days in the Northeast. Part of the story about the Roosevelt Glass Company, and what had happened there, could only be repeated from what he had been told himself.

About the Atlanta troubles he told them he had been a hard working engineer who labored ten hours a day for several of the small railroads which ran through and around the city. He was twenty-six years old at the time and had been married for almost two years to a woman he had met his last year of college. She was slim and shapely with dark brown hair, so dark some thought it was black. Her name was Rosalina and she was the center of Winston's life. Her dark brown eyes were the most beautiful he had ever seen. As far as he was concerned the sun rose and set in those eyes.

They had met at Harvard while Winston was working on his degree in engineering. The attraction was mutual and almost instantaneous. Neither Winston or Rosalina were seeing anyone else at the time of their introductions, both were too involved with their studies. Winston carried a tremendous load with his classes in the engineering department and Rosalina was studying to become a doctor.

Rosalina, two years younger than Winston, was charmed not so much by his appearance but by the sound of his voice and mannerisms. When he spoke she would almost always blush. His voice was deep and smooth. She described it as distant thunder and smoothly sweet like warm honey.

When classes were over that spring Winston graduated at the top of his class. He had been a child prodigy, breezing through and graduating from high school at the age of fourteen. He had attended classes at a small college in New York while working in a plate glass warehouse to help pay his expenses. Within a few months at the warehouse his skills with numbers had been noticed by a few of the men who ran the drafting department. When picking up specifications for an order he could do most of the calculations in his head as the drafters used rulers, pencils, and paper, to formulate the same results. He could call out the size and quantity of glass needed before the men at the drafting tables could tabulate their own answers. And he was always correct.

Chester's Last Ride

It wasn't long before others in the plate glass department took notice of the young man with the amazing mind for numbers. The owner of the company was a wealthy New Yorker whose name was Roosevelt. Upon hearing the rumors of the mathematical genius, Roosevelt arranged for Martin to join him and a few of his partners for lunch the very next day. The next morning, just before noon, Winston was brought over from the glass warehouse across the street to the companies rather austere offices. Being dressed in his warehouse working attire Winston felt completely out of place. He was led to the meeting room where the company executives met for lunch each day at one o'clock sharp.

Already there were Roosevelt and four other men whom Winston had seen from time to time on the warehouse floor and in the drafting rooms. After introductions Winston was shown to his seat. Sitting in front of him was a fancy china place setting with real silverware, and also a folder and five sharpened pencils. He looked up to find the four gentlemen already seated and looking at him with sly smiles. Mr. Roosevelt spoke first. "Winston, we invited you here today for two reasons, first to dine with us and secondly for you to demonstrate your skill with numbers. In the folder in front of you are five pages numbered one through five. Each has a list of problems for you to solve. Page number one is the easiest and page number five is the most difficult. Do you follow me so far?"

Winston looked at the folder but did not open it. He studied each of the gentlemen seated at the table and then spoke, "Yes Mr. Roosevelt."

Roosevelt smiled and then continued. "The other gentlemen seated here, who you were just introduced to, are my colleagues. They have heard the stories about your abilities with numbers and are as amazed as I am. We have devised a procedure where you will, so to speak, be the founder of our feast here today. There will be four courses for lunch today plus dessert. If you can complete the first sheet of problems in that folder then the first course will be served. After each course we will wait for the next sheet to be completed before the following course can be brought out. Do you still follow me?"

Again Winston looked at the folder but did not attempt to open it. Once more his answer was, "Yes Mr. Roosevelt."

Roosevelt smiled and then looked at the other gentlemen at the table. "We all agreed to this plan earlier. I have added one more rule to our lunch today which none of these fine gentlemen know anything about, but which I am going to tell you now. If at any time during your calculations a problem is too difficult to finish or is finished with an incorrect answer then the meal will be over and we will spend the rest of the day with our stomachs growling. Either way there is a happy ending so to speak. If you finish all the pages correctly then you are truly the wonder boy I have heard of and each of us will have enjoyed a very fine meal. And if you fail, the only upside is that each of my colleagues, myself included, will have had a lighter lunch than usual. And as you can see by the looks of us it should not leave any lasting damage."

Winston had to agree, each of the other men seated at the table were showing the results of too many fine meals, but he dare not mention this to his host. He opened the top flap of the folder and asked, "When shall I start?"

"Why right now please, let's get this contest under way before we die of starvation." This brought a few laughs from the other men at the table.

Chester's Last Ride

Winston pulled out the top sheet of paper and closed the folder. He laid the sheet on the top of the folder and glanced down the entire sheet, it only took him sixty seconds to scan and solve every problem mentally. Winston picked up one of the pencils and examined the point, sharp to perfection. He began writing and within another sixty seconds he put his pencil down and looked at the other men. "I have finished the first page, how do you plan to check my solutions?"

Roosevelt was too anxious to wait for the paper to be handed down the table from one man to the next. He bounded out of his seat and rushed to the other end of the table to retrieve the paper with its problems and answers. As he walked back to his seat he was extremely impressed with the very neat and legible handwriting of the young man. He had helped to arrange the questions for the first four pages and already knew the solutions. After a moment he sat down and handed the sheet to the man at his right. He then picked up a small bell that sat beside his plate and gave it a vigorous shake.

Without a word being spoken the door opposite the entrance sprang open and in came six smartly dressed kitchen staff carrying the first course. Each of the waiters was dressed in black trousers and wore a white jacket. Winston was impressed with the precision the kitchen staff used in placing the first course in front of each of the diners. One on the attendants came back in to fill the wine glasses while another filled the water in each man's water glass.

The man who had received the finished paper from Roosevelt scanned it only briefly before reaching it to the next man to his right. After each man had scanned the paper and the kitchen staff had left the room Roosevelt said, with a smile that couldn't be suppressed, "Gentleman, you may proceed with your first course, after we settle up."

Nathan Wright

Winston, who had been admiring the plate that sat in front of him, looked up to see what Roosevelt meant.

Each of the four men reached into a vest pocket and pulled out a crisp five dollar bill which was then passed down to a beaming Roosevelt. Roosevelt smiled as he gathered the four bills and sat them on the table beside his plate. "Gentlemen, shall we begin."

The first serving was an extremely fresh looking salad. Winston had never saw vegetables in New York at this time of year with such color and crispness. These were undoubtedly brought north on an express train from the Deep South. He had always assumed that the elite of the city enjoyed a higher quality of food than the average city dweller, and his assumption was correct. Placed beside each salad plate was a small container of sauce. Winston wasn't quite sure what to do with the sauce until he noticed the others liberally pouring the concoction on top of their salads. Not to seem completely out of his element, which he was, he did as the others and poured a corresponding amount on his salad as well.

He noticed which of the three forks the other men were using and grabbed the same for himself. After cutting a small bite off of a bright red tomato he stirred it in the sauce and immediately popped it into his mouth. In his mind he could not find the words to describe the taste. The freshness, along with the flavor and texture of the sauce combined to make it the most delicious tomato he had ever experienced. He chewed with gusto as he hurried his fork back for the second bite. The other men were talking among themselves and Winston hoped they hadn't noticed the fortitude in which he attacked his food.

When the plates were finished the kitchen staff returned and removed them, but did not bring the second course. Winston knew that if it was as good as the first then he was in store for a treat. Each of the men at the table grew quiet. Roosevelt spoke first, "Now young Mr. Martin, I hope you enjoyed the first course. If you did then I am sure you will not be disappointed by the second, which is assuming you can complete page number two. And I must remind you that this next page, as we told you at the beginning, is more difficult than the first. If you are ready please open the folder again and remove the second page."

Winston reached for the folder which had been slid to the side of the table. He opened the top and removed the second page and then scanned its contents. As with the first it only took him a minute. When finished he put the sheet neatly on top of the folder and picked up a different pencil. After inspecting the tip he quickly answered each problem in order on that page. Once he finished he put down both paper and pencil. Again a very excited Roosevelt jumped up and hurried to retrieve the sheet. As he walked back to his place and sat down he scanned the answers. Once finished he again reached the completed page to the man on his right. Winston was glad to hear the ringing of the bell. He was forty percent finished with the test and knew he and the others at the table would be rewarded with the next course.

As the plates were delivered and placed in front of each of the men Roosevelt said, "Gentlemen, I think Mr. Martin here has won you each your second course and won me the second part of our wager." With that each of the other four men reached into his vest pocket and again pulled out a crisp new bill, this time in the denomination of ten, and passed it down to Roosevelt who gladly took the prize and placed it on top of the stack of fives he had won earlier. Winston knew now that each man had agreed to a wager on each and every page and subsequent course. The first bet had been five dollars and the second ten. It was progressive. If it followed suit and he completed the next page correctly then the bet would be twenty, only time would tell. He wondered though if the fourth bet would be for forty dollars, which was two times the third bet, or if it would be for fifty dollars, the next denomination after twenty.

This new course consisted of fresh boiled and peeled shrimp and accompanied by a red sauce that Winston had never before seen. As he watched the other men, who were again talking among themselves, they each picked up the shrimp with a smaller fork and ran it through the red sauce before plopping it into their mouths. He did the same. The sauce was the first thing he could taste. It overpowered the shrimp almost completely. It was tangy and complemented the seafood. He had to admit he could get used to eating at the long table but knew this would be his only experience to dine with these men.

After the second course was removed Roosevelt again explained the obvious. Winston removed the third sheet of paper and again scanned the list of problems to be solved. Indeed as he had been warned each new sheet was harder than the previous one. But the first two had been so extremely easy for Winston's nimble mind that even this third sheet was completed in no more time than first two.

The five other men at the table watched in amazement as the third sheet was quickly finished and neatly placed on top of the folder. Roosevelt was up again and hurried at almost a run to grab the page. He scanned it as he returned to his chair, again reaching the sheet to the man on his right and immediately ringing the bell. Winston knew he had successfully earned a third course at the long table. As the plates were set he was curious as to how much the third bet would be. If it followed the progressive, as the first two, then it would be twenty for each man. Sure enough the four pulled crisp new twenty dollar bills from their vest pockets and handed them down the table to Roosevelt who was all smiles.

After carefully placing the four bills on top of the others Roosevelt said let's begin. The plate now in front of Winston consisted of steak along with an assortment of sides. By the small size of the steak Winston knew it was filet mignon, the best cut available depending on your preference. Taking his first bite he knew it would be good but could not have imagined that it would taste this exceptional. Few words were spoken as each man enjoyed the meal.

Next came the fourth sheet and again Winston finished it in the same amount of time. Again there was the same routine, which Roosevelt enjoyed as much as a young child at Christmas. The ringing of the bell this time brought dessert which confused Winston. This was the fourth course. There was one more sheet of paper in the folder and then supposedly the fifth and last course. Dessert was a greenish pie of some sort which Winston had no idea of what it was. As he looked at the strange pie he noticed the four men again go to their vest pockets and retrieve fifty dollar bills. It was then that he realized these men had more money than they would probably ever need.

Winston felt the need to ask a question. "Excuse me Mr. Roosevelt, I have never seen a pie of this sort before, may I ask its name?"

Roosevelt smiled and said, "It is called Key Lime Pie Mr. Martin and I think you will find it quite delicious. It's a bit tangy and helps to settle the stomach after a heavy meal such as the one we've just had."

Nathan Wright

Winston picked up the last fork and took a bite. Mr. Roosevelt was right about the delicious part and also about the heavy meal part; this was the most he had eaten at one time in his entire life. No one spoke as each man finished the dessert and the plates were removed.

"Winston, we here who dine at the long table in the conference room like to finish our lunch with a Cuban cigar which is what we consider the fifth and last course. I will warn you though that the last sheet of paper in that folder was not prepared by me or anyone else here in this room."

Winston pulled the last sheet from the folder and scanned it. Then he said, "If it was not prepared by the men at this table, or by you Mr. Roosevelt, then who?"

The four suddenly broke out in smiles. Winston's question had confirmed what each man had hoped; the last sheet was truly more difficult and had stumped the poor boy. Each man, with the exception of Roosevelt, now knew they would more than likely win the final bet even if it did mean losing their after dinner smoke.

Roosevelt noticed the anticipation and thought it might be a little premature. "That last sheet you have in front of you Winston was not prepared by any of us here at the table that is true. We felt that if you could overcome the first four sheets, which by the way were concocted by the five of us, then it would be safe to assume that a more difficult set of problems should be built by our Chief Architect who you have never met. His name is Oscar Ramey and he works across town at another office. The first four sheets were sent to his office by special courier yesterday for him to examine. I then instructed Mr. Ramey to make the last sheet at least twice as difficult as any of the first four. He assured me that the problems he prepared would more than meet my requirements. Now if you are ready Mr. Martin please begin."

Winston scanned the last sheet the same way he had done with the first four. Again he took up a pencil, this one being the last and examined its tip. A couple of the men at the table had produced pocket watches and timed the completion of the last sheet. It took less than three minutes.

Roosevelt bolted to his feet again and raced to the other end of the table. Each of the five men had been given a sheet containing all the correct answers to each of the sheets in advance. This time after returning to his seat Roosevelt produced his answer sheet from inside his vest pocket and scanned the results. Suddenly at the bottom of the page he found what he most feared, a mistake in Winston's answers. Again Roosevelt scanned the answers and solutions hoping that he might have made a mistake himself trying to apply an answer to the wrong problem. But he had not. The proof was right there in front of him. Winston Roy Martin had got the very last problem of the very last page wrong.

The others at the table could read the disappointment on their boss's face. Usually disappointment shown by a superior would make an employee nervous and apprehensive, but not this time. The other four men at the table were not in the least bit worried at their boss's current discomfort. They were in fact overjoyed. Martin had failed the test; there could be no other reason for Roosevelt's sudden loss for words.

Finally Roosevelt looked up from the paper. He studied each face before him. He was a bit unsettled by the sly smiles on the faces of his four associates. They knew they had won the last bet without even a word being spoken. Finally he handed the sheet to the first man to his right.

Nathan Wright

"I'm sorry Mr. Martin but it appears you have not solved all the problems correctly, one of the problems on this last page you have missed." With that he reached into his vest pocket and pulled out an envelope and slid it to the center of the table. It was very thick and every one at the table, including Martin, knew it contained cash. All were silent as each man acquired the paper and scanned the results. Each could not resist a smile as they matched up the last problem with the last answer on the solutions sheet. Finally when each had finished, the page was handed back to Roosevelt.

"Well Martin, it was an exceptional effort you put forth to a rather difficult test. Although you and I have both lost I still think you should be congratulated. Not one in a hundred could have accomplished what you have done here today." Each man raised his wine glass to toast the young man who had just failed what was probably the most important test of his life, each man that is except Winston Roy Martin. He sat there looking at each of the other men with a slight smile of his own, finally Roosevelt spoke.

"Winston do you understand that we would like to congratulate you with a toast. Please pick up your glass and join us, no need to be a bad loser."

Again Winston sat motionless with only the slightest of smiles on his face.

Roosevelt was not a man to become irritated easily but this was becoming rude. "Mr. Martin, are you going to join us in a toast or am I missing something here?"

Finally Winston picked up his glass and held it as high as the others at the table.

"Now, that is much better. Gentlemen I would like to present this toast to our young guest here for a job well done. It was an amazing feat he has accomplished here today, we salute you." With that the five men raised their wine glasses and finished their toast.

It was then that Winston spoke. "And I would like to add a word or two if I might gentlemen."

Roosevelt finished his glass and sat it on the table. "Absolutely Martin, proceed when you are ready."

Winston stood and raised his untouched wine glass. The other five men at the table immediately stood and raised their own glasses. Roosevelt laughed and said, "Gentlemen can, we hold up just a moment, my glass has somehow become empty." Each man laughed loudly as a waiter hurriedly refilled Roosevelt's glass. Once the glass was refilled, Roosevelt instructed Martin to proceed.

"Gentlemen, I want to thank each of you for this wonderful lunch and the opportunity to become acquainted with you. The food was outstanding; as good as anything I have had in my entire life." Each of the men looked at each other and smiled. "Furthermore I regret that the four of you, other than Mr. Roosevelt have lost the first four wagers." Martin paused for effect as each man continued to smile. "I do though have regret in this whole affair for the four of you who have already lost so much and anticipate a final win. You will not win the final bet, you have lost."

Each stood in stunned silence, not accustomed to being told different by an underling. Roosevelt was at first shocked by the arrogance of Martin, although Martin had been very gracious and courteous in his reply. Then it dawned on the company's founder and President that possibly Martin was either confused by the wine or, could it be, he was correct and had finished that last problem correctly.

"Mr. Martin, could you be so kind as to explain yourself"

Nathan Wright

"I would be delighted Mr. Roosevelt; the last problem on the last page was answered correctly by me."

Now Roosevelt was truly amazed. No one at the table had told Martin which problem he had solved incorrectly. How had Martin guessed that it was the last one on the page? But then maybe he hadn't guessed. Maybe he knew something about that last answer that no one else did. "Mr. Martin, could you please explain how you knew it was the last problem of the entire test and also how you assume your answer is correct and the Chief Architect of the company, who devised that last sheet I might add, has come up with an incorrect answer?

"Yes Mr. Roosevelt. But instead of me explaining my answer would it be possible to have the Chief Architect explain how he came up with his answer? He could be summoned in a matter of minutes."

Roosevelt felt like he was dealing with a young Sherlock Holmes. Martin hadn't been informed where the Chief Architect was other than the fact that he worked across town. The most amazing thing was that the Chief Architect was actually sitting in the lobby in case he was needed for any reason concerning the test.

"I think that would be a great idea Mr. Martin. I will have someone send for him now. It may take thirty minutes for him to arrive though."

"It shouldn't take that long Mr. Roosevelt. He was sitting in the lobby as I entered for lunch."

"But how did you know the man sitting in the lobby was the Chief Architect?" Roosevelt asked.

"He had the finals for the job you are bidding in Ohio in his lap. He was scanning the numbers and was also using a slide rule. I knew he was the Chief Architect for the company for those reasons along with the fact that he was wearing a

Harvard lapel pin, and Harvard has the leading Architectural School in the country."

Again the room was silent as the men continued to be amazed by the gifts that this young draftsman possessed. Roosevelt laughed loudly as he turned to the waiter by the door. "Could you have Mr. Ramey come in please?"

Within a minute the door swung open and in came the man Winston had seen in the lobby when he entered the building earlier. Mr. Ramey was a tall angular man with thinning hair and glasses that made him look the scholarly type. Upon entering he proceeded to a side table and deposited his papers and slide rule. Roosevelt rose from his chair and greeted him. "Good afternoon Mr. Ramey, I hope we're not inconveniencing you too much today."

Ramey hung his coat and hat on the oak coat tree before he spoke. "Not at all Mr. Roosevelt, I got some quiet time in the lobby and used it to great advantage to look over the latest plans on the Ohio Project. What is it I can help you with here this afternoon?"

"As you know we are hosting a little lunch here today for one of our young draftsmen. You know the one we asked you to prepare the final draft of the test for, a Mr. Martin."

Ramey looked to the end of the table where Martin was seated and smiled. "Yes, I wondered if I would get to meet the young math prodigy you spoke of a few days ago." Ramey immediately rushed to the end of the table where Martin was seated and thrust out a hand. "Mr. Martin, my name is Oscar Ramey. I am the Chief Architect for the company. So much has been said about your extraordinary abilities with numbers. If I hadn't been introduced to you soon then I had made up my mind to search you out myself.

"I myself have admired the art of math since I was a young child. I find numbers soothing, the numbers never lie." He took Martin's hand and shook it vigorously. The other gentlemen at the table were not the least bit upset with the fact that their colleague had completely ignored them in his rush to speak to Martin. Apparently they were accustomed to the musings of the head of their Architectural Department. Academics could exhibit eccentric behavior at times. Roosevelt and his four associates were very aware of the ticks of Mr. Ramey.

"Thank you Mister Ramey. I hope your time today hasn't been wasted," Winston said.

"Not at all, it is my time to waste and Mr. Roosevelt felt this little test was of such importance as to ask my help in designing that last page for him. I hope it wasn't too difficult."

At this point Mr. Roosevelt stepped back into the conversation. "Oscar, the test has already been completed. All went perfectly fine until the last page, the one you prepared. It appears that you have stumped Mr. Martin. Upon checking the answers you prepared for us against the solutions, I found the last one to have been tabulated incorrectly by Mr. Martin here. He though, seems to think that he has gotten all the problems correct. That is why I had you stationed outside the door, for just such an event."

Ramey released Martin's hand and stepped back. With a curious smile he said, "Well, let's get to the bottom of this. Where would the last sheet be?"

Roosevelt retrieved the paper from the table and reached it to Mr. Ramey. "There you go; I do believe you will find the very last problem to be the culprit."

Ramey stood and examined the test sheet and then turned his attention to the answer sheet that had been filled out by

Martin. After a few moments he looked at Roosevelt. "Well, it appears that Mr. Martin has answered the question correctly."

The four associates looked on incredulously. Roosevelt looked at his Chief Architect with a frown. "Do you mean to tell me that this young man has out smarted a Harvard trained fox like you. I am disappointed in you Ramey. When I hired you I was certain I had found the best draftsman in the country." Roosevelt only stood there looking at his employee.

"Mr. Roosevelt, I assure you that your faith in me is not misplaced."

"But you have just admitted that you made a mistake on one of your problems."

"But Mr. Roosevelt, I admitted no such thing. I only said that Mr. Martin had answered the problem correctly. I never said that I had given up anything as incorrect on my part."

"Mr. Ramey, this is absurd. There is no way that both of you can be correct if the answer doesn't meet the needs of the problem. Please state, if you will, how it can be otherwise?"

Oscar Ramey went over and stood by the side of Winston Martin, both looking at the other five men in the room. Finally Oscar spoke, "Gentlemen, let's look at the situation for a moment. First of all Mr. Roosevelt has clearly pointed out that it is impossible for both Mr. Martin and me to be correct if we have different answers to the same problem. And if that be the case then it is safe to assume that we both should not be incorrect either. But gentlemen, I am telling you now that both Mr. Martin and I are correct in our answers."

All the men in the room, including Winston, looked at Oscar Ramey in confused silence. Finally Roosevelt spoke up, "Oscar, if you don't mind, I would like an explanation. What you are proposing simply breaks the laws of physics. You cannot be both correct and incorrect at the same time."

Oscar put his hand on the shoulder of Winston and said, "Young Martin, I think you know what has happened."

"Yes Mister Ramey, I do know but I think it would be better if you could explain it to these gentlemen."

"Well I think you have a point. And I have held them in suspense for too long. Gentlemen I will explain. First of all, the entire problem that Winston, excuse me is it alright if I call you Winston?"

Winston looked at Oscar and said, "By all means."

"The entire problem that Winston saw on his sheet was a terribly complex problem. When he tabulated his results he came to the proper and correct conclusion. The answer I have on the answer sheet is also correct."

Again Roosevelt spoke up, his annoyance beginning to grow, "Oscar you know that isn't going to fly. Now try again to explain how both of your answers are correct if they are both different."

"Winston, may I see the sheet which you used to work out your solutions?"

"Sorry Mr. Ramey, I don't have a sheet."

"You mean it was thrown away."

"No Mr. Ramey, I completed all the calculations in my head."

The look on Oscar Ramey's face was one of sheer amazement. "You mean to tell me that you have done the entire test in your head?"

Before Martin could answer Roosevelt spoke up, "That is correct; he has done the entire five pages in his head. And he never took more than five minutes on any of the pages."

"That is impossible. I know of no one who could work out these problems without the aid of pencil, paper, and slide rule."

Chester's Last Ride

Winston looked at Roosevelt. "There was no slide rule on the table, only a folder and five sharpened pencils."

"Yes, that is correct. I thought it over and decided before you got here to only give you the slide rule if you asked for it. At the speed in which you solved the problems it was apparent you could do quite well without it," Roosevelt said.

"Well then, no matter. I can still prove my point without using Winston's tabulation sheet." With that said Oscar reached into his pocket and produced two sheets of paper. He held both up for everyone to see, and then he put both on the conference table.

"Gentlemen, as you can see I have two handwritten pieces of paper here. These are the originals and they are in my own handwriting. Once I finished preparing these for the test I gave them to a secretary, who shall remain anonymous, to type up as per Mr. Roosevelt's instructions. If you will examine them and then do a comparison to the sheet used in the test you will find your solution to the dilemma we now face."

Roosevelt picked up the handwritten papers as well as the typed paper used in the test. His eyes immediately went to the bottom of the page. "The question at the bottom of the page is different." He then reached the sheets to the other men. "What has happened Oscar?"

"When the page of questions was transcribed by the secretary she failed to copy it correctly. Look here, two of the words are reversed in the sentence. It still makes for a complicated problem, but one with a completely different answer. My answer to the handwritten problem is correct. Winston's answer to the incorrectly typed problem is also correct for that particular problem. Gentlemen, Winston's answers are correct."

Oscar walked over to the table and said, "Mr. Roosevelt, would you mind if I had a glass of water, it has been a long morning.

Roosevelt smiled and said, "I am sorry Oscar for keeping you waiting so long." With that a waiter was summoned and told to bring out a place setting for Oscar. The entire meal and wine was placed before a smiling Oscar who immediately began to dig in.

Roosevelt said, "Gentlemen, in light of what has happened I am calling all bets for this day null and void." With that he reached for the fat envelope in the center of the table and stuffed it back into his vest pocket. The other four separated the cash on the table and deposited the loot in their own vest pockets, each glad to have escaped without a monetary loss.

Roosevelt spoke up first, "Gentlemen, I think each of us has earned our fifth and last course." He turned and motioned for a waiter to bring in the selection. No more had the waiter left than he was back with a selection of twenty fat Cuban cigars of four different varieties. The tray was shown to each man in the room and each took a smoke of his own choosing. Winston noticed that each man knew exactly which his favorite was, for no one took more than a second to decide. Even Oscar, whom Winston assumed rarely visited the conference room, chose quickly. The last to be presented the tray was Winston who looked at the fourteen remaining cigars and had not a clue as to which he might enjoy. Roosevelt noticed the quizzical look on Winston's face and walked over.

"If you will allow me to assist you, I will help you select one that might suit your taste."

"Thank you Mr. Roosevelt, I am only accustomed to domestic cigars. These look completely foreign to me."

"Which tobacco do you prefer of the home grown variety?"

Chester's Last Ride

"There is one which is produced in Kentucky by a man named William Haskell Conley. He raises his own tobacco and has some men employed who roll a very fine cigar. They are called Kentucky Rolled Bourbon. The bourbon is also a Kentucky specialty of Mr. Conley's."

Roosevelt smiled and said, "Again Winston you have impressed me. I have heard of this William Haskell Conley you mention, but I didn't know he was in the cigar business, or for that matter the bourbon business. He is big into horses and cattle and from what I gather he is the largest land owner in the state of Kentucky." Roosevelt looked at the remaining selection on the tray and selected a very dark brown cigar. He reached it to Winston. "Try this one, it isn't soaked with Conley's bourbon but I do know it is an excellent cigar."

Winston took it and held it close to his nose. "Smells nice, I'm anxious to try it." With that Roosevelt picked up the desk lighter and went around the room to each man and lit each cigar with Winston being the last. Winston puffed and after a second exhaled.

"Well Winston what do you think?" Roosevelt said.

Winston held the cigar in front of him and without taking his eyes off of it he said, "Very nice, it kind of reminds me of the WHC cigar I mentioned earlier."

"That is the second time you have mentioned that particular cigar. How would a man manage to come by a box of these Kentucky cigars if he were to so choose?"

Winston looked at his cigar for a moment before answering, "The tobacco store at the corner of the street on which the plate glass warehouse is located has two boxes sent in once a week. I have a standing order for three of those Kentucky cigars every Monday morning. By Wednesday they are completely sold out of WHCs. Anyone who hasn't picked his up by then is out of luck until the following Monday when the train arrives that delivers them. I have always asked the tobacco store owner why he doesn't order more. He said if you want something to be a good seller, just keep it in short supply. If you want something to peak in sales, and then start dropping off, then keep it overstocked and underpriced."

Roosevelt took another puff of his cigar. "You know Winston, it sounds to me like I need to hire the tobacco store owner and put him in charge of sales at the window plant." Everyone in the room laughed except for Chad Parsons who Winston suspected was the current man in charge of sales. Roosevelt slapped Parsons on the back and said, "Sorry Chad, you know I was only kidding." Parsons laughed but was still noticeably nervous.

"Well gentlemen, I'm sure each of you has some work to do. I want to thank you for taking part in my little test of Mr. Martin here today. And I want to thank you Oscar for clarifying the issues with that last problem. It had each of us stumped."

With that each of the men started for the door. "Oh Chad, could you run down to that tobacco store Winston spoke of and check on those WHC cigars. Please put in a request for five boxes and check when they will arrive. I find my curiosity has been aroused and I am anxious to sample some Kentucky tobacco."

"I certainly will Mr. Roosevelt. And while I'm there I'll try to pick up a few pointers on how to be a better salesman." Everyone laughed.

"Winston, I would like for you and Oscar to stay for a moment if you could. I have a couple of things I want to run by you." Both men nodded in agreement as the other men exited and Roosevelt closed and locked the door. The three talked for a while longer as Oscar finished his meal and then lit his cigar.

Chester's Last Ride

Roosevelt turned and led the two men into his spacious corner office through a side door in the conference room. It was a large affair with nearly floor to ceiling windows on the two walls facing the river. The other two walls were covered with floor to ceiling book shelves. Beside the oversized desk were two tripods containing drawings of buildings that Roosevelt Glass was currently bidding on. He motioned to two of the wing back leather chairs in front of his desk. All three men sat and puffed on their cigars for a moment. Finally Roosevelt spoke. "Oscar, what did you think of our little test today and even more importantly, the performance of our man Winston here?"

Oscar took another puff and then crushed out his cigar on the floor stand ashtray that stood between the two wing back chairs. "Well Mr. Roosevelt, I am amazed by the fact that Winston here completed the problems using no props such as the slide rule, or for that matter even a pencil and paper. I spent years in some of the best schools in the land and could never have accomplished what he has done, and might I add, in the matter of minutes you said it took him. Also I feel compelled to add the fact that I never studied with anyone who possessed these skills. But let's ask Winston himself what he attributes to these remarkable feats he has just accomplished."

Roosevelt puffed on his cigar and looked over at Winston. No one spoke for several minutes. Finally Roosevelt put his cigar in the ashtray on his desk but did not extinguish it as Oscar had done with his. "That was truly an amazing feat you pulled off in there Winston. Is there anything you can tell us about how you learned to do what you can do or any idea how anyone can do what you have just done with only their wits and nothing else?"

Nathan Wright

Winston thought deeply about the question. No one had ever questioned his abilities with numbers. But then again he had never been tested as he had just been. These two men he was seated with were both men of importance. Both held significant positions in the new industrial age.

"My story is not much to talk about. As a child I was forced to work for my keep, I don't remember my parents. I never went to school on a regular basis until I was at least twelve, but when I did go I would listen to what the teachers had to say. But everything I heard seemed familiar to me. Not that I had ever experienced what was being taught. It was as if what they said, as soon as they said it, I could recall not just at that moment, but even now I can hear their voices, see their faces. I can sense the smells from the coal oil lamps, the wood burning in the fireplace, the blooming of the flowers just outside the classroom windows.

"When I was able to make it to the city I was fortunate enough to get a job in your glass plating warehouse. I worked hard. Anytime extra work was needed to be done in order to complete a job, I volunteered, not just for the money which was nice, but for the experience. Every job I completed became part of my experience. Soon the superintendent of the glass factory took notice and allowed me to fill in anytime someone was absent. One day a draftsman did not show up for work. It was later found out that the draftsman had died from an unknown ailment, most likely a heart attack.

"That first day of the draftsman's absence I volunteered. The superintendent at first laughed. To do well as a common laborer was one thing but drafting was a learned skill and no one could just sit down and take up where a previous draftsman had left off. I told the superintendent to give me ten minutes of his time on a trial basis and if I couldn't prove myself in that time I would apologize and return to the warehouse floor. He said he would give me some time to prove myself as a reward for the hard work I had put in on that same warehouse floor."

Roosevelt interrupted Winston at that point. "What made you think you could accomplish the tasks of a trained draftsman? You had no experience, nothing to prepare you for the job that you had requested."

Winston looked back at Oscar. "While I was filling orders on the warehouse floor I came into contact with the prints and plans for the jobs that were being filled. When I saw a plan it remained in my memory. After work I would go over the plans in my head. It didn't take long until I figured out there was a pattern to the mathematics of each plan."

Both Oscar and Roosevelt could only look at Winston in amazement. Before Roosevelt got the chance to speak, Oscar blurted out, "Do you expect me to believe that you can remember the details of a set of plans by only looking at them? And then hours later after a grueling day of pulling orders on the warehouse floor you can retrieve the plans from your memory and completely analyze these same plans and understand them?"

"Oscar, I know what I have told you is hard to believe. If you doubt me, you can check with the superintendent at the warehouse. He will verify what I have just told you."

Roosevelt looked at Oscar and held up a hand. "Oscar, I know this is hard to believe but let's you and I hear the young man out. I think when he has finished we will have more understanding as to what his abilities are and how they have gotten him to where he is today."

Winston continued, "The superintendent took me to the drafting room and put me at the desk of the absentee draftsman. On the desk were several sets of plans for portions of the Ohio job the company was bidding on. He picked out a sheet of drawings that were probably the easiest of the lot. He told me to take as long as I needed to estimate the amount of glass, the weight of the entire order, and then if I had any time left to figure wind loads and acceptable thicknesses for load tolerance.

"He left me with my work and went to consult several of the other draftsmen about progress on the job. After five minutes I left the desk and went to find the superintendent. I found him four desks down and told him the task he had assigned me was finished. He laughed and said he knew I was in over my head and couldn't finish the plan. I never spoke, he and I just walked back to the desk. He never sat down; he just picked up the papers and looked at the plans. The expression on his face was one of total amazement."

Roosevelt looked up from his thoughts and said, "You mean you did finish the plans as you were instructed to do by the superintendent?"

"That is correct. The plans were finished. The quantity of glass, weight, and wind loads, were right there for the superintendent to inspect. When he finished inspecting the papers he just stood there and didn't say a word for the longest time. Finally he looked at me and asked if I had actually figured the solutions out or just written down numbers to make it look like I had finished the problems. I told him to take the sheets to another draftsman and he could verify my work."

Oscar asked, "Is that what he did?"

"Oh yes Oscar. He went immediately to a desk which was staffed by a draftsman he had the utmost confidence in. He placed the plans on the desk and asked the draftsman how long it would take him to verify the figures on the page. He was told it would take no more than forty-five minutes. The superintendent told him to proceed."

Roosevelt now asked the obvious question. "It would take one of the most experienced draftsmen on the floor forty-five minutes to go over the numbers you had completed in five minutes? Are you serious man?"

"Yes Sir Mr. Roosevelt, I was finished and the proof of whether I knew what I was doing or not was about to be verified by one of the best draftsmen that worked in the facility. That man sat down and immediately went to work."

"And what was the conclusion, and did it really take him forty-five minutes to verify your work?" Roosevelt asked.

"It didn't take forty-five minutes Mr. Roosevelt; it was more like an hour. The results he came up with were exactly the same as mine. Everything was exactly the same. Quantity, weight and wind load all checked out the same."

"My Lord Oscar, this man, who is not even a draftsman and never had any experience on the drafting floor, was able to finish an hours' worth of complicated mathematical equations in five minutes time, five minutes?"

Oscar sat in silence. He was in deep concentration. Neither Roosevelt nor Winston spoke, they just let Oscar think. Finally he looked up and said,

"I believe I will go over to the drafting floor and have a chat with Chief Draftsman Briscoe. I do not doubt what you have told us for one minute Winston, I just want to look over the plans you completed for Mr. Briscoe that only took five minutes. I want to see for myself, do you understand what I'm saying Winston? I just want to get a little more information."

Winston looked at Oscar. He could tell the older man was having a hard time wrapping his thoughts around what he had just heard. He almost felt sorry for the Chief Architect. It wasn't the first time someone had observed Winston's abilities with numbers and felt overwhelmed by what they saw.

"I understand completely. If it were me and I was in your shoes I would do exactly as you say, go over and have a chat with the Chief Draftsman." Winston had no doubt what Oscar would find when he talked to Briscoe. He just wanted to reassure Oscar and hope the older man could grasp what had happened.

Roosevelt stood and went over to one of the large windows. As he looked over the river he said, "Oscar, I think what you have mentioned is the right course of action. Do you intend to go there now?"

After a few more seconds of reflection Oscar responded, "Yes Mr. Roosevelt, I will go at once. My other duties for the afternoon have been covered by my staff. I took that precaution because I didn't know how long I would be occupied here today."

"That is great Oscar. After you have spoken to Briscoe and verified everything, I would like for both you and the Chief Draftsman to come back to my office. I have a few questions as to how to proceed."

"I will be back in a short while and I am sure Briscoe will be delighted to come along also." With that Oscar stood and reached out a hand. Winston rose immediately and the two men shook. "I look forward to taking up this conversation again soon Mr. Martin. I think there is much we can learn from each other." Winston noticed that Oscar had called him Mr. Martin this time instead of Winston. Apparently once a meeting was at its conclusion the names used would be more formal.

"I would be glad to speak to you anytime you wish. I can most always be found at my desk in the drafting room," Winston said.

Chester's Last Ride

"If I have a say in your position here at Roosevelt Glass Winston then your days at that small desk are numbered. Your abilities can be utilized in a much more productive fashion over at my architectural offices. We could certainly use a man with your skills."

"Why thank you Mr. Ramey." Oscar noticed the use of Mr. and realized that Winston was a man who picked up on things quickly. Oscar retrieved his hat, coat, and gloves, from the adjoining conference room. After putting them on he picked up his slide rule and papers and went out through the conference room door into the lobby, closing the door behind him.

This left Roosevelt and Winston in the large office. Roosevelt turned and asked Winston, "What are your plans Winston?"

"I don't have any plans Mr. Roosevelt."

"You don't understand. I am asking what a man with your extraordinary talents plans to do with his life. You know your goals, your ambitions, and your plans for the future."

"Why, I had really never thought of it in that way. I only do my job and go home at night. I have been taking as many classes as I can at the city college, other than that I don't have any plans."

"What do you do with any spare time you have? Do you have hobbies? Do you do any sporting activities?"

"No sir, none of those. I spend any additional time, if I have any, at the library. I find it soothing to read the histories. After dealing with numbers all day I try to broaden my knowledge by reading history. I have little use for fiction; I find it a waste of my time, although I did read Don Quixote. I read it as a factual account of history with fictional characters. It was a use of my imagination that I was unaccustomed to. It turned out to be very enjoyable reading."

"How long have you been taking classes at the city college?"

"For three years, sir. I have taken a little of everything they have to offer with no subject in particular at the forefront of my thoughts."

"And how do you handle your assignments and homework with all the other duties you have just mentioned?"

Winston suddenly looked puzzled. "I don't do anything after class. I finish everything before I leave the building at night. I have yet to take anything home."

Roosevelt expected as much. He reached into a desk drawer and pulled out a pencil and paper and slid them across the massive desk toward Winston. "Would it be all right if I inquired at the college about your classes and your grades?"

Winston glanced at one of the large windows as he answered, "That would be perfectly alright. The gentleman who assists me with my class selection is Cecil Sterling. He is also over the office of student files and grading."

"If you don't mind, please write his name and position on that sheet of paper. Also, if you would, please write your acceptance in allowing my firm to acquire a copy of your classes and grades. I will need that in order to proceed."

Winston wrote the name of his advisor and also the permission for his grades to be shared with the Roosevelt Plate Glass Company. Once finished he signed his name at the bottom and slid the paper back across the desk to Roosevelt who immediately picked it up and read what Winston had written. Once finished he folded it in half and rang a buzzer to alert his secretary to come into the office.

"You have very neat handwriting Winston. And I find your signature to be of a rather artistic design."

Chester's Last Ride

Winston smiled and responded. "One of my classes last year was a calligraphy class. I found it very interesting but not very practical. About the only use I found for it was to improve my signature, after all a signature will inhabit almost anything a person writes."

Roosevelt again thought about what the young man had said. It seemed that almost everything he said had some sort of practical use. It was as if Martin's every effort had a way of bettering the young man's situation. No missteps had been revealed in his life. All his efforts were solidly on a path that should lead him toward a very promising future. No wasted effort, no missteps or sidesteps. Just a steady forward motion, but to where?

There was a knock at the door. Roosevelt asked for the person to please come in. The door opened and a slight woman in her early twenties came in. She nodded at Winston as she crossed the room to Roosevelt's spacious desk. "Margarete, this is Winston, he is an employee in the drafting department. I have a signed document here allowing us to have access to his grades at City College. Please have a courier sent as soon as possible to retrieve them. Once they have arrived please have them sent in to me."

Margarete took the paper from her boss and turned to Winston. "Hello Winston, it is a pleasure to meet you." She held out her hand and Winston sprang to his feet. He took her hand by her fingers and each gently shook.

"Hello Margarete, it is my pleasure." She smiled a very bright and cheerful smile. They released hands and she exited the office. Winston stumble stepped back into his chair. Roosevelt had worked with Margarete for nearly two years and thought he knew her as well as anyone at the office. He was amused at her because he was sure he noticed a blush as she shook Winston's hand. He knew she was single and lived with her mother. Also he could tell that Winston had noticed her beauty. Oh, to be young again.

"Well Winston, I think I have occupied enough of your time today. Could you come over tomorrow, say around ten in the morning? In the meantime I will go over your grades and also meet with Oscar again this afternoon."

"I can be here Mr. Roosevelt. May I ask you something?"

"Please Winston, ask me anything."

"Sir, I am flattered by all that has happened here today, and I want to thank you very much for the wonderful lunch we had earlier. I am confused though as to all the fuss over me. I feel that I am just an employee and not deserving of all this attention."

Roosevelt relit his cigar and took a puff. As he exhaled, the smoke slowly rose to the ceiling. He looked at Winston and wondered how he should proceed. Finally he spoke, "Winston, I am going to tell you exactly what I'm thinking. You are an exceptional young man with exceptional abilities. You have gifts that I don't think you are aware of. I say this because you have lived with your gifts all your life and take little notice as to how extraordinary they are. The reason for all the fuss is that I do not want you to go through life and not realize all you are capable of achieving. I believe a man with your abilities can accomplish great things. And those great things can help many people. Now you show up at this office tomorrow at ten in the morning and I will have a plan that I think you will find acceptable."

Roosevelt rose from his chair and walked around the desk. He held out a hand and said, "Let's shake on it, what do you say Winston?"

Chester's Last Ride

Winston rose had shook Roosevelt's hand. "I will be here Mr. Roosevelt and I do hope I don't let you down."

Roosevelt released Winston's hand and proceeded to the door. He opened it and allowed his guest to exit. As Winston walked through the lobby he caught the eye of Margarete who smiled and quickly turned back to her work. He felt she was watching him as he exited the building to the sidewalk outside.

After reaching the street Winston let out a collective sigh. He was both relieved at being released from his test and also excited about the prospect of being allowed to blossom. All his life he had felt smothered by the lack of prospects which were available to him. Now that could possibly all be in the past. He could study and learn at a pace that suited him. He nearly ran down the street in anticipation of what this all could mean in his life.

Roosevelt had closed the door after Winston left. He went back to his desk and began a list of things that would need to be done. He made a second list of the things that would need to be considered. He felt that he had experienced the presence of pure genius. He could not remember anyone in his life that had such mental capacity. He had known many men in his long career who were extremely intelligent but none who could do what Winston had just done.

After considering all his options Roosevelt completed the two lists, got up from his desk and walked back to the large windows overlooking the river. He felt he had covered everything that needed to be done. He was going to assist the young Winston Roy Martin in becoming fully anything he was capable of becoming.

Nathan Wright

After a moments reflection he turned from the window and returned to his desk. He took the action list and added; Contact the President of Harvard University and begin a dialog about the prospect of enrolling a student in the prestigious school who has very little formal education. It was unheard of for a person to enroll without some sort of previous extensive training, it just wasn't allowed. Roosevelt thought an exception would be allowed once Winston was interviewed by the acceptance committee and he was allowed to exhibit his skills.

Confident he had covered all the bases he again stood and walked to the door. He took his coat and hat and headed for the street. He needed a brisk walk to help clear his head. As he walked down the sidewalk he decided to go over to the drafting shop and have a talk with Oscar and Briscoe. He would see what these two were up to and run a few of his ideas by them in the process. After such a long lunch and meeting he needed the exercise. Once he reached the warehouse he nearly ran up four flights of stairs. As he entered the Drafting Department he took off his hat and coat. A young draftsman who saw him enter jumped to his feet.

"Mr. Roosevelt, may I take your coat."

Roosevelt, breathing heavily from his vigorous walk and exertions in the stairwell, gladly reached his coat and hat to the young man.

"Thank you very much. Have you seen either Mr. Ramey or Mr. Briscoe?" Roosevelt asked.

"Yes sir, they are both in Mr. Briscoe's office. It is the one at the end of the hallway on the left."

Roosevelt smiled as he headed down the hall. By the time he reached the end of the hallway his breathing had almost returned to normal. He stood outside the office door for a moment to make sure his demeanor was relaxed. He raised his hand and knocked on the door. On the other side he heard the words, "Enter Please."

Roosevelt turned the knob and opened the door. As he entered he saw Briscoe, Ramey, and another man he recognized from the Drafting Department but didn't know his name. Both Briscoe and Ramey were seated and the third man was standing.

"Good afternoon gentlemen. I thought I would take a walk after our long and might I say very productive lunch today, and I ended up here. I hoped to sit in on your conversation about the events where Mr. Martin sat in for the poor draftsman who passed away."

Briscoe jumped to his feet and retrieved a chair from the corner and slid it over to the desk so Roosevelt could sit down. He then went to the side office where his secretary worked and asked her if she could bring in a tray of coffee for the men in his office. He had noticed that his boss, Mr. Roosevelt, didn't look in the best of shape. Briscoe always noticed that when Roosevelt climbed the stairs to the Drafting Department he looked tired out.

"Mr. Roosevelt, please join us, would you have a seat? I had only started to explain to Mr. Ramey and Mr. Akers the events that led us to where we are today. And please let me introduce you to Frank Akers here, he is one of our best draftsmen." Frank Akers went over and shook Roosevelt's hand. Briscoe noticed that his boss didn't rise from his seat; he shook Akers hand from a seated position. Again Briscoe wondered if his boss was in some way not in the best of health. He made a mental note to investigate the matter further. He was friends with both Mr. and Mrs. Roosevelt and the next time he bumped into her he would find a way to broach the subject.

Roosevelt released Aker's hand and said, "Hello Mr. Akers, I have seen you on the warehouse floor before but never had the opportunity to speak with you. I hate to interrupt a man who is doing his job."

"Thank you Mr. Roosevelt, I try to do as good of a job as I can."

Briscoe saw the secretary coming down the hallway and cleared a portion of his drafting table so she would have a place for the tray. "Mrs. Reed, you may put the tray here. And if you don't mind please prepare each of us a cup of that wonderful coffee that you are so noted for."

Nancy Reed sat the tray down and turned to Mr. Roosevelt. With a big smile she asked, "How do you take your coffee?"

Roosevelt was beginning to feel a little more like himself after having sat for a few minutes. A cup of coffee was what he needed and he was grateful to Briscoe for thinking of it. "Just a little cream if you don't mind."

Once completed she reached Roosevelt a steaming cup of coffee and then asked the others how they took theirs. Roosevelt held the cup and noticed that his hands were cold and the warm cup felt good. He slowly sipped his coffee and was pleasantly surprised. It was as good as any he had ever tasted.

"Mrs. Reed, I want to compliment you on the coffee. It is very good. Does the Drafting Department use the same brand as the Executive Offices up the street?"

"No Sir Mr. Roosevelt. We did use the same coffee up until about six months ago. I thought the previous brand was acceptable but knew of a better brand and a better way of preparing it. So I asked Mr. Briscoe if I could change and he said he would allow me to try a new brand for one week only and then a vote would be taken among the men in the Drafting

Chester's Last Ride

Department. I found out after I started here that Drafters drink a lot of coffee during each shift."

Roosevelt took another sip and said, "Please continue, I want to hear the whole story."

"Well, I purchased the brand that I liked and brought it back to the Drafting Department's small kitchen. And by the way, it isn't just the coffee but also the preparation. You can take the best coffee in the world and if it isn't prepared properly you will not get the results you wish. So I made the first pot and brought a cup to Mr. Briscoe. He sampled it and asked if I would mind making more for the rest of the Department. I did as he asked and after a week of drinking the new brand of coffee a vote was taken."

Roosevelt took another sip of his and asked, "And how did the vote turn out?"

"Well Mr. Roosevelt, each man in the department was asked to write out a small slip of paper with either a yes or a no on it. Yes meaning they liked the new brand, no meaning they didn't. All forty-five employees in the department chose the new coffee, not a single vote for the old brand."

Roosevelt looked at Briscoe, "I think the entire department made the right decision. I wonder if you could spare Mrs. Reed for a few hours tomorrow and allow her to share her recipe with the kitchen staff at the Executive Kitchen. This is truly a treat. I may start drinking more coffee and a little less wine."

"That is exactly what I will do Mr. Roosevelt, but with one condition."

Roosevelt smiled, not knowing what to expect from his Chief Draftsman. "And what is your condition Mr. Briscoe?"

"My condition is that once your kitchen staff has the recipe and has been taught the process in preparing it you will release her so she can return to her station here. I would hate to lose a good employee because she is too good."

Roosevelt paused for effect and humorously thought over the condition. After he thought enough time had passed he said, "Well Mr. Briscoe, I agree to your condition."

Now it was Briscoe's turn to have a little fun. "Thank you Mr. Roosevelt. I will have the papers drawn up and sent over to your office for your signature. Oh, and by the way, I would like an additional signature, that of a witness." With that everyone in the room had a good laugh.

Nancy Reed finished with each of the men's coffee and picked up the tray. Roosevelt sprang to his feet and opened the door for her. As she exited she said, "Thank you Mr. Roosevelt. I look forward to meeting your Executive Kitchen staff." With that she proceeded down the hallway.

"Now Briscoe, what do we know about the day when Martin filled in for your missing draftsman?" Roosevelt asked.

Briscoe went back to his side of the desk and sat down. "Well, it would be better if Frank here told you what happened. Frank, go ahead and tell us the events of the day when Winston Martin filled in at Jack's desk."

Frank stood and looked at Mr. Roosevelt. "Well Sir, when my boss, Mr. Briscoe, came to my desk he asked if I could look over some work and make sure that it didn't contain any mistakes."

Briscoe asked the next question. "When you finished do you know how long it took you to verify the numbers on the page?"

"Well Sir, I never actually timed myself," Frank told him.

"Could you estimate the amount of time it took then?" Briscoe asked.

Chester's Last Ride

"Well, I guess I could. It was before lunch, say about eleven o'clock in the morning. And when I finished it was probably fifteen minutes before the lunch bell."

"So you're saying it took you an hour and fifteen minutes to verify the work that Martin took only five minutes to complete?"

"I would say that it took at least an hour and fifteen minutes Sir. Wind load on glass is a bit difficult to estimate. And I usually go over some of my figures twice. But it did take more than an hour. And I hear that Martin completed the estimate in less than ten minutes, is that correct?"

"Yes, that is what it took him, an unbelievable ten minutes. I first thought he didn't do the work and had only guessed at the answers. But after you told me that all his answers were straight on the money I didn't know quite what to think. I came back to my office and sat for at least thirty minutes before I decided to report it to Mr. Ramey. I didn't wait any longer after I had made my mind up, I just put on my coat and went straight to Mr. Ramey's office. Luckily for me he didn't have anyone with him and I was allowed to go straight in. After I told him the story he decided to bring it to the attention of Mr. Roosevelt. I had only told Mr. Ramey the basics of the story, not wanting to take up to much of his time. But it was enough to excite his curiosity. When he came back here today and told me what had happened during lunch I told him the entire story. He was as amazed as I had been. It is quite a story," Briscoe said.

When Winston left Roosevelt's office he didn't know what he was going to do for the rest of the afternoon. It was going on three o'clock and after the heavy lunch and intense discussions about his life he just couldn't bring himself to go back to the

301

drafting room to continue the quotes he had been working on for the last few days.

If what the Chief Architect had said about his days at the drafting desk being numbered then what was the point. Winston had always been a pragmatic man. When something was about to change for the better he just wanted it to happen, and happen soon. He wasn't one to hang on to a situation if the benefits weren't justified.

As he walked down the street he approached the glass warehouse where on the fourth floor his coworkers would be working away at their desks. His desk would be vacant. Nothing he had been working on was due for at least two more days. He could finish it all in two more hours if he chose. Sometimes he felt his great ability to consume numbers and finish tasks was a burden, because if he rushed and finished all his tasks, he would be left with nothing to do. His mind wouldn't allow that, he could never remember a time when he had nothing to occupy himself.

The problem was there was nothing else for him to do. Once finished he might lend a hand to a couple of the other draftsmen who he had become friends with, but he was very cautious about that. If he accomplished too much of the other men's work then it might be thought that some of the draftsmen were not needed and their jobs would be terminated. These were men that worked very hard and if they lost this job it was doubtful they could find another that paid as well. If someone lost a job, someone who had a family with children to feed and care for, it would be a tragedy. Winston could not take that chance.

These were things Winston thought about as he walked right on past the guarded entrance to the plate glass warehouse. He also didn't want to be in the Drafting

Chester's Last Ride

Department, knowing that Oscar Ramey was there talking to Briscoe and probably Frank Akers as well. Frank had been the man who had gone over Winston's work to check for mistakes and found none. Winston was a bit amused that it had taken Frank more than an hour to do a job that had only taken him ten minutes. Winston knew Frank was a hard worker but found the man dull and unamusing. It wasn't that he didn't like his coworker; he just felt he plodded along in too much of an uninterested fashion.

Once past the entrance Winston continued walking down the crowded sidewalk. He knew of a small grocery two blocks down that made coffee and sandwiches. He wasn't hungry but did want something to drink. He walked into the grocery and approached the counter. On the other side was a man wearing a shopkeeper's apron, the kind that covered the person wearing it from the neck to the knees. The man looked up and with a cheerful voice that had a strong Italian accent said, "Good evening sir, what may I do for you today?"

Winston looked around but didn't see, or for that matter smell, any coffee.

"Do you still make coffee here to sell?"

"Oh yes Sir. We make coffee every day. My wife, she's in the back, she makes the coffee. She also makes the sandwiches. She will make you one, which one do you like?" He was pointing up at a chalkboard behind the counter. On it was written a variety of sandwiches and soups. "We have small tables and chairs in the back, you can relax and no one will bother you. Newspapers are there also to read while you eat."

Winston had never actually been in this shop before. He had been told by one of the other draftsmen about the coffee. He wished he had come in before, he found the place to be interesting.

"I had lunch at work a couple of hours ago and am just not hungry at the moment, just the coffee please."

"Oh that is okay, I understand. She make you a sandwich and wrap it up in brown paper, you take it home with you for later."

Winston smiled at the shopkeeper. Food was the last thing on his mind but he couldn't resist the enthusiastic efforts of the short man in the white apron. Why couldn't others show such interest in their work?

"Here comes Margo now, she is my wife and she make you the most delicious sandwich you will find in New York. You choose from the board and she will make it for you. I think that after you try it you will be upset with yourself that you didn't get two." With that the shopkeeper laughed. Again he pointed at the chalkboard. Winston looked over the selection of meats and cheeses. As he read he realized it was making him feel a bit hungry. He settled on sliced ham and farm cheese on a hard roll.

"What vegetables and sauce do you prefer," asked the man's wife, also with a heavy Italian accent.

Winston scanned the board again but didn't see any other ingredients listed just meats, cheeses, and breads. "I don't know, what would you suggest?"

The woman smiled and said, "I make it for you as a surprise. You will like what I put on your sandwich." She turned and started for the back.

The shopkeeper watched her go. Before she was out of sight he said, "Also coffee, and he would like you to wrap the sandwich for later." She waved her hand in the air indicating she knew what to do.

Chester's Last Ride

The shopkeeper looked back at Winston. "That will be fifty-five cents. You pay and then make yourself at home at one of the tables in the back."

Winston was surprised, a sandwich and coffee for only fifty-five cents. If the food was good he would start taking his lunches here. He could leave work, walk down, have lunch and be back at his desk in well less than an hour. He reached the shopkeeper a dollar and waited for his change.

As he walked to the rear of the store he took in his surroundings. There was a little bit of everything in here. Besides the usual grocery items he noticed a substantial selection of hardware. He assumed that in the city most of the inhabitants walked anywhere they wanted to go. It only made sense that a neighborhood shop would need to carry most of the things that a family would need. As he got to the back he even noticed a selection of men's and women's clothing. Nothing fancy mind you, just the basics for all the factory workers who passed by the front of the shop each day.

In the back were five small tables, two chairs per table. There was a door which led to the small kitchen. Also beside the door was an opening with a bar attached. Food could be prepared in the back and then placed on the counter top. Winston picked the table in the very corner and pulled out a chair. He placed the chair so as to be able to observe everything about his surroundings. After being seated he scanned the stack of newspapers on the shelf to his left. He checked the dates and found that all were today's papers, another pleasant surprise.

He selected a copy and thumbed through the pages until he found something interesting. As he read he was unaware that the shopkeeper's wife had come from the kitchen and was standing beside the table. "Excuse me, your coffee is ready."

Nathan Wright

She sat the coffee down, along with what looked like something wrapped in brown grocer's paper and tied tightly and neatly with seagrass string. "I prepared your sandwich. Please try to eat it before two hours are up. If it sits too long then the sauce will soak into everything and make it soggy." She smiled and then returned to her kitchen.

Winston took a sip of his coffee and looked at the brown package. He picked it up; it was heavier than it looked. Another sip of coffee, he pulled his pocket watch out and observed the time. It had been more than two hours since lunch. Again Winston picked up the neatly wrapped sandwich. He put the sandwich back down and pulled at the string, it was a bow-tie knot. He slowly untied the string and opened the paper. He wanted to look at his supper. It was an oval bun cut in half with ham piled thick and covered with three pieces of cheese. There was lettuce on top of the cheese and on that was some sort of sauce.

Winston sat and admired the sandwich. The more he looked the more he knew it would never make it to be his supper. He picked it up and took a small bite. He chewed slowly and took it all in. The hard texture of the roll was pleasant. The abundant amount of ham and cheese was satisfying. But it was the sauce that made the whole thing outstanding. It was interesting, tangy like mustard, slightly sweet and thick. He took another bite, better than the first. That was it; he had found the spot where he would be taking his lunches from now on. And if the soup was anywhere near as good as the sandwich then he was in store for quite a treat.

The storekeeper's wife returned from the kitchen. She noticed the empty wrapper for the sandwich and smiled. "So do you like? Was the sandwich as good as you hoped?"

Chester's Last Ride

Winston took the last drink from his cup and stood. "It was delicious; I couldn't wait until later after seeing what you had prepared." The woman smiled and went up front where her husband was helping some customers. Winston reached into his pocket and pulled out the change the shopkeeper had given him earlier, forty-five cents. He laid the change on the table. As he walked past the front counter he smiled and said good-bye. The couple wanted to know if he planned to return another day for lunch. "I plan on having lunch here again tomorrow." With that he turned and exited the shop.

He decided to go over to the library at the city college. He would find something to read for a few hours and then call it a day. He would go home after that and get a good night's rest. Tomorrow he had a ten o'clock appointment with Mr. Roosevelt and he wanted to be prepared. Tomorrow would prove whether he was to be taken seriously about his skills, or would there be another test to prove again what he already knew. All his life, people he met had assumed that his only skill was some sort of magic, some kind of trick.

The library was busy as usual. There were lots of late evening students trying to finish reports or studying for tests. Winston chose a volume on the war of 1812 and went to his favorite seat.

The next morning Winston was up early and prepared for his meeting later in Roosevelt's office. For his first meeting he had been brought straight from the Drafting Offices and directly to the large conference room for lunch. He had been wearing some of his shabbiest looking clothing, not that he had anything very nice, but still he wished he had been dressed differently. Today he would be clean shaven and his clothes would have the wrinkles pressed out.

Nathan Wright

He was at his desk at seven-thirty and quickly finished up everything he had neglected the previous day. After finishing he took all the plans to the accounting offices and dropped them off. Finished with his work he headed down to the meeting that would change the future of his life, although he didn't know it at the time.

"And that is the story gentlemen. That is how I made my way from a lowly warehouse boy, to draftsman, to Harvard Engineering school graduate. And here I am." With that Winston leaned back in his chair and looked at the three lawyers.

Rooms looked at his other partners and smiled. "That is one of the most amazing stories I have had the pleasure of hearing in my entire life." The other two attorneys agreed.

The three lawyers deposited their guest back at the Beckley, said their goodbyes, and then went to their own homes. Each of the prosperous attorneys, at least for the moment, was a changed man. It seems that the hobo from down south had single-handedly taught the three wealthy attorneys a lesson in humility. The three attorneys had also taught Martin that there were still some people in this world that were willing to help a man down on his luck.

The next morning Martin was met in the lobby of the hotel by Rooms. Martin had all his belongings in the same bag he was given at the clothing store the day before. Rooms had realized during the evening that Martin would need a suitcase and had brought one of his from home this morning just for that purpose. As Martin transferred his belongings into the case Rooms asked him what he had done with the clothes he was wearing the previous day.

Chester's Last Ride

"I left them in the trash can in my room. I don't need any reminders of my rotten luck of the past few months. The past is now truly the past as far as I'm concerned."

Rooms nodded in agreement and felt again that his new friend was well on his way to a happy and prosperous life. With that the two men headed for the train depot. Rooms bought a one way ticket to Prestonsburg, Kentucky. Martin would be met there by a representative from the Conley ranch and escorted on to his final destination.

As he boarded the train Martin stuck out his hand. "I would like to thank you Mr. Rooms for all you have done for me. Someday I will try to repay you."

"You take care of the tunnel project for Mr. Conley and that will be repayment enough."

"You got a deal Mr. Rooms."

Before Martin boarded the train, Rooms reached him five twenty-dollar bills. "This should see you through to the Conley farm. " Winston put the money in his pocket and boarded the train.

He walked down the center aisle and found a seat by himself on the depot side of the car. He watched as Stanley Rooms walked back into the depot and out of sight. He was very excited about the new job prospect before him. He also wondered if he would ever again be in Beckley, West Virginia so he could thank the man who had changed his life.

After about twenty minutes he heard a double toot on the engine's whistle and a few seconds later the train jerked into motion. It wasn't long until a uniformed conductor entered the car and began asking for tickets. As he approached Martin he said, "Hello sir, may I see your ticket?"

Martin reached him the ticket that Rooms had given him not more than an hour before. As the conductor scanned the ticket

Martin asked, "How exactly does the train travel from here to a town in Kentucky called Prestonsburg?"

The conductor punched the ticket with a special little device that took out a small piece of paper and left a hole in the shape of a star. As he reached the ticket back to Martin he said, "Can't get to Prestonsburg, Kentucky from here."

Martin took the ticket and stuffed it back into his pocket. He looked back up at the conductor ready to ask if he had boarded the wrong train when he noticed the look on the man's face. He figured then that the conductor must have been having a little fun at Martin's expense.

"I was only kidding; I never get tired of that old joke." And with that the man burst into a loud laugh. Martin smiled and then he too began to laugh as well. After a few more chuckles from the conductor Martin said with a straight face, "Should I be starting from somewhere other than here in order to reach Prestonsburg?" At that the conductor couldn't control himself any longer and went on down the car punching other passenger's tickets as he went, laughing all the way.

After the man had exited the rear of the car Martin turned back in his seat and sat quietly looking out the window. Without an answer to his question there was no way of knowing how long or in which direction the journey would take him. Not long after that Martin was rocked to sleep by the steady swaying of the passenger car and the rhythmic clicking of the train's wheels going over the joints in the track. He didn't know how long he had slept when he was awakened by the same conductor.

"Train will be pulling into town in about thirty minutes. Be filling up with water and coal. Enough time for you to get a bite to eat before we pull out again. You might want to pick up a bag of something for supper too. Next stop after this one is about six and a half hours."

Martin rubbed his eyes and then asked the conductor, "What town will that be, the stop after this one?"

Martin fully expected another smart answer but this time was surprised when the conductor answered, "Charleston, be staying there overnight and leave first thing in the morning." With that said the conductor turned and proceeded through the car before Martin could ask the time of day it was. No problem, it is what it is, Martin thought. Someday he was going to buy himself a nice pocket watch. That someday being after he was earning a paycheck.

Martin made his way to Prestonsburg, Kentucky, without any troubles. He was met at the depot by a representative of the Conley farms. He settled in quickly and soon oversaw the project that he had been hired for. Little did he know that within a few short years he would be in another fight, this one though could take not only his life but also the lives of all the men he oversaw at the tunnels.

The Conley farm and ranch lay no more than eight miles from the tunnel project. On horse it was less than a ninety minute ride at just an average trot from old man Conley's sprawling front porch to the project offices. As the crow flies though, it wouldn't be more than four miles, straight shot.

The explosion was heard a few seconds before the shock waves that ran through the earth could be felt. It was a few minutes past five o'clock in the morning. The tunnel crews wouldn't enter the actual tunnels themselves until first light, that wouldn't be for at least another hour. The noise of the blast woke most of the ranch hands but not Conley. He had been in his study for more than half an hour. He had found sleep more difficult these last few days.

His son Zeke was overdue from out West. Help from his friend the judge in Cincinnati may not arrive in time with the answer that might just save Conley and all he had worked for his entire life from being taken from him. Now the sound of an explosion from the direction of his tunnel project could mean only one thing. Saboteurs had infiltrated the project and somehow managed to set off an explosion. Conley knew that his attempts to guard the works would be insufficient; there was just too much to guard.

Conley, upon hearing and feeling the explosion, went from his study and was standing on the front porch as some of his men began to gather around. Within fifteen minutes more than a dozen men were in front of the house and all were looking in the direction of the tunnels. Through the thin fog and the early morning light a column of black smoke could be seen lifting skyward. Conley knew the implication of the explosion. Having been unsuccessful so far in being able to buy him out the Trust would now attempt to destroy all he owned with guns and dynamite.

Conley now knew he must prepare for the worst. His eyes scanned the crowd of men for his ranch foreman.

"Has anybody here seen Riley?"

"No sir Mister Conley," Replied one of the ranch hands. "He was due back day before yesterday but never made it. He was probably caught downstream by the flood."

Conley had sent Riley to Prestonsburg the previous week to check on things in the county seat. His orders were to spend two days in town and make contact with a stranger from New York before heading back to the ranch. It was dangerous to send him alone but Riley was a dependable man who knew how to take care of himself. The flood no doubt had prevented him from returning to the ranch.

Conley scanned the faces of the men who stood before him. He chose two from the group and sent them on fast horses toward the tunnel project. Their orders were to find out what had just happened and return with all speed with a report for their boss. They saddled two of Conley's fastest mounts and then rode out at a full gallop.

"The rest of you men, listen up. Until we know for sure what happened at the tunnels we have to assume that it was no accident."

The men shuffled on their feet, but no one spoke except Conley.

"If that explosion was an accident then so be it. But if it was a deliberate act of sabotage then we have to assume that the ranch will be the next target."

Conley looked over his men and decided then and there he wasn't going to let his ranch go unprotected. He came off his porch and went to the bunkhouse, his men following. Off to the side and in the back was a heavy metal door with two hasps that were secured with large railroad locks, one at the top and one at the bottom. The men had always wondered what was kept in that room but no one knew for sure.

Conley removed a key from his vest pocket. When he unlocked the big door and swung it open all the men in the room stood in amazement. The room was like a bunker filled with weapons and ammunition. Conley went in and came out with a Winchester rifle. Sammons, the bunkhouse cook came forward. He had been an ordinance man during the war. Conley had heard of his skills and hired him as the cook for his ever growing enterprise. It was also his job to maintain the small arsenal that only he and Conley knew about.

"Sammons, draw a revolver and fifty Colt rounds for each man. Every man here also gets a Winchester rifle and two boxes of cartridges. Meet me back at the house when you're done." With that Conley turned and left the bunkhouse. As he walked away he could hear the booming voice of his cook giving orders. He went to his study and grabbed his pipe. When the men returned from his hidden stash of weapons he was standing on his front porch smoking.

As the men gathered around for instructions a horse could be heard down past the big front gate riding hard toward the house. The men turned around and faced in the direction of the front gate. A horse topped the rise and entered the yard. On the horse was one of the two men Conley had sent to the tunnels not more than an hour before.

The man was slumped in the saddle, holding the saddle horn with his left hand. His right arm hung to the side and was stained red with blood that was still dripping from his fingers onto the ground.

Several men grabbed him and eased him from the horse. Conley was there in only a second. The man was gently lowered to the ground. His wound was in the chest. How he had managed to stay in the saddle was anyone's guess.

The man opened his eyes and looked at Conley who had knelt beside him.

"They got Wayne boss. Shot him in the head as we were half way to the tunnel. He went down in a heap. They were waiting for us Mr. Conley. We rode right into a kill box. When I tried to return fire I got hit. Don't even know how I made it back."

"Who was it Pete, who shot you?" Mr. Conley asked the dying man.

Pete looked up at Conley and with a gurgling sound said, "Baldwin men bushwhacked us." Pete eased his head down and took a long raspy breath. As he exhaled, dark red frothy blood ran from the side of his mouth. He slowly closed his eyes and went limp. He was dead.

Conley stood and looked at his men.

"Sammons, how many scopes we got?"

The cook Sammons stepped to the front of the crowd and looked at Pete lying in a small pool of blood. "Only two have arrived so far Boss. The rest won't be here for another month at least. I mounted both on .45-.75 Winchesters. I spent some time sighting them in and they're both accurate, real accurate."

Conley and Sammons had expected that the situation would deteriorate to this as far back as January. Both men had put together an order for the best scopes available and rushed it off to Lexington. The order had only been partially filled with the arrival of the two scopes and three large caliber Winchester rifles. Sammons had mounted both scopes on two of the new rifles. Over the last few weeks he had spent several hours sighting them in while the rest of the crew were occupied with the ranch work. None of the crew had seen the new rifles or scopes.

Conley thought about his plan of action, but only for a second. His experience in the war had given him a good tactical mind.

"Sammons put a man on each slope in a good position to cover the drive and front gate. Every other man here team up. No man goes out alone except the two snipers. Take up positions on the ridges and stay in sight of the next pair. One thing we don't want is for anyone to attack us from behind. Sammons, you and three of the men guard the front gate. Whatever they got in mind will most likely start with the front gate. No man fires unless fired upon, is that understood?"

With that the men hurried from the front of the ranch house and took up positions to protect the house and barns. If anyone tried to burn the ranch he would be met with hot lead. Conley went inside and strapped on his old Colt revolver. He hoped he wouldn't have to use it.

He stayed in his study just long enough to write down what had happened. He dated and signed the document even including the hour of the day and locked it in his big fireproof safe. If anything happened to him at least the truth would be on paper. He then turned and went back outside to be with his men.

No more than an hour later riders could be heard coming up the long front drive. Conley approached the big stone and brick columns of the front gate where Sammons and his three men were positioned. Conley stepped to the center of the gate between the big stone columns and waited.

Four riders appeared at the end of the long approach that led to the gate. Each wore Baldwin-Felts uniforms with rifles unsheathed and carried in their right hands. Conley eased the strap from the Colt at his side and slid it out and then back into the holster, smooth. Sometimes a gun sticks a bit if it's been in a holster for too long. Conley hadn't put on a gun in more than ten years. The feel was no different. It's funny how a man can leave something so far behind in his life only to find that he never left it at all.

Conley stood straight and tall. His hat pulled low to block the morning sun. The four men kept coming. Conley, without turning around, said to Sammons and his men.

"Stay behind cover. Don't shoot unless you see me go down. Let's see what their business is before we do anything hasty."

"Sure thing boss," Sammons replied.

Chester's Last Ride

Conley felt good knowing that Sammons was backing him up. If anything happened to him he knew the four men on the horses would pay with their lives.

The four riders rode up and stopped short about twenty feet from the big gate that Conley stood in front of. One though eased his horse a little further than the other three and stopped. He sat his horse and looked at the man he faced in the road. He also took into account the other four men on either side of the big gate.

"I need to see William Haskell Conley," the man said.

"You just found him," Conley said in a cool tone.

"Mr. Conley, you're under arrest."

Behind him Conley heard the distinct ratchet of four Winchesters. The smooth click of a cartridge being chambered in each rifle had both a reassuring and frightening effect, depending on which side of the gate you were on. The four riders heard the same thing and stepped their horses back a few feet.

Conley looked at the man and asked. "And just what would I be arrested for this morning Mister?"

"Complicity to murder," said the man as he pulled out a paper and tossed it at Conley's feet.

Conley looked at the man on the horse and then at the papers. Not taking his eyes off the four riders he bent at the knees and retrieved the paper. It was an arrest warrant signed by a federal judge in Ashland, Ky. It stated that Conley was knowingly and willfully harboring a fugitive by the name of Zeke Conley who was wanted for the murder of a Baldwin-Felts detective and a storekeeper in Elizabethtown, KY.

Conley folded the paper and put it in his vest pocket.

"Zeke Conley is not here. Not been here in several years. This judge that signed these papers, is he on your payroll too?"

Nathan Wright

The man on the horse looked at Conley and smiled.

"Don't make assumptions that you can't back up Conley and that warrant in your pocket is not for Zeke, it's for you," the Baldwin man said.

The other three men on the horses lowered their Winchesters at Conley at the same time. The man on the horse spoke again, "You four behind the gate. Step out and drop your weapons or the old man dies here and now."

Conley knew his men could take out the four riders with no trouble at all. But one or two would be killed and he for sure would die. He could have kicked himself for not staying behind the cover of the gate. Haskell told his men to stand fast and maintain their weapons. He hoped his sharpshooters on the hill and the men positioned behind the gate could deal with the four standing in front of him. Just when it looked like hell was about to pay a visit on old man Conley, riders could be heard coming up the drive behind the Baldwin men.

The four Baldwin men on the horses didn't dare turn around and take their eyes off the men in front of them. The leader of the four said, "Don't take your eyes off of them boys." And then he turned to see who was coming up the drive.

Two horses came up the rise at a full run. One carried a young man wearing worn out trail clothes. The other carried an old man who was wearing what looked like a peg leg. The older of the two was riding one of the most remarkable horses ever seen. Beside the two ran what looked like a wolf, but much larger.

Zeke and Haywood had made camp about ten miles from the Conley farm at the Pike-Floyd County line. Just before sunup they hit the trail, easy at first but the last two miles had been all out. Ben had lagged a bit about a mile into the run but caught his second wind just as they were reaching the ranch. Rusty had been staked out before the two mile run, knowing someone could be sent back for him later.

Zeke and Haywood could see four riders in uniform holding Winchesters on a man at the gate. Haywood unsheathed his Greener and held it as he had held his sword during a Cavalry charge back in his war days. Zeke pulled out his .45-.75 and held it in the same fashion. As the two rode up they took in the scene and slowed their pace a bit. Zeke and Haywood pulled up short about ten yards from the Baldwin men.

Conley, who hadn't seen his son in several years smiled and drew his Colt. The four men behind the gate stepped out and leveled their rifles at the four riders.

The four Baldwin-Felts men knew they were in a bad way. Gunmen in front and back and outnumbered seven to four was a recipe for disaster. And they never knew that two of Conley's best marksmen were high on either ridge, each with a scoped rifle aimed at them. The tension was high, very high.

The quiet was broken by the sound of a double hammer Greener being cocked. Haywood leveled the twelve-gauge at the nearest man and smiled. The leader of the four lowered his weapon and ordered his men to do the same.

He looked at Conley and said, "I've got forty of my best men over at that illegal tunnel project you've been building with more on the way. If you don't order your men to step aside and come along peaceably then I will have no choice but to come back with my men and wipe you out."

Conley holstered his Colt. "You come on back. I'll have the coffee hot."

With that the four turned their horses and eased past Zeke and Haywood. Ben nipped the closest horse as it went by and nearly started the four into a stampede. Leave it to Ben.

Nathan Wright

When the four were out of sight Zeke dismounted his horse and walked over to Conley. The two men embraced, father and son. Conley was happy to see his son. Life is short and the years are few. No man should live without the company of his son for so many years.

"Good to see you Paw. Are things always this exciting around here?"

Conley looked at his son and said, "We lost two good men this morning, shot by those murdering sons-a-bitches that just left."

Haywood dismounted and hobbled over to Conley. Conley looked at his old friend and asked, "You didn't happen to bring any of that shine you're famous for did you Haywood?"

Haywood rubbed his stubbly chin and said, "Yeah I did, but me and Zeke got awful thirsty a day or two back and drunk it."

Conley laughed and said, "Come on in, I got some Tennessee Whiskey or Kentucky Bourbon, your choice, not as good as your stuff Haywood but it will have to do. We might try both later but right now I need coffee and by the looks of it both of you could too."

As the three headed for the house they could hear Sammons tell his men, "Stay here and don't let anyone through this gate. This may be our only chance to fix up some grub. Not a man has eaten today. If you cusses are like me then you'll fight a little better on a full stomach."

Sammons headed toward the bunkhouse to stoke the stove. He would send food to the teams that were guarding the ridges. No man could be spared from his position today.

Conley, Zeke, and Haywood, went inside the big house and to the kitchen. Conley filled the coffee pot from the hand pump at the sink and put it on the stove. All three then went into the study and sat down. Conley grabbed three cigars from the humidor and handed one to both Zeke and Haywood. The third he clipped with his Barlow knife and lit with a match. The other two did the same; Conley knew how much Haywood enjoyed a good cigar. The three just sat for a few minutes, saying nothing.

Ben had followed Sammons to the bunkhouse. The big cur could always tell where there might be a meal waiting and he wasn't wrong this time. Sammons cut a thick slice of cured bacon and tossed it to Ben. Ben sniffed and swallowed. Sammons laughed and said, "Dog, that's all the raw bacon you're getting this morning. You can have it cooked if you wait a little while." Ben walked over and sat down by the door. He could wait.

Conley filled his son and Haywood in on the events up to and including what had just happened that morning. Both men sat and listened. Before long the whistle of the coffee pot led the three back to the kitchen. Each man, cup in hand, then went to the front porch and took a seat facing the front gate. Even from where they sat each of the three could smell the faint scent of bacon cooking in the bunkhouse kitchen. Zeke stood and whistled for Ben. The big dog ran from the bunkhouse and made his way to the front porch.

"Paw, I'd like for you to meet Ben. We've been riding the trail together almost the whole time I've been gone. Found him caught in a snare a few years back. He was nearly dead when I cut him free. We have both saved each other's life a time or two over the years," Zeke said.

Ben had heard enough. Feeling that he had paid his respects to old man Conley he ran back to the bunkhouse where the smell of bacon on his nose was like a magnet to steel. Haywood laughed, "He sure does like bacon, don't he Zeke?"

Zeke looked at his father and asked, "Now what will happen, Paw? You heard what that Baldwin-Felts man said. He's coming back here with an army, forty men at least, maybe fifty or sixty."

Conley thought a minute.

"I got fourteen men on the ranch today besides me and you two. Everyone else is on the other farms or at the tunnels. Anybody at the tunnel now I figure is either a prisoner or dead and of no help to our situation. It's just us."

"Can we hold out against that many men Paw?" Zeke asked.

"For a while we can. I was in West Virginia a couple of weeks ago, had a hell of a time getting back. I paid a visit to my lawyers over there. I couldn't send a wire or letter from here or anywhere near here for that matter. All the mail and telegrams are controlled by that detective agency. They have known in advance every move I've made for the better part of a year. My attorneys in West Virginia sent one of their own, Stanley Rooms, to Cincinnati, Ohio to meet with an old friend of mine who just happens to be a federal judge now. If he can get an order signed and delivered here then it will be a matter for the court system to decide, and they will decide in my favor. That trust up in New York will stop at nothing, and that includes murder, to get what they want." Conley thought a minute before adding, "I think we got trouble from Chicago too. I believe there are men from both cities that are after the coal business."

Haywood looked out over the gate and then said, "We heard about your little trip into Virginia and West Virginia Haskell. Me and Zeke here were helped out by another friend of yours, one Judge Joel Stratton over in Virginia. He sent the sheriff and another deputy along to help us get here. We parted company with those two yesterday evening and they are heading back to

Norton as we speak. Stratton said it's the same way he got you back into Kentucky not long ago."

Haskell was surprised to hear that Stratton had again managed to get a Conley back to the ranch safe and sound. "That's right Haywood. Stratton came up with the plan to make it look like I was missing. Sheriff Gannon went out of his way to see me back here too. I owe those two and if I survive this then I plan to put in a good word to the Governor of Virginia on their behalf."

Zeke wondered about the legal side of things. "If the judge's order you mentioned doesn't get here in time, then what happens?"

Haskell took a sip of coffee. "We hold them off for as long as possible. If they break through our defenses and kill us off then they have accomplished what they came for, bring me in dead or alive. If I'm dead they win. Any story they care to make up will put us as the ones who started the trouble. Everything I have worked for my entire life will magically be sold to the trust for a pittance of what it's really worth after I'm dead and gone. The trust has the law and the judges in their pocket. But worst of all is that damn Baldwin-Felts Detective Agency. They are actually owned by the trust and will stop at nothing to see their plans through."

"Can we hold out until Rooms gets the federal judge's order signed and delivered to us?" Zeke asked.

"Maybe we can! Daytime is the worst. They wouldn't try anything at night, too risky. We know the lay of the land and they would be afraid of walking into an ambush at night. We hold them off a few days and give Rooms a chance to work the law."

Sammons got one of the men from the gate and sent him to deliver food to the ridges. Conley, Haywood, and Zeke, ate in the kitchen. Zeke listened to stories and tales he had missed out on while he was gone. The ranch had grown considerably in the few short years he had been away.

During the remainder of the day the Conley farm was transformed from an everyday working ranch into a fortified island. The men transformed the ridge posts into bunkers using deadfalls for protection and foliage to hide their positions. The front gate was closed and the positions on either side were strengthened with barrels and timbers to afford the men guarding it a little better cover. The only positions that weren't changed were those of the two snipers, they would simply shoot from cover hoping to keep their locations as hidden as possible. Extra ammunition was delivered to each of the men on the ridges.

While preparations were being made on the farm's perimeter Sammons prepared food that would keep a few days and portioned it into sacks. Hard tack and beef jerky was sent to each man on the fortified ridges, at least no one would starve. The men settled in for a siege but knew they could never possibly hold out against the Baldwin-Felts men. They could only hope that Rooms could get an order signed and delivered before it was too late. Haskell and Zeke had visited each position and spoken to every man during the day.

No more attacks came as night fell on the valley. Conley knew his adversary was probably using this time to prepare for an assault on his farm which would most likely take place in the next few days.

About an hour after dark two riders came out of the timber just behind the bunkhouse. They had traveled from the tunnel project along a little used trail that went along the ridgeline and ran through virgin timber that was dense and made the two riders nearly invisible to anyone who wasn't familiar with the area. Two of the sentries had challenged the riders when they came out along the trail and ran into their position. The men recognized each other and were sent on down to the farm.

Conley was in his study preparing a document that told of the murder of his two men that morning and also the attempted arrest by the four riders later in the day. He was notified of the two riders and immediately ran outside. From the front porch he could see the two men approach from the direction of the bunkhouse. There was light enough from a quarter moon to see the men's faces when they got close to the house, it was Cecil Duffey and Joey Fletcher.

"Boy it's good to see you two, I was afraid everyone at the tunnel project was dead, come on in," Conley said.

He headed the men into his study and sent Zeke to get some coffee, once seated he asked what had happened and how the rest of the men were.

Cecil spoke first, "Not good Mr. Conley. We got hit about five this morning. Some men had penetrated the project and placed dynamite charges on all three tunnels right at the supports that braced the openings. Martin had sentries placed in all the spots we thought a man might try to enter, but that was to keep out a man or two that might be trying to cause trouble. When they hit us it must have been with thirty men at least. They shot the sentries before anyone suspected anything, all we heard was a lot of shooting. As men came out of the bunkhouses they were sprayed with rifle fire. We lost a lot of men in the first few minutes alone.

"While we were pinned down more men went and placed the explosive charges at the mouths of the tunnels. While all this was going on Winston was gathering what men he could in order to put up some kind of defense. Most of the weapons we had were at the guard posts and that left very little for the rest of us to fight back with.

Winston and the men with him grabbed what guns they could find and went after the bastards that were attacking us. He had maybe eight men and they only had four Winchesters between them, the rest had Colts and two Greener shotguns. When the first explosion went off that was when Winston and his men made their escape from the bunkhouse shooting anything that moved." The man's hands were trembling as he told his story.

Zeke came in from the kitchen holding two cups of coffee. Conley got up and retrieved two glasses from his liquor cabinet and a bottle of whiskey. He poured a liberal amount into each glass and reached them to Cecil and Joey. "Here men, have a little something to steady your nerves." Both men gladly took a glass.

Now Joey spoke, "Well Mr. Conley, when Winton and his men made their move the rest of us that had guns began returning fire. We tried as best as we could to cover the eight men that were heading for the tunnels."

Conley looked at Zeke and then at Joey. "Are you telling me that Winston Martin was making a run at the tunnels with only eight men even after one of the openings had been blown up?"

"That's right Mr. Conley and he made it too. Apparently he split his men into two groups. He sent four men to the second tunnel and as they approached they saw two men in black uniforms lighting a long fuse that ran to a big bundle of dynamite that was placed under one of the main supports. If that had gone off it would have brought down half the mountain. They shot at the two and hit at least one before they ran off. One of the four yanked the fuse out of the bundle of dynamite. Winston looked at the fuse later and figured it had maybe a minute, probably less before it would have set off the charge." Joey stopped and took a long pull on the whiskey.

"What happened to Martin at the other tunnel?" Conley asked.

Now Cecil spoke, "Well, Winston said that those four had saved the second tunnel by pulling that fuse. Anyway he made it to the third as some of them tunnel blowing bastards ran into the woods. They managed to capture one after Winston shot him in the leg. When they got to the face of the tunnel they found another big bundle of dynamite and a burning fuse. They were able to pull that fuse out and save the third tunnel."

"What were the casualties Cecil, how many men killed and wounded?" Conley asked.

Cecil hung his head as he said, "Five men killed Mr. Conley. Fourteen more wounded, two are pretty bad but the good news is the first aid station at the end of the bunkhouse wasn't hit and the two medics are alright too. They have been patching everybody up as best they can. The men that are able are being put to work guarding while others are barricading the place. It was starting to look like a fort when we left to come here."

Conley looked at Zeke and the two men as he thought. "How well have you been able to hold out during the rest of the day, have any more attempts been made on the tunnels?"

"Well, it was about noon when a group of riders approached and one came into camp waving a white flag. We all thought they were going to surrender but Winston said that was silly. He told us to cover him while he went out to speak to the man," Joey said.

About that time Haywood came inside. He had been in the big barn squaring away the horses. He looked at the group and said, "Well if we're having some kind of meeting over drinks then count me in." Zeke poured the old man a shot of the Tennessee Whiskey and reached it to him.

"Got a little good news Haywood, most of the men at the tunnels are alright. Got five dead though and a bunch wounded but I had feared it would be much worse than that," Conley said.

Cecil asked, "What do you mean by much worse Mr. Conley?"

"I feared they might have killed every man there to get what they wanted, and to also eliminate any witnesses," Conley said.

"You mean they would have killed us all if Winston hadn't driven them off with his little eight man army?" Joey asked.

"That is exactly what I'm saying. This Baldwin-Felts bunch will stop at nothing now. I had hoped it wouldn't come to this but after the events of this morning their intentions are now clear. Kill everyone and take over the tunnel project," Conley said.

"But that is murder Mr. Conley, how could they get away with something like that?" Joey asked with a shaky voice.

"They have a federal judge backing their play. As it looks now we are the ones who initiated the trouble. I intend to find this federal judge when everything is over and whip his federal ass. In the mean time we have got to defend ourselves. Zeke go and find Sammons and get him here as quick as you can, he is the cook at the bunkhouse." With that Zeke went off at a fast trot. Ben was on the front porch snoozing when Zeke came out and he jumped up to follow. Ben had rested up from his run this morning and was ready for some more fun.

Within a few minutes Zeke, Sammons, and Ben, were back. When they came into the study Ben went over and sat down in front of the big fireplace.

Chester's Last Ride

"What have we got left in the way of guns and ammunition Willis? Do you think we got enough here that we might be able to spare something for the tunnel crew?" Conley asked.

"Got maybe twelve more Colt forty- five revolvers and lots of ammunition. I knew how you liked them Smith and Wesson thirty-eight revolvers so I had eight of them sent in about a month ago. Each has a ten inch barrel, good gun for anybody that can't shoot very straight. Ten Greener twelve gauge shotguns and six more Winchester rifles. Shotgun ammunition is in good shape but Winchester ammo is thin, got maybe two hundred rounds. Seems our orders have been getting intercepted and changed somehow. Instead of Winchester rounds they have been sending thirty-six caliber rounds for a Whitney revolver, who in their right mind would carry a Whitney?" the old cook asked.

Zeke remembered the Whitney he had taken from the Baldwin-Felts man and laughed to himself. Now he wished he had kept the gun instead of throwing it in the river, at least there would be lots of ammunition available.

"Did anybody see you leave when you two headed over here?" Conley asked Cecil and Joey.

"No sir Mr. Conley. Winston waited till dark and had us use the back trail over the ridges to get here. He had some of the men on the front side of camp fire a few shots to distract anyone that might be watching. It must have worked, we never seen anyone and within an hour we were here. We pushed our horses as hard as the rough terrain and timber would allow."

Conley thought about this and then looked at Sammons. "Keep two Winchesters two Greener shotguns and three Colts here along with half the ammunition. Pack up everything else and put it on that spare horse we brought in a little while ago.

The one Zeke and Haywood had tied about two miles out. Zeke you mind if I borrow Rusty for a little job tonight?"

"What you got in mind Paw?" Zeke asked.

"I want you to ride back to the tunnel project with these two men and deliver these weapons. Then I want you to return and bring back two men with you, probably Cecil and Joey here if they agree? I think Winston has plenty of men, just not enough weapons. If we can reinforce him with the firepower he needs then we can sure use the two extra men here, but only if he agrees. He knows the tactical situation there and I am only guessing."

The two men who had ridden in from the tunnel project looked at Conley and indicated they would return if needed.

"While you're there find out what he thinks and whether or not he can hold out. If it is bad and he wants the three of you to stay then he has my blessing," Conley added.

"You think I should tag along Haskel, Zeke here does a lot better if I'm telling him what to do," Haywood said.

"No Haywood, I think you and me need to work out a few things here concerning the defense of the farm. Zeke do you intend on taking that monster of a dog with you? That back trail is shorter than the main road but you're still talking about six miles each way."

Zeke already had an answer. "Ben will stay here with you and Haywood. He could probably make the trip but it's a long way and he has done enough traveling for one day. His hip might still be a little tender too, not been that long since he was shot."

Within an hour Sammons had Rusty packed up with the weapons and part of the ammunition. The rest was put on the other three horses that the men would be riding. It had turned out to be a pretty good load and Zeke didn't want Rusty loaded too heavy in case some fast travel was called for.

The men headed out at a little after ten o'clock. The night had grown cool and a slight breeze was blowing. This was welcome news to the three riders. The horses would function a lot better in the cool than in the heat of the day. Ben protested when Zeke headed out of camp without him. Sammons though had anticipated this and had cooked up ten thick slices of bacon for the dog. As Zeke and the two other men rode up the slope toward the back trail Ben wagged his tail as a goodbye and lit into the bacon. He knew Zeke would be alright without him, and he would be alright with this bacon. Everything looked about even to Ben.

The three men and four horses travelled in silence. All were keeping a keen eye out for any sign of trouble. Each was armed with a forty-five caliber Colt handgun and a Winchester rifle. The travel along the ridgeline was mostly easy. The trees all along the way were not closely spaced and the brush at the top of the mountain was minimal. There was enough light from the quarter moon to allow the men to pick and choose their path. The horses were allowed to walk the pace that suited them as they weaved around trees and rocks, their vision at night being much better than a man's.

After about thirty minutes the three turned down a slope into a big valley that was used by Conley to raise tobacco. The men rode around the edge of the field staying close to the tree line before heading up another steep hill. This was done twice more and a little before midnight the group approached the tunnel camp from the back side. All the men stopped short of the camp so Cecil could give the signal. He rode in front of the others and whistled the first few notes of Dixie. After a minute he could see a man walking toward him carrying a shotgun.

"Is that you Joey?" the man asked.

"It's Cecil; I got Joey and another rider with me."

The three men rode into camp and were met by Winston. "You boys come on in and get some coffee."

"We got a pack horse loaded down with guns and ammunition," Zeke told him.

"That is about the best news I've heard all day," Winston said.

"You look familiar Zeke, that wouldn't be because you are the long lost son of Haskell now would it?" Winston asked.

Zeke held out a hand, "You guessed right." The two men shook.

Within minutes the horses were unloaded and the weapons taken into the bunkhouse which had been transformed into a sort of command center. He sent four men with the horses to the barn to rub them down and then stable them for the night. Zeke informed Winston of the plan for the three men to return to the ranch as soon as he could be informed of the situation at the tunnels.

"You men, get those horses inside as fast as you can, rub em down and strap on a small feed bag. Have them ready to move out in thirty minutes." The four men trotted off, each leading a horse.

Winston went into the bunkhouse followed by the three riders. In the four hours Cecil and Joey had been gone the room had changed significantly. All the windows had been boarded up with heavy wood and then covered with crating material so no light could escape. A heavy burlap cloth had been hung just inside the door to allow a man to enter without having his silhouette broadcast to anyone outside.

"Mr. Martin, my name is Zeke Conley; I'm the oldest son of Haskell Conley as you have already guessed. I need to know what happened here today and what preparations you have made to hold onto the tunnels and protect the men and yourself."

"You three men get some coffee and have a seat; this is going to take a few minutes," Winston said.

Winston went over to give instructions to a man that had just came inside and after sending him back out he grabbed a cup and went to the coffee pot himself. He filled it three quarters of the way full and then finished it off the rest of the way with sugar. After sitting down across from the three he went into the story.

"About five this morning, or a few minutes after, there was a tremendous explosion. Most of the men were either up already or just rolling out of their bunks. Luckily none of the workers had made it into any of the tunnels yet. The crew has breakfast at five-thirty each morning and then are in the tunnels no later than seven. We got three tunnels going and all but the last one has been punched through.

"We service the entire project from here. The entrance to the first tunnel is no more than a hundred yards from here and is for the most part finished. The second tunnel is three hundred feet past the end of the first tunnel and is approximately sixty percent complete. It's punched through to the other side but still needs to be widened and the height increased. The third tunnel is the farthest away being a thousand yards from the far side of the second tunnel. That is the tunnel they dynamited first, but it wasn't a big loss. It's only driven about four-hundred feet underground and has no exit on the other side yet.

"Mr. Conley had me to set up a twenty four hour guard about five weeks ago. I basically have six things to cover, the construction yard here, which includes the bunkhouse, and the five tunnel openings. As I said, the third tunnel hasn't been driven through so it only has one opening. The night shift guards consisted of one man to each opening and two at the yard here."

Conley thought this over a minute before asking, "How did they set the charges if you have guards posted?"

"They sent men in wearing miner's cloths. Groups of three to four came into camp and made it to the three tunnels, no one tried to blast the exit end of the first two tunnels, their plan was to dynamite the openings on the side closest to the construction yard to prevent further work. The three guards that survived said the men waved as they came through camp and approached the tunnels. Once they were close enough they used knives to kill four of the five tunnel guards. The three that survived were the two men guarding the construction yard and one tunnel guard. Those three said the culprits waved and spoke as they were heading toward the tunnels. With two-hundred men working it is nearly impossible to recognize every man walking around camp, and remember, it was still dark.

"After the first blast I ran out with some of the men who had guns in hopes of finding out what had happened. We encountered some gunfire but pressed on toward the first tunnel. We saw some men there and I knew they were placing something at the base of the entrance supports. We exchanged gunfire and killed two of the vandals before the other two ran off. One of my men was killed and another wounded. I yanked the burning fuse out of the dynamite and told two of the men to stay and guard the opening. The four remaining men, and myself, ran through the tunnel as fast as we could, the whole time wondering if another charge had been lit at the other end. After a quick inspection I determined that there had not been

---

334

an attempt on that end of the tunnel. Again I left two men to guard that end and proceeded on with the two remaining men.

"When we approached the second tunnel we were fired upon but luckily no one was hit. The men at the entrance to the second tunnel ran off into the woods and I quickly checked for a burning fuse. At first none could be found and then I saw the bundle of dynamite. I ran to it and gently pulled out the fuse and traced it back to the end. There was only about five feet left and it was a fast burning fuse. They had covered it over with a scrap of wood to conceal the burning end. I figure we had thirty seconds before that fuse had blown, killing the three of us and destroying the entrance to the second tunnel. I left those two men to guard that entrance and then headed back to the construction yard where gunfire erupted. The explosion had occurred at the third tunnel and it was too far away for me and what men I had left to inspect. If another charge had been set then there wasn't anything I could do about it at the time."

Zeke asked the obvious question next, "What about the exit end of the second tunnel, couldn't it have also been blown up?"

"It could, but that end is only about the width of a wheelbarrow and as tall as a man. We push through from the finished end, if they had tried to blow that end then the most damage that could have been done would have been minimal. My concern was not for the already blown up third tunnel or the end of the unfinished second tunnel, it was for the men and the construction yard. If we didn't mount some kind of a defense then everyone to a man might have been killed," Winston said.

"What happened next?" Zeke asked.

"Well, when I made it back through the first tunnel the construction yard looked like a battlefield. There were bullets bouncing off everything in sight. Men were taking cover behind anything that would stop a bullet. I made it to the largest group and asked if anyone was armed. Of the thirty or so men there, only seven had weapons and these were of every variety imaginable. I had the seven to form up behind whatever was available and return fire but only enough to convince whoever was out there not to charge the camp.

"I made it back to the bunkhouse and there were at least forty men lying flat on the floor trying to not get hit. Bullets were coming through the back windows which faced the timber. Of the men in the bunkhouse only eleven had a weapon of any type. I had five of the men with weapons to fire a shot every now and then out those windows to let the shooters out there know we could shoot back. The seven others with weapons were sent out to assist the other men at the front of camp. My main concern now was to prevent a charge from the front which would have overrun our positions here.

"I went into the office and slid out the crate of Winchester rifles that Mr. Conley had sent over a few weeks back. Inside were four rifles and three hundred rounds of ammunition. The four best shooters in the bunkhouse were given a rifle and fifty rounds. I kept one of the riflemen in the bunkhouse and sent the other three out to the front of camp. After we got those Winchesters into the fight the men who were attacking the camp drifted away into the woods and also across the creek. I really don't think they thought we would have anything to fight back with."

"What do you think they will do next?" Zeke asked.

"They will kill us to a man if we don't surrender. A rider came up carrying a white flag and I went out to have a little chat with him. He said I along with everyman on this project was under arrest for trespassing on private land and destruction of private property. I asked him what the alternative was if we didn't surrender and allow ourselves to be arrested. He said he would be back with a hundred armed men and wipe us out. I couldn't speak for the lives of the men who work here so I told him to give me thirty minutes to talk to the men and then I would give him an answer, he agreed."

"And what did the men say when you talked to them?" Zeke asked.

"Well, after the initial battle everyone was mad as hell at being attacked for no reason other than a bogus arrest warrant. By then everyone in camp had gathered every weapon that would fire. We have almost eighty armed men in camp with everything from twenty-two caliber hunting rifles to Winchesters and Colts. I have even got three men with black powder rifles and one man with a bow and arrow. He said he is half Cherokee and uses his bow to hunt squirrels. I figure if a man can hit something as small as a squirrel running through the trees then he can surely hit something as big as a man.

"I told every man who wanted to leave that he would be promised safe passage by the man with the white flag. Not a man jumped camp and for that I am grateful. I didn't believe the promises they made and I really don't think anyone else did either. These extra guns you brought should bolster our defenses immensely. The men not on guard duty have spent the day building barricades with railroad cross ties. The next time they attack I think we can answer with some fireworks of our own. The rule of thumb is that an attacking force needs an advantage of at least three to one. To overcome our defenses that would mean it would take two-hundred and forty men to overrun our positions here."

"Well, I think I can tell Paw that the tunnels are safe for now. I don't think the farm is nearly as well off as you are here though. We got plenty of ammunition and enough guns but we number maybe twenty men total. I guess me and these two better be getting back," Zeke told Winston.

"You said you got extra rifles and I got extra men. How about I ask for five more volunteers to accompany you three back to the main ranch, you think that would make a difference?" Winston asked.

"Have you got horses to spare for the five?"

"We don't, the only horses we have are the two that Cecil and Joey used to make it to the ranch. All our stock was corralled down near the creek in some good pasture. The men who attacked us turned them all loose and made sure they were run out of our reach. The two we had left were in that big barn we use to store mining supplies. That is another reason none of the men surrendered. If those Baldwin boys took the horses then they didn't intend for any of us to leave here alive anyway," Winston said.

"We can't ride that far doubled up, the horses are tuckered out as it is. The horse we used as the pack horse is actually a fine animal and one of the five can ride him back. Let's head out now, four on horseback and four walking. Don't send any weapons back with the five, you need them here. Me, Cecil and Joey each came in with a Colt and a Winchester. We will let three of the best shots have the rifles and that makes six of us with weapons. We never met any trouble on the way over here and as dark as it is I think we can make it to the farm alright, shouldn't take more than a couple of hours, maybe three at the most," Zeke told Winston.

Volunteers were asked for and nearly every man in the building raised a hand. Winston picked five men he knew were dependable and told them the plan. After the horses were brought back from the barn the men loaded up. Four men on horseback left the camp followed by the other four men on foot.

As they headed up the slope behind camp all the men were a little apprehensive. Had the Baldwin-Felts men had time to reinforce their ranks and if they had would they send armed patrols out into the hills? After thirty minutes the eight men began to feel a little better about their chances. They were well into the mountains and were following the peaks as much as possible. As the eight walked along the high ground of the mountains Zeke couldn't help but let his mind wander. Men had died trying to steal everything his father had worked his entire life trying to build. Men had also died trying to defend it. What could be worth so much as to cost so many lives?

These were troubling thoughts. How much was he to blame for arriving so late. How much was his father to blame for not making better preparations. Zeke knew he and his father were now only reacting to events that were totally out of either man's hands. The culprits were the northerners who had invaded the coalfields with total domination in mind. His father had only responded because he was forced to defend his land and the jobs of the men who worked that land. Zeke put these troubling thoughts aside and tried to concentrate on the task at hand, getting safely back to the farm.

The night was cool with a slight breeze that rustled the branches of the trees and swayed the early spring foliage. Visibility was not the best but it wasn't the worst either. The men's eyes had grown accustomed to the darkness and each felt he was hidden from anyone that might be about, and anyway, who would be up on these ridges at this time of night? Zeke knew he and the men who traveled with him were going to arrive at the farm later than his father would have anticipated and hoped that nothing more had happened during his absence.

William Haskell Conley had spent the time that night checking on his men. The gate along the front of the farm was reinforced with whatever could be used to stop a bullet. Barrels and timbers were used to make gun positions for the few men that were available.

The men on the ridges were taken food and extra ammunition. In those positions one man slept while the other one stood guard. By two o'clock in the morning Conley was becoming concerned. Zeke and the two other men had been gone four hours. He couldn't send anyone looking for the three men, he didn't have anyone to spare and he also didn't want the two groups to stumble upon each other in the middle of the night and start firing away at each other in the dark. He filled a cup with steaming coffee and went to the front porch. Haywood and Ben joined him there and the three sat in silence.

Sammons had been busy in the bunkhouse kitchen preparing enough food for the coming day. He filled sacks with biscuits and ham he had fried to a dry texture. This would be sent out an hour before daylight along with thirty more rounds of extra ammunition for each location.

He wanted to do something special for the men's meals today but couldn't figure out what, and then he remembered something from his war days. After one big battle he and his gun crews were brought honey biscuits. This was nothing more than biscuit batter that was mixed with honey instead of water, although it still contained the buttermilk in the batter. They had substituted the honey for the little water in the recipe. When the concoction was baked it made for a sweet biscuit that was much appreciated by him and his crew.

Chester's Last Ride

Sammons went through the stock he had on hand and discovered he didn't have honey but had something similar, sorghum. It was like honey but much darker and thicker. He also found a sack of dried peaches and that gave him another idea. He knew he couldn't bake pies, time just wouldn't allow. To make what he wanted would require a little help and everyone else was busy either sleeping, working on defenses, or guard duty. One of the men who had the nickname of Slappy happened into the bunkhouse to catch his allotted two hours of sleep. Sammons nabbed the man and had him to take a sharp knife and cut up a batch of peaches into very small pieces. The man wasn't too happy about losing his meager ration of sleep and he let the cook know about it.

"You can sleep when you die Slappy, now shut the hell up and chop up them peaches, and be quick about it. If you can finish in thirty minutes then you can still get your precious beauty sleep," Sammons said.

As the man cut and chopped the peaches and complained about what kind of a bastard would take away his two hours of sleep, Sammons tended to his biscuit batter using the sorghum. When the batter was ready and the dried peaches cut to the appropriate size he mixed the two together.

"Why are you putting those peaches into that batter Sammons?" Slappy asked.

"Because I want to, that's why," Sammons snapped as he worked up the dough and when it looked about right he patted out the biscuit batter into big chunks of dough on a flat greased pan. He then placed the pan in the hot stove. After fifteen minutes he pulled the pan from the stove and placed it on the table. The biscuits were dark from the sorghum and had small orange specks from the dried peaches.

Slappy, who hadn't gone to his bunk because of the sweet smell, reached and grabbed one of the piping hot biscuits and placed it on the wooden table to cool a bit. Only seconds later he tore off a small portion and popped it in his mouth. He just stood there and chewed as Sammons looked on.

"Well how are they Slap or do I have to guess?"

Slappy swallowed and picked up the remainder. He tore it in two and reached half to Sammons, both men took a big bite. The outside was firm and tasty like a pie crust but the inside was softer and sweet from the sorghum. The peaches gave it a very fruity taste. Both men chewed and smiled.

"Sammons, that is about the best thing I ever had, how on earth did you ever come up with the idea of peaches and sorghum in a biscuit?" Slappy asked.

"An old cook from the war made us a treat like this one time. That was over twenty-five years ago and it would be my guess that he is dead by now. They say you will never die as long as someone remembers you and I would say that old cook is alive as ever by the taste of these biscuits he invented, wouldn't you Slappy?" Slappy shook his head in agreement.

Slappy finished his biscuit and then went to his bunk to grab some sleep. Sammons baked up the remainder of his batter into the sweet biscuits and then headed over to the big front porch to try out his recipe on Conley and Haywood.

Ben saw someone coming out of the bunkhouse and perked up his ears, it was Sammons. He got up and went off the porch and met him half way. He could smell something but knew it wasn't bacon, probably just something silly that people would eat. After checking out Sammons and what he was carrying he hurried back to the front porch to continue his nap. Sammons walked up the big front steps and reached each man a sweet biscuit. Both men took a bite in the dark expecting it to be just a biscuit.

"Did you forget how to make a peach pie Sammons; you went a little skimpy on the filling?" Conley said as he chomped away.

"Haywood chewed and said, "You know, we had something similar back in my younger days. Put fruit in the batter along with a touch of honey. This brings back fond memories Sammons. I think you'll make someone a good wife someday." Sammons and Haskell just shook their heads.

Sammons took a seat in one of the rocking chairs and looked out over the front gate. "You reckon they will come again this morning Haskell?"

Conley chewed his treat and said, "I figure they didn't finish off the tunnels yesterday so they will probably hit there first. We can expect their full attention though once that is accomplished."

Haywood added, "You think they can go up against that many men at the tunnels and be successful. They got over a hundred and fifty men over there."

"Those men at the tunnels are numerous as you say Haywood but remember, they are miners and laborers not soldiers, this Baldwin-Felts bunch are trained killers," Conley said.

Ben sat up and listened. The three men on the porch noticed and each picked up his gun. The three walked off the porch and followed Ben who was heading for the back of the bunkhouse. The big dog hadn't made a noise and that was a good sign. He must have smelled the horses and knew Zeke was back.

The four riders came down the slope behind the bunkhouse and headed for the house. Ben broke into a run, followed by Conley, Haywood, and Sammons, Haywood though was more hopping than running. They stopped at the side of the bunkhouse and waited. The four men on horseback looked like they were leading men on foot. This must be some prisoners they were bringing back for interrogation, but if they were prisoners then Zeke wasn't guarding them very well Haywood thought.

"Howdy Ben, you behave yourself while I was gone?" Zeke asked.

Ben was running and bouncing along beside the horses until Hazel bent her head down and knocked the big dog off balance and to the ground. Ben jumped up and pulled the horse's mane with his mouth, it was just the way the two greeted one another.

"Who are the four stragglers you got behind you there Zeke?" Haywood asked.

Zeke looked back at the four tired men. "That engineer you got over at the tunnels sent them. He didn't have weapons for all the men he has over there so he loaned us five. You think we can feed and arm them?"

Sammons looked the four men on foot over along with the man riding Rusty. "It looks like we got five extra men Mr. Conley, that should bolster our defenses a bit if they're any good."

"Winston said they are some of the best he has when it comes to gunplay," Zeke added.

Conley walked over and shook the new arrivals hands. "Sammons here will take you to the bunkhouse and get you fed. He can arm the five of you and show you a bunk. Eat and rest up a bit. About an hour before first light he'll assign each of you a position."

Sammons walked off in the direction of the bunkhouse with the new men. "Cecil, why don't you and Joey take the four

344

horses to the barn and rub them down. After you get everything squared away head over to the bunkhouse and get some food, and then some sleep, tomorrow promises to be a long day," Conley told the men.

The two men grabbed the reins of the horses and headed toward the big barn as Haskell and Haywood headed for the front porch followed by Zeke and Ben. All three men went to the study as Ben headed to the front of the big fireplace. Zeke filled his paw and Haywood in on what he had learned at the tunnels. They particularly liked the part about the half Cherokee with his bow and arrow.

"Sounds like Winston had a pretty rough time of it this morning, although he recovered well and seems to have a good defense set up. You think he can hold Zeke?" Conley asked.

Zeke shook his head, "No way to tell Paw. He has enough men but he is limited on guns even with what we took over. He says he will be alright as long as it don't last too long, food and ammunition will start to run low in a few days. That many men will take a lot of vittles to keep fed."

Haywood thought about what he had just heard. "I believe they will leave the tunnels alone from now on boys."

Zeke thought Haywood knew something that wasn't yet apparent, or obvious, to the rest of them. "You were in the war Haywood, and in the Cavalry at that. What do you think will happen next?"

"Let's go out to the front porch and talk, I want to get some fresh air," Conley said.

After the three men were outside and situated Haywood explained what he thought would happen. "Yesterday they hit the tunnels and tried to blow all three to hell. They only damaged one and took a few causalities for their efforts. I don't believe they expected to be met with any resistance, especially the kind that your chief engineer and some of his men were dishing out. They know that by now that Martin feller has been building bunkers for his men and another attack will only result in a lot of dead Baldwin-Felts bastards. They won't try the tunnels again."

The three men sat in silence and pondered what Haywood had said.

"So you think they will hit the farm instead of the tunnels?" Zeke asked.

"The tunnels can't be taken as long as that Winston feller is guarding it with all them men he's got. He may not have enough weapons for half his men but that still ain't such a bad thing. He can have half the men resting while the other half is guarding. Be hard to sneak up on a bunch of well rested mountain boys and those Baldwin bastards know it, they will not try the tunnels again.

"They will concentrate all their attention on the farm, and anyway, this is where Conley is. They capture and arrest old Haskell over there and the gig is up. This whole thing revolves around capturing Conley and putting him before that crooked Federal Judge up Cincinnati way. I tell you right now once that happens they have won and Haskell over there knows it don't you Haskell?" Haywood said.

"Boys, I'm going in to get me a cigar, one of the ones that is soaked in bourbon, how about I bring you two one as well?" Haskell asked.

Both agreed and Haskell disappeared inside. When he came back out he was followed by Ben. As the men lit the cigars and got situated, Ben walked down the steps and headed for the bunkhouse.

"I think that dog of yours has taken a liking to Sammons over at the kitchen Zeke," Conley said.

Chester's Last Ride

"Ben would take a liking to just about anyone who gives him bacon. I believe Sammons has made a friend for life," Zeke said.

Haskell toyed with his cigar as he thought about what Haywood had said. "I figure you told it about the way it's going to happen Haywood. The tunnel would take a few hundred men to overrun now that Winston and his men are prepared and expecting it. I believe they know we are short of men here at the farm and this place ain't exactly a fortress. They will use all the men they have and hit us next."

"Can we hold out with the men we have Paw?" Zeke asked.

"I don't think so. We can make it hard as hell on them but when the last gun is fired I don't see how we can win," Haskell said. "Let's get some rest and meet back here on the front porch at five o'clock. They won't try anything while it's dark."

At a little before five in the morning Haskell and the rest of the men that weren't on guard duty met at the ranch house. The old cook Sammons hadn't slept more than a few minutes and spent his waking hours preparing breakfast for all the men at the farm. The total now numbered twenty five counting the men on top of the low hills that surrounded the farm on three sides. As soon as everything was ready the food was sent to the ten men on the ridges and the two snipers. It was crucial that the snipers be supplied under cover of darkness as not to give away their positions.

Including Haskell, there were only thirteen men left to guard the front gate and the valley that faced the big house. He really needed more men at the gate but knew he couldn't spare anyone else from the ridges. The possibility of an attack coming from behind was just too great. With the thirteen men here and help from the two men on either side of the hill with the scoped rifles he hoped they could hold out.

Nathan Wright

By the time the sky had begun to lighten everyone had been supplied with food and ammunition. As Conley sat at his desk and considered the events that had happened over the last two days one of the men from the gate ran up the front porch steps and said there was a rider coming up the front drive with a white flag. Haywood, who had been in the study taking a nap, said they were probably surrendering and then laughed.

Conley, Zeke, and Haywood, walked outside and then down to the front gate.

Sammons, who had now joined the men at the gate, saw his boss coming and said, "Remember what happened yesterday Haskell, don't let yourself get caught out in the open where they can get a shot at you."

Haskell stayed near one of the big stone columns and waited for the rider to approach.

"What do you think this is about Paw?" Zeke asked.

"My guess is that once it got light enough for them to see what Winston had waiting for them over at the tunnel project they decided to give us all their attention. In a minute or two we will know for sure," Haskell said.

The rider approached with extreme caution and it was apparent he was unarmed. "Hello the gate," the man shouted.

Haskell stepped from the protection of the column and told the rider to approach. He also added that if he tried anything he would be shot. The rider approached the men and stopped his horse about twenty feet from the gate.

"I have a message from my boss," the man said.

Haskell didn't speak; he just waited for the man to say what the message was.

"I have been sent to ask you to surrender your positions here. We have overrun your men at the tunnels and they have all been placed under arrest. If you do not surrender here then we will have no choice but to overrun your positions here and place each of you under arrest also. We have taken casualties at the tunnels and as of now everyone arrested over there has been charged with murder. If you resist and any of our men are killed here then you also will be charged with murder. What is your answer?" the rider asked.

Haskell was stunned, his tunnels had been overrun and his men arrested. How could this be possible? If Winston had truly been defeated with the number of men he had then how could the men at the ranch hold out. And if it was true then a lot of his men would have been killed and wounded during the battle.

"What evidence do you have that you have actually taken the tunnels?" Haskell asked.

The rider looked a little nervous. Could it be that he had lied and now didn't know how to respond.

"We have the bodies of over twenty of your men. If you want you can accompany me back and see for yourself," the rider said.

Haskell turned to Sammons who was nearest and asked, "You believe what he just said?"

Without a seconds pause Sammons responded, "If what he says is true then they must have hundreds of men. There is no way in hell that you or anyone else can go with him to see if he is telling the truth or not. They will kill you for sure."

Zeke came over to where his father and Sammons were standing and said, "I heard everything Paw; I don't believe a word of it. If they had attacked the tunnels again then the battle would have lasted for hours. Winston and his men wouldn't have given up. It has only been daylight for an hour. If they would have attacked at first light and defeated Winston then it would have still taken the better part of an hour to get here at a full gallop. Look at that man's horse. It isn't winded or even sweating. He is lying Paw, I know it."

Haskell drew his gun and turned to the man. "You may step down now mister; I am keeping you here until we can figure out what is going on."

The man looked surprised at what he had just heard. "You can't keep me here; I rode in under the protection of a white flag."

Haskell drew back the hammer of his Colt and the noise it made was a game changer for the man on the horse. He immediately threw up his hands and said, "Don't shoot, I surrender."

"Sammons, take this man to the bunkhouse and interrogate him. Find out if he is telling the truth about Winston's men at the tunnels," Haskell said. "Zeke why don't you and Haywood go along too, he might feel more like talking if he sees how well Haywood likes to whittle with that sharp knife of his."

Haywood grinned at Haskell; he knew he was trying to scare the Baldwin man. "Sure thing Haskell, I been wanting to do a little carving on me a Baldwin-Felts man ever since this started."

As Sammons pushed the Baldwin man toward the bunkhouse Zeke grabbed his horse and headed for the barn. It wasn't much of a horse; apparently the Baldwin Company hadn't been able to acquire any Conley stock.

"Put that animal in the barn with the other horses Zeke. Meet me back on the porch after you get through with the Baldwin man, if he doesn't tell us what we need to know then kill him," Haskell said.

Haskell had only said this to get the man to talk. He would never in his life have a man killed that was defenseless. It must have worked because within minutes Sammons came from the

Chester's Last Ride

bunkhouse, along with Haywood and the Baldwin man, who had now been tied at the wrists.

Haskell stood as they approached.

Sammons pushed the Baldwin man down in a chair on the front porch and said, "He was lying. He said they were afraid to attack the tunnels again for fear of damaging them anymore. Said the man who ordered them to be blown up yesterday was fired and run out this morning. Apparently their bosses up in New York want the tunnels taken undamaged so they can use them for themselves. Your property is all to be confiscated after you are caught and forced to sign some new deeds. After you have done that then they have orders to kill you and dispose of your body as to leave no clue. The story would be that you sold out and then hit the road."

Conley looked out over the front gate. "Bring his horse from the barn. Put him on it and run his ass out of here." With that the old man turned and went back inside.

Nothing further happened until about three that afternoon. There was a gunshot but no one knew where the shot originated. A few minutes later there was another shot that hit the bunkhouse. Still no one could spot the shooter.

"Zeke, why don't you go and check on the horses, make sure they are all in the back stalls where a stray bullet won't hit them. You better put Ben in there too and fix it so he can't get out. I don't believe they will shoot the horses but I am sure they would like nothing better than to shoot Ben," Haskell said.

Zeke thought this was probably a good idea. The barn had stone exterior walls up half way and it was doubtful if a bullet, or for that matter a hundred bullets, could penetrate it. There was a saddle room to one side and it had a sturdy door. Ben protested at first but finally sat down as Zeke closed him inside. He hated to do it but knew it was the safest place, all the

Baldwin men knew about Zeke and his big dog and would like nothing more than to kill both.

As Zeke made his way back to the house he had to take cover here and there because of the random shooting. Haywood and Haskell were back at the front gate and trying to figure out what was happening. As everyone was watching the front gate and road a Baldwin man had slipped in through the timber and made his way to the bunkhouse and eased inside without being noticed. He took a lantern and poured the contents out on the wooden floor and then struck a match. He was out the door and back in the timber before anyone knew what he had done. Within minutes the fire had spread up the walls and was working its way into the loft.

When one of the men at the gate happened to see a little smoke he shouted, "Fire in the bunkhouse."

Everyone turned to see smoke coming from one of the vents at the end of the roof.

"Everyone stay here," Haskell said.

He knew none of his men could fight a fire now. The building was all wood and couldn't be saved anyway.

"They want us to tend to the fire so they can attack," Haywood said.

There was another gunshot but this time it sounded like it was from one of the men with the scoped rifles. A minute later a man staggered out of the timber. It wasn't any of the ranch hands. Blood could be seen on his shirt and he had both hands clasped to his chest. He made it a few steps and then fell, never to get up again.

"Looks like whoever started that fire got himself shot by one of the snipers," Haywood said.

By four o'clock the bunkhouse had fully caught and flames could be seen coming out every window. The building was built of heavy timbers and Haskell knew it would burn for days.

"What do you figure is going to happen next?" Haywood asked.

Before anyone could answer there was heavy gunfire heard from one of the positions up on the ridge. A moment later and the other ridge posts opened fire.

"Sounds like they tried to outflank us and got caught by the men on the hill, I just hope they can hold out," Haskell said.

The gunfire on the ridges continued as men could be seen taking positions across the valley in front of the front gate. "Hold your fire men until we figure out what they are trying to do," Sammons told the men he was in charge of.

It didn't take long before heavy gunfire erupted in front of the gate from farther down the road where the tree line helped hide the attackers. Sammons and his men took cover and let the bullets have their way with the barricades.

"They are trying to feel us out men. Don't a one of you return fire? Let them shoot all they want," Haywood said, and he was right.

The Baldwin men had been told to shoot five rounds apiece to see what kind of response they would get, but when you are talking about forty or fifty men that would amount to more than two-hundred rounds. After five minutes the shooting ended without Conley or his men firing a single shot. The shooting stopped as abruptly as it had started. The only sounds that could be heard were the men firing on the ridges and the burning of the bunkhouse.

The peace didn't last long. As Conley waited he explained to his men that they could not afford to let any of the Baldwin men breach the front defenses. If it went to close quarter fighting and hand to hand combat then they would all die. There just weren't enough defenders.

Without warning fifty men jumped from cover and advanced on Conley's men. There must have been twenty or thirty more Baldwin men giving covering fire with rifles. Sammons and his men soon started returning fire before they were overrun. Conley and his men also joined the fight. Baldwin men were going down but not without cost. Slowly the defenders were being picked off. When it looked like the ranch would be overrun the Baldwin men turned and fled back to cover. The gunfire from Sammons men along the fence line and also Conley's men at the gate had taken a toll on the attackers. Gunfire from the sniper positions had also proven accurate and the attack by the Baldwin men had faltered.

Conley quickly checked on the men. His crew had taken casualties. Part of the area that Conley and his men controlled included a shed off from the main gate. Conley checked on the men there and discovered one man dead and another one wounded. There were other casualties among Sammons men. It had been a ferocious fight and Conley feared that what ammunition they had wouldn't last until dark. A lot of Winchester and Colt rounds had been lost when the bunkhouse and ordinance room had burned.

Conley stayed at the shed and fired on a man he could see in the distance. It appeared that a few of the Baldwin bastards had stayed behind to harass the ranch while the others prepared for the next attack. He surveyed his surroundings; it appeared that damage had been done to every building in sight. Conley was cautious to keep an eye on the area in front of his position, firing whenever he found a suitable target. Ammunition was going to be the determining factor now and he knew it.

Chester's Last Ride

Conley kept looking at the bunkhouse which burned with an intensity that startled him and the men who had once called it home. He knew that part of the fire was being fueled by the powder and ammunition stored in the ordinance room. The walls of that room were of thick stone and cement but you could still hear the sound of rounds cooking off. The heavy timbers that were used to build the rest of the bunkhouse added to the fire. Thick black smoke filled the sky and drifted over the mountains.

The fire had been burning for hours and smoke could be seen for miles around. It was still an hour and a half until dark. Conley and his men knew that they couldn't hold out that long. Three of his men were wounded that he knew of and one man was dead. Up on the ridges he could still hear gunfire but it had grown sporadic. Those men had held out against repeated assaults and had without a doubt taken casualties. The good news was that they were still in the fight. This kept the bandits from coming over the top which would have put the men guarding the main front entrance of the farm in a cross fire. The next attack would without a doubt come from the front.

The battle that day had been nearly as tough as anything Haywood had experienced during the war. The house had been riddled with gunfire. The barns though had been spared except for a few stray bullet holes here and there. The Baldwin-Felts men had orders from higher ups to spare the prized stock. Great care had been taken not to shoot at the two barns, especially the main one that housed the horses.

Zeke ran over to where his father had taken up a position near the wood and concrete shed used for sharpening implements.

"Paw, do you have extra Winchester ammunition anyplace other than the ordinance room?"

Nathan Wright

Conley fired twice more at the man trying to outflank his position.

"There might be just a box or two in my study. When that is gone we can try to hold them off with our Colts." Old man Conley and Zeke both knew that men with revolvers stood little chance in a firefight at this range against men with Winchesters. Conley looked at his son and said, "I don't think we can hold out until dark Zeke. If worse comes to worse you and the rest of the men can make a run for it through the high timber. No one with a brain would try to flank a position on you in there. The two men on the ridge with scopes will keep you covered until you make it to the big timber."

Zeke knew his father would die fighting before he would be taken by the detectives. It was a given that the Baldwin men would kill any prisoners in order to silence the witnesses.

"Won't happen Paw, I'm staying right here with you. If we die, we die together."

With that Conley loosed another round with his Winchester. Precious minutes were slowly sneaking by and with each one that was gone the safety of darkness was that much closer.

"Zeke, if we're going to die here then I say we take as many of those son's-a-bitches as we can with us. Can you make your way back over to where Haywood and Sammons are?"

"I think so, what have you got in mind?"

"If I see this right, they will mount a Cavalry charge just before dark. If they come pouring through that gate you and Haywood give them a hot reception. I'll cover from here and try to take care of any that get through. They know we must be low on rifle ammunition and a man on a fast horse ain't that worried about a revolver. They might lose a man or two but they will sure as hell overrun the ones of us that are left."

Chester's Last Ride

Zeke patted his old man on the shoulder, "We can do this Paw."

With that Zeke sprinted in a zigzag motion back to where he had left Haywood by the front gate, Sammons had moved further off to check on the other men by the fence. Conley and Haywood both gave covering fire. Rifle shots rang out and dirt was kicked up but Zeke was too fast. He slid into his previous position beside Haywood completely out of breath.

"What's the old man got planned Zeke?" Haywood asked as he fired another round from his revolver.

Zeke filled Haywood in on the possible Cavalry charge of the Baldwin-Felts men. Haywood hung on every word.

"A Cavalry charge huh. Zeke, that is about the same thing I had figured. Those boys want this over today before anyone else makes it in here to lend us a hand. I think your old man has it figured out. But I've been around long enough to know that a man on foot with just a revolver against a Cavalry charge is a dead man." With that the old man stood and started for the barn, oblivious to the battle that was taking place around him.

"Come back here Haywood, you wanna get yourself killed?" Zeke shouted.

Haywood never looked back. He just pegged his way into the barn. Gunshots filled the air and dirt was kicked up everywhere around Haywood but the old man never got a scratch.

Conley looked up at the ridgeline. The gunfire there had dwindled to nearly nothing. He figured at least half of his twenty five men were either wounded or dead by now and it was still thirty minutes until dark. Suddenly a cloud of dust could be seen at the end of the road in front of the gate. Old man Conley yelled with all his might, "Here they come boys. Wait until the last second and let them have it."

Nathan Wright

At least fifty Baldwin men on horseback were headed at a full gallop toward the last of Conley's men. There were still Baldwin men taking cover in front of his position and they had also started firing. Conley knew that none of his men would survive. He for some reason thought of Custer.

As the cloud of dust got closer the defenders could see at least twenty five riders with rifles, the others carried revolvers. All of Conley's men were holding their fire until the last minute. It would be only a matter of seconds now until Conley and his men were slaughtered. At that moment the Baldwin men let loose with every gun they had.

Suddenly from behind, Conley could hear the sound of hoof beats. He turned in time to see Haywood Jones, riding Chester, coming from the barn at a full gallop. Haywood held the Greener in one hand and his old navy Colt in the other. There was another Colt stuck in his holster. He carried the reins in his teeth. As that big Chestnut Stallion came by Conley swore Haywood was smiling.

When Haywood and Chester cleared the front gate the old Cavalry man let the big horse have its wind. The big stallion lowered his head and charged forward at a full gallop. All firing from the advancing squad of detectives seemed to have stopped. They must have been too rattled by the sight of one lone rider on a fast horse bringing the fight to them.

The Baldwin man in charge of the assault screamed at his men, trying to spur them back into the battle at hand. The detectives heard their boss and leveled their weapons again. With that all hell broke loose as a wall of lead was unleashed toward the farm entrance and at this lone ancient cavalryman riding toward them on a massive chestnut horse.

Haywood's days in the war were many years in his past but now he felt alive and young again as he drove his horse in a

Chester's Last Ride

headlong charge at the enemy. He and Chester went straight toward the onrushing horses in order to split the Baldwin men's advance. By this time the Baldwin-Felt's charge was within range of the surviving Conley men at the gate and the fence line. Every man, including the wounded, added to the fight. Men started to fall from the Baldwin ranks.

As the Baldwin advance split, Chester and Haywood drove for the middle. Haywood fired the revolver with one hand while holding the Greener with the other. Suddenly Chester jerked as a bullet found its mark. The big horse recovered quickly and pressed on. Then another shot hit the big stallion. Chester slowed for a moment and seemed to realize that the end was near. The hoof beats slowed and fell out of rhythm but again Chester lowered his head and with a last burst of energy drew down into the onrushing horses and men. Haywood had felt both shots hit his horse and knew he and his old friend were near the end of the line. He raised the Greener toward the thickest group of uniformed murderers and fired both barrels at the same time. Four of the Baldwin men went down just as a bullet hit Haywood in the shoulder.

Haywood fired the single action navy as fast as he could and emptied it into anything that threatened. Once empty he dropped the gun and pulled the other Colt from his holster and continued to fire. A bullet grazed his side and then another hit him in the chest and he was knocked from the saddle. Both Haywood and Chester went down at the same time. As the dust settled Haywood could be seen crawling the last few feet to where Chester had fallen. He lay with his back against his fallen horse and fired the last two rounds from his Colt.

Zeke had seen Haywood and Chester go down and without thinking he ran from cover and headed toward the two. He had seen Haywood fire his last two shots and when he saw the old man's head slump and the gun fall from his hand he knew that both man and horse had just died. Zeke continued to fire as he headed to where the two lay. In his fury he hadn't noticed that the Baldwin men were turning from the fight, they had had enough.

The charge from the Baldwin men had faltered, Chester and Haywood had saved the day but it had cost both their lives.

As the surviving Baldwin agents made their retreat from the murderous fire of Conley's surviving men and the desperate charge of Haywood and Chester, there was the appearance of five more horses and riders coming up the road that led to the big front gate. The Baldwin men had stopped firing and were out of accurate range for the Conley men still in the fight. Conley stepped from the gate and held up a hand to stop his men. The sudden silence was thunderous.

The Baldwin riders stopped and waited for this new group to reach them. It didn't take long before each could see the badge of a Federal Marshal hanging on the chest of the man in the lead. As he approached he pulled his gun and ordered all the men from their horses. The marshal held his gaze on the man he assumed must have been in charge of the Baldwin-Felts men. That man returned the stare and then spoke.

"Marshal, we are agents for the Baldwin-Felts Detective Agency. We're here on official business."

The marshal pulled back the hammer on his Colt. Before he could speak another man behind the marshal stepped his horse forward.

"Are you the man in charge here?"

"That's right. I'm chief detective Simon Reynolds of the Baldwin-Felts…"

Before he could finish the man stepped his horse a little closer and said, "I heard who you worked for the first time you said it Mr. Reynolds. I am Judge Longston Gunnels, and you sir are under arrest, along with the rest of your men."

The detective looked around at the shocked faces of his remaining men and said, "This is an outrage. We are here on official business and I demand that you and the marshal step aside."

The judge rode his horse up to the Reynolds horse and produced a warrant signed by the Governor of Kentucky himself. The charges were listed. It had been a known fact that Kentucky's young Governor was a stout opponent of the New York and Chicago men that were invading his state and it didn't take much convincing for a Federal Judge to sign the warrant. The paperwork had been rushed from the Governor's desk in Frankfort to Judge Gunnels hand by a series of riders in a little less than two days.

"Marshal, disarm and arrest these men. And if anyone of them gives you any trouble you have my full authority to use any means at your disposal to carry out your duty," Gunnels said.

With that the marshal said, "Yes Judge, it will be my pleasure." The Baldwin men threw their guns to the ground and stepped off their horses. The judge and the other three riders made their way to the front gate. The scene was one of pure hell. There were dead and wounded everywhere. Some of the unwounded men had begun to give aid to the wounded, at the gate stood William and Zeke Conley, along with a few more of the farm's survivors.

As he approached the judge said, "We got here as fast as we could Haskell. The flood and all has held us up a good two days."

Conley looked at the Judge and said, "You missed a real war Gunnels. I don't care about the two days but I do wish you could have gotten here an hour earlier." All the men were looking at Haywood and Chester.

Gunnels also looked back at the horse and fallen rider, "Who is the man who charged that army of Baldwin men Haskell?"

"His name is Haywood Jones and the horse is named Chester. The two of them saved our lives here today Judge."

"Well I would say courage like that is rare," Judge Gunnels added.

"Haywood knew what he was doing Judge. He died making something right." After some silence Haskell added, "It was Haywood's last battle and 'Chester's Last Ride'."

Made in the USA
Coppell, TX
07 December 2023

25589948R00199